Settling back, determined to have nothing more to do with such an outrage, Nicholas, Lord Vexford, reached for his brandy. At that moment, the blankness went out of Miss Seacourt's eyes. She was looking straight at him.

Nick saw her expression warm and her body somehow soften. Instantlt, he could feel her in his arms again. Forcing his gaze upward, past those soft breasts, past her slender throat and softly rounded chin to her lips, he felt his breath catch when she licked them. He could see her small, even, white teeth, could almost smell again the freshness of her gentle breath.

The auction was heating up. Men were shouting bids with the same fervor one saw when Tatt's auctioned off a prizewinner. The room had come alive, but Miss Seacourt appeared completely unaware of the lust-filled arousal she had ignited.

She looked only at him. Her lips curved in a gentle, flirtatious smile. Her hands rose slowly to her waist—whether consciously or unconsciously, he could not tell—one stroking the other gently, caressingly, before they parted, poised and cupped, as if to move upward again.

Nick's body stirred in urgent response.

"Eight hundred pounds!" Tommy shouted hoarsely.

"You haven't got eight hundred pounds," Nick snapped.

"Borrow it from you," his friend declared. "God, what a wench! Must have her."

She smiled.

Nick stood, caught her eye again, and said in a clear, carrying voice, "Twenty thousand guineas."

. . . Nicholas, Lord Vexford, had just bought himself a wife.

AMANDA SCOTT

DANGEROUS GAMES

PINNACLE BOOKS
KENSINGTON PUBLISHING CORP.

PINNACLE BOOKS are published by

Kensington Publishing Corp.
850 Third Avenue
New York, NY 10022

Pinnacle and the P logo Reg. U.S. Pat. & TM Off.

First Printing: June, 1996
10 9 8 7 6 5 4 3 2 1

Printed in the United States of America

To Bryan and Tracy,
Best huggers in town

Contents

One

First Player Sets the Stakes

Thursday, 29 April 1824, Scotland

At the moment that Melissa Seacourt's life changed forever for the second time, she was watching a thick gray fog bank creep into the Firth of Forth from the North Sea. The distant clamor of Edinburgh's church bells ringing in celebration of the King's birthday muffled other, nearer sounds, and she paid no heed to the rattle of iron wheels on the gravel drive leading to Penthorpe House. Naturally shy of strangers, and expecting no visitors in the absence of her mother and stepfather, who were visiting friends in the Highlands, she had already dismissed the vague, familiar noise as most likely being a tradesman's cart.

Although the chilly breeze that stirred her fine, long flaxen hair lacked the power to penetrate her thick blue wool cloak, there was dampness in the air. She could smell the fog. When the bells fell suddenly silent, a pair of gulls overhead dove and screeched at each other in apparent fury. At the sound, memory transported her—as it had with diminishing frequency over the past nine years—to the many times she had stood in stolen solitude on a much higher bluff in Cornwall, overlooking the English Channel from Seacourt Head. How long ago those dim, dark days seemed now.

The wheels had fallen silent.

Dragging her thoughts from Cornwall back to Scotland, she fixed her memory on another darkening day only two years since. All Edinburgh had turned out then, crowding the hillsides to watch the royal yacht steam into the Firth through a downpour of rain, at the start of King George IV's historic visit to Scotland. It had been the first such visit by a sovereign in the hundred years since unification with England.

"Melissa?"

Her mind flashed Cornwall and Edinburgh into one disoriented, terrifying image when the masculine voice startled her. Turning, she caught no more than a brief glimpse of the tall, fair-haired man who approached so silently before she sensed another presence behind her and foggy daylight disappeared into silent blackness.

Melissa's first conscious awareness was unnamed fear accompanied by a throbbing ache at the back of her head. Her second was that she was in a coach that rocked and swayed in a manner suggesting that she ought not to open her eyes before her headache eased and her stomach settled. Confused and frightened, she kept still, trying to gather her wits before facing what lay ahead.

She was not alone. Her cheek rested against the rough cloth of someone's hard, muscular shoulder, and the scent of citrus mixed with snuff wafted to her nostrils above the lavender fragrance of her own clothing. Something about that scent was familiar, awakening those dark memories of Cornwall buried in the nethermost regions of her mind. Forgotten images stirred, then flared to life when she remembered the figure she had seen so briefly before everything went black. The unnamed fear exploded into terror. Her heart pounded, and her breath caught in her throat. Headache and unsettled stomach were forgotten.

"So, you are awake at last, are you?" Hearing his voice again, she thought she must have recognized it at once, although she had heard it pronounce only the three syllables of her name. When she still did not open her eyes, he added with sardonic amusement that raised the hairs on the back of her neck, "It is of no use to continue pretending to be out of your senses, you know. An unconscious person does not tighten her lips like that. That's better," he added when, fighting for calm, she opened her eyes at last and straightened in her seat.

Sliding away from him, she turned slightly in the hope he would believe that she had moved only so she could face him, and said quietly, "Hello, Papa."

"So you know me, do you? After so many years apart, I was afraid you might have forgotten." Sir Geoffrey Seacourt smiled, and she realized instantly that one thing she *had* forgotten about him was how charming his smile could be. His even white teeth glinted, and his eyes crinkled at the corners, lending his expression a deceptively engaging warmth.

Still terrified but exerting herself to keep her voice calm, she said, "No, sir, I-I hadn't forgotten you." She hoped her countenance did not betray her fear.

"Well, it would not surprise me if you had," he said. "I don't expect your mother encouraged you to remember, and certainly that scoundrel Penthorpe did not. I suppose they have both filled your head with nonsensical notions about me."

"I do not think they have done that, sir. Indeed, I cannot think when they last mentioned you at all."

Just as a long-dormant but rapidly awakening instinct warned her that he might take offense at such an unflattering choice of words, he chuckled and said, "Now that does *not* surprise me. I doubt very much that they ever told you the truth about what happened nine years ago. Perhaps they chose silence as their best recourse."

She thought she caught a speculative gleam in his eyes as

he spoke, as if he wondered if she believed him, but the expression vanished so quickly that she could not be certain. The swaying of the coach made her headache worse. She reached to touch the lump on the back of her head, wincing when she did.

He said, "I'm sorry you were hurt, darling. I'd intended to visit you first and explain matters, but seeing you outside and alone like that made me realize how much I've missed you. I acted quite impulsively; however, my man ought not to have struck you so hard. I don't mind confessing, it frightened me witless to see you collapse at my feet. Is the pain very great?"

"It will ease." More dark memories stirred with his apology, but she could not grasp them. She knew only that his remorse did nothing to ease her fear.

The carriage lurched in and out of a pothole, and as she grabbed the strap to steady herself, she realized from passing scenery that they were heading south. "Where are you taking me?" Despite another surge of panic, she strove to speak quietly.

His expression changed to boyish ruefulness. He said, "The fact of the matter is that I'm in the devil of a hobble, darling, and I need your help to extricate myself."

"I-I will do what I can," she said, "but surely it would be better to return to the house to discuss the matter. My disappearance must have distressed the servants, and the children. That is," she added, watching him carefully, "it did unless you explained who you are, and reassured the household of my safety."

"I must say, you have grown into a lovely young lady, my dear," he said glibly. "Even more beautiful, I think, than your mother was in her prime. Your eyes are a clearer blue and your features far more delicate than hers. But you were such a silent, reserved child that I feared you might have grown into an insipid woman. I am pleased to see that you have not."

"Thank you. You have not answered my question, however."

"What question is that?"

"I have asked two. Where are you taking me, and did you tell anyone at home that I am with you?"

"At home, you say." He frowned. "Your home ought to have been with your father, not with that scoundrel who snatched you and your mother away from me."

"Penthorpe has been very kind to me," Melissa said. "I am sorry if you were made unhappy by our leaving, but Mama did tell me that when you agreed to let her take me with her, you promised never to demand my return."

"They took advantage of my good nature," he murmured. Once again she noted the speculative look, but again it was fleeting. The muscles in his jaw tightened. He said, "You'll never know how difficult it was to let you go, you and your mother both."

"Papa, you still have not answered my questions," she said, trying to gather her dignity. "I really must insist—"

"Don't be impertinent, Melissa." His tone had changed, and remembering the new one all too well, she felt herself go still, just as she had in the old days. He added flatly, "I'll explain everything when I believe it is appropriate for you to know my plans. For now, you must be content knowing only that we are heading for the border."

"But you can't—"

"I can do as I want where you are concerned," he retorted. "I'm your father."

"But Mama divorced you," Melissa said. "The Commissary Court in Edinburgh granted her a divorce, and she is married to Penthorpe now. He is—"

"He is a bounder and a scoundrel, and I do not want to hear his name on your lips again." There was no mistaking the menace in his voice now.

Fighting returning terror, reminding herself that she was no longer a child but a woman grown, she nonetheless bowed her head, looked at him through her lashes in the old way, and said, "I-I'm sorry, Papa. Perhaps I do not properly understand. After all, I was a child when it all happened, but I did think that Pen—that is, that he had become my legal guardian when he married Mama."

"Well, he did not. Even in Scotland, with its very peculiar laws, they could not alter the fact that you are my daughter, subject to my will and my will alone."

"Then why—" Recognizing that her temper, nurtured by nine years of freedom to speak her own mind, had betrayed her again into speaking forcefully, she broke off to say in a more docile tone, "I am no doubt being very stupid, sir, but I don't understand why you did not simply explain your wishes to me. If you mean to take me across the border, you should at least have given me time to pack clothes for the journey, and to reassure our people at home . . . that is, at Pen—" Again she broke off. Biting her lower lip, she hoped she looked only confused and had not betrayed the increasing exasperation that threatened to overcome her better judgment.

To her relief he smiled again and said, "I have made things difficult for you. I can see that, but you must understand my feelings too, darling. Once I had seen you, it was as if all the frustration and anxiety I've experienced these past years just overwhelmed me. I acted without thought. You are right to chide me for carrying you off in such a mad way, but please remember that I lost you in much the same fashion."

She wondered if perhaps he was taking her so swiftly south because Scottish law would prevent his taking her at all if he did not seize his opportunity. She said casually, "I hope when we stop to change horses, you will allow me time to tidy myself, sir. I must look as if I've been dragged through a hedge. I'll be grateful for a restorative drink by then, too."

Her real hope must have betrayed itself in her expression, however, because when he smiled again, the expression not only lacked its usual charm but chilled her to the marrow.

"This team is good for two stages," he said in clipped tones. "We won't stop before Galashiels, and then only for the change. There is a passable inn just south of the Carter Fell turnpike where we can pass the night. Your appearance need not concern you before then."

Panic flared again. She swallowed, wondering if it would do any good to point out to him that Nature might make it necessary for them to stop longer than that at Galashiels. As if he read her thoughts again, he said gently, "If you require a private moment, we can arrange for one at the roadside where I can keep my eye on you."

Heat flooded her cheeks. Hoping there would be no need for such a stop, she decided she would not eat or drink. Fortunately, at this time of year the Great North Road allowed for speed, so to reach the border would take only three or four hours unless the gathering fog slowed their pace. The farther they moved from the sea, she knew, the less likely that was to occur.

Silence reigned for several moments before she said quietly, "You said you require my assistance, sir. Will you tell me how you think I can help you?"

"I'll tell you later," he said, "but make no mistake, Melissa. I will be most displeased if you create a scene at Galashiels when we change horses. Believe me when I say that you are legally bound to obey me, regardless of what anyone else may have told you. The fact that I chose to remove you abruptly rather than await the return of your mother and that fellow she lives with can have no legal bearing in this matter. They could not have prevented my reclaiming you."

"You knew they were away?"

"Yes, I took the liberty of inquiring about them before we drove to the house, but as I said, their presence would have made no difference. He might have had the effrontery to insist upon a hearing before a magistrate, but although Scotland allows women to divorce their rightful husbands, it does not attempt to deny a father's lawful authority over his own daughter. That scoundrel might have delayed matters, but he cannot stop me."

"I-I see."

"I hope you do, because if you embarrass me at Galashiels, I will make you very sorry. Even at this distance of time and place, I expect you can recall the folly of arousing my displeasure."

Icy terror raced up her spine. Shivering, she said, "I-I won't disobey you, sir."

He reached over to pat her knee. "That's my good girl. Now, address me as Papa, as you were used to do—not sir—and we shall get on very well." Glancing out the window, he added in a more cheerful tone, "How very green these hills are."

"Yes, w-we've had a lot of rain."

"That's the one thing I remember vividly from my last visit to this country," he said, still looking out the window. "It seemed to rain the entire time I was here."

"The last time—! W-were you in Scotland before, sir—Papa?"

Smiling at the hasty amendment, and relaxing again, he said, "Does that surprise you? It should not, when you must know the greater part of the English gentry and nobility accompanied His Majesty on his historic visit two years ago. I saw you twice, in fact, once at Dalkeith and then at the King's Drawing Room. I must tell you, I thought at first that they intended you to wed the young Duke of Buccleuch, but when you were not presented at the Drawing Room, I realized that could not be the case."

"I was only sixteen," she protested.

"Old enough to suit ambitious parents, and as I recall the matter, His Grace the duke is almost exactly your own age. I distinctly remember His Majesty refusing to allow him to drink the liqueur that was served after dinner at Dalkeith. Too strong it was, he said, for a lad so young."

"I remember that dinner at Dalkeith Palace, of course,"

she said, "and the Drawing Room, too, but I don't recall seeing you."

"Both events were dreadfully crowded, and I took care to keep out of your way," he said, "especially since I doubted that I could meet that scoundrel your mother lives with without punching him in the nose. Hard enough to know I was in the same house with him, but I bore with it in order to catch a glimpse of my pretty daughter. It pleased me very much to see you dancing with the young duke."

"Well, I like him well enough," she said, "but not enough to want to marry him. In all fairness, I've never had the least hint that anyone expected me to do so."

"That's just as well. You won't marry him."

"Goodness, you sound very certain. Do you not approve of His Grace?"

"I scarcely know him, but you are going to marry someone else."

"I daresay I shall, one day, but—" Breaking off, she regarded him with dawning apprehension. "What do you mean? Is that why you—? No, no, I am being foolish."

"Not at all, my dear, if what you believe is that your father has arranged your marriage. I am sure that to do so is no more than my paternal duty demands."

His tone was gentle, but the look in his eyes challenged her to deny his authority, and feeling panic stir again, she knew she lacked the courage to do so. Striving for calm, she said, "I daresay such arrangements are still made, though I do not know anyone whose father has arranged her marriage without so much as telling her that he intended to do so. Such customs have gone out of fashion here in Scotland."

"Perhaps they have," he agreed, adding in a harder tone, "but even in Scotland, I believe a daughter does not defy her father's will."

"N-no, sir." Another shiver raced up her spine.

Silence fell again. She knew there was no hope that Penthorpe might be hard on their heels, for he and Susan had not intended to return for four more days. Nor would the servants act on their own to follow her, even if they could pick up her trail. The most she could hope was that someone would ride to the Highlands and urge her mother and stepfather to return at once. Even then, they could have no notion of what had become of her. She would remain wholly in Sir Geoffrey's power unless and until she could manage to escape on her own.

Longingly, she wished she were more like her cousin Charley. Charley would know what to do. A year older than Melissa, Charley had always protected her from the consequences of their childhood mischief. Of course, Melissa reflected now, Charley had always been the one who led her into mischief in the first place. Still, her cousin had never let her suffer for their misdeeds. In those long-ago days, Melissa had followed Charley like a shadow and had benefited greatly from their friendship. That she was an expert horsewoman now was certainly due to Charley. Their Aunt Daintry—Susan's younger sister and the present Lady Abreston—had taught both girls how to ride, but it was Charley who had helped Melissa overcome her initial terror of horses.

She was still thinking of her intrepid cousin when the coach rocked into an inn yard in Galashiels and she heard the coachman shout for a fresh team. Charley, she decided, would somehow manage to overcome both Sir Geoffrey and the coachman, and escape. She would never sit meekly, as Melissa was doing now. However, Charley had small acquaintance with Sir Geoffrey's temper, while Melissa remembered too well the dreadful consequences of arousing it. Moreover, although Sir Geoffrey treated her with attentive consideration for the benefit of the bustling inn servants, even asking if she wanted a glass of lemonade brought out to the coach, he gave her no chance to escape. She declined the lemonade with quiet dignity, and glanced at the watch cunningly set into the gold bracelet she wore. It was four o'clock.

"That's a pretty bauble," Sir Geoffrey said.

"Aunt Daintry sent it to me from France on my eighteenth birthday," she said. "She and Deverill ordered it made by the same jeweler who fashioned a much more expensive one years ago for the Empress Josephine."

He showed no more interest in her watch, and silence fell until the coach was rattling along the road at speed again, when she summoned up a smile and said, "I wish you will tell me what lies ahead, sir—Papa. I cannot imagine that you've gone to all this trouble for the pleasure of my company."

He shifted his weight, settled back comfortably against the squabs, and said matter-of-factly, "Since you seem willing to accept the situation with becoming serenity, I see no reason not to explain now. You will want time to become accustomed to the notion, after all."

"What notion is that?" The words sounded calm enough, she thought, but her nerves were raw.

"Why, the notion of marriage, of course."

"I hope you are jesting, but I own I do not find that very amusing."

"I made no jest." He regarded her speculatively for a long moment. Then he sighed and said, "Matters have come to such a pass that I have no choice about this decision, darling. You must just understand that and forgive your papa when he says that what must be must be."

"*What* must be, then?"

"I suppose you know that you are a considerable heiress."

Surprised by the apparent change of subject, she said, "Am I? I didn't know."

"Well, I have no son, so when I die, you will inherit Seacourt Head and everything else I own."

"But you are not old, Papa. You will live for many years. I'd be a fool to depend upon such an expectation when you may well marry again and produce a son."

"I cannot marry again," he said.

"Good gracious, why not?"

"Because a man can have only one wife."

"Do you mean to say you *did* marry again? When? Why did no one tell me?"

"Because I did no such thing, of course."

"But then . . . Do you believe you are still married to my mother, sir? Because I must tell you that she did divorce you quite legally in a Scottish court."

"I'm aware of that, but that relatively insignificant detail does not alter the fact that I have never divorced her in England."

"But I don't understand. Her marriage to Pen— Her marriage is quite legal. Why, I have a brother and a sister now, sir—twins—and they are certainly—"

"Call me Papa," he snapped, adding in the same abrupt tone, "It is only by the idiotic laws of Scotland that your mother's true marriage was dissolved. In England, I am still her lawful husband. I could have applied for a Parliamentary divorce when she ran off, of course, but the procedure is lengthy and expensive, so I never bothered with it. I still love your mother," he added softly, "and in England, she is still my wife."

"I-I see," she said, suppressing another shiver. "Still, what has my being your heir, or your being still married to my mother in England, to do with anything else?"

"You are not just *my* heir, you see, but also heiress to a significant portion of Lady Ophelia Balterley's vast fortune."

"Great-Aunt Ophelia?" She remembered that outspoken lady with fondness, though she had not laid eyes on her in a number of years. Lady Ophelia was quite elderly and did not enjoy traveling. "I know she means to leave her fortune divided among the females in her family because she has a poor opinion of men, but I do not know the exact amount of her fortune or how, precisely, it is to be divided. As I understood the matter, Mama and Aunt Daintry stand to inherit most of her money."

"You need not mention that fact to anyone else, however," he said, glaring at her. "Look here, Melissa, I'm going to be frank with you. I owe a great deal of money to a man who is not willing to wait until my finances are in better trim to collect his due. When I told him that you are a considerable heiress, he agreed to accept you as his bride in place of the money I owe him."

Oddly, she was tempted to ask how much he owed the man. Just what was she worth as a bride? However, aware that such impertinence would infuriate him, she said only, "Who is this man, sir?"

"Yarborne," he replied. "Lord Yarborne. He's no more than a baron, I'm afraid, and I know little about his antecedents, for he popped onto the London scene only a year or so ago. Small pickings for a girl who has danced with a duke, I grant you, but Yarborne is very wealthy, which ought to make up for that small defect. He is a perfectly suitable match for you."

"What is he like?" She felt suddenly as if they discussed something of no more moment than the weather. *Will it rain tomorrow, Papa?*

If her calm surprised him, he did not show it. He said, "He is not quite as tall as I am. I suppose he must be two or three years older, for he has a son a couple of years older than you are—at Oxford, I believe. But Yarborne is widowed, of course."

She gazed at him for a long moment before she said, "I am persuaded that you must be teasing, sir. You cannot expect me to believe you really want me to marry a man old enough to be my father merely to repay him for lending you money."

"He did not lend me money. It is a debt of honor."

She had heard the term before. "In fact, you lost the money to him, gambling."

"How I came to owe the money is not your concern," he said curtly. "I do not propose to explain my actions. I expect your obedience, Melissa, and I will have it."

Though her terrors had eased somewhat, she did not argue. Instead, as the miles passed, carrying her farther and farther from home, she tried to think how she could escape. If he was taking her to London, as she assumed he must be, they had five days or more of travel ahead. Even if she found herself unable to devise a plan in that time, it was now the end of April. Not only would Lady Ophelia be in town but Charley as well. Surely, they would help her avoid the horrid fate Sir Geoffrey intended for her.

Conversation in the coach grew desultory after that. They changed horses again at Jedburgh at dusk, crossed the border an hour later, and shortly after nightfall reached the inn Sir Geoffrey had mentioned. As he handed her down from the carriage, Melissa looked around curiously, assessing her chances for making an escape that very night.

The inn was small, its yard lighted by torches. It was by no means as busy as inns she had seen at Galashiels and Jedburgh, but laughter rang from its taproom, and ostlers scurried to and fro. When Sir Geoffrey ushered her inside, she had a sudden fear that to prevent her escape he would insist that she share his room, even if to do so he had to declare her his wife. To preclude that horrifying prospect, she said clearly as the landlord hurried to greet them, "What a cozy inn this is, Papa, to be sure."

When Sir Geoffrey gave orders for two bedchambers and a private parlor for their dinner, she took hope. With a room of her own, she would surely find opportunity for escape, and as a first step, she said, "I'd like to tidy myself before we dine, Papa."

"Yes, darling, of course," he said. "Landlord, have you a maidservant who can attend my daughter and perhaps sleep in her bedchamber? We were unable to bring her maid with us today, and she is not accustomed to looking after herself."

Bowing obsequiously, the landlord said, "To be sure, sir, I've a wench who'll look after her. Won't be the sort Miss be accustomed to, but Mag will see to her well enough." He shouted to the nether regions of the inn, whereupon a plump young woman with crisp brown curls spilling from beneath her mobcap came hurrying in response, wiping her hands on her apron.

"Lawks-a-mussy," she exclaimed, "ain't I a-comin' as fast as me legs will carry me?" Seeing Sir Geoffrey and Melissa, she bobbed a hasty curtsy.

The landlord said, "Mag, you're to look after Miss Seacourt here whilst she refreshes herself afore dinner. Put her in the yaller room at the top of the stairs, and her da in the next. They kin use the wee parlor beyond it fer their supper."

"Right you are."

Sir Geoffrey said, "As a matter of fact, landlord, if you agree to the notion, I'd like to hire this young woman to accompany my daughter for the three days remaining of our journey. She looks capable, and I'll see to it that she gets back to you safely."

"Lawks-a-mussy," Mag exclaimed. "Me? Go to Lunnon-town?"

"Oh, I'm afraid not London," Sir Geoffrey said, "only to Newmarket."

Melissa gasped. "Newmarket!"

Raising an eyebrow, Sir Geoffrey said, "Did I forget to mention where I am to pay off Yarborne, darling? Since he, like every other sporting man in England, is in Newmarket now for the annual Spring Meeting—the horse races, that is—we're to meet him there."

Neither Charley nor Lady Ophelia could help her now. She was on her own.

Two

The Dice Are Cast

Monday, 3 May 1824, Newmarket

"Main of seven, gentlemen, five thrown," declared the groom-porter at the hazard table in the crowded main gaming room of Newmarket's famous Little Hell. "Odds three to two against the caster. Chance of five to win; seven loses." Collecting the dice from the table, he looked up at the large, dark-haired man who had just cast them. "Will you increase your stake, my lord?"

Nicholas Barrington, elder son of the Earl of Ulcombe and presently styled Lord Vexford, nodded. Taking the dice from the porter, he dropped them into the dice box and set two more rouleaux with his markers on the table. "Adding twenty guineas," he said in a deep voice that carried easily to the other players.

"Thank you, my lord. Who covers, gentlemen?"

When most of the others—some fifteen in all at the table—moved to cover Vexford's stake, the much shorter, rather plump gentleman beside him said plaintively over the rumble of their voices, "By Jupiter, your luck's in with the bones, Nick, but love's another matter, ain't it? As I hear it, the Hawthorne's been out of sorts ever since the pair of you arrived in Newmarket. Daresay you've just got bored with her, but to hear her tell it, you're being purposefully cruel, and folks are bound to believe it, since she uglifies any other chit unfortunate enough to be seen in her company."

"Do you believe her, Tommy?" Vexford murmured.

Lord Thomas Minley said hastily, "Dash it, Nick, she cites dozens of instances of your cruelty. Names dozens of witnesses, too. But though other folks are bound to say even *you* can't expect your luck to hold with women and gaming all at one and the same time, I say you're just bored with her."

Smiling lazily down at him, Vexford said, "I'm increasingly bored with the whole game of life, Tommy, but what makes you think I'm bored with Clara?"

"Plain as a pikestaff," Lord Thomas said. "At the Heath, she clings to you like a limpet whilst you watch the damned horses, and where is she right now, I ask you? At some dashed assembly or other, wondering where the devil you are, that's where she is right now. And, like I said, she's named dozens of witnesses."

"Clara always names dozens of witnesses, particularly when she's lying through her pretty teeth," Vexford said. "She knows better than to expect me to do the fancy here, however, and as to my watching the horses, everyone does. That *is* why one attends the Newmarket Spring Meeting, after all."

Lord Thomas snorted. "That's one reason, but it ain't the only one, and that's a fact. Gambling's the main reason they come, and don't say it ain't, my lad, not when you've had a monkey off me in less than an hour right here in Little Hell and another this afternoon before the first subscription heats were over and done."

"But I need the money," Vexford said in a dulcet tone. "The lady's damned acquisitive. Are you covering my stake, Tommy?"

"I am, though only a fool would believe you need my blunt to pay for Clara's baubles. Dash it, I saw that ruby bracelet you gave her." His gaze narrowed shrewdly. "Is that what it is? She asks for too many pretties? I can believe it. Too demanding by half, I'd say—for my taste, anyway. But then, I could never afford her in the first place. Be done up just paying for one of her shoe buckles, and don't tell me she don't wear 'em. That chit flaunts glitter wherever she can manage to put it. Now I come to think of it, Nick, maybe you'd best get rid of her. You've enough luck and to spare, even for finding a new light-o'-love."

Vexford looked pointedly at the other gamesters who were waiting for Lord Thomas to cover the stake. When he had done so, Vexford gave the dice box a shake, then cast a three and a two.

"There, you see," Thomas said in disgust. "Odds against it, and you throw chance. No doubt you'll call a new main now and nick the board."

While the groom-porter called the odds, Vexford added to his stake again, and Thomas, albeit shaking his head at his friend's incredible luck, covered again when the others did. Vexford threw an ace and a four.

Thomas groaned. "That's done it. Someone ought to call for new dice."

Vexford looked at him. "Do you want to do so?"

"By Jupiter, no! Just thinking someone might. Serve you right if they had, right in the middle of your cast, so you'd have had to throw over with new ones. And it's no use looking daggers at me, for I'm damned if I'll cover you again. When you're in vein, old lad, there's none as can touch you, not even Yarborne. Look, there he is now. I'll confess, I've wondered about him. Rich as Midas, yet I never heard his name mentioned before last year or so. Still, one sees him everywhere, and there he is now, collecting more blunt. Must have made a private wager that you'd cast chance again."

"You suspect everyone of something, Tommy," Vexford said, "and while I'll grant you that Yarborne's got more money than most, he also gives as much as any man in London to the poor and needy. Not only is he rich but he must choose his wagers well, for he's said to be more of a gamester than I am."

"Dash it, that can't be true. You live and breathe cards and dice, and Yarborne's forever organizing musicales, ladies' supper parties, and concerts to raise money for the poor. But I'm not the only one who don't trust him much. My father says he's just trying to build a reputation for himself, to work his way into the highest circles, and has taken your father as his example. One no sooner hears Yarborne accused of some dashed scurvy thing like usury than one learns he lent money to some fool, interest free, just to keep the bailiffs from the chap's door. But— Good Lord," he exclaimed when his errant gaze fixed suddenly on the entrance to the crowded room, "here comes Dory! Don't tempt him to play, Nick, I beg you. It ain't right to take advantage of a man of God under any circumstance, and certainly not when he's my brother."

The Reverend Lord Dorian Minley, ten years older than Lord Thomas, strolled up to the table and watched with polite interest while Vexford threw the dice again. When most of those gathered around groaned in much the same way that Thomas had earlier, the vicar said with a chuckle, "I collect that you've thrown in, Nicholas."

Thomas said with a snort, "He has. If he don't nick the board with his first cast, he throws chance three or four times running. Goes against all the odds, Dory. In his position, I'd throw chance and then the main, which would mean—in case you don't recall—paying off each and every man at the table. That would serve Nick right if it ever happened, but he throws only winners. If I didn't know him for an honest player, dashed if I wouldn't call for a hammer to break those dice. But when did you arrive in Newmarket, old man?" he added in a more genial tone.

"Earlier this afternoon," the vicar replied with a singularly sweet smile. The two brothers looked a good deal alike despite the difference in their ages, for both had the same hazel eyes, curly brown hair, and sturdy, plump figures. The second and fifth of the Marquess of Prading's six offspring, both were of average height, but standing next to the tall, broad-shouldered, loose-limbed Vexford, they looked nearly diminutive.

Lord Thomas exclaimed, "Dash it, how could you have arrived this afternoon, Dory? I never saw you at the Heath."

"As it happens, I took a walk along the Devil's Dyke," the vicar said, "and the oddest thing happened to me there. I shall tell you about it later, for it is too noisy by half in here to engage in a proper conversation."

Thomas said at once to Vexford, who had been keeping an ear on their conversation while he added to his growing stake, "Look here, Nick, I'm famished. If you want to have supper with Dory and me, you'll have to pass that box on soon, or else I'll just toddle off along with him now to the supper room."

In response, Vexford called a new main and cast again. Once more the result was greeted with a groan, but this time, when the porter asked if he would increase his stake, he shook his head. "My luck can't hold much longer," he said, "so I'll take Tommy's excellent advice and pass the box." Handing the dice box to the man on his left, he gathered his winnings, saying over his shoulder, "I'll be delighted to join you and Dorian for supper, Tommy."

"The devil if you'll just *join* us," Lord Thomas said tartly. "You'll bloody well *pay* for the supper."

Chuckling, Vexford followed the two Minley brothers to the supper room, where they were fortunate enough to find a corner table unoccupied. As they took their seats, Lord Thomas said to the vicar, "I've just been advising Nick here to spend some of that luck of his in finding himself a new mistress, Dory. The one he's got now is too avaricious by half. But no doubt you'll remind him that the Church of England frowns altogether on such sinful liaisons."

The vicar smiled. "I could do that, of course, but I should hate to imagine myself responsible for any young woman's being cast adrift without support or shelter." He shot Vexford a quizzical look, adding, "However, I daresay that our Nicholas would not abandon any friend of his to such a fate."

Thomas grimaced. "Good Lord, no! Clara could live for a lifetime on the proceeds of the bracelet he gave her last week, and heaven only knows what else she's managed to cozen out of him. It's more likely that she'll refuse to accept her congé. Woman's a dashed limpet, like I was telling him before."

A servant approached, and conversation lapsed while the gentlemen discussed the evening's menu with him. Once he had gone, Thomas said as if there had been no interruption, "Mind you, I don't say he ain't been fair to her. I'm just saying—"

"You're saying rather a lot, actually," Vexford interjected gently but in a tone that caused the experienced Lord Thomas to fall instantly silent. "I'd prefer," Vexford went on, "to hear what the vicar has been up to of late. I don't think we've encountered each other since last year's Spring Meeting."

"That is perfectly true," the vicar said with an understanding smile at Thomas, who seemed to have no more desire at the moment to speak. "It is difficult for me to get to London these days, you know, let alone into Hampshire, although I did meet your estimable sire right here in Newmarket at the Calver Stakes a fortnight ago. I collect that he has not returned for the Spring Meeting, however. At least, I have not yet laid eyes on him."

"No, he and my mother are at Owlcastle," Vexford said, referring to the Earl of Ulcombe's primary residence, which occupied vast parklands in Hampshire. "He is presently engaged in building a home for blind orphans in Upton Grey, on the edge of the New Forest, but they will return to town by week's end, I believe."

"I have heard of this latest enterprise of his," the vicar

said, nodding approval, "and though I am sorry not to see him again, I shall doubtless do so when I visit London next month. It has been far too long since I did, and so I mean to attend the Epsom Derby. I have not enjoyed that exciting spectacle since my Oxford days."

The servant returned with their wine, filled their glasses, and went away again, leaving the bottle on the table, before Lord Thomas said, "Look here, Dory, didn't you say something odd happened to you today in the Devil's Dyke? Can't think why anyone would want to go for a walk in a ditch rather than watch the heats, after coming to Newmarket for the races."

"Call it an impulse," the vicar said, "but indeed, the strangest thing happened. I really cannot account for it. I thought I was quite alone, you know, and didn't expect to meet another soul, but as I rounded a curve, I heard a chap talking. Found him rather shortly after that, sitting cross-legged on the ground, chattering away to himself. I bade him good-day, and took the liberty of inquiring about what he was doing there."

" 'Why, sir,' says he, 'I am at play.' "

" 'At play? With whom?' I asked. 'I see no one.' "

" 'My antagonist is not visible,' says he. 'I am playing with God.' "

Lord Thomas exclaimed, "The devil he did! What did you say to that, Dory?"

"I asked what game they were playing, of course."

Vexford chuckled. "Good for you, Vicar. What game did he say?"

"Chess."

"And did you see a chessboard?"

"None. Indeed, I pointed that out to the chap, and then— just funning a bit, you understand—I asked if he and God had placed any wagers on the outcome."

"And had they?"

"According to my newfound acquaintance, they had.

And—would you believe it—when I mentioned that he did not stand a chance to win such a wager, since his adversary must be the superior player, he said, 'He takes no advantage of me, sir, but plays as a mere mortal.' Being naturally rather stunned, I asked how they settled accounts. 'Very exactly and punctually,' says he. 'And pray, how stands your game now?' I asked, whereupon the chap admitted that he had just lost to his opponent."

"And how much had he lost?" Vexford asked.

"Twenty guineas," the vicar said with an enigmatic smile.

"By Jupiter, Dory," Thomas exclaimed, "the poor fellow must be all about in his head! You didn't leave him out there all alone, did you?"

"Patience, Thomas, I have not yet come to the end of my tale. When I asked how he would manage to pay what he owed, he said the poor were his treasurers. He said his opponent always sends some worthy person to receive the money lost, 'And,' says he to me, 'you are at present His purse-bearer, sir.' "

Thomas stared. "You're hoaxing us, Dory, admit it! Dash it, it ain't the thing for a man of the cloth to be telling such Banbury tales."

In response, the vicar reached into the pocket of his coat and withdrew a handful of guineas. "See for yourself. I would offer to pay for our supper, but I am honor-bound to contribute it to the poor box. I just wanted to share my tale with someone else before I did so. Passing strange, is it not?"

Thomas gaped at the golden coins in his brother's hand, then looked at Vexford.

Though Nick might have suspected another man of lying, not for a moment did he think the vicar had done so. And although he knew that innocents were frequently duped by sharps of one sort or another, who allowed them to win money at a gaming table in order to draw them back again to play for higher stakes at a later date, this was clearly not such a case. Such dupes were, in his experience, more greedy and less honorable than the worthy vicar. And no matter what devious thoughts might have been in the strange chess player's mind, the fellow could have nothing to gain by giving the vicar money for the poor box.

The servant soon placed their supper before them, and conversation became desultory until they had finished eating. Then, when a second bottle of wine had been placed on the table, the vicar asked casually, "How does young Oliver fare at our alma mater, Nicholas?"

Nick shrugged and said with a hint of amusement, "Haven't heard of any earthquakes or fires in Oxford of late, Vicar, so my guess is that he's been locked up or dug six feet under and they just haven't got round yet to telling the family."

The vicar chuckled, but Lord Thomas said with a grimace, "That brother of yours is a damned menace, if you ask me. I still remember that awful fortnight I spent with you at Owlcastle during a long vacation, when that brat put honey in my shoes and then made me pay him to guard my door against some villain or other who supposedly enjoyed putting tacks on the door sill each morning. Dashed if I didn't catch that scalawag, Oliver, with tacks in hand the very next day!"

"That was years ago, Tommy," Nick said, grinning at him, "and you asked for it by treating him with all the disdain of your superior years and education, you know."

"Well, you didn't treat him so well yourself, as I recall," Lord Thomas retorted. "When he snipped the seams of your leather breeches to make them fall apart when you mounted your horse, you pinned his ears back good and proper."

"Yes, that was to teach him respect for his elders. You might have done the same with my goodwill."

"Well, I might if I'd been a Goliath like you, but even then young Oliver was near as tall as I am. Moreover, though I might have had your goodwill, I'd not have had Ulcombe's." Lord Thomas gave an exaggerated shiver. "Your father's not a man to cross, and he fair dotes on that scapegrace brother of yours."

"He might have doted on Oliver then, Tommy, but the lad is fast losing his charm, I'm afraid. You may not credit the news, but my father complained recently that Oliver's been wasting the ready at an unbelievable pace and said he means to put an end to it. If I'm not mistaken, the long vacation began nearly a sennight ago, so I won't be surprised if the lad's crest isn't soon lowered a bit."

The vicar said tolerantly, "As I remember that boy, he was always full of juice and ginger."

"He's spoilt rotten," Lord Thomas said, not mincing matters. "Oh, he don't trouble you any, Nick, but you mind my words. If they've let him out of Oxford, London's where he'll be, and you'll have your hands full. Just you see if you don't."

"Oliver doesn't trouble me," Nick said amiably, "because I don't allow anyone to do so. I go my own road, Tommy, and let others go theirs. You said a while back that my father is not a man one chooses to annoy. Would you say perhaps that I am the more easily crossed, old friend?"

Lord Thomas choked on his wine, and the vicar pounded him on the back, saying sternly to Vexford as he did so, "I have never thought you a heedless man, Nicholas, so I shall not pretend to believe you spoke as you did just now without thinking. Nor do I hesitate to tell you to your head that it don't become you to speak like that to Thomas."

"I'll speak as I choose when he plays the fool."

"No one expects you to cherish fools, but neither would anyone who knows you believe you could harm a friend. Indeed, I believe I know you as well as anyone does, so I shall go further and dare to say that no one who knows you would expect you to ignore any fellow human being who appealed to you for help."

"I'll take issue with that, Vicar, for it would depend upon the particular human being in question. In my experience, most petitioners want only to have their paths smoothed for them without having to exert themselves in any way. In the idealistic days of my youth, I lent money to friends and put myself out in other ways to help those I thought deserving. In most cases, not only was the money not repaid, but my so-called friends never expressed any gratitude, and made it clear that they expected to be able to put a hand in my pocket whenever the fancy struck them. I soon learned to be more wary, I promise you, and in the end decided it was best to be and let be."

"But surely you would not refuse a friend in need," the vicar protested, looking at him with a worried frown.

"Perhaps not, if he were really my friend and really in need," Nick said with a sardonic smile. He stood up, adding, "It is nearly eight, I believe, and my man will have returned to the inn from the racing stables by now. Since I've got horses running tomorrow and Friday that are both favored to win, I ought to have a word with him before he goes to bed."

Lord Thomas looked surprised. "Do you mean to say you don't intend to go back to the tables? But, Nick, your luck is well and truly in vein tonight!"

Vexford smiled. "One reason my luck does not desert me, Tommy, is that I don't push it when it's been strained. Considering what I've won the past two nights, I'd doubtless be wise to take to my bed now and get some sleep. However, you needn't fret, for I don't intend to be wise, only to meet with my trainer. I shall return after I've spoken with him."

The vicar rose and shook his hand. "I daresay you are staying at the Rutland Arms, Nicholas. I shall have taken to my bed before you return, but I look forward to seeing you tomorrow. I shall put my money on your horses to win, too," he added with a smile. "Then, perhaps, next time I'll also be able to afford the Rutland Arms."

Melissa's room at the Rutland Arms Inn was small but well appointed and tidy. However, although she recognized the inn as a first-class hostelry, she was anything but comfortable. The past three days had been one long exercise in self-discipline, and she was exhausted from what seemed to be an unceasing need to gauge Sir Geoffrey's unpredictable and often dangerous moods, and to adjust her demeanor accordingly.

Mag had provided some relief, but not as much as might have been expected, for she had not the least notion of the true situation, and her hearty cheerfulness and frequently expressed delight in things she saw along the road irritated Sir Geoffrey. At one point, he had demanded that she ride up front with the driver, leaving Melissa alone to try to assuage his bad humor.

Even now, Melissa found his outrageous plan nearly unbelievable. However, when she had dared suggest that he had no right to marry her off to a stranger merely to repay his gaming debts, he had slapped her, a reaction that had reminded her instantly of how dangerous it was to cross him. After that, she had not even dared to ask for more information about Lord Yarborne, nor had she met with the least opportunity for escape. And although she had considered enlisting Mag's assistance, she soon realized that the girl was neither clever enough nor discreet enough to trust with such a confidence. Moreover, Mag was utterly in awe of Sir Geoffrey, and Melissa did not think she would entertain for a moment the notion of defying his orders.

Not until now, in fact, had Melissa managed to have more than a brief few moments of solitude, for Mag had slept in the same bedchamber with her at each inn, and Sir Geoffrey had scarcely let the pair of them out of his sight at any other time. But shortly after sunset, he had set out in search of Yarborne, ordering Melissa to remain in her room until his return. An hour later, when Mag had suggested ordering supper served to them there, Melissa quickly pleaded a headache and begged her to take her meal below in the coffee room. Mag, as anxious for freedom as Melissa herself, had made no objection, and so it was that Melissa had found herself alone at last.

Shuddering at the thought of what her father would do if

he caught her, she waited only moments after the sound of Mag's footsteps faded away to silence before she snatched up her cloak and threw it round her shoulders. Then, drawing on her gloves, she hurried down to the torchlit inn yard, taking care to avoid the coffee room.

Pausing on his way back through the gaming room to exchange a few brief words and another drink with friends, Nick made his way to the exit at last, stepped outside into Kingston Passage, and shouted for his horse.

Though darkness had fallen, a half moon perched high above, making it unnecessary for him to request a boy to light his way. The Rutland Arms, located on Newmarket High Street halfway between the town center and the Heath, was a popular inn for the racing set. Since Nick had stayed there from the time of his first visit to Newmarket, he thought that even on a darker night, his horse would know the way, and that was just as well, for the fresh air made it clear that he had taken more wine than he usually did. A steady stream of traffic crowded the road, but the cool night breezes soon cleared his head, and he enjoyed the ride. By the time he reached the arched gateway approaching the two-story inn, he felt refreshed and decided he might linger in the taproom a while if he found any acquaintance there after he had spoken with his man. First, however, he had to see his horse safely into its stall.

Though the stable area appeared to be temporarily deserted, he knew well that he had only to shout for a stableboy and one would appear without delay. But though he did not make a habit of looking after his own animals, he did not mind doing so. Thus it was that he rode straight into the dimly lighted stable.

He was conscious of movement near the back of the building, and heard unmistakable sounds of horses that had been disturbed. Dismounting, he peered into the dimly lit interior. "Who goes there?" he called, stepping ahead of his horse.

Silence greeted him. As he moved farther into the stable, he saw that one of his horses had been saddled, but there appeared to be no one near it. Then suddenly, a hooded figure enveloped in a long cloak threw itself into the saddle, leaned forward, and kicked the horse, which immediately sprang forward toward the open stable doors.

Although Nick stood directly in its path, he did not jump out of the way but only stepped a little to one side. Just as the horse would have shot past him, he reached out, grabbed the bridle, and held on until the animal plunged to a halt beside him.

An infuriated shriek was the rider's sole response.

"One ought not to ride full tilt out of a stable," Nick said calmly. "Such lack of consideration for others might well result in an innocent person's being run down."

"Let go!" The angry, frightened voice came from low in the rider's throat.

In the dim light Nick could not see a face, but the emotion in the voice intrigued him. "I think you had better get down," he said, "and explain yourself to me."

Instead, the rider wrenched at the reins and kicked the horse, trying by brute force to yank the bridle from his hand.

Shaking his head, Nick reached for the figure and unceremoniously lifted it from the saddle. The lightness of the body in his arms surprised him, but not nearly so much as did its soft, slender shape as it squirmed frantically to escape his grasp. The hood fell back, and even in the gloom he saw at once that his captive was female and a very pretty female at that, with long flaxen hair.

"What the devil!" he exclaimed.

"Oh, please, sir, let me go! You must."

"Oh, no, I don't think so," Nick said, grinning at her. "I think I've just taken the biggest prize of the night, my pretty little horse thief, and I've never been a man to throw away good winnings."

Three

Vexford Rejects Chance

Melissa stared at her captor in dismay. She had worried that Mag might catch sight of her as she crept past the coffee room, or that she might meet Sir Geoffrey in the inn yard. She had even worried about what she would say to a groom or stableboy with effrontery enough to try to prevent her from leaving. But it had not once occurred to her that her escape could be thwarted by a total stranger who believed she was a thief. Certainly, she had never expected to meet one large enough and strong enough to hold her straight out in front of him with her legs dangling, in order to examine her as if she were no more than an irksome child.

He was not only powerful, but dressed as he was, in a close-fitting dark riding coat and buckskin breeches, he looked both muscular and athletic. He had a rugged, handsome face with deep-set eyes and an aquiline nose. Despite the dim light, she noted a hint of a dimple near the left corner of his mouth, and she could see that his eyes were dark blue.

He set her down but took the precaution of retaining his hold on one arm, and though his grip was light, she could tell that his intention was to keep her there.

Gathering her dignity, she said with forced calm, "Release me, please. You have no right to interfere with me."

"Oh, but I do," he replied, his voice deep and melodic, his tone lazy but certain.

"You do not," she snapped, trying to ignore the odd effect his voice seemed to have on her body, as if its deep vibrations rippled right through her. Straightening, she added firmly, "I can be of no concern whatsoever to you."

"That horse is mine."

"Oh." Deflated, she tried to imagine what Charley would reply now, had she been the one to find herself in such a case, but her imagination boggled. The stranger was watching her curiously, and despite the stern set of his countenance she thought she detected a glint of amusement in his eyes. Lines etched their outer corners, as if he were a man who laughed frequently, and she took courage from that but could discern little else about him. His dark hair was carelessly tousled, so he was not a member of the dandy set, and if he was a sportsman, he was not one who prided himself upon being a devil to go in the hunting field. He was far too large for most hunters.

He was clearly waiting to hear what she would say next, and his silence, despite the twinkle in his eyes, was daunting.

At last, quietly, Melissa said, "I beg your pardon for my error, sir. I thought I was merely borrowing one of the inn's hacks."

"Borrowing?" His eyebrows shot upward in disbelief.

"Yes, borrowing," she said firmly. "I intend to ride only to Cambridge, where I am persuaded I can easily arrange for its prompt return. I am no thief."

"Then you simply made a mistake and took the wrong horse. Is that it?"

"That's it exactly. Now, if you will just excuse me—"

"One moment." His grip remained fixed on her arm, and despite the thickness of her cloak, she could feel the warmth of his hand now. His nearness was disturbing. He did not frighten her, but he seemed to fill the space around her, to take up much more space than even his great height and breadth warranted. His voice, too, seemed larger than life. It seemed to her that it resonated through the stable, though he did not raise it, when he said reasonably, "No doubt my host will know which horse you ought to take. Shall we just step inside and ask him?"

"No! That is," she said, forcing calm back into her voice, "I do not wish to return to the inn, sir."

"Then you are not, in fact, a guest here."

"Yes, I am. Or I was. It's just that . . ." Struggling to think how to continue, she caught his gaze again and, seeing patent disbelief in his quizzical expression, fell silent, nibbling her lower lip and wishing he would step back, if only a foot or two.

"Just so. You did not, in fact, previously arrange with my host to borrow one of his horses. Perhaps," he added when she did not contradict him, "you had better explain the whole matter to me. I must warn you, however, that my time is short, for I have formed the intention of speaking with my trainer before he retires for the night, and he does so rather earlier than usual on evenings before important races."

"Do you breed racers?" The question leapt from her tongue before she could stop it. Horses, particularly highly bred horses, were ever of interest to her.

"So you are an enthusiast," he said, smiling. The smile made his dimple more noticeable, softened his features dramatically, and was infectious enough to stir an instant urge in her to smile back. Then another thought seemed to strike him, for the smile faded, replaced by curiosity, and he said, "If that is the case, why are you determined to leave Newmarket on the eve of the biggest day of racing?"

Noises of arrival outside in the yard stirred her tensions anew, and she became increasingly anxious to get away. Trying to think of something that would convince him to let her go, she said distractedly, "Is tomorrow the biggest day?"

"It is." Again he was watching her, but he said only, "I

expect I should call for a stableboy to look after these horses of mine."

"Oh, please do not, sir. Could you not very kindly lend me that one for just a short time. I promise to send him back the moment I reach Cambridge. I-I cannot explain the whole to you, but really, I am in the most dreadful hurry. I must get away from here at once. I-if I do not . . ." She definitely heard men's voices in the yard now. Looking back at the large gentleman, who maintained his inflexible grip on her arm, she saw him shake his head, and said beseechingly, "P-please, sir."

"Don't be foolish," he said, looking into her eyes in a way that made her want to weep with vexation. "You are far too young and unprotected to ride off at night on your own."

"You say that only because I am female," she retorted, fighting through increasing fear to retain her tattered shreds of dignity. "I'll have you know I am an excellent horsewoman, sir."

"No doubt you are," he said calmly. "But though I do worry more about a female, particularly one as small as you are—"

"I am no such thing!" But she felt very small next to him, certainly, and she was not surprised to see him smile again.

The smile was rueful. He said, "To me you seem petite, I'm afraid, although I daresay your height is probably average for a female. That makes no difference to the point at hand, however. Riding off alone after dark on an unfamiliar route would be foolish for anyone, even a large, strong man. There are any number of dangers out there that you cannot have considered properly."

"I haven't got time to consider them," she said. "Please, sir, you must let me go. What might or might not become of me is not your affair, just as I told you at the outset of this conversation."

"Nevertheless—"

"Melissa! What the devil are you doing here?"

Frozen in place by the sound of Sir Geoffrey's voice, despite the fact that her increasing tension had warned her that she might expect momentarily to hear it, Melissa felt as if the breath of life had been knocked from her body. It was as if somehow she had turned into a phantom or shadow that swooped up to perch above the three figures in the stable, looking down as the scene unfolded. Though no portion of her body had moved, she knew the expression on her father's face as clearly as if she gazed at him in a bright light. She knew how his jaw had tightened, how the lines around his mouth had deepened. She knew the thinning of his lips as he pressed them together, and the way his eyes narrowed and their expression chilled. She sensed, too, the exact moment he collected his wits and became fully aware of her large companion.

"I am Sir Geoffrey Seacourt," he said in a firm but much calmer tone. "I do not believe I have the honor of your acquaintance, sir."

"I'm Vexford," the tall stranger said casually in his deep voice, the very sound of which recalled Melissa to her senses. His tone indicated that he had no doubt that his brief identification of himself would suffice.

Apparently it did, for Sir Geoffrey said warmly, "Are you indeed? I have met your father, of course. Ulcombe is a member of White's, as I am myself."

"I also claim membership in that august establishment," Vexford said with some amusement, "though I do not believe I have set foot in the place since my honorable sire first presented me there."

"No doubt you prefer Brooks's," Sir Geoffrey said, chuckling. "I know how it is with the younger set, you see, but you will no doubt change your attitude once you have succeeded to your father's earldom, you know, for that generally is what happens in such cases as yours. Go inside now, Melissa," he said, adding in a caressing way, "You will catch your death out here, darling. Indeed, I cannot think what brought you to the stables tonight, but his lordship and I will excuse you now."

Melissa stood still for another long moment. The hand gripping her arm had released it the moment Sir Geoffrey first spoke. At the time, she had felt oddly abandoned by the gesture, though it had freed her spirit to take its odd flight of fancy. Taking courage now from the mildness of Sir Geoffrey's manner and the fact that the sensation of having left her body had disappeared, she began to turn toward her father, pausing briefly as she did to look up into Vexford's eyes. Seeing not only curiosity in his expression but the same strength she sensed in his very nearness, she shifted her gaze to Sir Geoffrey, saying as she did, "I would prefer not to go in just yet, sir. I was speaking with his lordship, and our conversation had not yet ended."

Sir Geoffrey stood just inside the stable door, his horse's reins in one hand, his riding whip in the other. When her eyes met his, she realized instantly that his charm was false. Wondering how she had dared to defy him, she could only hope that Vexford would not do or say anything to make the situation worse than it was.

Flicking an imaginary bit of lint from his left breeches' leg with the tip of the whip, Sir Geoffrey said evenly, "You will do as I bid you, darling." Smiling again at Vexford, he added, "You will excuse her, I know. She is young and does not always know what is best for her. I daresay you were considerably astonished to meet her out here alone at such an hour—unless, of course, you were previously acquainted and had made some sort of assignation with her." His smile widened as if he were certain that was not the case, but Melissa, oversensitive to his moods now, noted that the steely glint in his eyes did not match the lightness of his tone.

Vexford said smoothly, "I'm not acquainted with the lady at all, I regret to say. We encountered each other but moments ago when I rode into the stable. However, if she does not wish to return to the inn, I can see no reason why she should, and I am quite willing to see that no danger befalls her here."

"The decision is not hers to make," Sir Geoffrey said, looking at Melissa.

Although nothing in that look would have warned anyone not well acquainted with him, she remembered the expression she saw now as clearly as if they had never been parted. Her knees threatened to betray her, and she swayed dizzily.

A large hand gripped her elbow, steadying her, and she heard Vexford say with an edge to his voice, "I do not understand you, Seacourt. Have you some particular claim on this lady that you so cavalierly make such decisions for her?"

Melissa looked up at him in surprise, realizing only then what he must have thought, but Sir Geoffrey chuckled and said, "I collect that the wicked minx exerted herself to charm you, just as she has charmed others before you, rather than tell the truth. She likes to get her own way, you see, and never hesitates to employ a vast array of feminine wiles to that end. At another time, Vexford, I might hesitate to intervene in what I'm persuaded can be no more than innocent dalliance—on your part at least—just to teach her a lesson. However, in this particular instance, my darling daughter was specifically commanded to remain in her bedchamber until my return."

"Your daughter!"

Sir Geoffrey laughed. "I ought to have known she did not mention her surname, because you did not recognize it when I identified myself to you. Since I collect, as well, that she failed to mention even that she is here at the inn with her father, just what *did* she tell you, if I may inquire?"

Melissa stiffened, trembling, but the warm hand at her elbow did not stir as Vexford said on a note of surprise, "I think you misunderstood the situation, Seacourt. We had, as I said, but just met when I rode into the stable. That Miss Seacourt did not make me a gift of her name or circumstance is therefore quite understandable. I daresay she must have been taking the air before retiring, but our conversation had not advanced to the point of exchanging any details whatsoever."

Sir Geoffrey said skeptically, "When I came in, I distinctly recall that you had your hand on her arm, just as you do now. If you had only just met and had not yet introduced yourselves . . ." Though he fell silent, he looked pointedly at Vexford.

"I'm afraid I took her by surprise when I came inside, and—"

"Excuse me, mister." A wiry stableboy appeared opportunely (in Melissa's opinion) out of the dark doorway behind Sir Geoffrey, and reached to take the reins he held in his right hand. Pausing, the lad looked in bewilderment from one man to the other and said, "I were told ter come put up a horse fer the night. Be it this 'un or one o' them others, or all of 'em? 'Cause if it's all of 'em, I'd best shout up some'un else, so as not ter leave any of 'em standing too long."

Sir Geoffrey looked at the horse Melissa had saddled for herself, then at Vexford's, and a brief but pregnant silence ensued. Melissa racked her brain for something to say that would explain away the presence of a second, saddled horse, but nothing useful occurred to her.

Vexford said casually, "You may certainly look after mine, lad, and if you like, I'll have someone else sent out to help you. That second horse was probably saddled in the belief that my trainer would visit the racing barn again tonight, for it is certainly the horse he rides. He will not be going out again, however, so you can put it up now."

"But, m' lord, no one—"

"That will be all for now," Vexford said. "Just see to these horses. I'm beginning to feel a distinct chill out here, and I've no wish to linger to discuss the matter. Shall I tell the landlord to roust out another lad to help you?"

"No need for that, m' lord. I'll just shout. The lads sleep

when they can in the back loft, because we've got gentlemen coming in all night long, but 'tis a wonder none of 'em heard us afore now. Ye ought ter know ye'd only to call out."

As the boy moved to collect the three horses, Melissa said, "Before you go into the inn, my lord, perhaps I might just have another brief word with you."

Sir Geoffrey said, "No need for that. You are coming with me, darling, and there will be no more roundaboutation. His lordship will excuse you."

Desperately, praying he would support her, Melissa said to Vexford, "Please, sir, you must hear me out. This is wrong. He may be my father, but he has abducted me from my rightful home and forced me to come here in order to—"

"That's enough," Sir Geoffrey said sharply enough to silence her. Turning to Vexford with a sigh, he said in rueful exasperation, "I am sorry for this. My daughter is unfortunately both imaginative and fanciful. Merely because I have made a decision on her behalf which she does not like, she has led me a merry dance, but I'll not allow her to trouble you or anyone else with her feminine nonsense, I promise you."

Melissa, indignant at hearing her behavior described in such an outrageous way, opened her mouth to object, but the words were stopped on her tongue when Vexford said flatly, "He is your father, is he not?"

"Yes, he is," Melissa said, "but—"

"Then you must obey him."

"But you don't understand!"

"Yes, darling, he does understand, more clearly than you do, I think," Sir Geoffrey said in that maddening, amused tone he had used before. "As your father, I have the legal right to command your obedience to my will in any and all things. That is the law of England, and although I have always exerted myself to consider your wants and desires, I need not ever do so, you know."

As he spoke the last few words, he looked right into her

eyes, giving her to understand that those words, and the fact
that the law would support his every move, were the only
things that would concern anyone. Looking at Vexford, she
saw with dismay that he would not help her.

While she hesitated, her gaze still fixed on Vexford, Sir
Geoffrey stepped forward and put an arm around her shoulders, saying gently, "Come along now, darling. You don't
want his lordship to think you ill-behaved. You have taken
up quite enough of his time already. We'll just go inside and
have a little talk, the two of us, and I'm sure I'll convince
you that the proper course is the one I've laid out, but if you
still have some uncertainties, you know you have only to
express them to me." She could smell liquor on his breath
now, and the odor increased her fears, though she could not
have explained why it did.

"I'll walk in with you," Vexford said.

Melissa's knees felt weak again. Not for a moment did she
believe that Sir Geoffrey intended to have reasonable speech
with her. She remembered only too clearly how he reacted
when his will was crossed, and she had certainly crossed it
tonight. But when she did not move instantly to accompany
him, he gave her a hard nudge, unseen by Vexford, and she
obeyed, believing from what she had seen in the larger man's
eyes that he was completely convinced of Sir Geoffrey's
kindly intent.

Melissa would have been surprised to know, as they
walked back into the inn, that Nick was anything but convinced of her father's amiable character. He had, in fact, taken
an instant, albeit apparently illogical, dislike to Sir Geoffrey
Seacourt, although he would have agreed with anyone who
said the man seemed no more than ordinarily concerned
about his daughter. Having discovered her alone in a barn
with an unknown and unmarried man, his concern was reasonable. Even the overbluff heartiness in Seacourt's manner

was understandable, since he knew the Earl of Ulcombe wielded considerable influence both in the political world and in the *beau monde*. The attitude was one that Nick had encountered frequently, even in persons who were otherwise perfectly likable. Still, he did not like Seacourt.

Instincts honed by uncountable hours at gaming tables told him that the man's bluff heartiness was a facade, but what lay beneath the surface remained a mystery. Though it had become clear to him that Seacourt had taken a drink or two over his limit, the man was not ape-drank. In any case, Nick told himself, he was the girl's father, did not mean real harm to her, and she had earned a scolding. He also decided that, despite his instincts and the way he had felt drawn to help her, he had no good reason to interfere in what was, after all, no business of his.

When they parted company near the taproom door, he caught Miss Seacourt's frightened gaze once more, and felt again the unusual urge that had stirred him to lend her his protection. She was a disobedient daughter, one clearly accustomed to doing as she pleased. Nothing else could explain the mad attempt to ride to Cambridge on her own. Even if she spoke the truth about Seacourt's having uprooted her from her rightful home—though what she could have meant by such a statement, he could not imagine—she had no business stealing horses or riding off in the dark of night. He did not doubt that she was a minx or that her frail flaxen beauty hid a spoiled and willful nature. Why then, he wondered, watching her go dejectedly up the narrow stairway ahead of her father, did he feel as if he had abandoned her to a dreadful fate?

Putting his concerns ruthlessly aside, he entered the taproom to find his trainer comfortably seated at a table with his groom, a pint of foamy beer before each of them. Nick said to the latter, "So here you are, Artemus. Go out to the stable, will you, and help them put up my hack and the gelding Drax rides."

The trainer, a slender but muscular man twenty years Nick's senior, with grizzled hair and eyebrows so thick they threatened one day to hide his eyes altogether, said, "I never had that bay out after six, my lord. Put him away myself."

"Nevertheless, Drax, he's wearing a saddle now, and the lad has three to deal with. Your beer will keep, Artemus. I want a word with Drax now, anyway."

"Aye, m' lord."

When the groom had gone, Nick sat down in his place, called to the tapster to provide him with ale, and turned back to Drax. "How are Quiz and Florrie?"

"At their peak, my lord, just as I promised. They both ought to win their early heats. As to whether Prince will carry the day tomorrow against the Duke of Grafton's nag, I can't say till we pair them. I like Wilson's colt for the Friday race, but His Grace insists that Whizgig will win, and he's put his blunt down pretty heavy, I'm told."

"So have I, Drax, not to mention my hundred-pound subscription just to enter, so don't let me down. His lordship will never let me hear the end of it if you do."

Drax did not misunderstand him. In his view, there was only one lordship worth mentioning. " 'Tis a pity he ain't here, Master Nick. He'd like to see your horses win, even if he's teased you something unmerciful for naming the black Prince Florizel."

Nick chuckled at the memory of his father's reaction to the name. "I did it in honor of His Majesty's erstwhile nickname," he said with a false air of virtue.

Drax smiled and rubbed his bristly chin, watching the tapster serve Nick's ale.

Nick's thoughts drifted upstairs, and he was just wondering what might be happening between Miss Seacourt and her father when Drax said, "Do you mean to tell me how you came to find that bay saddled again in the stable, Master Nick? I don't need to tell you I never left him that way when I got back from the Heath."

"I know you didn't," Nick said. "I did tell someone that the lads out there had saddled the hack up for you, thinking you would return to the racing barn tonight, but I doubt that he believed me. For that matter, it was a stupid gambit," he added musingly. "Too easy to check. I don't want to discuss it further, however."

Drax looked curious but made no more attempt to question him, which did not surprise Nick. Over the years, he had discouraged his retainers from inquiring too carefully into either his actions or the reasons for them.

When he finished his ale, he bade his trainer good-night and, feeling restless, decided to walk back to the Little Hell. He told himself the exercise would do him good. The drinks were excellent there, his friends would still be gathered around the tables, and action would be running high in anticipation of the next day's heavy betting at the Heath. He would not stake his money at the tables, however, for instinct warned him that his luck had run its course. Still, the activity was bound to take his thoughts off what he was rapidly coming to believe had been a most unfortunate encounter. The sooner he forgot the silly chit, the better it would be.

Entering her bedchamber with her father right behind her, Melissa silently cursed her untimely meeting with Vexford. If only—

"Lawks-a-mussy, miss, I were just beginning to think you musta been carried off by gypsies!" Mag jumped to her feet from the bench in the window embrasure where she had been curled up awaiting the return of her mistress. "I'll fetch your hot water straightaway, for I don't doubt you'll be wanting to get right to bed."

"Get out," Seacourt said.

"Well, lawks-a-mussy, sir, didn't I just say I was going?"

"Don't come back here tonight unless I send for you."

"But I sleep here," Mag protested.

"Not tonight, you don't. Tell the landlord to find you a pallet in the attic with his own servants. If he cannot, he must provide you with a room of your own near this one. Your mistress will not require your services any longer tonight." He held the door open and Mag fled without another word. Shutting the door with a bang, he said grimly, "And now, my darling daughter, we will discuss your failure to obey me."

"Sir, please, you must understand how I feel about this," Melissa pleaded, stepping toward him with her hands spread.

He slapped her face.

The blow brought tears to her eyes and sent her stumbling back again, but she pressed a hand to her stinging cheek and did not cry out.

He snapped, "I understand that you have somehow come to believe, in the past nine years, that you can set your will against mine with impunity. You will soon learn the error of such misguided thinking, however. Just where the devil did you think you were going?"

Without thinking, she blurted, "Nowhere, I swear! It was just as his lordship said. I-I was taking some air before retiring, and— No, please don't hit me again!"

He lowered his hand. "Then don't lie to me. That horse was not saddled in error, Melissa. I heard the stableboy perfectly plainly when he tried to say that no one had left it saddled for Vexford's man. You saddled it yourself, didn't you? Tell me the truth now, or I'll make you wish you had."

"Very well, then, I did saddle the horse." she said. "I-I want to go home, Papa. Please, let me go home to Scotland!"

"Home is with me until you are married," he said, adding on a different note, "I missed seeing Yarborne tonight, but perhaps that's just as well, because before I turn you over to him, I must teach you to obey those in authority over you. You may consider it my wedding gift to your husband."

Raising the riding whip he still held, he stepped purposefully toward her.

Four

Increasing the Stakes

Outside the entrance to the Little Hell, Nick tossed his reins to a waiting lad. It occurred to him that although Clara, Lady Hawthorne, had known better than to expect him to dine with her that evening, she did expect him to put in at least a brief appearance at the assembly she was attending. She had said as much before leaving the Heath earlier that day when she had also expressed displeasure with his lack of attention to her since their arrival in Newmarket. Her ladyship, he reflected as he mounted the steps, was proving to be more demanding than was consistent with his hedonistic nature, not to mention a bore. No doubt Tommy was right, and he was no more than a selfish trifler, but Clara had understood the game well enough when they first met, so she had little to complain about now. He had been exceedingly generous.

Miss Seacourt had more cause to be provoked with him, because she had asked for help and he had refused it. The truth was, of course, that there had been little he could do for her. Seacourt's authority over her, as her father, was indisputable. Still, Nick could not forget her fear. Reminding himself that Seacourt had not projected an impression of violent anger did not help, for heaven knew, the Earl of Ulcombe seldom raised his voice, yet he was a terrifying figure when his displeasure was aroused. Furthermore, although Nick could not remember the last time he himself had shouted or employed violence against a fellow man, more than one friend had declared his temper one to be avoided at all cost.

Seacourt simply had not appeared to be infuriated, only exasperated; and considering that his daughter had tried to ride to Cambridge on what could only have been a female's foolish whim, he had been well within his rights to be annoyed. If he subjected her to a severe tongue-lashing, it was no more than she deserved. So why, Nick wondered as he gave cloak, gloves, hat, and whip to the footman waiting inside the door to receive them, did he continue to feel as if he had shamelessly abandoned a drowning kitten?

Many gentlemen in the card room had dressed more formally for the later hour. They wore the stiff white neckcloths, brass-buttoned coats, embroidered waistcoats, and elegant pantaloons that one might see at any fashionable London club. The noise level had risen since his departure, however, to a point well beyond the decorous low hum one encountered in the august chambers of White's or Brooks's. It had, in fact, risen to a din that must preclude any rational conversation.

Men crowded around the hazard and faro tables, while others played whist for high stakes, or macao, or piquet. With the advantage of his superior height, Nick scanned the crowd and soon spotted Lord Thomas, once again at the hazard table. Making his way there, pausing now and again to exchange a greeting, and then to order a bottle of his favorite brandy from a passing servant, he found himself, more than once, pushing the memory of Miss Seacourt out of his mind.

When he stepped to the table beside Lord Thomas, that gentleman's cheerful round face broke into a broad grin. "Couldn't stay away, I see," he said, raising his voice to a near bellow to make himself heard. "Cover my stake, will you, Nick? English rules. Main was five, chance is seven, which is three to two in favor of the caster. Just look at that stake! If I throw the main now, I'll have to apply to you for a loan to pay off everyone, but if I throw chance, I'll be rolling in filthy lucre."

"I'll watch, thanks. You're more likely to lose your shirt than to throw in, and it sounds to me as if I'd lose in either event."

"Doubter." Carelessly, Lord Thomas gave the cup a shake and spilled the dice onto the green velvet plain.

May the devil fly away with those ivories!" he cried when they came to rest with an ace and four showing. "If I'd wanted five, I could have thrown all night and never got it."

"I told you, you'd lose your shirt. Do you really need a loan?"

"No, dash it, but it's low tide with me now."

"Then come away and play piquet with me instead."

"Don't you mean to play hazard?"

"No, something tells me I'm bound to be as out of vein now as you are," Nick said. "Pass the cup like a good chap, and come along. I saw an unoccupied table near the door to the hall."

"Very well, but I don't know how you can say you're out of vein when you were winning every throw you cast before supper," Thomas complained as they made their way to the table.

"That was, as you say, before supper." The servant approached with the brandy Nick had ordered, and at their request, he soon provided them with a second glass, a fresh thirty-two card piquet pack, and a wooden piquet marker. "You deal, Tommy," Nick said. "I shall pour the brandy."

"Right you are," Thomas said, removing the binding and shuffling the cards with practiced speed. "I should tell you at the outset that, although I haven't altogether lost my shirt, my pockets are well and truly to let for the duration unless your nag wins the sweepstakes tomorrow."

"I'll frank you for now. We'll play for chicken stakes if you like."

"Are you feeling quite the thing?" Thomas said, dealing them each twelve cards and fanning out the rest in the center of the table.

"I'm well enough." Having poured generous amounts into both glasses, and resolutely ignoring the recurring memory of a slim and supple body squirming in his grasp, Nick set the bottle down, drank deeply, and picked up his hand.

Watching him curiously, Thomas said, "Look here, old son, if Drax gave you bad news about Prince Florizel's chances, I wish you would tell me before the nag turns tail on the course tomorrow and runs off into the Dyke with my wager."

"There's naught amiss with Florrie or Quiz," Nick said as he sorted his cards and mentally scored the hand. "I'll take five," he added, discarding that number and taking the top five cards from the stockpile. Looking at them, he grimaced, thinking it was just as well that he had decided not to try his luck again at the hazard table.

"Dealer takes the remaining three," Thomas said, doing so.

Nick drank more brandy and finally blinked away what seemed to have become a tenacious mental image of Miss Seacourt. "I declare a point of five," he said.

"Value?"

"Forty-four."

"No good."

"Three kings?"

"No good."

Resigned to a second-rate hand, Nick led his ace of diamonds.

Lord Thomas declared, "Point of five, tierce in spades, fourteen tens." He followed suit with the eight of diamonds, while Nick marked the score on the board.

Having no second ace with which to take advantage of the nine points down, Nick played a seven. By the end of the hand, the unguarded king of spades he had kept in hopes of drawing the fourth king caused him to lose seven tricks, leaving him a net score for the hand of eight to Lord Thomas's forty.

"Take care you ain't routed," that gentleman said, grinning.

Nick gave him a look, shuffled, and began to deal the cards.

"Good evening, gentlemen."

They looked up as one to find Lord Yarborne standing beside them. A man with more than fifty summers behind him, he was fashionably dressed in a dark blue coat, light pantaloons, highly polished shoes, and snowy white linen. Looking from one to the other with a benign smile, he said, "Forgive me for interrupting your game, but I've not had a spare moment since I saw you today at the Heath, Vexford, to inquire after the health of your estimable sire."

"He is perfectly stout, sir, thank you."

Despite Tommy's earlier suggestion that Yarborne was acquainted with Ulcombe, Nick had not been aware that the two were particularly friendly. He could not recall Ulcombe's ever mentioning Yarborne's name, and that fact must have reflected itself in his expression, for Yarborne said, "I had the honor to be of some service to him, you know, in his recent arrangements to endow a home for blind orphans, and I believe he said I could expect to see him here at the Spring Meeting."

"To be sure, one can generally rely upon him to attend," Nick agreed, "but he's spent so much time of late with the orphanage that estate matters required his presence at Owlcastle this week. He won't miss the Epsom Derby, however. You can be sure of meeting him there."

"I daresay I shall see him in town before then," Yarborne said easily. Turning to Lord Thomas, he said in a bantering, almost avuncular tone, "I hear your luck was out tonight at the hazard table, my boy. Hope you haven't gone and earned yourself a lecture from that parson brother of yours. I'm told he arrived this afternoon."

"Oh, yes, Dory's here, all right and tight," Thomas replied, "but he's not one for chafing a fellow, you know. Got his own trials to bear."

"Altogether a most worthy man, I'm told, though I've never had an opportunity to become formally acquainted with him."

"Oh, he's worthy enough, is Dory," Thomas said with a chuckle, "but just now he's more concerned with dancing round a parson's mousetrap than with accomplishing deeds of rectitude or poking his nose into anyone else's affairs."

"He is ten years your senior, is he not? Do you say that he has formed an attachment at last with an eligible female?"

"Worse," declared Lord Thomas, eyes atwinkle. "A predatory widow's taken a fancy to him. That's why he took it into his noddle to take that dashed foolish walk along the Devil's Dyke today, Nick," he added with a wide grin. "Told me he was afraid of encountering her at the Heath, because she's formed a dashed nuisancing habit of following him about, wherever he goes. He told me that after supper. You'd gone back to the Rutland Arms."

Yarborne said, "I had the good fortune to dine tonight with my son, who's come down from Oxford for the long vacation. I had expected him to accompany me back here, but he'd got himself invited to some assembly or other instead."

"There are any number of assemblies this week, I believe," Nick said. He thought ruefully again of Clara, only to have her glittering image replaced at once in his mind by that of a slender figure in a voluminous cloak, with silvery flaxen hair highlighted by the golden glow of stable lanterns.

"There are all sorts of entertainments," Yarborne said. "Women need something to amuse them while their husbands and sons are racing and gaming."

"Some of the men must be dancing, too," Thomas pointed

out, "or else the ladies would have no partners. Don't dance much myself, mind, but someone must."

Yarborne smiled. "True enough. But I've interrupted your play long enough, gentlemen. You ought to bring Vexford along to the Billingsgate one evening when we're back in town, Thomas."

Lord Thomas looked surprised. "You've played at the Billingsgate Club in St. James's Street, have you not, Nick?"

"Once or twice."

"I thought so, by Jupiter. It ain't but a few blocks from Barrington House."

Yarborne's smile widened. "We must put your name up for membership, Vexford, though the powers that be won't thank us for the gesture if you break their bank. I'm told your luck is quite extraordinary."

"It is thought to be so only because I generally stake myself against the house, and don't accept every wild bet that's offered to me," Nick said mildly.

"Is that how you built your reputation? Perhaps I should follow your example—though I've had very good luck of late," he added with a glint of sardonic amusement. "Enough now. Get back to your cards." And he vanished into the milling throng.

"What was that in aid of, I wonder," Nick said musingly.

"Your father," Thomas said, looking surprised. "Said so himself. Managed to be of service to Ulcombe, he said. Daresay he wants to pursue the acquaintance. Like my father said. Happens to *him* all the time. He's surrounded by toadies."

"But one can hardly think of Yarborne as a toady if he already has built nearly as great a reputation for good works as my father has."

"Works too hard at it, and he's dashed expensive, Yarborne is. He's got his finger in a dozen pies besides his charities. I don't like him much though, when all's said and done. May be a warm man financially, but otherwise, he's a cold fish if you ask me. Walks as if he's soiled his smalls and can smell it. Ulcombe ain't like that."

"No, he's not," Nick agreed. "Have you aught to declare?"

Thomas picked up the hand he had put down out of courtesy when Yarborne interrupted them, glanced at it, and said, "Point of five."

"It's good." Nick sighed and poured a generous amount of brandy into his glass. His luck had clearly deserted him.

When Sir Geoffrey grabbed Melissa and pulled her across his knee, she went limp. She did not try to struggle or to fight him, focusing her energy instead on enduring the punishment, and on doing nothing more to fan his anger. Long ago she had learned that struggling produced dreadful consequences. In the terrible moments that followed, each stroke of the riding whip laid a line of fire across her body, but though she sobbed, she did not scream or cry, or stir from the humiliating position.

When he stopped at last, she remained exactly where he had placed her, tense and frightened, until he said grimly, "You may get up now, Melissa."

She stood carefully, choking back sobs. Nine years had dimmed her memory of the pain he was capable of meting out. She had not remembered, either, how difficult it was to maintain an appearance of submission. She kept her eyelids cast down, knowing that to look at him would be foolhardy, since he might choose to read insolence or antipathy in her expression even if both were absent.

He said quietly, "I am sorry you forced me to be harsh with you, Melissa, but you ought to have remembered that I never tolerate disobedience."

"Yes, Papa."

"That is not a proper apology."

"I am sorry I disobeyed you. P-please, forgive me." She stared at the floor as she spoke, knowing that if she were to look at him now he would surely see her resentment. It was all she could do to keep her voice from betraying her feelings.

"That's better," he said, putting an arm around her and giving her a hug. "It would not do for me to be giving Yarborne a disobedient bride, now, would it?"

She stiffened. Then, to cover the involuntary movement, she slipped from his embrace and turned to pour water from the washstand ewer into the basin. The water was tepid. She splashed some on her face, realizing only when she straightened that Sir Geoffrey had moved up beside her and was holding out her towel.

"Thank you." Taking it from him and patting her face dry, she moved away toward the fireplace.

She could sense him watching her, could feel the silence lengthening uncomfortably, before he said lightly, "You know, my darling, I don't believe you are entirely reconciled to this marriage."

"I do not want to marry a stranger old enough to be my father," she said, struggling to keep her voice calm. "Surely that is n-not so odd."

"Are you thinking of disobeying me again?" His voice, soft and silky smooth, sent icy prickles of fear shooting up her spine.

"N-no, sir." She could manage little more than a whisper.

"I did not quite hear you."

She did not think she could utter the words again. Recalling a similar scene in the distant past, she remembered wishing then that she had a fairy godmother who would whisk her away to a distant country, preferably one where females were not ever burdened with fathers or husbands.

"Look at me, Melissa."

From somewhere deep inside, drawing on long buried instincts, she summoned up the strength not only to turn and face him but to manage a small, rueful smile as she did. Tears clung to her lashes, and her smile lacked confidence. She moistened her lips and said, "I have not behaved well,

Papa. No doubt you were right to say I have become spoilt over the years. I will try to do better."

"You must do more than try," Sir Geoffrey said. "Yarborne will know how to manage you, I expect, but I'll be very much displeased if you embarrass me when you meet him, or do anything to disgrace the Seacourt name. Do you understand?"

"Yes, sir." She understood that he intended to beat her into submission if she defied him, and she knew he was perfectly capable of doing so. Using her fingers as makeshift combs to push her hair back from her face, she said as matter-of-factly as she could, "Did you say you've had no chance to speak with him yet?"

"He is staying at the White Hart, but he did not dine there tonight and the porter did not know where he could be found at that hour. I had a few drinks to pass the time, not wanting to traipse all over town, but I came away when the fellow told me at last—as he ought to have done at once—that Yarborne wouldn't return before midnight."

"Then you will speak with him in the morning," she said with relief. Perhaps she might yet find a means of escape.

Sir Geoffrey did not respond at once, and she realized with a flutter of fear that he had been watching her. She smiled again, smoothing her skirt with nervous hands, before he said, "I think perhaps it would be wise to look Yarborne up tonight. After all, one does not like to put off settling one's debts of honor."

A glimmer of hope stirred. "As you please," she said, striving to look and sound submissive as she turned to pick up her brush from the dressing table. "Perhaps you could ask someone to send Mag to me before you go. I would like to go to bed."

"You will not require Mag's services."

Confidence surged through her. If he left her alone while he went to find Yarborne, surely she could manage to slip out to the stables again. This time, with no large stranger to stop her, she could be well away from Newmarket long before Sir Geoffrey returned. Knowing that she must not agree too quickly, however, lest she renew his suspicions, she peeped up at him from beneath her lashes and said in a coaxing voice, "You give me too much credit, Papa. I am dreadfully unhandy, and I'd prefer to have her assistance. I'd like some hot water as well."

"You are not going to bed yet, I'm afraid."

"I-I don't understand. Do you want me to await your return before retiring?"

"No, Melissa. You are going with me."

She said in dismay, "You cannot mean to drag me all over town while you search for Yarborne!"

"I have no intention of giving you a second chance to escape."

"I won't," she said desperately. "I'll give you my word if you like, but please don't force me to go with you. What on earth will people think?"

"I don't care what they think, but perhaps Yarborne will have returned to the White Hart by now. Under the circumstances, no one could think it outrageous for me to present his betrothed to him there."

"But they would. At such an hour as this, the very idea is outrageous."

"Not if I say it is not, Melissa." The grim note had returned to his voice, and the look he gave her dared her to contradict him. When she remained silent, he said, "That's much better. Now, if you are going to brush your hair, do so at once."

Obediently, she dragged the brush through her tangled hair, but though she would have drawn the process out as long as possible, he soon took the brush from her and wielded it with energy enough to bring the tears back to her eyes.

"There," he said at last. "Now, pin it up or whatever you do, but do it quickly if you don't want me to do it for you."

Stepping away from him without a word, she twisted the

silken strands swiftly into a knot at the nape of her neck and pinned it in place. Then, seeing that he held her cloak ready for her, she did not point out that her only gown was wrinkled and needed both washing and pressing, but allowed him to drape the cloak around her shoulders. When he opened the door she said, "My gloves, Papa?"

"Yes, yes, put them on."

"Must you not order horses saddled for us, sir?"

"We'll walk."

"But—"

"We'll walk, I said. It is no more than a few blocks, and if you don't want to suffer another lesson in obedience before we leave, you will hold your tongue. In fact, don't utter another word until we find Yarborne."

Believing he would do what he threatened, Melissa pressed her lips tightly together. Downstairs, when they encountered a surprised look from the landlord, Sir Geoffrey said, "Going to take my daughter for a little stroll up the street. Been cooped up here all evening, you know. She will be the better for a breath of air."

"To be sure, sir, but you won't want her walking along the public street. You'll find the small garden behind the stables much more to your liking. You won't see my rib's flowers a-blooming in the dark, but there's a moon up, so you'll see the path well enough without needing a lad to light your way."

"Thank you," Sir Geoffrey said, giving a clear impression that he intended to take the advice. In the yard, however, he did not so much as turn toward that garden behind the stables, urging Melissa forward to the High Street. She put up her hood to hide her features from passersby, knowing that no one who saw her walking there at such an hour would take her for a gentlewoman. Fifteen minutes later, when they arrived at the White Hart, she kept her face down and her hood up as Sir Geoffrey hustled her inside.

When a porter approached to ask how he might serve them, Sir Geoffrey said, "Has Lord Yarborne returned yet?"

"Oh, it's you, sir. Well, the fact is, he ain't back and most likely won't get back yet a while. Even with the sweepstakes tomorrow, many gentlemen won't leave the tables before dawn. Not that his lordship generally stays out so late, but as I said before, I doubt we'll see him before midnight. Do you want to wait for him? I cannot offer you a private parlor, for they're taken, and without his lordship having warned us to expect you, I can't let you wait in the one he hired for himself."

"No, no, I won't ask that of you," Sir Geoffrey said. "What I would like to do, however, is to seek him out, if you know where I might find him now."

"As to that, I can't say for certain, sir, but I do know as how he's partial—like so many other gentlemen—to what they call the Little Hell. He don't like the food there, which is why I didn't send you round before, knowing as I did that he meant to dine with his son, who arrived today from Oxford."

"Thank you, we'll look for him there," Sir Geoffrey said, reaching into his waistcoat pocket and handing the man a coin. "Back up the High Street, is it not?"

"Aye, sir, in Kingston Passage. The entrance is on the right just before you reach All Saints Street."

Melissa watched the porter through her lashes and saw that he was regarding her with curiosity. Since he made no attempt to dissuade Sir Geoffrey from taking her with him to find Yarborne, she decided he believed her to be a strumpet.

Out in the street, she said quietly, "Please, Papa, don't make me go with you. A place with a name like that cannot be one where I ought to be seen."

"Then keep your hood up, and take a lesson from this, for it is all your own fault. Had you obeyed me earlier, you would not now find yourself in such a case."

"Please take me back. I'll stay at the inn, I promise."

"I'm not letting you out of my sight until I've kept my bargain with Yarborne."

The passageway to which the porter had given him directions was a narrow, cobbled alley. When a man stepped out of the shadows to confront them, Melissa drew her hood more securely into place.

"Beg pardon, sir, but this be no area to walk with a lady."

Sir Geoffrey said haughtily, "I am expected here, my good man, if this is the place known hereabouts as the Little Hell."

"It be that right enough, sir. I'm their orderly man, you see. No females admitted, I'm afraid."

"This one is expected just as I am, fellow, and I certainly cannot leave her out here in the street." To Melissa's dismay, Sir Geoffrey chuckled then and added in a conspiratorial way, "She is by way of being a gift for Lord Yarborne, you see."

The man grinned appreciatively and said, "Well, in that case . . ." He led them to where the passageway opened into a cobbled courtyard and light spilled from a number of windows, then ran nimbly up a set of narrow steps to open a tall door crowned by a lighted fanlight.

Digging in her heels, Melissa said desperately, "Don't do this, please!"

Sir Geoffrey pulled her past the grinning orderly, into the house.

They found themselves in a narrow but elaborate entry hall. It was unoccupied, but from a room ahead of them came a rumble of conversation, punctuated by frequent shouts and laughter. Sir Geoffrey hustled Melissa toward the doorway.

Numerous chandeliers and wall sconces lighted the room. Melissa saw only men present, and tried again to pull away from Sir Geoffrey, but his grip tightened around her arm. Pausing just inside the doorway, he said in a carrying voice, "I say, Yarborne, I've been looking for you. I've come to deliver what I owe you, sir!"

Five

A Win Reveals False Play

Tommy exclaimed, "What the devil?" Other men made similar exclamations, and play came to a halt when everyone in the room turned to look at the newcomers.

Nick, too, had glanced up at the disturbance, and watched through narrowed eyes as Sir Geoffrey Seacourt dragged the girl past their table, through the crush of gamblers parting before them, to the opposite side of the room. He had recognized Seacourt's voice at once, but he did not think he would have recognized the girl.

The sable-trimmed hood of her blue cloak fell back as Seacourt yanked her along. Flying wisps of flaxen hair, loosened from the twist at the nape of her neck, framed her flushed, oval face. She looked frightened and untidy, like a child dragged after midnight from her bed. The heavy cloak concealed her slender—and memorably supple—figure in its swirling folds.

"Who is that fellow?" Tommy demanded, putting down his cards and getting up.

The din diminished abruptly to a buzz of curiosity, and Nick's calm voice carried easily when he said, "Sir Geoffrey Seacourt."

"Oh, yes," Tommy said, nodding. "Seen him at the Billingsgate, I think."

Nick said, "Not a stunning recommendation of the place, f that's where he learned to drag females about, or to enter a room shouting a man's name for all to hear. But no doubt you're right. He seems to know Yarborne, at least."

"Yes, yes, I remember him. Must be in his cups now, for as I recall, he's a pleasant fellow. Plays deep, but so do we all. Still, what the devil is he about to be bringing his peculiar into the Little Hell?"

"I think you will discover that she is not his peculiar." Nick wished that he had not drunk so much brandy. His mind was not working in its usual reliable way. He dragged his gaze from the girl back to Seacourt. The man's lips were moving, but Nick could not hear the words.

A hush fell when the rest of the men realized Seacourt was speaking, and his words floated across the room. ". . . and I always pay my debts."

"Do you indeed?" Yarborne said evenly. "I don't recall that our agreement included such prompt or public delivery, however."

Tommy looked astonished. "Delivery?" he muttered under his breath. "What can he mean by that?"

"Hush, rattle," Nick said, "I want to hear this."

So, apparently, did everyone else, for aside from the astonished muttering that accompanied Tommy's exclamation, not another sound was heard until Seacourt said, "As I recall the matter, Yarborne, I agreed to fetch the chit and deliver her to you here at Newmarket." He glanced away, seemed to become aware of his audience, and smiled, saying to the room at large, "Yarborne agreed to accept an heiress in exchange for those of my vowels that he has collected to date. This is she."

When a collective gasp greeted this announcement, his smile widened, but he said, "Now, now, gentlemen, no need for that. Yarborne intends to marry her."

Yarborne, looking at the girl with a sneer, said, "You over-step yourself, sir. As I recall our agreement, I agreed to accept this little bird as payment for your debt, but I don't believe I am bound in any way to marry her. She is but a prize in the game, fairly won, so I can do as I please with her, can I not? When she begins to bore me, would you not agree that I can simply discard her or stake her as the prize for another hand?"

Nick realized he had clenched his teeth, and consciously relaxed his jaw. It was, after all, no business of his what Seacourt did with his daughter. Reaching for his glass, he sipped. The girl had squared her shoulders at the end of Yarborne's discourse. She no longer looked like a child. When she tossed her head and reached to push strands of her silky hair back from her face, he saw a bruise darkening her cheek, and stiffened, wishing he might be granted a few moments alone with Sir Geoffrey Seacourt.

Unruffled by Yarborne's speech, Seacourt said with a shrug, "She is yours to do with as you please, Yarborne, but you'd do well to remember the reason you agreed to take her in the first place."

"Ah, yes," Yarborne said, "the inheritance. I must say, if she is the great heiress you declared her to be, I don't know why you would display her to all and sundry in this fashion. I'm by no means certain that I want a wife who has been exhibited as a public spectacle."

"Perhaps I was impetuous to deliver her to you at once," Seacourt said in the same smooth tone that Yarborne had employed. Clearly enjoying himself now, he added, "You may certainly do as you please with the chit once you have her, but her inheritance will do you no good if you don't marry her."

"That's a point to you, certainly," Yarborne said, shifting his gaze to the girl. "What is your given name, my dear?"

She hesitated, and Nick could almost feel her trembling. He resisted an impulse to stride across the room and snatch her away from both men. Though he did not doubt he could do it, he knew that such an act would accomplish little. Not

only did he not have the slightest idea what he would do
with her once he had rescued her but Seacourt would still
be her father, with the right to give her in marriage to anyone
he chose, or to slap her again. The bruise on her face showed
plainly that he had already done that at least once. The most
Nick could accomplish would be to remove her from the
present humiliating situation, and if his action resulted in
more of the same Turkish treatment she had already endured,
she would be unlikely to thank him.

Just then, she looked at Yarborne and said with grave dignity, "My name is Melissa, sir, but you should know that I
am here against my will."

"Are you indeed?" Yarborne said. A cynical smile touched
his lips. "Do you know, my dear, that does not surprise me.
I cannot imagine any lady of gentle birth setting foot in Little
Hell by choice. You are clearly an obedient young woman,
who will make an equally obedient wife."

"But not your wife, sir," she said. "No clergyman will
force me to marry where I do not want to."

Another wave of murmurs met this remark, but they
hushed when Yarborne said, "Your reputation has suffered
merely by your presence in this place, my dear, and I have
agreed publicly to accept you in exchange for Seacourt's
debts. It is of little moment to me if I marry you or not, but
I think you will agree that the best course for you under the
circumstances will be to accept marriage if I do choose to
offer it."

The general murmuring stirred again, its tone making clear
that nearly everyone present agreed with his statement.

Miss Seacourt flushed deeply, but Nick could see that she
still met Yarborne's gaze directly. She said, "I do not agree
that my only course is to marry you, my lord, although I can
see that I will be ruined if I don't. However, you should know
that my inheritance is not nearly so certain as you have been
led to believe."

"That's enough, Melissa," Seacourt said sharply. "You

don't know what you are saying. Women know nothing about financial matters."

She kept her eyes fixed on Yarborne and said, "I have no money of my own, sir, beyond the pin money my stepfather allows me. My expectations derive from the possibility that Sir Geoffrey will predecease me without having sired a son, and from my mother's great-aunt, who is a woman of independent means."

"A singularly wealthy woman of great antiquity," Seacourt said. "Now, be silent, Melissa, or you will displease me excessively, which I am sure you don't want to do. If his lordship has questions about your inheritance, he will discuss them with me."

"Who the devil is that chit?" Tommy demanded. "If she's his stepdaughter, he's a damned rogue. That's all I can say."

He's worse than that, but hush, I want to hear this," Nick said, realizing from his friend's question that neither Yarborne nor Seacourt had yet identified her as the latter's daughter.

Yarborne said, "Well now, Seacourt, if I understand the chit, she suggests that I might not ever get the money you promised. What have you to say to that, sir?"

"She exaggerates," Seacourt said smoothly. "She dislikes having her will crossed, but you will find her obedient enough when she does not enjoy such a large audience. Perhaps if we were to retire to a more private—"

"You chose the stage," Yarborne reminded him. "I would have the matter plainly. Just how old is this great-aunt of hers?"

"She is eighty-six, for God's sake! She can't last much longer."

"She is in excellent health," Miss Seacourt said, "and even if she should die, my mother inherits before I do. You would have to await her death as well."

"Is that true?" Yarborne demanded.

Seacourt shrugged, but Nick thought he looked nervous. "A portion of the estate does go to Melissa's mother, but a good portion goes to Melissa, as well. I would not cheat you, Yarborne. The woman is decrepit. She is presently in London, no doubt seeing her doctor. You can see her for yourself whenever you choose."

Nick saw Miss Seacourt bite her lip, but she was not defeated yet, for without a glance at Seacourt, she said, "I have not seen Great-Aunt Ophelia in some years, my lord, but I receive a letter from her once a month. She is not decrepit. Indeed, she is as mentally acute as she has ever been, and if she is in London, it is because she accompanies my cousin, who is there for the Season. Moreover, my great-aunt is still quite capable of writing both my mother and myself out of her will, if only to spite my father. She does not like him, and has already taken steps to see that he can never touch her money, by setting up trusts for us through the Chancery Court."

A shift in the tone of the murmuring told Nick that many men in the audience had finally deduced Miss Seacourt's identity. He heard Tommy mutter but paid him no heed, having ears now only for what was said by the principal players.

"Is that true about Chancery, Seacourt?" Yarborne's expression hardened.

Seacourt spread his hands and exclaimed, "Good God, Yarborne, what if it is? All the more reason the old lady won't do anything to alter the matter. Think of all the fuss and bother she'd have to endure! And if you are thinking—"

"What I'm thinking is that you tried to cheat me, sir. If her fortune is tied up by the Chancery Court, what chance have I ever to control a penny of it?"

"A man controls his wife, Yarborne. What more can you want? Believe me, though she has clearly forgotten her early lessons in obedience, I would point out to you that she has been living in Scotland these past nine years. You will be able to remind her very quickly of who is master, I assure you." The look he gave his daughter boded no good for her future.

Nick noted that she was careful not to look at Seacourt again, almost as if she feared to lose what little resolve she had mustered if she did. She looked at Yarborne instead, her silence like a challenge to him.

Gazing back steadily, Yarborne's expression became calculating.

At last she said with forced calm, "My great-aunt assured me, sir, that I will have control of my fortune no matter whom I choose to marry. Though you are doubtless right to say I will be forced to accept an offer of marriage, unless you are prepared to employ drastic measures, I will not relinquish that control to you or to anyone else."

"I see," Yarborne said. His hard gaze shifted back to Seacourt. "We seem to have reached an impasse, sir. Your offer of payment is insufficient."

"But you agreed! Good Lord, Yarborne, do you imagine you cannot prevail against a mere female?"

"What I believe, sir, is that until her great-aunt dies, I shall not even know whether she inherits. Even if she does, I'll have no control over her money unless I'm willing to beat her into submission. That is not my nature, I'm afraid." He paused, looking at Miss Seacourt, his gaze sweeping over her in the manner of a man assessing a prize mare. He said, "She is certainly lovely. I'll readily admit that I'm drawn to accept her. I have agreed to do so, in fact, and thus am I bound to. Nonetheless, I daresay everyone here will agree that your debt to me is by no means repaid in full."

Without realizing that he meant to speak, Nick said impulsively, "I'll buy her from you, Yarborne, for one-half the sum of the gentleman's losses."

He heard Tommy's shocked protest, and saw the audience turn as one to stare at him. Wondering what had possessed him, he nonetheless looked right at Yarborne.

Yarborne bowed slightly and said, "I must decline your offer, Vexford. I think I'd do better to keep the girl and await full payment from the debtor."

Some wag in the audience cried, "Auction her off, Yarborne! That'll get you your money. By God, if it won't. Here, I'll bid ten pounds!"

Someone else shouted, "He don't want the money. He wants that tender little pigeon caged for use in his own bed, but I'll raise your bid, by God. Fifteen!"

Yarborne hesitated, looking around the room, his expression calculating again. "I'll admit," he added, slowly smiling, "you gentlemen do suggest a better and far more entertaining remedy. The woman is mine now, as everyone must agree, so what say you all if, in the excellent tradition of Newmarket, I do offer her as a filly at auction? After all, fine horses are auctioned here by Tattersall's every day."

Tommy cried, "You're daft, Yarborne! What a thing to suggest when one can see at a glance that she's gently bred!"

A few others echoed his distaste, one going so far as to shout, "Outrageous!"

Seacourt laughed and said, "Many of the fillies at Tatt's are gently bred, too, so why the devil shouldn't he auction her if he likes? She's his fair and square, and if the bidding goes well, he'll recover my debt and make a profit, as well. And whoever gets the girl will get his money back when she inherits her fortune."

More protests were heard, but since the general reaction to auctioning Miss Seacourt was amused tolerance underscored by unholy glee, no time was lost. Seacourt picked her up bodily and stood her on the hazard table, snatching off her cloak to reveal her slender body clad in a thin, pale pink muslin gown. The life had gone out of her eyes. She stood erect and stiff, staring straight ahead, as if she no longer dared look at any of the men.

Yarborne said abruptly, "Make your assessments quickly, gentlemen. What am I bid on this pretty pink filly?"

"Fifty guineas," one man shouted with a laugh.

"A fair beginning," Yarborne said, "but I warn you, I won't

be much interested until the amount begins to approach the ten thousand Seacourt owes me."

Nick saw Seacourt flush with embarrassment but thought it served the man right to hear his debt shouted to the whole company. Settling back, watching, but determined to have nothing more to do with such an outrage, he reached for his brandy. At that moment, the blankness went out of Miss Seacourt's eyes and her demeanor changed. She was looking straight at him.

Pausing with the glass at his lips, Nick saw her expression warm and her body somehow soften. She looked unbelievably yielding. Instantly, he recalled the supple curves of her waist and imagined the yielding plumpness of her breasts. He could feel her in his arms again. Forcing his gaze upward, past those soft breasts, past the delicate creamy bare skin above the lacy white edge of her bodice, past her slender throat and softly rounded chin to her lips, he felt his breath catch when she licked them. His gaze rested, waiting for her to press her lips together again. Instead, her small pink tongue darted out again, just touching the lower one. He could see her small, even, white upper teeth, could almost smell again the freshness of her gentle breath.

Inhaling deeply, he realized the auction was heating up. The price had soared, and men were shouting bids with the same fervor one saw when Tatt's auctioned off a prizewinner. The room had come alive with a seething, ardent vengeance, but Miss Seacourt appeared completely unaware of the lust-filled arousal she had ignited.

She looked only at him. Her lips curved in a gentle, flirtatious smile. Her eyes glinted with intent. Her hands rose slowly to touch each other at her waist—whether consciously or unconsciously, he could not tell—one stroking the other gently, caressingly, before they parted, poised and cupped as if to move upward again.

Nick's body stirred in urgent response, making him devoutly glad that no one else was watching him. All belief in her innocence vanished. No innocent child could excite him this way.

"What a wench," someone exclaimed, and the tension in the voice informed Nick that he was not the only man physically aroused by Miss Seacourt's behavior. Even Yarborne looked hungry for her now. What on earth did she think she was doing? Was it possible that Seacourt had driven her over the edge into madness? What else could account for a girl of obviously gentle breeding behaving so seductively at a time when she ought to have been screaming with fear and revulsion?

"Eight hundred pounds!" Tommy shouted hoarsely.

"You haven't got eight hundred pounds," Nick snapped.

"Borrow it from you," his friend declared, not taking his eyes from Miss Seacourt. "God, what a wench! Must have her."

"You won't get the money from me."

But Tommy's bid had already been doubled and redoubled, and within minutes, Seacourt's debt was paid and Yarborne was on his way to a profit.

Nick saw that Miss Seacourt had not shifted her gaze from him. Her expression warmed noticeably when she caught his eye again. She smiled.

Instantly there was another surge in the bidding, and the sum soon reached fifteen thousand. When someone stepped in front of Nick, cutting off his view of Miss Seacourt, he stood, caught her eye again, and said in a clear, carrying voice, "Twenty thousand guineas."

Startled silence greeted his bid, and the blank look returned to Miss Seacourt's eyes. Once again, Nick thought she looked like a frightened child. Gathering his wits, his gaze sweeping the room, he saw that most of the men looked more confused than annoyed by the sum he named. They were shaking their heads, as if to clear them.

Yarborne's voice snapped the spell of silence. "Does anyone else care to bid?"

No one did.

"Very well, Vexford, the girl is yours. I'll accept a draft on your bank."

Dumbfounded but determined not to reveal his consternation to the others, Nick nodded and said, "You'll have it first thing in the morning."

"I'm at the White Hart. Come collect your winnings, lad."

Nick looked around at the others again, sternly. "Though I'm sure it is not necessary," he said, "I'll remind all of you to take care what you say about this incident outside these four walls. Miss Seacourt now enjoys my protection."

For a moment, in the brief, breathless hush that followed his warning, Nick wished he had stuck by his earlier resolve not to enter any more of the gaming that night. He had been right to believe his luck was out of vein.

Watching Lord Vexford approach, seeing him clearly for what seemed like the first time, Melissa felt disoriented, as if she had been somewhere else and suddenly found herself in the midst of a gaming hell. She remembered why she was there, but she seemed to have lost her train of thought in the past moments. She wondered why Vexford moved so purposefully toward her.

Somehow she was standing above them all, but even as she began to wonder how she came to be there, she remembered defying Sir Geoffrey. The words she had spoken came back to her then, and with a shudder, she wondered where she had found the strength to utter them. Clearly, nine years spent in the safety of Scotland, away from his brutal temper, had stiffened her backbone. Still it had been foolhardy. Despite that bravado, she knew she would never be able to stand up to a domineering man who demanded control of her money.

It was all very well for Great-Aunt Ophelia and Charley to assure her that she would retain that control. They were stronger than she was, and had never been in the power of a ruthless man. She remembered how easily her father had controlled her when she was young, and she did not believe for a moment that she would find the strength to hold out against any man willing to beat her into submission.

When she saw Vexford still walking toward her, she trembled. Others were watching him, too, but her father stood with Yarborne. Vaguely she could remember that men had been shouting—creating a veritable din—but the room was quiet now. Yarborne took a step toward Vexford, then stepped back again. Others turned back to the tables. As Vexford reached up, lifted her carefully down from the table, and put her cloak around her shoulders again, someone nearby rattled a dice box and said, "My cast, I believe. The stake is set. I call a main of five."

Standing on the floor beside the tall, broad-shouldered Vexford, Melissa felt as if she stood beside a solid wall, sheltered and safe from the storm around her. When he put a hand on her shoulder and urged her toward the doorway through which Seacourt had dragged her a short time before, she obeyed at once and without question. By the time they reached the door, the noise of the gaming room had returned to normal levels.

When they emerged from the courtyard passageway into the High Street, as fog-ridden air swirled damply around them, she said, "Thank you, sir, for rescuing me."

"I didn't rescue you," he said bluntly. "I bought you at a damned long price, so don't chatter at me. I loathe chattering females."

"Where are you taking me?"

"Where do you think? To the Rutland Arms."

Panic-stricken, she exclaimed, "You can't mean to give me back to Papa!"

"Don't be daft. I've just paid twenty thousand guineas for you. I'm certainly not giving you back. I'm staying at the inn, too, if you'll recall."

But she had stopped listening. "Twenty thousand guineas! For me? That must be nonsense. No one can purchase another person."

"I just did, and you know it. I'll admit you had me fooled. I'll admit, too, that if I hadn't overindulged in the brandy, I'd never have bid so high. But, having teased me to it, madam, I expect you to make good on the enticing promises you made back there."

"Promises? I don't know what on earth—"

"I told you not to chatter," he snapped, and for the second time that night, she found herself being dragged willy-nilly along Newmarket High Street.

Deciding that any attempt to argue with him in the street would prove fruitless, she held her tongue until they reached the inn yard. However, when it became apparent that he meant to haul her right inside, she said quickly, "You need not drag me in like something the cat caught in the yard, sir. I am quite capable of walking on my own."

He released her, pulled open the main door, and made her a mocking bow, saying politely, "After you."

"Thank you," she said, attempting to gather her dignity. She was not quite successful. The entry hall was reassuringly empty, but when she reached the stairs, she realized she had no idea which chamber was his.

When she hesitated, he said, "Second door on the left at the first landing."

Feeling warmth in her cheeks, she looked around and saw with relief that although candles burned in the wall sconces, and a plain brass candle holder lighted a nearby desk, the hall was still empty.

"At this hour, one rings the bell if one wants assistance," he said.

She did not respond, too much aware that she was going with a man to his bedchamber, and fearful of what he might expect once they got there. She had been pondering what to do next from the moment he began hurrying her along the street. When she reached the door he had indicated, she dismissed a brief hope that she might somehow convince him to take her back to Edinburgh, and began to wonder instead if she could persuade him to escort her to London and to Great-Aunt Ophelia.

He reached past her and opened the door, revealing a bedchamber much like the one she had shared with Mag. A candle in a glass lamp burned low, lighting the room and revealing the bed. It was larger than hers. An elaborate green and gold dressing gown lay draped over a chair back, and a pair of Moorish slippers rested beside the bed. The coverlet was turned down invitingly.

Taking her cloak, Vexford said, "Do you need my help to take off your dress or can you do it yourself?"

She turned toward him, shivering, although embers glowed red in the fireplace. "Take off my dress?"

"Yes." He turned away, picked up the poker, and stirred the fire to life.

"But—"

"Look here," he said over his shoulder with an exasperated sigh, "I just paid twenty thousand guineas for you, and although you showed great skill at playing the game, I doubt that I'll get my money's worth. Still, one does not play and not pay, so I want no games from you now. I'm a better choice than Yarborne, certainly, and if nothing else, I've damned well bought your unquestioning obedience."

Feeling colder than ever despite the reviving fire, Melissa saw from the stubborn look in his eyes that he would not listen to argument, and experience with Sir Geoffrey warned her that she might well infuriate him if she objected. She knew she could never win a physical battle with a man of Vexford's size, and just the thought of what he could do to her if she angered him was enough to stop the protest on the tip of her tongue. He clearly was not sober. Moreover, he had said he loathed chatter. Swallowing hard but moving slowly, she reached back to untie her sash.

"Here, I'll do it," he said impatiently.

His big hands were warm where they touched her, though he treated her more like a doll than a woman. When he whisked her gown over her head, a sleeve caught on her bracelet, but he freed it quickly, and she soon stood facing him in her cambric chemise and her sandals.

He reached for the chemise.

"Please, sir, I-I'm chilled. May I keep it on?"

"If you like." He knelt to deal with her sandals, then stood again and looked at her for a long minute, during which her heart hammered in her chest and she knew herself to be incapable of speech even if she could think of something to say.

He touched her shoulder. "Your skin is soft," he murmured.

Heat from his fingertips sped to the center of her body, lighting a fire there, surprising her with its intensity. Despite the horrors of the evening, despite Vexford's undeniable size, power, and present, nearly tactile irritation with her, she discovered that she trusted him. More than that, she wanted him to touch her. She stood perfectly still, aware, despite her predicament, of that odd, lingering sense of being protected. Anticipating the moment his fingers would move, looking into his eyes, she licked her lips, feeling strangely exhilarated by the dawning lust she saw in his expression.

He caught both shoulders in his large hands and pulled her close, bending to kiss her. She could smell brandy on his breath now, but the heat she felt in his fingers was as nothing to what swept through her when his lips touched hers. Her body pressed against his, and a hunger awoke in her such as she had never known before. When he picked her up and carried her to the bed, she did not protest, not even when he put her down and the welts and bruises left by Sir Geoffrey's whip nearly made her cry out. Vexford's touch continued to stir feelings she had never imagined, and burning curiosity soon blotted out the pain. Knowing she could not stop him, she wanted to feel his hands caress her body, to learn what he would do and how he would do it. She wondered, too, what he would expect of her.

He was impatient. His hands moved swiftly once he had laid her on the bed, catching the hem of her chemise as he moved over her, and pushing the garment to her waist. His right hand slipped between her legs. Her breathing stopped. She felt a little like she had in the stable, as if she were watching, not participating. Then she felt his fingers, tentative at first, before they moved more purposefully. They opened her, slipped inside, then suddenly went still. He, too, seemed to stop breathing. Then, slowly, a finger moved, and an aching pain made her gasp and cry out.

Snatching his hand back as if it had been burnt, Vexford leapt to his feet. "Good God, you're still a virgin!"

She sat up, bewildered. "Well, of course I am."

"There's no *of course* about it," he snapped, pushing his left hand through his hair to the back of his neck and glaring down at her. "Hell and the devil confound it! What am I going to do with you now?"

Six

Melissa Fails to Calculate the Odds

Quickly refastening his breeches, Nick stared down at the disheveled Miss Seacourt, trying to collect wits still fogged by brandy, and swearing to himself that he would never touch the stuff again. He had been feeling its effects more and more ever since he had entered the warm room.

Looking up at him, wide-eyed, her lower lip trembling, her clothing still rucked up around her waist, she seemed to realize that she was partially bared to his view, for she reached quickly to cover herself, wincing as she did.

He said gruffly, defensively, "I didn't hurt you, did I?"

"No, *you* didn't, not really."

The emphasis bolstered his suspicion that she was in pain, and he remembered the way she had winced and nearly cried out when he had put her on the bed. He had thought at the time that she was merely playing more games, but now he wondered if it might not have been something else.

"Who did hurt you?" he demanded.

"That is not important now."

"I'll decide what's important. If you've been hurt, I want to know."

"It's none of your affair," she said, wincing again when she sat up and tried to arrange her clothing.

"Everything about you is now my affair," he said grimly. "I just bought you at auction, in case you've forgotten."

"You said that before. You can't really own me, you know."

"The devil I can't. I've just paid twenty thousand guineas for the privilege."

"I don't believe you. Did you really pay that much?"

"Of course I did! You were right there. You heard the whole thing. By heaven, you begin to make me think you must be demented."

"Perhaps I am," she said, moving cautiously, apparently undecided as to whether to stand or not.

"What the devil do you mean by that," he demanded, "and why are you squirming about like that if you are not hurt? Come now, let me see."

"No!" she shrieked, scrambling away on the bed when he reached for her.

With a snort of exasperation, Nick caught her, dragged her off the bed, and stood her upright. "Stand still," he ordered, giving her a shake. "It will do you no good to fight me, for I mean to know what's wrong."

"You've no right!"

"We've already plucked that crow." He turned her with one hand and reached down to raise her shift with the other.

Desperately, she yanked the shift from his grasp, dancing back to keep him from catching it again. He still held her arm, and her gyrations were making him dizzy. Straightening in an attempt to regain his equilibrium, he glowered at her.

Quickly she said, "I'll tell you! Papa was angry when he found me in the stable. H-he had told me to stay in my room, and he . . . he . . ." She paused, licked her lips and looked away, then said flatly, "If you must know, he whipped me."

"Good," he snapped, releasing her arm. "Stout fellow. Didn't think much of him before, but now I make him my compliments. You undoubtedly deserved it."

"Well, it was your fault," she retorted, pushing a loose strand of hair from her face and glaring back at him.

"It was no such thing."

"It was. If you hadn't stopped me, I'd have been safely in Cambridge by the time he returned, instead of still standing there in the stable with you."

"You have an exaggerated notion of how fast that hack would have taken you to Cambridge, my girl. Even Prince Florizel and Quiz don't run fast enough to have carried you there that quickly."

"I suppose they are your racehorses. Maybe I couldn't have got there so fast, but you know what I mean."

"No, I don't. How badly did he hurt you?"

"I am quite all right, thank you."

"Miss Seacourt, you are trying my patience. I want to know how badly you are hurt, because I need to decide if I should send for a doctor."

"I do not need a doctor." Her words were tensely measured, and he could tell she was angry, but she also seemed wary, as if she were afraid. The thought startled him. He knew that many men feared his temper, but he did not think he had ever frightened a woman. He had certainly never done so purposely. And he was not even angry now, not with her. Exasperated, perhaps, but not angry. She was too small and feminine to stir real anger in any man. He wondered what sort of a fellow Seacourt was, that he could whip someone so slender and fragile-looking. Although he had told her he could understand her father's action, he did not understand at all. He had snapped at her out of aggravation, nothing more, and he had not meant the words he had spoken. What he thought of Seacourt did not bear repeating.

She was still watching him. Realizing that if she really was the gently bred young woman she appeared to be, she might well believe she had reason to fear him, he said, "I won't hurt you, and if you don't want a doctor, I won't send for one. You will have to forgive me if I do not seem to be acting sensibly tonight, but the fact is that, thanks to the way you behaved earlier, I took you for a different sort of female."

"Doubtless a sort more to your liking," she said.

He rubbed his forehead, aware of an incipient headache, and decided the excess brandy had been incredibly stupid, not just a grave mistake in judgment. Smiling ruefully, he said, "Let's just say that if I am going to be stuck with a female in my bedchamber at two o'clock in the morning, I'd prefer to have one who understands the rules of the game, and who can play her hand with confidence."

"I do not understand you, sir. I am not here by choice, and I'm certainly not playing any game. I cannot imagine why we are even talking about this, for there is nothing to discuss. At this point, there can be only one acceptable course to take."

"You are right," he said with a sigh. "Have you got a maid?"

For a moment she looked startled, but then her countenance cleared and she said, "Papa hired a girl from a posting house near the Carter Fell turnpike to serve me during our journey."

"Why on earth did he have to hire an inn servant? What happened to yours?"

"W-we left her behind." She bit her lip, and he was sure she was leaving out the greater part of her explanation, but he had small interest in servants at any time, and no time to delve into such details now.

"Where is she?"

"I don't know."

"Now, look here—"

"Papa told her to find somewhere else to sleep tonight—other than my bedchamber, that is—and said I would not require her services. He sent her away because . . . because of what he meant to do to me, and he told her to ask the landlord for a pallet in the attic or some such thing."

Restraining himself with more difficulty than ever from expressing his opinion of Seacourt, Nick said, "I'll have to roust out my man in any event, so I'll tell him to find her. What's her name?"

"Mag, but why do you want her?"

"I want her to accompany you to London, of course."

"Are we going to London?"

"Immediately," he declared. "The sooner we're away, the better, for I certainly cannot keep you here."

"I suppose not," she agreed. "Could we perhaps go to Edinburgh instead?"

"Good God, no! Why on earth would I want to do that?"

"Well, my mother and stepfather live there, you see, and—"

"A stepfather, eh?" He dimly remembered that she had mentioned one before.

"Yes, I have lived with him these past nine years. What I told you in the stable about being abducted was quite true, you see. Papa came and took me away."

"As your father, he had every right to do so, however. In any event, I am not driving you to Edinburgh or anywhere else that would keep us on the road for three or four days, so you can put that notion straight out of your head. You've got family in London, too, haven't you? Didn't Seacourt mention a great-aunt?"

"Well, Great-Aunt Ophelia does go to London for the Season, so I expect she will be there soon if she is not already, but—"

"For the Season! I know you said that earlier, but Seacourt said the woman is eighty-six years old. Surely, you must be mistaken."

"No, I'm not. For the past few years she has accompanied my cousin Charley."

"Accompanied a young man to London? Now, see here—"

"Not a man. Charley is female. Her name is Charlotte, but everyone except Papa calls her Charley. He never held with boyish nicknames, you see, but Charley never liked him much, either. She does not think much of men in general, so she and Great-Aunt Ophelia get on quite well."

Nick frowned. "She's that sort, is she?"

"What sort?"

"Never mind. If you don't know—"

"But I want to know. It sounds like a sort you don't approve of, and I assure you, Charley and Great-Aunt Ophelia are both quite respectable. They just don't care much for men. Great-Aunt Ophelia says women are misnamed the weaker sex, that in truth, it is men who are weak. In fact, Great-Aunt Ophelia says—"

"I don't think I want to hear more of what Great-Aunt Ophelia says," Nick said, cutting her off without a qualm. "Great-Aunt Ophelia sounds like a crazy old lady to me, but since she is your relative I shall try to refrain from disparaging her."

"Thank you," Melissa said dryly.

"Now, about that maid of yours—"

"She is not my maid, exactly. I told you—"

"I know what you told me. She will have to do, however. Although," he added thoughtfully, "it occurs to me that we might meet with a problem if she considers herself to be in Seacourt's employ."

"Oh, I don't think Mag will care a rap about who hires her, sir. She has served me well enough, though she cries 'lawks-a-mussy' at everything."

"I trust you have not also picked up that habit," he said.

"No." She smiled at him then, and he remembered how easily she could stir him sexually. Abruptly, he said, "Have you got much baggage to collect?"

"No, none. He did not give me time to pack anything."

"I see," he said grimly. "Well, there is a comb on that dressing table. Put it to some use, if you please, while I turn out my man and order up my phaeton. I do not at all like being seen in the company of bedraggled females." Smiling to take the sting out of those last words, he turned on his heel and went to find his valet.

Alone, Melissa moved obediently to the dressing table, drew a deep breath, and tried to assess her situation. Though she picked up the tortoiseshell comb on the table and did what she could to smooth her hair, she did not sit down. Sitting was, as she had discovered when she sat up on the bed, really rather painful.

Despite what Vexford had told her, she still could not remember any auction or his paying the amazing sum of twenty thousand guineas for her. She did not doubt that he had done so, for he had given her no cause to think him a liar, but she remembered nothing between speaking up in her own defense and finding herself atop the table, watching him walk toward her. The latter moment was indelibly imprinted on her mind. Just by closing her eyes, she could see him even now, coming toward her through the crowd, taller than anyone else, his shoulders broader, his walk that of a man who never let anyone order him about. She remembered hearing him tell the others that she was now under his protection, and that memory calmed her now.

Moments ago, she had been afraid of him. When he glowered at her, her knees had turned to jelly, her heart pounded in her chest, and she had told him instantly what he wanted to know. That thought brought another on its heels, making her shudder when she suddenly imagined herself married to Yarborne instead, trying to tell him she would not let him spend her money.

At least Vexford was young and handsome, and did not talk to her in the disdainful way that Yarborne had, so if she had to marry, marriage to him would prove a far better fate. The fact was, however, that she did not want to marry anyone just yet.

Not that the notion of marriage had never crossed her mind, for it had, many times, albeit like a dream with little substance. She had supposed that one day she would marry, that she might even fall in love with the man first, but she had not met any man with whom she could imagine spending the rest of her life. Certainly, she had never met anyone who made her feel the way her mother, Susan, so clearly felt whenever her gaze came to rest upon Viscount Penthorpe.

Melissa had often wondered about that look. She liked Penthorpe. He had always been kind to her. But she could not imagine what made Susan adore him, for he was not in the least her notion of a romantic figure. His attitude was casual in the extreme, he had no strong likes or dislikes, and although he had been a soldier at the Battle of Waterloo, he was the world's worst procrastinator, never doing anything at once that he could put off until later, or until he need not do it at all.

Fortunately his servants adored him and saw to it that things that needed doing did get done. Everyone liked him. Melissa had never heard his voice raised in anger, except perhaps once. She thought Penthorpe might once have spoken sharply to Sir Geoffrey, and it would not have been amazing if he had, for it happened the day she and her mother had left her father to run away with Penthorpe. She remembered little about it now, however, having buried the memory deep at the back of her mind.

She made a face at her reflection in the glass. Her gown was creased again, and she yearned for something else to wear. Mag had done her best to keep both gown and shift clean for her, but another day's wear, added to the strains of the night, had not improved them. With a sigh, Melissa picked up her cloak and draped it over her shoulders. At least, the cloak was still presentable. When Vexford returned, she was pulling on her gloves.

He said, "We leave in ten minutes if Lisset can get my gear together by then."

The dignified man following him was a foot shorter than Vexford. He did not look at all as if he had been shaken from his bed, and if he thought it odd to find a young female in his master's bedchamber at two o'clock in the morning, Melissa could detect no sign of it. She decided that he did not find it unusual at all.

He bowed and said, "Good evening, miss." His movements as he collected Vexford's gear were efficient, and except for a quiet request to know if his master wished to change clothes before their departure, his work was accomplished in silence.

Vexford, writing at the dressing table, denied any desire to change, for which Melissa was grateful. She was certain no power on earth could keep her in that room while he did so, and she knew of nowhere else to go. Only when they were ready to depart, did she remember Mag and ask where she was.

"Lisset told her to meet us in the hall," Vexford said. "Since you have no clothing to pack, I thought it would be easier for you if she did not come here."

She knew he meant she would have fewer explanations to make if Mag never saw her in his room, and she smiled at him gratefully.

Lisset said, "Will Artemus accompany us, my lord?"

"He is bringing the phaeton around, but he does not come with us. We'll be crowded enough without him. Don't stow my pistols," he added, standing up. "We'll keep them at hand in case of would-be robbers. I've told Artemus to stay here and assist Drax, then return to London on Friday." Turning, he said to Melissa, "Drax is my trainer and Artemus my groom. Are you ready to go, Lisset?"

"Yes, my lord. I will carry these bags down at once and send a lad up to collect that portmanteau."

"Never mind the lad," Vexford said, picking up the portmanteau. "I'll take it."

"But, my lord—"

"Don't jabber, Lisset. I won't lower my consequence, or yours, by carrying one bag. Come along, Miss Seacourt."

Moments later, Melissa stood in the inn yard beside an excited Mag, staring at the vehicle in which she was expected to travel to London. She had supposed Vexford must have a closed carriage, but the light crane-necked phaeton before her was no such thing. Worse, it was harnessed to a team of blacks that even in the shadows of the yard looked powerful enough to draw a vehicle ten times larger and heavier.

"Lawks-a-mussy, Miss Melissa! Be we driving all the way to Lunnon in that?"

Gathering her dignity as best she could, Melissa turned to Vexford, who was handing something to his groom, and said, "Do you really expect me to travel such a distance in that sporting vehicle, sir?"

"I do, and I hope you won't enact me any tragedies at this point in the game, because I'm devilish tired and likely to lose my temper if you do. See that Lord Yarborne gets that first thing in the morning, Artemus. The White Hart."

"Aye, m' lord."

Melissa said, "Really, sir, would it not be better—?"

That was as far as she got before he picked her up bodily and thrust her onto the back seat of the phaeton. Landing with enough force that, even on the upholstered seat, she had to stifle a cry when her backside made contact, she did not attempt to complete her protest. Clearly, he would not listen to complaints, justified though they might be.

Lisset helped Mag climb up beside her, and the young woman said with astonishment, "Did you see that, miss? He put me up just as if I was a lady. Oh, but look, miss, how high we are! Lawks-a-mussy, I ain't rid this high off the ground since me and me brother rode atop a hay load when we was just nipperkins."

Watching as Vexford swung himself onto the driver's seat and Lisset climbed to the seat beside him, Melissa said clearly, "Yes, Mag, we are very far from the ground. We must just hope his lordship does not turn us over before we reach London."

Mag gasped, and Melissa saw Lisset cover his mouth, but the groom standing by the lead pair's heads, looked back and said indignantly, "His lordship won't never have you over, miss. Drives to an inch, drunk or sober, does his lordship!"

Vexford, gathering the reins, said evenly, "Much as I appreciate your compliments, Artemus, I shall appreciate your silence more."

"Aye, m' lord, and when you change that team at Bishop's Stortford, mind you tell Alfred Clint I said he was to look after them blacks like they was his own children. They be a far cry from them bays he's been a-looking after these past few days."

"If Alfred weren't capable, Artemus, I should not keep him in my employment. Stand away from them now."

The groom jumped back, and Vexford gave his team the office. He drove slowly until they cleared the archway leading from the inn yard, then held them to a trot along the nearly deserted High Street. Melissa held her breath when they passed first the Kingston Passage and next the White Hart Inn, but she saw only a pair of gentlemen staggering along the footway, neither of whom was in any case to recognize his companion, let alone anyone else.

When the phaeton left the cobbles for the Cambridge Highroad, Vexford urged the team to greater speed, and Melissa soon found cause to be grateful both for the vehicle's thick upholstery and its excellent springs. Without them, she was sure she would have been battered beyond bearing. As it was, each bounce was painful, and there was little to distract her mind from the pain, for conversation was next to impossible over the rattle of wheels and clatter of hooves on the hard-packed road.

Nevertheless, the cool night air was invigorating, and the light fog did little to impair their view of the moon, and nothing to impair the view of the road ahead. There were, to be sure, patches of road that passed through forested areas, and Melissa decided Vexford must have eyes like a cat's. She was glad to know that he had pistols at hand, but he did not slow the horses until they reached Bishop's Stortford. When he drew into an inn yard there, Lisset obligingly took a yard of tin from beneath the front seat and blew up for the change.

Before Vexford had pulled the team to a halt, a lad came hurrying from the stable, tucking his shirt into his breeches as he ran. He skidded to a halt when he saw the phaeton, and shouted, "So it's your lordship, is it? I'll just get Alfred then."

"Tell him to look sharp, lad," Vexford said, wrapping the reins around the brake handle and jumping to the ground. "I'm in the devil of a hurry." He stepped quickly to the leaders' heads.

Without a word, Lisset got down and moved to begin uncoupling the team. By the time the lad returned to help, followed by a second man leading a team of powerful-looking bays, he had them unfastened, and Vexford was leading them from the shafts. The boy exclaimed, "You didn't ought to 'ave done that yourself, m' lord!"

Vexford ignored him, saying, "Step lively, Alfred. Keep the blacks here, and rest them till Friday when Artemus will come to help you get them to London. He said to warn you he'll cut out your liver and lights if any harm befalls them before then."

The man leading the bays grinned widely and said, "I'd let him do it, too, my lord. It's a pleasure to see them again, but I see you've been a-driving 'em hard. Hope there ain't nothing amiss with the earl or her ladyship, sir."

"Nothing that I know about," Vexford said, "but I am in a hurry, and I'll not be coming back."

"You'll never miss the final heats, my lord!"

"I *am* missing them," Vexford said grimly, swinging back to his seat. "Quiz and Florrie will do well enough without me."

"They will that." Alfred had been working as he talked, and he was soon finished and the phaeton back on the London Road.

Two hours later, despite the rapid pace, Melissa was beginning to nod off when the carriage wheels rolled onto cobblestones again. Startled, grabbing for the seat frame to steady herself, she realized that it was dawn and they were in London.

Vexford looked over his shoulder at her. "Ever been in London before?"

She shook her head, looking around her with awe. The city was larger than Edinburgh, and far noisier. Mag, too, was staring, her mouth agape, her eyes wide with amazement as she tried to take it all in. "Lawks-a-mussy, miss, just look at the place. How come you never been here before? I thought all the quality lived in Lunnon."

Melissa said, "My parents used to come each year, but they always left me behind. We lived in Cornwall then, Mag. London is truly an astonishing place, but I don't know how anyone can be sleeping now. It's so dreadfully noisy."

Vexford apparently heard her, for he looked back again and said, "It will be quieter when we reach St. James's Square."

Melissa made no further attempt to speak, but she listened with interest as Mag pelted Lisset with questions about the city. Obligingly, he identified the Oxford Road and certain other landmarks, including Tyburn Hill, making Mag shriek with dismay when he told her it was where felons had been hanged in days of old. It was not long, however, before they entered a quiet square surrounded by stately mansions, and Vexford drew up on the southeast side before one of the most imposing of them.

Extending over a good deal of ground, for all the world as if it were in the country, the three-story central block was linked by means of long colonnades to large wings, similar in character but only two stories high. Exceptionally intricate carved stonework and wrought iron graced the front, the crowning glory of which was a high pedimented entrance. A youth came up the stairs of the railed-off areaway to the left of the entrance, and ran to the leaders' heads to hold them.

"Lawks-a-mussy," Mag exclaimed, inevitably.

Vexford wrapped the reins around the brake handle and turned to Melissa, gesturing toward the house and saying, "My great-grandfather, like many men of his time, was an amateur architect, a Palladian of the Burlington school, who couldn't seem to decide whether he wanted Barrington House to resemble a villa or a palazzo. His most immediate influence, we believe, was William Kent, but by and large, it's a cheerful place, anyway. Come, I'll take you inside."

Broad, shallow steps led to the large, ornately carved door. It opened before they reached it to reveal a porter dressed in cream-colored breeches and a dark coat.

"Good morning, my lord. Welcome home. Mr. Preston is busy in his pantry, so I did not disturb him, but I've rung for men to fetch your baggage in at once."

"Thank you, Figmore. Have my parents returned?"

"No, my lord, but Mr. Preston did receive a message warning of their return tomorrow. Oh, and Mr. Oliver is here, sir."

"Is he, indeed?" Vexford said, urging Melissa into a magnificent entrance hall, constructed largely of white marble, and adding, "Were we expecting him?"

"The long vacation, my lord."

"Ah, yes, I do recall that it has begun." Clearly as an afterthought he added, "This is Miss Seacourt, Figmore, who will be staying for a short time. I trust the blue guest room can be made available to her, and perhaps an adjoining room would be suitable for her maid."

"Yes, my lord," the porter said, bowing to Melissa, who had been admiring the spacious domed hall and its arched arcade of white Corinthian columns, echoing those outside. "I shall have their things taken up straightaway, sir," the porter added.

"As to that," Vexford said glibly, "Miss Seacourt's baggage was most unfortunately mislaid. Her servant does, however, possess a bandbox, I believe."

"I do," Mag said instantly. "Lawks-a-mussy, m' lord, that white staircase there in the middle must be all of twenty feet wide. 'Tis the finest I ever did see."

"Thank you," Vexford said dryly.

Melissa noticed that he avoided his porter's gaze, and she could not blame him. No servant in such a grand London house would believe for a moment that Mag was maidservant to a lady of quality. Though Melissa could scarcely blame her for being amazed by the soaring, white marble split staircase, with its ornate wrought-iron balustrade picked out in French gilt, her cheeks burned, and she was grateful to the porter for not staring. When Vexford moved to a marble side table to look at a pile of cards on a gilded salver, she followed him and said in an undertone, "Pray, sir, why did you tell that man I am to stay here for only a short time? You made my arrival seem most peculiar, and I should have thought, since he is clearly an old retainer, that you might have introduced me to him properly."

"Properly?" He looked at her. "I did introduce you properly, Miss Seacourt."

She glanced over her shoulder to be sure the others would not hear her and said urgently, "Surely, you ought to have made it plain that I am your intended wife."

"But, my dear girl," he said, visibly surprised, "I do not have the smallest intention of marrying you."

Seven

Play Continues With Pockets to Let

Melissa stared at Vexford in dismay. However, before she could demand to know how he could refuse to marry her after what he had done, he grasped her arm and turned her around, reminding her that they were not alone in the huge entrance hall.

He said to the porter, "I will go up with Miss Seacourt myself, to be sure she is satisfied with her bedchamber."

"Yes, my lord."

"I suppose Mr. Oliver is still abed."

"Yes, my lord." The porter allowed himself a smile. "He returned home only an hour or so ago, sir. He's like to sleep till noon, I should think."

"Returned home an hour ago? Do you mean he only just arrived in town?"

"Oh, no, my lord. Came home on Sunday, he did. I meant only that he was out and about very late last night."

Vexford frowned. "Where was he? Do you know?"

"As to that, sir, I believe he spent the greater part of the night at . . ." The porter glanced at Melissa, then went on with scarcely a pause, ". . . in Bolton Row, I should say, my lord."

"The fishmonger's?"

"Aye, my lord. In point of fact, that is just how he put the matter. Said he'd gone from the fishmonger to Billingsgate and would next be going to— But I oughtn't to repeat that, I expect," the man said with another glance at Melissa.

"No." Vexford also glanced at her, then said, "I'll let him sleep, for I intend to do the same myself. I daresay Lisset will soon have my traps stowed, and I can see that Miss Seacourt is having trouble keeping her eyes open, so we'll take ourselves upstairs. Be a good fellow and tell Mr. Oliver, if you see him before you see me, that I want a word with him before he leaves the house. He can wake me if he likes."

"Yes, my lord."

Melissa waited until Vexford had guided her to the left-hand branch of the swooping staircase before she said in an undertone, "Who is Mr. Oliver?"

"My brother."

A sardonic note in his voice made her look at him. His face was set, but she could not tell if he was annoyed or only tired. She said, "I never heard of a nobleman spending a night at a fishmonger's before, sir."

He smiled and said, "That was a tactful way of telling me that my younger brother has taken to patronizing certain gaming establishments. The fishmonger in question is a chap named Crockford. He did indeed used to sell fish on the streets, but now he runs a very successful hazard bank in Bolton Row."

"And Billingsgate?"

"Also a fish market, but in this case, my brother's sleepy attempt at humor. The Billingsgate Club is another establishment that caters to the gaming set."

"Are you not a member of that set, sir?"

"Here is your bedchamber, Miss Seacourt," he said, reaching past her to open a door. Pausing in the doorway, he said to Mag, "Go along to the room next door. It will be yours until we can arrange to send you back to Carter Fell."

Mag hesitated, glancing from him to Melissa and back again, but when Vexford looked stern and seemed about to speak again, she bobbed a curtsy and fled. He urged Melissa into the bedchamber, followed her, and shut the door with a snap.

She stared at him. "You can't come in here!"

"Don't be missish. I want to know what the devil made you think I intended to marry you. I know I never said any such thing, and I don't want you running all over town giving people the impression that I gave you a slip on the shoulder."

"I just assumed . . ." She saw by the look on his face that what he had said was true. He had never had the least intention of marrying her. "Why did you pay such a long price for me if you did not intend marriage?"

"Good Lord, you might as well ask why I was even there! It just happened. I had a deal too much to drink, and though I can generally drink most of my companions under the table, the stuff must have affected me more than usual last night, for I was clearly out of my senses. I can only say that I am fervently grateful that my father no longer oversees my bank accounts. I should never hear the end of it, and if he didn't order me down to Owlcastle to rusticate—"

"Owlcastle?"

"Our family seat in Hampshire. But to return to the point at hand, Miss Seacourt, I would be grateful to hear you admit that you had no good cause to believe I intended marriage."

"I certainly thought that was what you meant! How could you . . ." She cleared her throat. "How could you do what you did to me in your bedchamber and *not* expect to marry me?"

"Look, I explained about that. If you suffered some embarrassment, I am sorry for it, but it was your own behavior earlier that led me to think you were a different sort of woman. In any case, I did nothing, even then, that requires me to marry you."

She sighed. "Well, in honesty, I must agree that you never said as much, but good God, sir, what am I to do now? Every man who was there will tell everyone he knows about that disgraceful auction. I shall never be able to hold up my head again."

"Nonsense. Not one will speak of what happened. Each one knows he would have to answer to me if he did."

"If you believe that, you must be all about in your head," she said bluntly. "I cannot imagine they will all keep such a tale to themselves. It begs to be repeated."

"It may beg repeating," he said, "but there was not a man in that room who is not fundamentally a gentleman. Nor," he added grimly, "was anyone present who does not know me well enough to understand his peril if he does speak."

"Are you so fierce then, sir?" Although he did not reply, she remembered the look on his face when he had demanded to know what Seacourt had done to her, and remembered, as well, that she had immediately yielded to his will. With a shiver, she said, "I suppose I must trust you to know those men, sir. Still, I can neither take myself back to Edinburgh nor repay the huge sum you say you spent. You said yourself that you own me. If you don't intend marriage, what do you mean to do with me?"

For the first time she saw him look uncertain. With a grimace, he said, "As to owning you, you know that is not possible, whatever I might have said. Although I can give no good reason for what I did at the auction last night, it was solely my own doing. I don't hold you responsible for my foolhardiness."

"I am grateful to you," she said quietly. "I just want to know what to do next."

"We are both going to get some sleep," he said. "While we do, you will give that dress and anything else you are wearing to a maid to refurbish for you. Which reminds me," he added, "I sent Mag away so I could ask you without offending her if you want her to continue to serve you for the present. I can arrange for one of our maidservants to look after you if you'd prefer."

"Mag wants to see London, sir. I think the least I must

do is to allow her that. She can serve me until you arrange for her return to Carter Fell. But you did not answer my question."

"Because I do not know yet what to say. I mean to find that great-aunt of yours, if you will give me her direction, but not until we've had some sleep."

"She resides in Berkeley Square, at my grandfather St. Merryn's house," Melissa said. "If she is not there, they will know when to expect her, but I'll go with you, of course. I can just stay there until she arrives. The servants will look after me."

"No," he said. "You won't leave this house until I know you will be safe."

"Safe? How could I not be safe in my grandfather's house?"

"We'll talk about that later, when I know more about the situation. I can be fairly certain no one will mention what happened last night, but if you are widely known to be staying here before my parents return, tongues may wag, anyway. Don't trouble your head about that now, though. Just get some sleep. I'll send Mag to you now." And with that, he was gone, leaving Melissa to glare after him in frustration.

A few minutes after Mag rejoined her, a maidservant brought an ewer of hot water and offered to look after Melissa's clothing, saying as she held out a flowery silk robe she had draped over one arm, "I am Lucy, miss. His lordship sent this robe for you to wear. It belongs to her ladyship, but she won't mind if you wear it. Then we can wash your chemise as well. Oh, and I'll have that lovely cloak brushed up for you, and your shoes and stockings, too. What a bother to have lost your baggage!"

"Yes, wasn't it?" Melissa thanked the maid, and asked to have a bath prepared when she awoke. Upon being assured that Vexford had already ordered one for her, she climbed gratefully into the tall blue-silk draped bed and fell quickly asleep.

Awakening much later, she felt disoriented until she remembered where she was. The curtains had been closed, though she did not remember Mag having closed them, and the room was dark. Slipping from the bed, she found the robe the maid Lucy had brought, and put it on, enjoying the sensation of the cool silk against her skin.

Guided by a sliver of gray light peeping through a crack in the curtains, she moved to the window and pushed the curtain aside to look out. The bedchamber overlooked a large, grassy inner courtyard, its center and borders abloom with spring flowers, their colors dimmed just then by lack of light. At first, she assumed that clouds must have rolled in over the city, but she soon realized that much of the day had passed. Annoyed, since she had asked Mag to awaken her by early afternoon so she could enjoy her bath before Vexford left for St. Merryn House—in the hope that she might still persuade him to take her—she picked up her watch-bracelet from the table where she had left it, and gasped to see that it was nearly six o'clock.

Gathering the robe tightly about her, she searched for a bell cord and pulled it. She paced impatiently until the maidservant came, then said rather more sharply than she had intended, "Where is the girl who came with me, if you please?"

"Why, in the servants' hall, miss. I came up to see if you still want a bath. It's a bit chilly, but we can stir up the fire and have hot water up here in a trice."

"Yes, thank you. I should like that very much. Has his lordship awakened yet?"

"Oh, goodness, miss, he was up and gone out of the house by four o'clock."

"Then why did no one wake me?"

"His lordship said you was very tired, miss, and that we must let you sleep until you wakened on your own. He sent me in to close your curtains when your woman said she hadn't done so. You was sleeping like the dead then, miss. It would have been right heartless to wake you."

"Very well," Melissa said, resigned. "Order hot water and a tub brought up, and send Mag to me now."

"Yes, miss."

Mag hurried in a few minutes later, carrying a bright green garment over her arm. Pushing the door shut behind her, she held up the garment, saying, "This will keep you warm after your bath, miss. Much better than that silk thing. Lawks-a-mussy, but this wool is as soft as can be."

"But where are my clothes?"

"This be another of her ladyship's robes, miss, which that Lucy said you was to wear after your bath. I'll just put it here on the dressing chair. Lawks-a-mussy, but this be a well-run house, miss. Servants everywhere! Now, I'll just move this screen out, so's we can put it round the tub when it comes. Then I'll stir up yon fire."

Noting that Mag was talking faster than ever before and seemed reluctant to meet her gaze, Melissa said, "Mag, what's amiss? Where is his lordship?"

Mag looked surprised. "Why, he's gone a-looking for Mr. Oliver, miss. That be his brother, down from Oxford, and a rare limb of Satan by what's said of him in the hall. Seems his lordship done told Mr. Figmore—that be the porter, miss—that Mr. Oliver wasn't to leave the house afore he spoke to him. But Mr. Oliver said as how he didn't have nothing to say to his lordship, and so—"

"I see," Melissa said, cutting off the flow. She was not surprised to discover that Mag had learned so much in her short time at Barrington House, for she was well aware that the servants in any great house knew as much as the family, if not more. But she knew she ought not to quiz Mag about Vexford's family. Her gaze fell upon the green wool dressing gown on the dressing chair, and she said, "But surely, in such a well-run house, my dress and other things ought to have been cleaned by now."

Again Mag avoided her gaze, saying, "Well, that they ought, miss, but looks as if they ain't now, don't it?"

"Mag, look at me."

Mag bit her lip, then looked remarkably relieved when a rap sounded on the door, and a male voice said, "Your tub and bath water, miss."

"Miss, quick, behind the screen. You ain't wearing nearly enough to be seen by no menservants."

Melissa obeyed but waited only until the tub was in place and the men had gone before stepping out and saying sternly, "Now, Mag, without more roundaboutation, where are my clothes?"

Mag looked as if she might prevaricate, but then she said with a sigh, "Well, I knew I ought to tell you, but he said to keep it mum if we could, so I tried, but lawks-a-mussy, miss, they's your clothes when all is said and done."

"Perfectly correct. Where are they?"

"I don't rightly know. His lordship told that Lucy girl she wasn't to give them to you till he gets back from wherever it is that he's gone to. Said you wasn't accustomed to town ways and might try to go out and about on your own without proper protection. Said it would be as well to let you stay in your bedchamber for the time, and so you're to have your supper served to you here as soon as you've had your bath."

"Oh, am I?" Melissa resisted a nearly overwhelming urge to tell Mag exactly what she thought of his lordship's tactics.

Mag did not seem to think Melissa's comment required a response, for she busied herself stirring crushed lavender into the warm water. Melissa could smell it, and the scent calmed her outrage. "Where did that come from?"

"Lucy said his lordship give it to her, miss."

"Oh, did he?" He had chosen well, for it was her favorite scent, but she wondered how he happened to have some at hand. Mag took the flowery silk robe, and Melissa got into the tub and slipped down in it, relaxing, enjoying the sensation of warmth spreading through her body. Taking the bar of French milled soap Mag handed her, she lathered herself, letting her thoughts take their course. By the time Mag had washed her hair and wrapped it in a cotton towel, Melissa had decided she had nothing to fear from a man who thought of details like lavender bath water and French milled soap. By the time she stood to let Mag pour rinse water over her, she had made up her mind not to let the arrogant Vexford believe for a moment longer than necessary that she would submit quietly to his dictation.

"Tell me, Mag," she said, as she stepped out of the tub, "do you happen to know where his lordship's room is to be found?"

"Aye, miss, for Lucy showed me about. She's kind, is that Lucy. I want to be as good as her, and maybe work in a great house one day. She said she come from an orphanage, she did, and begun as under-housemaid down at Owlcastle, which is the earl's big house in the country."

Only half-listening to her, Melissa said, "Where is it?"

"In Hampshire, I think she said."

"Not Owlcastle," Melissa said, keeping her patience. "His lordship's room."

"Oh, the big corner one's his bedchamber, miss," Lucy said. His dressing room and Mr. Lisset's room be the next ones after the turning, and the earl and his lady be in the southwest wing. Mr. Oliver—"

"Then his lordship's rooms overlook that courtyard out there," Melissa said, with satisfaction.

"Aye, miss."

"And Mr. Lisset? I suppose he must be in the servants' hall, having his dinner."

"Oh, no, miss. That is, he wouldn't be, because Lucy said Mr. Lisset takes his meals in the housekeeper's room with Mr. and Mrs. Preston—them's Lord Ulcombe's butler and housekeeper—and Mrs. Gretton, which is her ladyship's dresser, and Mr. Plenmeller, which is Lord Ulcombe's ditto. But Mr. Lisset has gone out, Lucy said, on account of his lordship said he wouldn't be home most likely till long after midnight, and wouldn't need Mr. Lisset when he did get home." Mag looked at her curiously, as if something in Melissa's tone had given her thoughts away.

Melissa smiled innocently back and said, "We must dry my hair quickly, Mag. Time is flying by, and my supper will be ready soon."

"Aye, miss."

Melissa thought about confiding her intentions but decided not to, fearing that Vexford might punish Mag—if the girl would even agree to help her. She could not be sure Mag would, for she seemed to have come to the belief, ill founded though it was, that Vexford was some sort of god who had whisked her to London and was going to whisk her back to the north again, doubtless with her pockets generously filled.

Mag was still brushing Melissa's hair dry before the fire when Lucy entered and began setting a table for supper. The meal arrived soon afterward, and Melissa insisted that Mag run off with Lucy to enjoy her own dinner.

"I shall do very well alone," she said. "I see books on the table by the door, so after my supper, I shall take one to read by the fire. I shan't even need you to put me to bed, for there is practically nothing left to be done."

Lucy said, "Just you ring when you want someone to collect them dishes, miss."

The moment they had gone, however, Melissa put down her fork, pushed the table away, and hurried to the door. Peeping both ways down the corridor, she was delighted to find it unoccupied. She was even more pleased, a few moments later, to find both his lordship's bedchamber and his dressing room in a like condition.

Nick was not in a pleasant mood by ten o'clock, when he entered the main subscription room at the Billingsgate Club. Having discovered that the ladies residing in St. Merryn

House had gone out before four and were not expected back until the small hours, he had left a message saying he would call at eleven the next morning, and had gone looking for his brother. So far his search had been unsuccessful.

He had already visited Mr. Crockford's establishment in Bolton Row, where he had dined with a friend. Then he had gone on to various and sundry other places that enjoyed a popular reputation similar to Crockford's. He had not gone to White's Club or Brooks's, for although he knew his brother could gain entrance at either of those esteemed gentleman's clubs, he did not think either would attract him. For that same reason, he had not sought him at the Billingsgate until he had looked into every hell he could think of, for he knew from his own brief acquaintance with the place that the play was high and the atmosphere generally more dignified than Crockford's. One visit, in his opinion, should have warned his brother that the stakes were too rich for his pocket.

Most of the houses he visited had proved thin of company, since most of the sporting men were still in Newmarket. Thanks to carrier pigeons taken to Newmarket for the express purpose of returning with such news, he knew that Florrie had lost his race to Wilson's colt, just as Drax had predicted. That disappointment, coupled with increasing displeasure toward his brother, must have shown in his expression, for when he encountered an acquaintance just inside the subscription room, the man exclaimed, "Good Lord, Nick, I hope I'm not the one who's stirred that damned temper of yours."

Nick blinked, then smiled ruefully and held out his hand. "Evening, Mereworth. Do I look like thunder?"

"Worse than that. Who's put you out of temper?"

"My own ill luck," Nick said with another smile. "I had to come back to town, so I missed today's heats. Had one running, and just learned he didn't place. Got another one running in the King's Plate on Friday though. You haven't seen Oliver about, have you?"

Mereworth nodded toward the far side of the room. "Young fool's yonder, at the hazard table. Hope you don't object to me calling him a fool."

"Not in the least. Playing deep?"

"Like the son of a nabob. Not that Ulcombe can't stand the nonsense, but if he were my son . . ." Tactfully, he added, "Not my affair, of course."

Nick made no reply to that, merely thanking him and turning to make his way across the room. He went slowly, not wanting to be obvious about looking for Oliver. Pausing twice to speak with acquaintants, he came at last to the table his brother graced and observed the play for a time without drawing Oliver's notice.

The younger man's attention was riveted on the dice. He was not as tall or broad-shouldered as Nick, nor was his hair as dark, but his eyes were as deeply blue. Their expression was generally merry rather than serious or stern, like Nick's, but he was not smiling now. And, although he generally favored high fashion and a natty appearance, his neckcloth was crumpled and he looked a little worn around the edges.

Nick soon saw that Oliver was losing. His losses did not appear to be enormous, but they were significant, and when he recklessly pushed a pile of notes out onto the table, crying, "I'll cover that if it breaks me," Nick muttered an epithet to himself.

When the caster threw out, Oliver turned to the man next to him and said, "I say, Freddy, will you frank me for the next cast? It's bound to be a winner. Dash it all, they can't come up crabs again, now can they?"

"Oliver," Nick said gently, "can you spare me a moment just now?"

Oliver jumped, and turned so sharply that he must have disarranged his neckcloth altogether, for he reached up to tug at it. His face was pale, but he said with forced cheerfulness, "That you, Nick? Thought you were in Newmarket."

"Did you, indeed?" Nick nodded to the other five gentlemen at the table.

The groom-porter said, "Will you cover the stake, my lord?"

"No, thank you," Nick said. "Oliver?"

Oliver opened his mouth as if to disclaim any intention of leaving the table, but when Nick caught his gaze and held it, the younger man said, "Oh, very well, if you wish it, but your timing is dashed inconvenient. Just look at that stake!"

"Yes, but I have not seen you in some time, you know. Humor me."

He had kept his voice calm, but he could tell that his brother was not deceived. As they left the subscription room, Nick urged him toward the stairway to the entrance hall, but Oliver dug in his heels. He said brusquely, "I suppose you are out of sorts because I didn't hang around at home to talk with you but came out for a lark instead."

"I am out of sorts, my dear fellow, because my horse lost its race today and I have searched this town high and low for you. You ought to have had the courtesy at least to leave word where I might find you. Avoiding me, Ollie?"

Oliver looked at him from under his eyebrows and said gruffly, "I don't need a nursemaid. I know you think you're top of the trees, Nick, and that I ought to cling to your coattails until I'm up to snuff, but I've friends of my own, and I want to go my own way."

"Certainly." Nick grasped his elbow and drew him into an alcove where they might be assured of some moments of privacy. Then in an undertone, he said sternly, "You'll go your way, my lad, straight out of this place."

"Well, it may not be Brooks's," Oliver began defensively, "but—"

"You can't afford Brooks's, either," Nick snapped, "but this isn't even Crockford's, although I hear you enjoy playing hazard there, too."

"Rigger says Crockford's and the Billingsgate know how

to treat a chap, and by Jove, I've seen that for myself. If I were to go into Brooks's or White's, Father's friends, or yours, would be looking over my shoulder, advising me and warning me at every turn, worrying about how much I'm wagering. Well, Rigger told me—"

"Who the devil is this Rigger?"

"A friend from school. He's—"

"He's giving you damned bad advice, Ollie. Now come away from here at once, and go home where you belong, or—"

"Or what, Nick? You'll tell my father? By Jove, I almost wish you would. He'd give you what for. He told me himself he was glad I'd be getting a bit of town bronze this Season, and dashed if I don't mean to do just that."

"As I recall, he has also told you he is tired of paying for your excesses. He certainly does not mean for you to lose a fortune at the tables."

"Oh, I don't lose all the time. I'm much more fortunate with cards than with the ivories. I just thought I'd have a go at the Billingsgate hazard bank because Rigger said I'd enjoy myself, and I did. I won quite a lot at first, too, and so—"

"Of course you did. That's how they entice you to stay, and to wager more and more until you've lost all you've got. Now, you listen to me, Ollie. . . ." For the next several minutes Nick spoke to some purpose, his words bringing deep color to his brother's face and a sulky look to his mouth, but Oliver did not make the mistake of attempting to interrupt him.

When he finished, Oliver glared at him, then said, "You needn't think you can order me about, Nick, for you can't. I know your temper scares everyone else to death, but I don't dance to your piping. It won't do the least good to look like you want to murder me, either, for I know you won't. Of course, if you are thinking you can knock me down, well, I know you can, but I doubt if you want to drag my limp body back to Barrington House. Even if you do, I'll just come back again tomorrow. I'm not a child anymore, and I'm dashed well old enough to set my own course."

"If you think I'm going to leave you here without so much as a pound in your pocket, to go begging from your friends, you are very much mistaken."

"Oh, I'll leave now. I haven't got a feather to fly with until I can get another draft on Father's bank. Moreover, having stayed up till dawn the past two nights, I don't mind going home and getting some sleep. I'll even allow you to take me with you if you promise not to lecture me all the way."

Repressing an urge to throttle him, Nick nodded and silently led the way downstairs to the street door. When he called for his tilbury, however, a lad ran up to him and said urgently, "I say, sir, be you my Lord Vexford?"

Nick nodded, and the boy thrust a sealed note into his hand. Reaching into his waistcoat pocket, he withdrew a shilling and tossed it to him, then broke the seal.

"Who's it from?" Oliver demanded. "No trouble at home, I hope."

"Do you think Preston or Figmore would send a street urchin with a message for me?" Nick asked sardonically, turning just enough to defeat Oliver's blatant attempt to read over his shoulder. "It appears that I am not going to take you home, Ollie, but if you will accept some advice, you won't go anywhere else. You may pretend to have no fear of my temper, but I promise you'll be sorry if you persist in maintaining the insolent attitude you assumed upstairs just now."

Oliver had the grace to look abashed. "I won't. I ain't a complete fool, Nick, but where are you going?"

"That, my dear fellow, is none of your affair."

"Then it's a female, I'll wager."

"Be off while you can still walk and talk," Nick advised him. He did not have any intention of telling him that for once he had hit the mark. The missive, reeking of some exotic perfume, was from Clara, Lady Hawthorne. Although she couched her demand in diplomatic terms, she was clearly incensed with him and expected him to present himself at her house at once to explain just what he had meant by abandoning her in Newmarket without a single word of explanation or farewell.

Eight

Vexford Throws Out, Twice

When Nick drew up his tilbury in front of Lady Hawthorne's tall, narrow house in Clarges Street, he found light pouring from every window. Had he not known better, he might have thought the lady was giving a party, if not a full dress ball, but he knew that Clara's house was always brightly lighted, and with wax candles. She did not think any more highly of the smelly new gas lighting than Lord Ulcombe did.

Leaving the tilbury with the under-groom who had attended it throughout his search for Oliver, he mounted the steps and rapped sharply on the front door. It opened at once, and the haughty-looking butler no sooner saw him that he relaxed and beamed at him, saying, "Good evening, my lord, and welcome. We have been expecting you these two hours and more. You will find her ladyship in her boudoir."

"Thank you, Greaves. I'll go straight up."

The door to her ladyship's boudoir was slightly ajar. He pushed it open, revealing a room decorated in moss green and pale pink. An Aubusson carpet covered the floor, its pink roses and pale green leaves echoing the pattern of the voluminous curtains at the windows and the upholstery of the exquisite Sheraton furniture. A cheerful fire in the Adam fireplace filled the room with warmth, but if Nick hoped for a similarly warm welcome from the room's sole occupant, he soon learned his error.

He had not, in fact, anticipated any such thing, and so he was not moved when the lovely woman curled up on a claw-footed sofa in the left window embrasure failed even to look up when he entered. She continued to read the book she held, its pages lighted by several branches of candles on the table beside the sofa. Her golden head glinted in the candlelight. Her hair, fashionably styled and adorned with jeweled clips, was the exact color of a guinea coin, but Nick found himself comparing it unfavorably with Miss Seacourt's smooth flaxen tresses.

Collecting himself he said blandly, "An affecting pose, my dear, but since you sent for me, I should think the least you could do is say hallo."

She looked up at last and frowned at him, saying in her low-pitched, sultry voice, "Nicky, you are a very naughty boy. I sent the lad to look for you hours ago. I had quite given up waiting, which is why you find me *en déshabillé.*"

"I generally do find you *en déshabillé,* my dear. No," he added, "pray, don't attempt to blush. Coyness does not suit you. And before you begin ripping up at me for leaving Newmarket, let me say that I found your note a trifle impertinent. Not only did I not escort you to Newmarket—although you seem to have told everyone I did—but I told you there was no use in your going, except for your own pleasure. With two horses running, I was of no mind to dance attendance on any female."

She pouted. "If you are going to be cruel, Nicky, you will distress me very much. I thought you loved me."

"You never thought any such thing, and I'll thank you not to waste my time playing off such fantasies."

"Why did you come then?"

"I came because you asked me to come, and because I occasionally find you amusing. I am not, however, amused by whining or by tantrums, Clara, so pray do not inflict such behavior on me now. I have had a very trying day."

"Trying?" She bristled, set her book aside, and stood up. "Despite having horses running both today and Friday—and Prince Florizel lost, in case no one told you— Despite that, and despite having no time for females, I was informed, Nicky *darling,* that you left Newmarket in the company of a very beautiful young female. Do you mean to pretend that's not true?"

"If it is, it is certainly no business of yours."

"But of course it is my business! Why, everyone knows you've been paying me a great deal of attention, and no fewer than six persons told me about this female. At least two of them said she was beautiful, Nicky, and would cast me into the shade."

"Now I know you are lying, Clara."

"Well, I'm glad you think she won't, but how dare you accuse me of lying!"

"Because you are. You give yourself away every time."

"How?"

"I shan't tell you that. But although you might have caught wind of a rumor, I'll go bail it was no more than that."

"At least *two* people told me who *must* have known the truth." She pouted again. "Don't you love me, Nicky? Truly? Come and put your arms around me. Because you abandoned me, I was forced to accept another man's escort back to London. Although he was charming enough to drive you mad with jealousy, we were driven at a wicked pace all the way, so even if he had wanted to make love to me, he had no chance. Then I hurried through my bath, just to smell good when you hugged me. Would you put all my effort to waste?" She spread her arms invitingly.

He did not respond. Frowning, he said, "You have become too imperious and too possessive for my taste, madam, and I do not relish petty attempts to make me jealous. If you have begun to pretend that I hold more than a slight affection for you, it would be as well to end matters between us here and now."

"Most of the *beau monde* believes you love me," she murmured, moving slowly toward him, her hips swaying seductively beneath the silken robe she wore. "Why, any number of people have asked when you mean to set a date for our wedding, and though I have assured them all over and over that we are only friends, so it is, Nicky. Would you make me appear to be the victim of a common jilt?"

He was annoyed, and apparently it showed, for she stopped in her tracks and her eyes widened warily. He said softly, "You understand the rules of the game we've played as well as I do, Clara. You will collect no winnings with this wild cast."

She stamped her foot. "You think all life is a game, Nicky, a hand of cards to be won or lost by the best player! I suppose you have no acquaintance with such common human failings as jealousy. Oh, no, and I suppose you are not at all displeased to learn that I danced with other men, or even that the one who escorted me here from Newmarket was extremely handsome and debonair. What do you say to that, sir?"

He shook his head. "Fortunately, I am not cursed with a jealous nature, my dear, but since you don't see that as a blessing, no doubt you are well rid of me."

"Nicky, no! You promised to buy me a gold bracelet, damn you!"

"And you shall have it, my dear, for though I am not entirely suitable as a lover, I am certainly a man of my word."

"Nicky, please don't go."

He went, and he did not turn back. Clara's affectations had long since ceased to amuse him, but he had found it easier to continue the relationship than to exert himself to end it. Ignoring her continued entreaties and—before he had reached the hall—her shrieks of temper, he left the house, feeling only relief to be gone.

As he climbed into his tilbury, he remembered the wary

look on Clara's face when she had angered him, and remembered, too, thinking not long before that he had never frightened a woman. Perhaps, he told himself now, he ought to be more careful about that—not with Clara, who had deserved to be frightened a bit, but with others.

When he drove the tilbury through the high archway leading from St. James's Square to the Barrington House stables, he was tired and yearning for his bed. Handing the reins to the under-groom, he jumped down and entered the house through a side door, using his key, since the servants had long since retired. A candle lay waiting for him on a mahogany side table in the anteroom, and lighting it, he made his way to his bedchamber. Without bothering to ring for Lisset or to do more than remove his clothing, he fell into bed and went right to sleep.

The following morning he was awakened betimes by his valet shaking him and saying, "Begging your pardon, my lord, but it is just upon seven o'clock now."

"So what?" Nick growled.

"You requested that I waken you, sir."

"The devil I did. Go away, Lisset."

"I found your note when I returned, my lord. Perhaps you do not recall writing it. I will get your shaving gear and clothing at once," he added, the sound of his voice indicating that he was moving away toward the dressing room.

"There's nothing amiss with my memory, damn you. Go away."

"I am merely following your orders, my lord," the valet said stiffly.

Recognizing offended dignity, Nick opened bleary eyes and looked at him. Lisset had paused on the dressing-room threshold with Nick's discarded clothing draped over one arm, and he looked as offended as he had sounded. He also seemed to be very much in earnest.

"Lisset," Nick said evenly, "I have sworn off brandy, and I was quite sober when I returned to the house last night. I came straight here, threw off my clothes, as you see, and fell straight into bed. I did not write any notes, to you or to anyone."

"I can show it to you, sir, in your own handwriting, just as soon as I—" He had turned and stepped into the dressing room, so Nick could no longer see him, but after a moment of stunned silence, Lisset exclaimed, "Good gracious me!"

Fully awake now, whether he chose to be or not, Nick sat up in the bed and said, "What the devil is amiss now?"

The valet returned to the doorway, his eyes wide with shock. "My lord, you will surely question my sanity now. Your clothing is gone."

"Nonsense, how can it be gone?"

"Well, I have not searched every drawer, but the doors to the wardrobe are open, and the drawers of the dresser, as well, and—" He broke off again. The startled look on his face quickly changed to one of exasperation, and he exclaimed, "Young Master Oliver! I ought to have guessed at once! Oh, how I'd like to—"

"Gently, Lisset," Nick warned. "I cannot allow even you to utter threats against my obnoxious brother. Moreover, while I am perfectly willing to believe that it was he who set you on to wake me hours before he knew I would want to be wakened, I refuse to believe him so lost to sanity as to have stolen my clothing."

Cocking his head as if he had heard something, Lisset said, "I beg your pardon, sir, one moment." He turned and went into the dressing room.

When an urgent murmur of voices ensued, Nick got out of bed and went to see what was going on. Just before he reached the doorway, he heard Lisset say, "Don't gabble so, girl. Tell me plainly what you know."

Nick saw that a scared-looking housemaid faced his valet. Visibly gathering her wits, she said, "Oh, Mr. Lisset, sir, I do beg your pardon, but 'tis the oddest thing, and Cook did say I were to run up here and tell you at once, sir."

"Then do, for heaven's sake, tell me."

"His lordship's clothing, sir, it be— Oh!" She broke off, covering her mouth with a gasp when she saw Nick standing in the doorway.

He stepped hastily back, but she made no attempt to continue until he looked round the door again and said, "What about my clothing, girl? Where is it?"

Blushing furiously, she said in a rush, "In the courtyard, sir, in heaps, like it were flung out the window, Cook says. A fearful lot of clothing, it is, too, m' lord."

Lisset collected his dignity and said with aplomb, "Thank you, you may go now. And mind, girl, I don't want to hear any of the other servants prattling about this."

"Oh, no, Mr. Lisset. I-I wouldn't!"

"See that you don't." When she had gone, he moved swiftly to the window overlooking the courtyard, flung open the casement, and stuck his head out. Then, looking grimly over his shoulder at Nick, he said, "Every stitch and button, sir. Even your shoes. Mr. Oliver must have quite taken leave of his senses."

"I would agree with you, Lisset, if I believed Oliver had done this, but I don't." He was perfectly willing to believe that Oliver's predilection for practical jokes had led him to forge the note Lisset had found. What he did not believe for a minute was that his brother could be so lost to a generally active sense of personal preservation as to have cast all of Nick's expensive clothing into the courtyard. He believed, instead, that such an act must have been perpetrated by someone much less well acquainted than Oliver was with his temper—someone destined, on the other hand, to become particularly well acquainted with it in the very near future.

Melissa was roused from her deep, warm sleep by a voice asking ever so politely if she had enjoyed a pleasant night. At first she refused to open her eyes, assuming that she must have dreamed it, since the voice was definitely a masculine one, and not one that an unmarried, gently bred lady expected to hear in her bedchamber before rising.

Taking on a disturbing edge, the voice continued implacably, "I can see that you are awake. You might just as well open your eyes so that I can judge for myself the truthfulness of your answers to one or two little questions I want to ask you."

There could be no question now. The voice was all too real. She could feel Vexford's presence looming over her, and in a flash she remembered what she had done in a fit of pique the night before. Sensing impatient movement from the massive figure beside the bed, and fearing to have the bedcovers snatched away at any moment, she opened her eyes at last, threw back the covers on the side opposite him, and scrambled to the floor. Someone had laid a fire in the room's fireplace, but since Vexford had given no orders for her comfort, no one had lighted it yet. The chilly morning air struck her with force through the thin lawn nightdress she wore, and she quickly stepped from the cold hardwood floor to the small throw rug beside the bed. "Get out of this room!" she cried. "You have no business in here."

"On the contrary," he said, glaring at her across the bed, "I have the singularly important business of discovering why you threw all my clothing into the courtyard. It was you who did so, was it not?"

"What if I say it was not?"

He moved toward the end of the bed, "I don't think I would believe you."

Eyeing him warily, she stepped back, only to step onto the cold floor again. Glancing behind her, she saw that the corner of the room offered no sanctuary and no weapon with which to defend herself. "Stay where you are," she said, trying unsuccessfully to infuse her voice with authority.

He continued his slow approach.

Glancing at the bed, she realized that if she could reach

the other side, the doorway lay just beyond. With a hope that he would not pursue her down the corridor, she edged nearer the bed again.

Vexford stopped several steps from her. Clearly exerting himself to keep his temper, he said, "You might at least give me an explanation."

"You took my clothes," she said. "I took yours in return."

"A rather drastic return of play, I think. Hardly an equal gambit."

"It was not a move in a game," she snapped. "I was angry."

He frowned, somehow looking larger than ever, and she suddenly felt small and defenseless. It was hard to believe she had once, even for a moment, considered him to be her protector. She stepped back, again seeking escape, until she bumped against the bed-step table. She heard the candle-stick's rocking rattle, but it did not fall over.

He said in an even voice that sent shivers of apprehension through her, "I know you were angry. I can't imagine any other reason to commit so destructive an act."

"Destructive? Don't be ridiculous. You have only to send a servant to collect them. They are hardly destroyed."

"I doubt that my valet will agree with you, but in any case, it is not a servant who is going to collect them but the person who threw them out the window."

"I will not!"

"I sincerely trust that you will change your mind," he said grimly, "for you deserve worse punishment. I prevented the return of your clothing only to deter you from leaving the house. I didn't think you would stay just because I told you to, but I knew you would if you had nothing to wear. I merely exerted reasonable caution. Your behavior was childish. I won't insist that you put my things back where you found them, because they are in no fit condition to be put away; however, you will certainly pick up every stitch of my cloth-ing, and carry it back to my dressing room."

"I won't!"

He stepped toward her, and quick as a flash she reached back, snatched up the candlestick from the table, and threw it at him. She missed, but the action diverted his attention long enough for her to leap to the bed, roll across, and slip off the other side. She landed, running, and made it to the door, but as she reached for the latch, a large hand clamped onto her left arm from behind. He scooped her up and carried her back to the bed. Struggling and kicking, she shrieked, "Put me down! How dare you!"

"I'm going to dare much more," he snapped, flipping her roughly over his knee as he sat on the bed. "I'll teach you not to throw things, Miss Seacourt, either at me or out of windows." The skirt of her nightdress had caught on the cloth of his sleeve as he turned her over his knee and when he raised his hand, he bared her nearly to the waist.

She went perfectly still.

So did Vexford. She heard his indrawn breath, and then the skirt of her nightdress was gently drawn down again. He did not say a word or move a muscle for a long moment, but she made no attempt to get up, still terrified and not knowing what he meant to do next. She was certain her ordeal was not over.

At last, in a quite different, audibly strained voice, he said, "What did he use?"

Only then did she realize that he had seen, not just her bare backside, but the marks of her father's beating.

"His riding whip. May I get up, sir?"

"Yes, certainly," he said at once, helping her to stand. "I can't think why you didn't fight like a wildcat to keep me from adding to that."

"I never do," she said simply, shaking out the lawn skirt.

"Good Lord, when you said he had whipped you, I imagined a child's whipping. How often has he beaten you like that?"

"Not at all in the past nine years, because that's when my mother left him and moved to Scotland with my stepfather.

They took me with them. Before then, he did so whenever my behavior displeased him."

"Is that why she left him?"

"Partly, but he was much more fierce with her. Once, he beat her so badly that we ran away to Grandpapa St. Merryn's house, but Papa followed us, and we had to hide. Then the magistrate made Mama go back with Papa. She told me the law holds that a woman *must* be better off with any husband, even one who beats her, than with no husband at all. Until we moved to Scotland, I thought most fathers were like mine, and I envied my cousin Charley because hers paid her no heed. She was used to do the most outrageous things, too, trying to draw his attention." She smiled a little then, remembering. Although her cousin's father had learned over time to pay more heed, Charley still enjoyed less restriction than most young women her age.

"So your mother obtained a Scottish divorce, did she?"

Melissa nodded. "We were very happy in Scotland, but then Papa came and stole me away. He said the law allowed him to do that, and that nothing Penthorpe—he's my stepfather—that nothing he could have done would have prevented it."

"He's right about that, I'm sure," Vexford said.

"I know, and I can't say that I want a husband who will probably be just like him, but I daresay you'll have to marry me now."

"Don't be nonsensical. I am not like your father, and we are not getting married. I thought I'd made that clear."

"But surely you can't bare a lady naked to the world, twice, and *not* marry her."

"I did not bare you to the world, either time, only to the ambient air," he said, looking her straight in the eye. "Moreover, I seem to recall that you yourself once pointed out that one cannot be forced to marry against one's will nowadays."

"That was when Lord Yarborne seemed to think my father

could simply give me to him without my consent, sir, and well you know it."

"So you remember that part, at least, but the fact remains that one would find forcing an unwilling man to the altar much more difficult than compelling an unwilling woman. After all, there are plenty of magistrates and parsons who still believe that a girl's father controls her until her husband takes over the job. Men like that would most likely choose to ignore a minor detail like her lack of consent."

She believed him. "What are you going to do?"

"I am going to deliver you as quickly as I can to Lady Ophelia. She will look after you. By the sound of it, she's fierce enough to protect you from anyone."

Melissa was not so sure. Lady Ophelia was elderly, and she had not seen her for some time, but she realized there was no use arguing. "Must I really collect your clothing?" she asked. "I will do so if you insist. I know it was a dreadful thing to do, but I was very angry. I don't always think before I act, I'm afraid."

"You had better learn to think about the potential consequences of your actions." When she sighed in resignation and turned toward the door, he chuckled, and she found it a welcome sound. He said, "Even at my most temperamental, I doubt I would make you go downstairs in your nightdress. As things stand now, I think we will let Lisset attend to it. After all, he needs to find me something suitable to wear to pay a morning call on an elderly lady. In the meantime, I will ring for Mag, and for some breakfast. I left word at St. Merryn House last evening that I would call at eleven, but I think we will depart as soon as we can. Send me word when you have eaten and dressed."

He left, and she sighed in relief, but it was with mixed feelings that she waited for Mag to bring her clothes. Much as she looked forward to seeing Lady Ophelia again, and Charley, the thought that she might never again lay eyes on Vexford depressed her. Though at times he frightened her a little—more than a little, if she were honest—and angered her a lot, the fact remained that from the moment she had first exchanged words with him, she had felt as if she had known him forever. The circumstances of their meeting accounted for much of that feeling, she knew, but she would be sorry not to see him again, and the chance that they would meet was slim. She doubted that she would attend any parties in the short time remaining for her in London, or meet with many members of the *beau monde*. Her recent experiences had undoubtedly relegated her to that class of persons who were better not seen in public.

Although she had to wait only a short time after she had dressed and broken her fast before Vexford was ready to depart, it was nearly nine o'clock by then. They went in style, in a comfortable town carriage, driven by a very respectable-looking coachman, and were soon set down before St. Merryn House in Berkeley Square.

The butler who answered the door did not recognize Melissa, nor she him, and his first, rather haughty reaction was to deny them entrance. "Her ladyship is not at home to visitors until after one o'clock," he said.

"I am Miss Seacourt, Lady Ophelia's great-grandniece," Melissa said. "Please be so good as to tell her I am here. If she has not left her bed yet, or is otherwise indisposed, pray inform Miss Charlotte of my arrival instead."

The man's brow cleared, and he smiled. "Begging your pardon, miss, I'm sure, but I've only been with Lady Ophelia these past five years. Still, I've heard your name spoken often and often. She will be ever so pleased that you are here. In fact— But what am I thinking? There is no need to stand upon ceremony with you. I'll just show you upstairs at once, and the gentleman, too." He looked pointedly at Vexford, who obliged him by giving his name.

"Is Miss Charlotte here?" Melissa demanded as they went upstairs.

"She is, indeed, miss, and has been this fortnight past. Her parents being on the Continent just now, visiting the Lady Daintry—or as I should say, with Lord and Lady Abreston—the old master brought Miss Charley to London himself, though he did not stay above two nights. He don't like town life much, you know, and Lady St. Merryn—your grandmama, that is—enjoying such indifferent health—well, he don't like to leave her, and that's a fact. Lady Ophelia," he added in his chatty way, "has another early visitor this morning, but I daresay you must know all about him. I don't know what's come over me, for I've been going on like a fiddlestick, which is not, I assure you, my normal habit. But here we are now." He pushed open a pair of tall doors, revealing a pleasant drawing room, stepped aside to allow them to pass, and said in much more dignified tones, "Miss Seacourt, my lady, and my Lord Vexford."

Lady Ophelia Balterley, seated stiffly erect on a sofa drawn near the fire, turned her head toward the visitors, and to Melissa's astonishment, she frowned.

"Aunt Ophelia," Melissa said hastily, "I hope I have not imposed upon your good nature by coming to you without warning like this, but when I have explained, I am persuaded—" She broke off when Lady Ophelia's other visitor, standing just beyond her immediate view, near the window, stepped forward. "P-papa!"

Sir Geoffrey said with his most charming smile, "Good morning, my darling. I daresay you are a little surprised to see me so soon, but you must have known I would come for you. I've just been telling Lady Ophelia I'd quite expected to find you here."

Lady Ophelia said dryly, "I see that you were not, as I had supposed, lying through your teeth again, Geoffrey. Don't stand like a stock, Melissa girl, but come in and sit down, and pray do not enact me any Cheltenham drama, for I've already been obliged to dismiss your cousin to her bedchamber for her impertinence, and I simply won't stand for any more of it."

Nine

Vexford Declares, and Wins a Main

Seacourt moved as if to embrace Melissa, but when she stepped quickly back beside Nick, the older man said with a laugh, "You see, ma'am, it is exactly as I said it would be, for here they are, albeit not as soon as I'd expected. Poor Vexford acted out of impulse or caprice when he helped her run away from Newmarket, and now he wants only to thrust her back into the bosom of her family." Although Seacourt's voice was touched with light humor, Nick noted that he was looking not at Lady Ophelia but at Melissa. He saw, too, that, despite the smile, his expression was unforgiving.

"Sit down, sit down, all of you," Lady Ophelia said tartly. "You are making my head ache, forcing me to look up at you like this." Frowning at Nick as they obeyed her command, she added in the same abrupt tone, "Are you Ulcombe's son, young man?"

Without taking his eyes from Seacourt, he said, "I have the honor to be one of them, ma'am."

"A good chap, Ulcombe, as men go. Are you much like him?"

Nick smiled at her then. "Not much, I'm afraid, but I will be delighted to extend your compliments to him."

"No need for that. What are you doing with my niece?"

"Handing her over to someone who can protect her from her father, I hope," Nick said, echoing her bluntness.

"Indeed?" She raised her eyebrows, but Nick saw that she glanced speculatively at Seacourt. "What has her father been doing that she requires protection from him?"

He, too, looked back at Seacourt as he said, "Beating her, for one thing. Attempting to sell her into matrimony against her will, for another."

The look Lady Ophelia shot at Seacourt then ought, Nick thought, to have incinerated him on the spot. "Up to your old tricks, are you?" she said. "No, don't bother to deny it. I can see the bruise on her cheek for myself. And don't bother explaining to me how it is your God-given right as a man to beat the women in your family, for I won't listen to you. You are a brute, Geoffrey, for all your charming ways, and it is of no use whatsoever to look at me as if I were merely a feeble old woman who don't have her wits about her. I am neither feeble nor demented, and I shall still be able to deal effectively with you in the five short minutes before they shovel me underground. You are a fool, and I am not. That's the long and the short of it. You represent the worst and weakest of your sex, sir, which is saying quite a lot."

"And you represent the best and strongest of yours, ma'am," Seacourt said instantly, his temper apparently unruffled. "However, since Vexford is returning Melissa to her family, she will go with me to Brook Street, and there is nothing you or anyone else can do to prevent it. That is not a God-given right but one granted by good English law. In fact, I want to know just what Vexford has been doing with her since he removed her from our inn at Newmarket," he added with a challenging look at Nick.

Nick did not reply at once. He had listened with interest to the verbal sparring, and recognized the pair as adversaries of long standing. Though he did not care a fig for Seacourt, the old woman fascinated him. He thought her remarkably well preserved for eighty-six. Although a stout blackthorn cane leaned handily against the near arm of her sofa, she wore no spectacles. The gray hair beneath her plain white cap was pulled ruthlessly into a bun at the nape of her neck. Her gown was also gray, but the material of the latter was a fashionable Levantine, trimmed with expensive lace, and the cut and style became her well despite a figure that, if not exactly stout, was solid and square. Her pale blue eyes were clear, their expression intelligent, even shrewd.

She was looking at him, obviously waiting to hear what he would say. Ignoring Seacourt, he said to her, "I brought your niece to London, ma'am, to my parents' house. I won't pretend that I entrusted her to their care, for as it happens they were in Hampshire, at Owlcastle, though they are expected to return today. Nonetheless, Miss Seacourt has her maid with her, and our servants looked after her as if she were one of the family. She was quite safe at Barrington House." Taking care not to look at Melissa, he hoped she would have the good sense not to contradict him. He did not fear Seacourt's revealing the true worth of her so-called maid, since he had, after all, hired Mag himself.

Melissa was silent.

Lady Ophelia, glancing at her and then at Seacourt, said, "Well, what have you got to say to that, Geoffrey?"

He shrugged. "I'll accept Vexford's word as that of a gentleman, and thank him for looking after Melissa, but there is no longer any reason for him to do so, regardless of what tale they tell. We can go now, Melissa," he added, standing again. "It is more than time that you became acquainted with our Brook Street house, I believe."

Seeing Melissa stiffen, Nick said, "I believe I've purchased the right to have a say in where she goes, Seacourt. I daresay she will prefer to remain right here."

Lady Ophelia said brusquely, "She is welcome to stay with me, certainly."

"As to that," Seacourt said with a superior smile, "I—"

"Lissa, you *are* here! Buxton said you were, and of course Uncle Geoffrey all but accused us earlier of concealing you, so I knew you were up to some mischief or other, but— Goodness, who are *you?*"

Melissa, facing the doorway, was half out of her chair before Nick turned to see the newcomer. When he did, he found himself staring at an extraordinarily beautiful young woman. Her black hair was as glossy as if she had polished each strand with the finest pomatum, and her blue eyes were so dark they looked black beneath long, curling ebony lashes. Though she regarded him briefly with open curiosity, she quickly forgot her demand to know his identity, and hastened to hug Melissa. Her movements were graceful and confident, her figure exquisite, and her personality so imposing that it was with surprise that Nick saw, when the two young women embraced, that she was not as tall as Melissa.

Melissa cried, "Charley! Oh, how happy I am to see you!"

"How you've grown! I'm a mere Lilliputian beside you."

"Never! Oh, how I've missed you."

"Very affecting," Lady Ophelia said dryly, "but I was under the distinct impression, Charlotte, that you had retired to your bedchamber."

"What you mean, ma'am, is that you sent me there in disgrace as punishment for my bad manners," she retorted with disarming candor and a twinkling look at the old woman. "You may scold me mercilessly when our visitors have departed, but you simply cannot have expected me to stay upstairs once I discovered that Lissa had arrived." She looked again at Nick, who had risen politely but without undue haste, and said, "But, pray, is no one going to make this gentleman known to me?"

Obligingly, Lady Ophelia said, "May I present Lord Vexford, Charlotte, who has been kind enough to bring Melissa to us. Miss Tarrant is Melissa's cousin, sir, and has not seen her in some years. Hence, her unbridled enthusiasm."

"How do you do, sir," Miss Tarrant said, dropping a slight

curtsy, "but ought I to know you? I don't believe we have met before."

Taken aback by such direct questioning from a young woman scarcely out of her teens, even one who clearly boasted an acquaintance with *Gulliver's Travels,* Nick said, "An oversight on my account, Miss Tarrant. You must forgive me."

"Oh, don't talk fustian," she said. "It cannot be any fault of yours that we have not previously encountered each other. I have no patience with such drivel. I merely wondered if your title ought to be familiar to me."

Seacourt said with an edge to his voice, "You see what comes of allowing girls too much freedom of expression, Vexford. My niece has been allowed to speak her mind and run free, right from the cradle. She spends too much time with her horses and not nearly enough learning the manners expected of a young woman of quality. The lack derives from having too-sociable parents and a too-generous and doting great-grandaunt, and that is precisely why I will not allow Melissa to take up residence in this house."

"Uncle Geoffrey, really, what a thing to say about Papa and Mama when you've scarcely exchanged a civil word with either one of them in nine years! Of course, Lissa will stay here. She certainly doesn't want to go anywhere with you!"

"Hush, Charlotte!"

"Oh, Charley, please, don't!"

"Charlotte, hold your tongue," Seacourt commanded, adding sternly, "you have even less to say about Melissa's future than Lady Ophelia or Vexford has. The plain fact is that by law I am still Melissa's father, and by law she must obey me."

"The law," said Charley, undaunted, "is a nonsensical lot of poppycock made up by men to suit themselves, with no consideration whatsoever for the rest of the world. No matter what anyone else says about it, I say the law is merely a way for men to keep everything of value in this world for themselves."

Perfectly true, my dear," Lady Ophelia said, "but we cannot indulge ourselves just now in reciting a litany of legal injustices. Geoffrey, there is one bit of information that you left out earlier, and Vexford has said nothing to make the point clear to me. Though you said that Melissa had run away from you in Newmarket, both my hearing and my memory are acute, and I'm certain I heard Vexford say something just before Charlotte came in about having *purchased* the right to have a say in Melissa's future. I should like you to explain to me just what he meant by that."

Seacourt looked disconcerted, but Nick, taking his cue yet again from Miss Tarrant and Lady Ophelia, said bluntly, "I purchased Miss Seacourt at auction in a gaming hell, ma'am. Her father, having abducted her from Scotland, presented her to Lord Yarborne in payment of a large gaming debt. Yarborne, not putting much confidence in Seacourt's assurance that she is a considerable heiress, put her up for auction to recover his money. I had the honor to outbid the others."

Lady Ophelia gasped. "Merciful heavens! And here I'd been led to think Yarborne a gentleman, almost as generous to the poor and helpless as Ulcombe is."

Even the indomitable Miss Tarrant seemed to have been stricken speechless.

Seacourt shrugged, shook his head, and said with a twisted smile, "You need not look so shocked, either of you. Yarborne is exactly the man you thought him to be, ma'am. It was merely a matter of business between gentlemen and not anything one expects mere females to understand. Vexford may have been fool enough to purchase Melissa at that sham auction, thus paying my debt to Yarborne for me, but he has clearly relinquished any claim by bringing her here. He would have to do so, in any event, even if the purchase itself were not utterly without standing in any court of law, which, of course, is precisely the case. England does not recognize slavery, after all."

"Oh, yes, England does," Charley snapped. "Women all over this country are trapped in a state of *sexual* slavery that's been virtually unchanged since the dawn of our *man*-made civilization!"

Seacourt said testily, "Don't be stupid, Charlotte. You don't know what the devil you are saying, and it's got nothing to do with Melissa, who is leaving this house with me right now. English law may not be to your liking, but it does recognize a father's authority over a minor daughter. That authority cannot be superseded by anyone."

Silenced, Charley shot a pleading look at Lady Ophelia, but Nick knew that the old woman would not be able to stop Seacourt if he was determined to take his daughter. Looking at Melissa, he saw that, although her father had turned toward her with the obvious intention of removing her forcibly if she did not go with him willingly, she was looking not at him but at Nick.

"Come along, Melissa," Seacourt said, taking her arm and giving Charley a look that dared her to deny his right.

Melissa licked her lips, watching Nick determinedly.

Surprising himself, Nick said, "One moment."

Seacourt glared at him. "What now?"

"There is, in fact, someone in a woman's life whose authority does supersede that of her father."

Seacourt chuckled. "There is always God, of course."

"I am speaking of a husband's authority over his wife."

"Oh, famous," Charley exclaimed, clapping her hands.

Melissa's gaze remained fixed on Nick, but Seacourt only laughed and said, "Damnation, Vexford, you can't have married her, and I'll wager you haven't got the least intention of doing so. I've learned a great deal about you since we met, sir, and the one thing everyone agrees on is that you are *not* hanging out for a wife."

"But I do intend to marry her," Nick said with a steadiness

that surprised himself as much as it must have surprised the others. "I brought her here because I'd learned that Lady Ophelia was in town. I realized it was far more suitable for Miss . . . for Melissa to stay here with her than at Barrington House until I can procure a special license and make other necessary arrangements."

"Ah, but you did not know that I was in town as well," Seacourt said. "It must be even more suitable for her to remain under her father's roof until she marries."

"I disagree," Nick said, "and while you may quibble over whether my purchase gives me any legal right to make such a decision, you cannot say that our betrothal gives me no such right."

"But I do not agree that a betrothal exists," Seacourt said, still calm. "I am her father, after all, and I certainly have not agreed to one."

Lady Ophelia said with annoyance, "Don't be absurd, Geoffrey. If selling her—auctioning her; whatever it was you did—don't amount to agreeing to her betrothal, I don't know what would. I should still like to know what you were about to promise Yarborne that Melissa is a great heiress. If she is to inherit anything from anyone other than myself—and you, of course—I am unaware of it. Were you expecting me to be so obliging as to pop off my hook merely so that you could pay your gambling debts?"

"No, of course not," he retorted. "Vexford has exaggerated what occurred in Newmarket, I assure you. His description is outrageous and must be utterly incredible to anyone of common sense."

Nick said nothing. Nor did he try to avoid the penetrating gaze directed at him. Lady Ophelia snorted in a most unladylike way and said, "We must certainly hope that others will think it incredible if rumors begin to fly, but if you think, Geoffrey, that I'll take your word over his just because you are in some small way connected to me, you very much mistake the matter. Melissa will stay here for the present."

"I don't think so. He cannot marry her at once, after all."

"Yes, I can," Nick said. "I will go from here straight to Doctor's Commons, and the moment I have the special license, we can go to St. George's Chapel. The rector there is a friend of my father's, and will be happy to marry us at once."

"No," Lady Ophelia said flatly.

Having expected her support in his mad gesture, Nick looked at her in disbelief.

"But, Aunt Ophelia," Charley and Melissa began in one and the same breath, only to fall silent when she glared at them and went on in her decided fashion, "No niece of mine will be married in such a scrambling way."

"Exactly so," Seacourt said. He had not released Melissa's arm, and now began to draw her toward the door, adding, "Until I am convinced that you mean what you say—"

"Release her, Geoffrey," Lady Ophelia said, getting to her feet and facing him without so much as reaching for her cane to steady herself. "You will take her nowhere. Vexford is quite within his rights as her betrothed husband to decide where she is to stay. And if he were not, I think I could still convince you that you would be wiser to leave her here. Aside from the question of her inheritance, I intend that Melissa shall have a proper come-out before she is married. I daresay you will not want to foot the bill for that."

"I see no reason why I should do any such thing."

"Well, you will see soon enough once Charlotte and I begin putting it about that you are keeping your daughter a prisoner in Brook Street rather than presenting her to the *beau monde*. People have, after all, been quite curious about Melissa and her mother these past nine years. So long as Melissa is seen to be behaving like a young woman of quality, which she is, little will be said about her by the gossips, but the moment the least whisper gets out that she is not quite what she ought to be, the rumor mills will begun to churn. If that happens, it will not be long before all the tidbits from nine years ago become common knowledge, even if we can manage to suppress the details of what occurred in Newmarket."

When Seacourt looked thoughtful, she added more cheerfully, "What a fortunate circumstance it is that His Majesty's gout has forced him to postpone his Drawing Room again. It's the first in two years, you know, and he has already put it off once, so it is only by the most uncommon good fortune that he is still indisposed. He was to have held it today, but now we shall have a sennight to prepare, and according to the rules for presentations published in the *Times* this morning, there is no reason that I cannot present Melissa next week. I presented Charlotte at the last one, of course. Exhausting business, but I do not begrudge an ounce of effort to see my gels well established."

Seacourt shook his head and said, "I still do not know why the King must hold such events at all. It was perfectly proper for the Queen to do so, naturally, but I am sure no other King of England has held Drawing Rooms, only levees."

"But why should he not?" Charley demanded. "He is King and can do what he pleases. Moreover, since there is no queen, how would young women enter society if he did not allow them to be presented? Oh, but, Aunt Ophelia, is there not some rule or other about when names must be submitted?"

"Yes, but we have until Wednesday at noon," Lady Ophelia said. "One used to hand in one's card at the door, but His Majesty will no longer allow presentations of unknowns by the Lord in Waiting, so now one must send a card to the Lord Chamberlain's office with the name of the lady to be presented, and that of the lady who will present her. I believe the best course," she said in a thoughtful tone, turning her attention to Nick, "will be for you to obtain your special license and to set the date for a week from Saturday. That will give a much better appearance than to marry in greater haste, don't you agree?"

He thought it all sounded too hasty, but to his surprise he had no real objection to her plan. He glanced at Melissa and saw that Seacourt still had his hand on her arm. Shifting his gaze, he caught Seacourt's and held it until, ever so casually, the older man raised the offending hand to smooth an errant hair, and stepped away from his daughter.

Charley said, "I never thought I'd encourage anyone to enter the matrimonial state, Lissa, but I think it will suit you. 'Tis a pity, of course, that you don't have a great deal of money and a house of your own, so that you could send them both to the devil."

Lady Ophelia said dryly, "I will acquit you, Charlotte, of desiring my imminent demise, but if that is the sort of comment you mean to fling into conversations whilst I am attempting to see your cousin launched into the *beau monde,* I pray you will not be dismayed when I begin to leave you at home."

Instead of being chastened, Charley laughed and said, "I will behave, ma'am, I promise. I wouldn't miss this for anything less than a chance to put females in charge of the world."

Lady Ophelia smiled at Nick and said, "I presume that you have received an invitation to the Northumberland House party tonight."

He grimaced. "I did, but I confess I had not meant to go. Indeed, I believe I may have sent my regrets. I expected still to be in Newmarket, you see."

"Well, you must attend. If it troubles you to go after saying you would not, just attach yourself to my party. I shall have to send a note round, in any event, telling the duchess that Melissa will be with me. It provides an excellent opportunity for her to make a first appearance. She needn't face Almack's till Wednesday, and what with the new exhibition at the Royal Academy, morning calls, and other entertainments, she will have her feet pretty solidly on the ground by the time I present her. Oh, and one other thing," she added. "She can be married from this house. No one will think that odd in the least, for it is much larger than Geoffrey's Brook Street house, and the garden court will be quite a lovely setting if it doesn't rain. So now that that's all settled, you men can go away. We females must discuss a few details."

Left with nothing more to say, an odd state for a man generally able to speak up even in the face of Ulcombe's temper, Nick made no objection to being shooed out of Lady Ophelia's drawing room. He half expected Seacourt to speak to him in the street below, but when the man turned his shoulder and walked away, he was not sorry for it. In the carriage, thoughtfully considering what had just come to pass, he realized that instead of suffering the shock he might have expected, he was looking forward to a party that only a day before he would have thought not worth his time or effort to attend.

Alone with her cousin and Lady Ophelia, Melissa felt as if she had survived a dangerous storm, but she was not left long to ponder her fate. With Charley demanding to know every detail of her life since their last exchange of letters and Lady Ophelia demanding the help of both young women to plan details for the next ten days—not least of which was to order clothes for Melissa—she was scarcely able to think at all.

Vexford's declaration had astonished her. She had looked to him for protection, even rescue, but her hopes had been vague, for since he had flatly disclaimed interest in marriage, she had no notion of what he might do to protect her. Now that it seemed he did indeed expect her to marry him, she felt numb and more disoriented than ever, but Lady Ophelia proved once again that her years had done nothing to diminish her ability. Shortly after eight o'clock that evening, Melissa, elegantly attired in a gown of clear book muslin over a pale blue satin slip, emerged behind Charley from her ladyship's town carriage at Northumberland House, a grand old pile facing the Strand with rear gardens that sloped down to the Thames.

"For such a great house, this entrance courtyard is singularly inadequate," Lady Ophelia said tartly, looking around the crowded yard as she allowed a footman to help her from the carriage. "I've told Northumberland over and over that he ought to enlarge it, but since he never has to enter his own house amidst a crowd, he pays no heed to those of us who do. Perfectly typical male."

Inside, Melissa followed in Lady Ophelia's wake. Grateful for Charley's presence beside her, she responded politely when she was introduced to her host and hostess at the top of the left wing of a grand marble staircase, but otherwise remained silent. It was not the first time she had attended a party in a grand house, but it seemed to her that Scottish parties were more relaxed and less clamorous. Everyone seemed to be talking at once, and she could not imagine how anyone made himself heard above the general din.

Lady Ophelia paused. Leaning closer to Melissa, she said, "They have just finished a number of alterations, including the staircase, my dear, which is the reason for this party, I daresay, and why there is so much commotion."

The staircase was certainly grand, Melissa thought, looking down. From the ground floor, a single flight led to a wide landing, from which two branches swooped up and back to the gallery above. Just then, she caught sight of Vexford, coming up the central stairs from the ground floor. Since she stood above and a little behind him, near the gallery railing, she could not see his face, but she was sure it was he. He was with another gentleman, and when they turned at the half-landing, she saw that the latter was several years younger. He looked as if he would rather have been elsewhere. She saw Vexford murmur to him, whereupon the younger man flushed, but he straightened and smiled as they approached the Duke and Duchess of Northumberland.

"Why did you stop?" Charley demanded, behind her. "We shall lose Aunt Ophelia in this crush if we don't stay near her. I think she went through that door ahead. My goodness me, just look at that room! That must be the glass drawing room one hears so much about. Why there must be eight or ten pier glasses, and windows everywhere."

The room was spectacular, and large enough so that as the crowd passed through the doorway, Melissa thought the party seemed less of a crush. The walls were paneled with shimmering red and green glass, framed and overlaid with delicate neoclassic motifs. She recognized them as the work of Robert Adam, for he had designed Hopetoun House, across the Firth of Forth from Penthorpe House. Nothing about the glass drawing room was understated. Because of the motifs, little space remained on the walls for paintings, but there was ample space for Adam's settees, chairs, and pier tables, which were scattered liberally throughout the room. On top of the tables, numerous candelabra lighted the scene, which was reflected many times over in the legion of mirrors.

"Impressive, is it not?" Vexford spoke from behind her, and Melissa turned quickly, hoping the warmth flooding her cheeks was not visible in the golden candlelight, and glad that Northumberland was not one of the few aristocrats who illuminated his town residence with the new, bright gas lights.

"Good evening, sir," she said, thinking he looked particularly elegant in the dark coat and pantaloons he wore. He was not so magnificently attired as the young gentleman beside him, but the simple elegance suited his height and breadth very well.

Beside her, Charley said, "So you did come, Vexford. Aunt Ophelia will be pleased, but don't you want to say something complimentary about Melissa's new gown? You would not believe what lengths we were put to, to acquire it so quickly."

Vexford said, "To be sure, Miss Seacourt, that dress becomes you well."

Melissa thanked him, repressing a wish that he had said something before Charley prompted him to do so. She turned a politely inquiring gaze toward his companion, who was openly looking her up and down.

Vexford said dryly, "May I present my brother, Oliver Barrington. Ollie, this is Miss Seacourt and her cousin Miss Tarrant."

"Well, by Jove," Mr. Barrington said, "I've been as curious as a cat all night to meet you, Miss Seacourt. Nick tells me you and he are to be buckled in little more than a sennight, and I swear today's the first I've heard about it." He looked around, adding, "I say, Nick, haven't they done something to this room, too?"

"Made it larger," Vexford said tersely, "but here is Lady Ophelia bearing down upon us. I wondered where you two had left her. How do you do, ma'am," he added when she joined them. "You see, I am here, obedient to your will. I have even dragged my disreputable brother, Oliver, along to meet you. Make your leg to Lady Ophelia, Ollie. We had expected our parents to have arrived by now, ma'am, but they had not yet done so when we left the house. We left word of our whereabouts, however, so they may join us here before the night is done."

"Well, I don't intend to stay long," Lady Ophelia said. "With such a sizable crowd this early on, I shudder to think what it will be like by ten. We should have to wait a good half hour after we called for our carriage before they could produce it. Moreover, we've a rout and a cotillion to attend before we retire for the evening. You may lend us your escort to them both, if you please."

Oliver Barrington looked dismayed to have his evening thus arranged for him, and although Vexford said they would be delighted, Melissa soon discovered that his delight did not include dancing attendance on them. When both gentlemen disappeared soon afterward, she asked her cousin where they had gone.

"Good gracious, Lissa, you can't expect them to sit in our pockets. That simply isn't done. Moreover, men always think that their desires must precede ours."

"But surely, true gentlemen—"

"Fustian! Any gentleman is still a man when all is said and done. He may follow certain rules, but he is still a selfish beast all the same. Just look at them now."

Following Charley's gesture, Melissa saw both Vexford and Oliver standing with a beautiful blond woman in a low-cut, emerald-satin gown, who glittered with a myriad of jewels. The manner in which she spoke and the intimate way she touched Vexford made it clear they knew each other well. Watching them, barely aware of creeping annoyance, she recalled Vexford's remarks about the sort of women he preferred. Knowledgeable women, he had said, women who knew the rules of the game and could play it with confidence.

"Melissa," Lady Ophelia said just then, "I should like to present Lord Rockland to you, my dear."

Turning, Melissa looked at the tall, handsome young man before her, lowered her lashes, and said demurely as she made her curtsy, "I am pleased to meet you, sir."

When she looked up again, a pair of laughing dark eyes twinkled back at her. Taking the gloved hand she held out to him, he assisted her to rise, giving her hand a squeeze as he did so, then pressing his lips lightly against it.

A stifled sound—half laughter, half irritation—reminded Melissa of Charley's presence just as Lady Ophelia said, "You know Miss Tarrant, of course, Rockland."

"I do, indeed," he said, adding sweetly, "Been gelding any stallions of late, my dear Miss Tarrant?"

Startled, Melissa looked from one to the other, and saw at once that Charley was keeping a rein on her temper. When it became apparent that she would not deign to reply, Melissa said hastily, "Have you been to this house before, sir?"

"I have," he responded, grinning at her, "and I happen to know that just beyond that door yonder an orchestra is striking up for some dancing. May I have the honor, Miss Seacourt?"

"Certainly, sir," she said, allowing him to draw her hand through the crook of his arm. They made their way to the far side of the room, but when Rockland opened the door he had indicated, and urged her through it, she saw at once that the room was unoccupied. "We've come the wrong way, sir. There is no one dancing here."

"I lied," he said, firmly shutting the door.

Ten

New Players Must Learn the Rules

Nick had allowed Clara to draw him into conversation as much to show Lady Ophelia that he would not dance to her piping as for any other reason, but Clara was behaving as if there had been no breach between them. The fact that others, including his restive brother, stood chatting with them had much to do with her attitude, he knew, but since they were members of the same set, he was bound to meet her frequently. Therefore, he intended to set the tone for those future meetings now.

She made a light comment to Oliver, adding with a laugh, "You need only ask Nicky if that is not so, or any of a dozen others. Tell him, Nicky."

"I'm afraid I was not attending," he said. He ignored her frown, but it did not last long, for her attention shifted toward the doorway into the stair hall. Following her gaze, Nick saw Sir Geoffrey Seacourt enter the room with Yarborne. When he realized that Clara had caught Seacourt's eye and was fluttering her lashes at him, Nick wondered idly if the charming, debonair companion who had escorted her from Newmarket might have been Sir Geoffrey.

He gave the matter no more thought, however, for he caught sight just then of Lady Ophelia and Miss Tarrant, and saw that Melissa was not with them. "Forgive me," he said to Clara as he scanned the throng, looking for Melissa's silvery blond hair. He almost missed her. He would, in fact have done so had the man with her not bent forward to open the door they approached, revealing Melissa just when Nick's gaze fell upon them. They were on the far side of the room, and since it was some time since his last visit to Northumberland House, a moment passed before he recalled that the door led into the State Bedchamber. Aware that that portion of the house was not open to view that night, he could think of no good reason for Melissa to be there. Then her escort turned slightly, revealing his profile, and Nick recognized him. Without another word to his companions, he strode after them.

The crowd parted before him as if his very annoyance warned others of his approach, though several people murmured greetings as he passed. He did not heed them. The door had shut long before he reached it, and he was as certain as he could be of what he would find when he opened it. Rockland was not to be trusted with an innocent female—no more, Nick thought wryly, than he himself should be.

Reaching the door, he pulled it open at once and stepped into the room, startling both occupants considerably.

When Melissa saw him, she began to move away from her companion, but Rockland's hands were on her shoulders, and although he looked astonished to see Nick, he did not release her. Instead, he said blandly, "You interrupt my little scene, Vexford. Do be a good fellow, and go away at once."

Nick snapped, "Take your hands off her."

Rockland snatched his hands back as if they had been scalded. Hastily, he said, "Like that, is it? Didn't know, old fellow. No way anyone could know, come to that. Haven't seen you in days, have I? Haven't seen this young woman before at all."

"You will, however, see an announcement in the *Gazette* tomorrow that will make matters perfectly plain to you," Nick said coldly.

"Will I, by God?"

Having stepped away from him the moment she was released, Melissa said with apparent calm, "Really, my lord, you have no reason to eat the poor man. As he was just explaining to me, he merely—"

"I will talk to you when he leaves. Get out, Rockland."

"Certainly. Your servant, ma'am." Without further ado, he left the room.

"Now, Miss Seacourt," Nick said grimly, reaching for her. To his surprise, she caught his hand with both of hers, and moved closer, looking up into his eyes with an intense, appealing gaze that reminded him of nothing so much as a hopeful kitten.

Still holding his hand, she smiled and said, "So fierce, my lord? I promise you, you have no cause to be. Lord Rockland is presently absorbed in engaging my cousin Charley's interest, and he had the misfortune to believe that by inviting me to dance, and then bringing me in here instead, he might somehow stir her to jealousy. He didn't, of course, but you must have seen the disconcerted expression on his face when he saw that it was you who followed us in here instead of her."

Making no attempt to disengage his hand from her gentle grasp, he said, "Rockland cannot have expected Miss Tarrant to follow the two of you."

"But he did, and when you know her better, you will see that although he was wrong to think she would, such an expectation is not so absurd as one might believe. My cousin is a most unusual female."

"Your cousin wants conduct," he said curtly, "and so, I'm afraid, do you."

"Are you very angry with me?" He could smell her lavender scent when she leaned a little toward him to ask the question. She looked anxiously into his eyes.

Afraid he might unintentionally have frightened her again, he said more calmly, "You deserve that I should be vexed, do you not? Surely you know better than to enter a room alone with a man you do not know."

"I didn't know where he was bringing me," she said. "He told me there was an orchestra." She frowned. "I suppose you must think me very stupid, but I still don't know all the rules of this game, and it will take some time for me to learn them."

"What rules? What are you talking about?"

"You said you prefer ladies who know the rules and can play their hands with confidence. I know I must have played this hand badly, since I seem to have displeased you, but I can learn quickly, I promise."

He stared at her, well aware that he had never mentioned the fact that he had much different expectations for the woman who was to be his wife than he had for women who merely amused him. She had caught him off guard, and he experienced an odd desire to kiss her and shake her at one and the same time. He settled for saying sternly, "We have a good deal to talk about, but this is neither the time nor the place. The announcement of our betrothal has not yet appeared in the *Gazette*, but even if it had, we would be unwise to stir gossip by lingering in such a private place as this. We must return at once to Lady Ophelia and your cousin."

Melissa went with Vexford willingly, relieved that he no longer seemed angry. When he had first come into the room, he had looked as if he wanted to murder someone, and when Rockland had abandoned her without so much as helping to explain matters, she had feared the worst. Now, however, although she sensed that the man beside her was still irritated, she no longer thought him dangerous.

They found Lady Ophelia and Charley without difficulty, and when the old lady said she was ready to leave, they agreed. As they made their way through the crowd, Melissa saw Sir Geoffrey and a man she recognized at once as Lord

Yarborne, both talking with the bejeweled blond lady who had been with Vexford earlier. Melissa's relief increased. At least, she thought, by leaving now, she would avoid a confrontation with either her unpredictable father or the man to whom he had meant to marry her.

Oliver Barrington joined them as they reached the stair landing, saying casually, "Saw you were leaving, Nick. I daresay you won't miss me if I go with my own friends now. Rigger ain't back yet, but a few of the other lads have decided to—"

"You'll come with us, Ollie."

"But I—"

"Do you desire Lady Ophelia and her nieces to think you don't enjoy their company?"

Flushing, Oliver begged their pardon and assured them that there was nothing he would like more than to escort them wherever they wanted to go. A link boy called up Vexford's tilbury, along with Lady Ophelia's carriage, and when Lady Ophelia gave her driver the direction for their next stop, Vexford assured her that he and Oliver would be right behind them.

However, by the time the three weary ladies were set down in Berkeley Square several hours later, having stopped first at a cotillion and then at two routs, Oliver Barrington had long since managed to escape. Melissa could not blame him, and Charley only laughed and said, "He will get his ears scorched for it, if not worse. Vexford does not seem like a man who easily dismisses the flouting of his commands."

"Most men," Lady Ophelia said dryly, "do not take defiance lightly, my dear."

Still chuckling, Charley said, "Grandpapa would say that's because the laws of nature ordain that males should dominate."

"There are many exceptions to the laws of nature."

Listening to them, Melissa was reminded again of childhood days in Cornwall, listening to Lady Ophelia argue with the old earl. Grandpapa St. Merryn believed in the natural superiority of the male as firmly as Lady Ophelia believed in that of the female. Their exchanges had been lively, to say the least, and remembering them as she followed the others upstairs to bed, Melissa realized that she had not appreciated her peaceful days in Scotland as much she ought to have.

Upstairs, she apologized to Charley for going off with Rockland but was not much surprised when Charley only shrugged and said, "Rockland is an ass. He teases me incessantly, but he proves useful when I want him to be, so I put up with him."

Bidding her good-night, Melissa went to her own chamber and soon fell fast asleep. It was not until the following morning, while reading the official announcement of her betrothal in the *Gazette,* that she remembered that Vexford's family consisted of more than just his scapegrace brother. Alarmed, she said, "Won't Vexford's parents be distressed to learn of his intended marriage in such a shocking manner?"

Lady Ophelia, sitting at her desk and writing in the latest volume of the journal she had kept since she was a girl, looked up and said, "If that young man has any sense, he must have informed them of his intention last night, my dear. If you recall, he said they were expected to return to London at any moment, so you may depend upon it that he will not have neglected to give them the news before they can read it in the papers."

"Do you know them, ma'am?"

"Yes, indeed. Ulcombe is a respectable man, who is much inclined to look after those more unfortunate than himself, and Arabella is a kindly woman, though I daresay she has not read anything more stimulating to the brain than romantic novels in years. Ulcombe possesses a vast amount of money, of course, but he has more sense than most rich men, except with regard to his dealings with young Oliver. The only person who seems to demand that scamp's obedience is his elder brother."

Charley was reading an account in the *Times* of the latest session in the House of Commons, from which she had already read bits aloud to them, but she had apparently been keeping an ear on their conversation. Looking up from her paper, she said with a laugh, "We saw last night how effective Vexford's commands are, ma'am, but I like Oliver Barrington. He has laughing eyes, and he doesn't seem to care a scrap for his brother's temper."

"That may well be," Lady Ophelia said, "but if I have taken Vexford's measure, I believe we will receive a visit today from young Mr. Barrington. You may see then if his eyes are still laughing. In the meantime, my dears, you must tidy yourselves, for if that announcement don't bring a horde of morning callers to have a look at the bride, you may call me a Dutchman."

Neither young woman would have dared to call her any such thing, but in the event, Lady Ophelia was right. Her more intimate friends began paying morning calls at ten, following one another in a steady stream until noon, when she gave orders that she was no longer receiving. The three ladies enjoyed a light luncheon, and then Lady Ophelia allowed her servants to admit visitors again.

Afternoon callers, as custom demanded, were generally more formal than those who visited in the morning, many doing no more than leaving cards at the door. Nevertheless, a good many came upstairs to the drawing room and sat with their hostess and her nieces for the requisite twenty minutes. Thus, when rain began to pour down in torrents soon after three o'clock, just as one set of visitors was leaving and before any others had arrived, all three ladies greeted the storm's arrival with relief.

Collapsing into a chair in a way that ought to have drawn censure, Charley said, "Tell them to deny us to anyone else, ma'am. My throat is sore from talking, but what a day, and how inquisitive certain people are! I wish I might believe that Lady Jersey came so early this morning only to pay her respects to you, ma'am, but I think she just wants to be able to say she met Lissa before others had become acquainted with her."

"Say nothing against Sally, my dear," Lady Ophelia said with a chuckle. "She had the goodness to provide your cousin with a voucher for Almack's."

"Oh, pooh, as if Lady Sefton would not have obliged you, or Lady Gwydyr."

"Who are they?" Melissa asked.

Charley said, "You met Lady Jersey. She believes she sets the moral standard for all Englishwomen. Lady Sefton is a dear, and Lady Gwydyr used to be Mrs. Drummond-Burrell before she became a baroness in her own right. She is very starched up, as much as Lady Jersey. They and some others are the present patronesses of Almack's Assembly Rooms. One must enjoy their favor if one is even to step across that important threshold."

"Does one so desperately wish to cross it then?"

"If one is to succeed in the *beau monde,* one does," Charley said with a sigh. "I was ready to tell them all to go jump in the Thames. I think it is perfectly idiotic to bend the knee to such arbitrary rules as they are constantly dreaming up, but Aunt Ophelia convinced me that I was being as selfish in my way as they are in theirs. In truth, to be shut out would be quite dreadful. But just look at that rain," she added, peering out the window. "One cannot even see across the square. Oh, there is a hack drawing up. Who can that be?"

"Charlotte, come away from there," Lady Ophelia commanded. "A lady does not gawk out of windows at passersby. I quite despair of you sometimes, my dear."

"No, do you, ma'am?" But Melissa saw that her cousin's eyes were twinkling, and Charley said mischievously, "Don't trouble yourself this time. The gentleman is too busy keeping his head under his coat to look up and see me."

By the time their visitor was announced, however, she was seated demurely beside Melissa on a sofa, pretending to apply herself to a waistcoat panel she was embroidering for her grandfather.

"Mr. Oliver Barrington, my lady."

All three ladies exchanged speaking glances.

Mr. Barrington had given his outer garments to the butler, and his well-cut blue coat and gray pantaloons looked fairly dry, but his hair curled damply. When Lady Ophelia welcomed him, he said with a laugh, "You behold me dashed well nearly drowned, ma'am, and my neckcloth has wilted. I must look a sight."

"No worse than usual," Charley said with a wry smile as she set her embroidery aside, "but how brave of you to risk your attire, sir, merely to pay us a call."

He looked sharply at her, saying with a curious look, "By Jove, you are the oddest female I've ever encountered. I am sure I've never known another one to say the sort of things you do. My brother says you want conduct, but—"

"Does he indeed," Charley interjected sweetly, "and what does he say of your conduct, Mr. Barrington?"

Melissa tried to think of a diverting comment to make before either of them said something unforgivable, but before she could think of one, Oliver flushed and said hastily, "You are quite right, of course." Turning to Lady Ophelia, he added, "I behaved badly last night, ma'am, and I've come to make my apologies. Don't know what came over me to abandon you like Nick says I did. I was just there alongside you one moment, and off with my own friends the next. Daresay I plum forgot where I was and who I was with. Won't happen again, I assure you."

"Oh, very pretty," Charley said.

Lady Ophelia said, "Hush, Charlotte. You are putting Melissa to the blush again. Not but what Charlotte is quite right, young man. You were doing well enough with your apology until your candor overcame your good manners. Honesty is all very well in its place, but you are scarcely demonstrating proper remorse for your behavior."

"Well, don't tell that to Nick," Oliver said quickly. "Dash it, I'm no hand at this sort of thing, and so he ought to know, but he said I had to come and make my best apology before he gets here. Oh, yes," he added, glancing from one surprised face to the next, "he's coming at five to fetch you to dine at Barrington House. It's in all the papers that he's going to buckle himself to Miss Seacourt, so it stands to reason he wants to present her to the parents straightaway. All of you are invited to dine, of course. I'm to be there, too, they said, even though a special friend of mine should arrive in town tonight, and I had made other plans."

"Well, I can't go," Charley said, adding with a quick look at Lady Ophelia, "I don't mean to be rude, ma'am, but you will recall that I am promised to Lady Sefton tonight for her party to the play at Drury Lane. I can easily go to Sefton House on my own, however. My maid will accompany me, and once I get there, I shall be in good hands. You must go with Lissa, of course. But, Mr. Barrington, it is now only twenty past three. Surely, you do not intend to sit with us for nearly two hours!"

"Don't see why not," he said. "Raining too hard for you to shove a fellow out the door, especially one who didn't come in his own carriage. Moreover, Nick expects me to be here. My position in this was a bit tricky, don't you see? Could scarcely wait till twenty minutes of five before telling you he would collect you at five."

Lady Ophelia said disapprovingly, "He ought to have sent a note round to us."

Oliver reddened. "Well, ma'am, the fact is that Mama intended to write a proper invitation, but Nick said he would take care of inviting you, and then I offered to bring his message round so he could attend to procuring the special license and such. Thought it would give me a way to ease into my apology, you see. Didn't expect Miss Tarrant to put me at a stand the moment I came in."

"And when did he expect you to deliver his message?" Charley asked.

Oliver glowered at her. "I didn't ask him, if you must know, just said I'd bring it round. Now that I think about it, he might well have thought I'd bring it straightaway, before noon, though he ought to have known I ain't well enough acquainted with you yet to pay a call so early in the day. I had other things to do, in any event, so I'll thank you not to throw a spoke in my wheel. He was fierce enough before."

"Are you frightened of your own brother?" Charley asked.

"Not in the least," Oliver said stoutly. "Not now that my father's back in town, at all events. But Nick can make things dashed uncomfortable for a fellow."

Melissa, feeling that it was more than time to change the subject, said quietly, "I doubt if we shall have any other callers if this rain keeps up. Perhaps, Charley, you can think of something we might do to entertain ourselves."

Lady Ophelia stood up. "I want to finish my journal entry. I've got behind these past two days and must catch up, and I must also change to my evening dress. Melissa, you and Charlotte ought to change now, too. We need not stand on ceremony with Mr. Barrington, since he will soon be a member of the family and can certainly look after himself for half an hour. Then you young people can think of something to entertain you until Vexford arrives—perhaps a game of some sort."

"By Jove," Oliver said, "cards would be the very thing! I can show you some famous tricks I've learned. I'll practice while you two change your clothes."

Obligingly, Charley pulled a table away from the wall, and found a pack of cards for him. Then the two young women went upstairs and hastily changed their attire for the evening. When they returned, they found that Oliver had drawn up two more chairs to the table, and that someone had provided him with a glass of sherry.

For the next hour, Melissa and Charley watched, fascinated, while he showed them a number of card tricks. When they complimented him on his skill, he said, "Oh, I'm a dab hand with the cards, right enough. You wouldn't believe some of the things I've learned. Look, I even carry my own pack with me." To their astonishment, he withdrew a pack of cards from his waistcoat pocket.

Indignantly, Charley said, "Then why did you make me look for new cards?"

"Well, these are special," Oliver said, winking at her, "not the sort one uses for simple parlor tricks, and certainly not with ladies of quality. Here, I'll show you. You and I will play a hand of piquet, and Miss Seacourt can watch. See if you can observe what I do, Miss Seacourt." He gave her a speculative look, then said, "Look here, we're soon to be brother and sister, like Lady Ophelia said. May I call you Melissa?"

"Yes, of course," she said, shooting a speaking look at Charley.

That damsel said quickly, "Just don't call me Charlotte, Oliver. I'm Charley to my friends."

"Good," he said, "now watch this. I'll wager you won't, either of you, see anything amiss."

Nor did they, although when he had won the third hand in a row, Charley said curtly, "You play the next hand with him, Melissa. My luck is either completely out or he is doing something quite unthinkable. If it's the latter case, I mean to catch him if I have to watch every move he makes."

But although she watched carefully, he continued to win, and she soon admitted defeat. At last, with a laugh, Oliver spread the cards out in front of them on the table and said, "Examine them closely if you like."

They obeyed, turning the cards over and holding them up to the light. They looked like any other cards. At last Melissa smiled, shook her head, and said, "You must be doing something very clever, Oliver. Please show us."

Grinning, he gathered the cards again, shuffled them, and

began dealing them into a pile face down, one at a time. As he did, he turned up four cards, apparently at random. Each was an ace. When he flipped the fourth one, Melissa and Charley said together in bewildered amazement, "How did you do that?"

"Want to see the kings?" Oliver asked smugly.

Melissa chuckled. "Odious boy. How do you do it?"

Grinning, he said, "They're fuzzed—shaved a bit on the ends and sides. I got them from a good friend of mine. When one plays with such a pack, one cannot lose."

"You cheated!" Again the two voices spoke as one.

"No such thing," he retorted. "We weren't playing for money. I was just showing you some card tricks. Any sensible chap has to learn about such things in order to be up to snuff, after all."

Confused, Melissa said, "I certainly don't understand the rules in London, sir. Is cheating not the same thing here as it is everywhere else?"

"Cheating is cheating, of course," Oliver said in a tone of one explaining a complex matter to persons of smaller mind than himself. "The thing is that if one wants to *avoid* being cheated, one has to be up to every rig and row in town. There are men—not gentlemen, of course—who don't hesitate to cheat at cards or at dice. One finds them frequently in the gaming hells, and the plain fact is that the best defense against such flat-catchers is for a fellow to know how they do the tricks."

"Ought a lady to know these things, as well?" Melissa asked.

Chuckling, he said, "What, to win at silver loo?" Then a thought seemed to strike him. With a look of pure mischief, he added, "Of course, if the lady were to marry a gamester of high renown who practically never, ever loses, and who ought to be taught a small lesson in humility, she might do worse than to learn to use such a pack as this—just for that one occasion, mind you."

Looking at Charley and seeing her own understanding of what Oliver was suggesting reflected in that maiden's roguish grin, Melissa felt a ripple of unholy amusement. To be able to beat Vexford at his own game, just once, would be glorious. He had said he liked ladies who knew the rules and could play with confidence. She knew the rules for whist and piquet and other such popular games, and generally played them well, but she did not think she was skilled enough to beat a man who bore the reputation of being both highly skilled and very lucky. "Would he not know at once that I was using such a pack?" she asked.

Oliver shook his head. "Bound to fool him," he said. "Fact is, he wouldn't think for a moment that you knew the first thing about fuzzed cards. Wouldn't do to make a habit of it, mind. Just the one time, privately, long enough to beat him. Then never again. I'll make you a wedding gift of this pack. Here, this is how it's done."

By the time Vexford arrived, both Melissa and Charley had learned all that Oliver could teach them. Neither thought herself his equal at deftly managing the pack of cards, but he had declared them skilled enough to recognize an attempt on the part of anyone else to cheat them. That, after all, as he loftily reminded them, was the real point of the exercise. He also expressed his firm conviction that Melissa could now fool Vexford long enough to beat him at a single game of piquet.

The pack of fuzzed cards disappeared into Melissa's reticule the moment they heard Vexford's carriage draw up outside. By the time the butler announced him, the card table had disappeared and the three conspirators were innocently discussing the likelihood of the rain continuing into the next day. Since, as they soon learned, he had received word within the past hour that his horse Quiz had won its Newmarket race, he was in an excellent humor, and the topic of conversation turned naturally to horses.

Melissa, Lady Ophelia, and the two gentlemen soon departed for Barrington House, where dinner proved more comfortable than Melissa had expected. Ulcombe, a man nearly as tall as, and much heavier than, his elder son, was even higher in the instep, but his manners were extremely cordial, and the same twinkle that lurked in Oliver's eyes lurked in his when he congratulated Vexford on his Newmarket win.

Lady Ulcombe, plump and cheerful, greeted Lady Ophelia as an old friend, and warmly welcomed Melissa to the family.

The meal was excellent, and the Barrington men did not linger over their port, but soon joined the ladies in the drawing room. Shortly afterward, the three members of the older generation had their heads together, discussing plans for the wedding.

Pleading his other engagements, Oliver won his father's permission to leave, whereupon Vexford drew Melissa discreetly aside, and she soon found herself alone with him in a small alcove on the far side of the drawing room. They sat side by side on a claw-footed Egyptian sofa, just beyond sight of the others, and his nearness and size seemed to overwhelm her. She could think of nothing to say to him.

He said, "I never even thought to ask if you wanted Mag to accompany you to Berkeley Square, but Lucy has promised to show her the sights of London, so I assume that you can have no objection if she returns to Carter Fell on Tuesday."

"No, sir."

"I'll see to it, then."

"Thank you."

After she had replied in monosyllables to two more conversational gambits, he said, "Tongue-tied, Miss Seacourt? You chattered quite happily at the table, I thought."

Turning, she looked up at him in surprise. "Did I talk too much, sir?"

"No, and I was not criticizing, merely wondering why you are so silent now."

She smiled then, moistened dry lips, and said, "I have never been betrothed before. If there are rules for that, as well as for all the rest, you had better tell me."

Smiling warmly back, he said, "We enter this part of the match as equals, for I, too, have never been betrothed. I think I had better warn you, however, that I will not take it kindly if you disappear into any more bedchambers with strange gentlemen."

"Bedchambers! But, except for you yourself, I have never—"

"The State Bedchamber at Northumberland House is where I found you with Rockland," he said, looking into her eyes. "Since it is a large, vastly overdecorated room, I realize that one does not instantly perceive the bed. Nonetheless, that is where you were. And as for the fact of your being alone with Rockland—"

"I explained about that."

"So you did." His steady gaze did not waver, and when he smiled, her body stirred in response.

Uncertain whether he believed her—although her explanation about Rockland and Charley had been the exact truth—she licked her lips again, trying to think. The way he looked at her now made that difficult, because her physical awareness of him seemed to impede her mind's ability to function. Just seeing him take a deep breath made her whole body tingle with anticipation of what he might say.

"Do you know," he said suddenly, in an altogether different, more intimate tone of voice, "now that we are betrothed, I have been promising myself something all day."

"Have you, sir?" Her gaze seemed riveted to his. Her mouth was dry again. "W-what is it?"

He did not speak, but his increasingly ardent expression made his intent quite clear. When he moved a hand to her shoulder, she felt its warmth easily through her thin muslin sleeve. She could still hear the others' voices from the main part of the drawing room, but only as a murmur, no more distracting to her than the crackling of the fire on the hearth. Vexford's eyes darkened and gleamed with purpose. She parted her lips in anticipation, moistening them yet one more time. She held her breath.

He lowered his head. "You always smell delightfully of lavender," he murmured, very close now. She could feel his warm breath touch her lips, and a light aroma of fine old port wafted past her nostrils. She could almost taste him.

"Nick," Lord Ulcombe called suddenly, "you do mean to have Oliver as your chief witness, do you not?"

With a speaking grimace, Vexford raised his head, then stood up and drew Melissa to her feet, saying in a voice loud enough to carry to the others, "No, sir. I'd like him to stand up with me, of course, but Tommy Minley and I promised each other when we were ten that we would each serve as chief witness for the other."

As they emerged from the alcove, Ulcombe said, "I should certainly think you would choose your brother over a mere school chum."

"Indeed, sir? Did my uncle serve as your chief witness?"

Lady Ulcombe chuckled. "He has you there, my dear sir. You said that you would see Harold damned and in—"

"Yes, yes, madam," Ulcombe interjected hastily. "No one wants to hear about that now. You will have Thomas if you want him, Nick, of course. I just made an obvious suggestion, that's all."

Vexford said calmly, "I think, if you were to ask Ollie, sir, you would find him happy to be given no responsibility other than to stand up and be counted."

"It shall be as you wish, naturally," Ulcombe said. "Come and sit down now, the pair of you. We've other details to discuss."

The moment of intimacy was over, and Melissa was not sure whether she was glad or sorry when Vexford drew her forward to join the others. They were planning her wedding, and she knew she ought to take part, but she believed, too, that stronger personalities than her own were bound to prevail. Still, she began to look forward to the marriage with much more enthusiasm than before, and she was more than a little disappointed that the interval with Vexford had ended so abruptly.

Eleven

Players May Form a Partnership

The weekend passed swiftly. Melissa rode in Hyde Park with Charley and Lord Rockland early Saturday morning. Having discovered that his lordship was her cousin's most persistent suitor, albeit apparently without persuading that young lady even to consider the notion of marriage, Melissa had accepted him into the ranks of her new friends. He paid Melissa little attention, however, once he discovered that his attentions to her went entirely unnoticed by Miss Tarrant.

He clearly knew better than to criticize Charley's riding, and Melissa was delighted to follow her intrepid cousin's lead in a mad gallop along the otherwise deserted Rotten Row, despite the stern rules posted against such behavior. They were expert riders, and each frequently rode at home, but that mad morning gallop whisked Melissa's mind back once again to Cornwall, where she had often followed Charley's lead over fences and walls, and across the grassy moor.

Saturday afternoon the two young ladies paid calls with Lady Ophelia, and all three enjoyed another round of parties that evening. They did not see Vexford or Oliver, but both were in attendance the next morning when the ladies joined Ulcombe and his family at St. James's Church in Piccadilly for morning worship. The afternoon passed quietly at home, and after a dinner shared with guests, whom Lady Ophelia had invited some time before, they made an early night of it.

A slight setback to Lady Ophelia's plans occurred on Monday, when a notice regarding the forthcoming Drawing Room appeared in the *Times*. Charley, an avid reader of that respectable newspaper, drew Melissa's attention to it soon after breakfast, in the morning room, by declaring with annoyance, "Well, if that isn't just like him!"

At the time, Melissa was looking through the recently delivered morning post in hopes of finding a letter from her mama, though she knew she was being foolish to hope for a reply to a letter sent to Scotland only on Thursday. She turned from her futile search, and said, "If what isn't just like whom?"

"The King, of course, to be still in the gout after weeks and weeks of coddling himself, which is *just* like a man. He means to make you put off your wedding, that's all. Only listen to this, Aunt Ophelia," she added, drawing the attention of the old lady from her daily journal entry. " 'The fact proves to be nearly as we predicted with respect to the state of the King's health. It now appears that His Majesty is not able to hold the Drawing-Room even on the thirteenth, and that a *farther* prorogation of a week is necessary.' So, you see, Lissa, although it has been two full years since the last Drawing Room, he has now put this one off again, till the twentieth of June. You will have to put off your wedding as well, I expect."

"No, she will not," Lady Ophelia said emphatically before Melissa had so much as opened her mouth to reply.

"But if she has not yet been presented, ma'am, surely—"

"The wedding will go forward as planned," Lady Ophelia said. "The King's health is no good reason to put it off, unless he pops off his hook, of course, and that does not seem to be an event that anyone anticipates. She can simply be presented on the occasion of her marriage, which is, after all, a perfectly good reason in and of itself. I must speak to

Arabella, however, to see if she will desire to act as Melissa's sponsor, which would be the most proper course after she marries."

Melissa had taken a strong liking to Lady Ulcombe and had no objection to put forward to such a plan, which was just as well under the circumstances, since no one asked for her opinion on that point or—as the days passed by—on any other. Though it was to be her wedding, her great-aunt and cousin both had decided notions about how the event should be arranged. It seemed easier in the face of their constant discussion of details to let them argue their way to consensus without muddling things by offering a third opinion. Melissa had no real objection to offer in any case, except that her life suddenly seemed to be moving much too swiftly.

If she had hoped to learn more about Vexford in the days before their wedding, she soon learned her mistake, for she encountered him exactly twice. The first meeting took place at the Theater Royal, Covent Garden, on Monday evening when he and his friend Lord Thomas Minley strolled into Lady Ophelia's box at the first interval. Vexford introduced Minley to them, exchanged a few remarks about the play, and the two gentlemen departed at the end of the interval.

The second meeting took place the following Wednesday afternoon when the ladies emerged from the exhibition at the Royal Academy. Vexford was driving by in his tilbury and, catching sight of them, was so obliging as to draw up at the curb. Melissa recognized the man perched behind him as his groom, Artemus, whom she had last seen in the inn yard at Newmarket. Lord Thomas was again at Vexford's side.

Vexford handed the reins to Artemus and jumped down to the pavement, saying, "Good day to you all. I see you have been admiring Lawrence's heads."

Melissa smiled. "Indeed, we have. He is very talented, don't you agree?"

He smiled back at her, the look in his eyes reminding her

instantly of Friday evening at Barrington House, but then he said, "Do you mean taken as an individual or by comparison with the mass of mediocrity and imbecility with which he competes?"

Biting back an unseemly retort, since she had liked not only Sir Thomas Lawrence's portraits but several of Mr. Constable's landscapes, and a splendid water piece of Mr. Callcott's as well, Melissa glanced at Lady Ophelia.

The old lady said with customary abruptness, "You've a good eye, young man. Anyone can see at a glance that the number of true works of art is by no means as great this year as in past years. One or two are an utter disgrace to the Academy, yet we are told that the men who selected them rejected multitudes of others."

"In justice to the managing committee, ma'am, we must then suppose that those which were rejected were outrageously bad indeed," Vexford said, smiling at her.

"Unless there was foul play," Lord Thomas added sagely.

With a sardonic look, Vexford said, "You suspect mischief when your breakfast is served five minutes late, Tommy."

"What better cause?" Minley demanded. "But we are keeping the ladies standing in this chilly wind, Nick." Turning to Lady Ophelia, he said politely, "May we send someone to fetch your carriage, ma'am?"

Charley said, "It's coming now, sir. We told Higgins two o'clock, and he is never late."

Glancing at her watch-bracelet, Melissa saw that her cousin was right. She found herself hoping that the gentlemen—at least one of them—would accompany them back to Berkeley Square. They did not, however, and she looked in vain for Vexford at Almack's Assembly Rooms that evening. Thanks to the efforts of her cousin and Lady Ophelia, she had, by that time, become acquainted with a number of people and did not lack for partners, but she was disappointed. To her astonishment, however, she had no sooner finished a set with Lord Rockland than she was solicited to dance by Yarborne. Although she blushed to recall their meeting in Newmarket, Yarborne behaved as if he had forgotten all about it.

"I trust you are enjoying your visit to the metropolis," he said smoothly as he led her into the nearest set. He acted for all the world, she thought, as if she had been introduced to him at a supper party by a mutual friend.

"Y-yes, sir. Everyone has been very kind."

"I observed the notice of your betrothal in the *Gazette*. Vexford is a luckier man than he knows, I believe."

"Thank you, sir."

His attitude was benign, and his friendly charm soon put her at ease. He identified people for her, describing them in terms clearly calculated to make her smile, and she found herself liking him, relaxing in his company in a way that she would not, days before, have believed possible. Thus, when the set was over and he escorted her back to Lady Ophelia, she was not as dismayed as she might otherwise have been to hear him say, "I am giving a ladies' supper party at my home in Bedford Square on Wednesday next. We'll provide a few amusing little games of chance to raise money for a most worthy cause, and I'd be most honored if you and your nieces would attend."

Lady Ophelia said coolly, "You may send us cards, sir, but I cannot answer for Miss Seacourt. She will be married by then, you know, and must—as one of the more absurd rules of our time demands—request permission from her husband."

Remembering that Vexford liked confident women, Melissa said impulsively, "I do not believe he will object, ma'am, if the cause is indeed a worthy one."

Yarborne chuckled. "Since the cause is one of Ulcombe's favorite charities, I do not think Vexford will dare to object."

Charley, grinning, said, "Perhaps, in that case, he will wish to accompany us."

"Ah, but that cannot be allowed, Miss Tarrant. 'Tis a supper for ladies only. Except for those of us engaged in organizing the evening, and porters and the like to see that it runs smoothly, no men will be allowed on the premises."

"That seems peculiar," Charley said when he had moved beyond earshot. "Why would his lordship not desire gentlemen to attend his charitable dinner?"

Lady Ophelia said, "Such events have become popular of late, although they are generally arranged by ladies engaged in charitable works. Silver loo suppers are most effective, and I daresay Yarborne believes that ladies are more easily charmed out of their money than their husbands are. If I were to hazard a guess, I'd say he's leaving the men out lest they curb the generosity of their wives and daughters."

"Well, if he thinks he will get more money than I think it wise to give him," Charley said, "he will find himself mistaken. Grandpapa gave me what money Papa had left me for the Season before he and Mama departed for the Continent, but he said he won't give me a penny more. Since neither he nor Papa puts the smallest rub in the way of my pleasure, I want to do all I can to show them I can be as frugal as a nun."

Melissa was still trying to imagine Vexford's reaction, both to Yarborne's invitation and to her acceptance, and she paid little heed to her cousin's remarks. Although he had told Lady Ophelia and Charley about the events in Newmarket, they had never discussed the details of what had occurred, and Melissa had no intention of telling them more. She had thought she could not bear to see anyone else whom she associated with that night, yet she had as much as told Yarborne that she would attend his supper. Just doing that, without asking anyone for permission, had given her an unfamiliar but invigorating sense of freedom. Now she wondered what Vexford would say, but she doubted that he would care a whit. Despite his attitude the evening he had surprised her with Rockland, he certainly had not proved to be a possessive suitor.

In truth, she wished he were more so, and the fact that he was not, puzzled her a little, for in her experience, men were possessive of what they owned. Vexford certainly thought of her as a possession, a prize in the game, albeit one acquired against his better judgment. Having been told that admission to Almack's was exclusive and that most applicants were denied, she had expected him to take a certain pleasure in escorting her there, but Charley had laughed when she noted his absence.

"Too pompous and humdrum here for the likes of him," she said. "You won't find Oliver either, I'll wager. Lady Ulcombe does not attend, and they have no sister to demand their escort. If they were on the catch for wives, that would be different, for Almack's is known as the Marriage Mart. But Oliver is too young to be thinking of marriage, and until now Vexford was not looking to marry either."

That Vexford had spoken impulsively when he declared himself, Melissa did not doubt. And having spoken without deliberation, he had undoubtedly regretted it since, though he had not said as much to her. She had noticed that he rarely expressed his thoughts or feelings aloud, and as a result, she found it hard to understand him. The incident with Rockland was a case in point.

Although Vexford had said he preferred women who played the game of life by the rules, and with confidence, he had assumed when he found her with Rockland that she did not know what she was doing. She had diverted him easily enough, and that thought comforted her now, because he did not seem like a man who clung buckle and thong to imagined grievances. Still, it was unsettling to know that once they were married, his authority over her would be as unquestionable as that of a father, with the right to force her obedience to his every whim and caprice.

These thoughts and others of their ilk plagued her from time to time in the next few days. However, dress fittings, shopping excursions, and an apparently unending round of calls, routs, parties, and plays filled her time, so that Saturday arrived in what seemed like the blink of an eye. That it dawned weeping, in a fierce downpour of rain punctuated at regular intervals by cracks of lightning and crashing thunder, was convenient. But since Lady Ophelia and Charley had taken it upon themselves to arrange everything else, Melissa was content to let them worry about the weather, too.

Lady Ophelia had gone to see what could be done to salvage their plans, when a footman brought the post to the morning room. Melissa searched quickly through the cards and letters, sighing in disappointment when she found none from her mother.

Charley, standing at the window with her arms akimbo, as if she could stop the rain by sheer strength of will, looked over her shoulder and said, "Still nothing?"

"No, I'm afraid they must have been delayed in their return from the Highlands."

"But there must have been the greatest commotion over your disappearance. Surely, the servants would have sent your letter on to them."

"Oh, yes, if they could do so, but if Mama and Penthorpe did not return when they had planned, I cannot think who in the house would know exactly how to find them. Their friends live in a most remote part of the Highlands, you see."

Lady Ophelia, returning in time to hear the end of this exchange, said cheerfully, "Don't trouble your head about such things, my dear. You must think only pleasant thoughts today, if only to make up for this dreadful weather. Where did I put my cane, Charlotte? If I must stand to direct those idiots in the drawing room—and I must, of course, because they've removed every stick of furniture to make room for our guests—but never mind that. Come away from that window and make yourself useful. Go and speak to that Frenchman in the kitchen, for I daresay he will have forgotten, in this dreadful weather, to send someone to Gunter's for the ices. Melissa, you should be upstairs. Your hair won't dry in time if you do not have it washed at once, and since your cousin has ordained that you shall wear it spilling all down your back—"

"That's traditional, Aunt Ophelia," Charley said. "Even if it were not, Melissa's hair is so lovely, she ought to show it off whenever she can do so without stirring comment." Glaring out the window one last time, she turned away, adding with a sigh, "I hate this rain, but perhaps it will stop before two o'clock."

"Even if it does," the old lady said flatly, "we are not moving the ceremony outside. The courtyard flagstones will be wet. In any event, since I have had to exert myself to arrange the thing indoors, indoors we will stay. Melissa, go up right now, and ask my woman to attend you. She will be quicker than any of the younger maids. You must arrange to hire your own, you know, as soon as you can do so."

Melissa agreed and as she moved to obey Lady Ophelia's command, she found herself hoping Vexford would not object if practically the first thing she did was to request a proper dresser. To do him credit, she did not think he would. Not only would he consider a personal servant a necessity, but it had been he, not she, who had thought of arranging for Mag to accompany her to London.

Before she reached the morning-room door, it opened and Lady Ophelia's butler said quietly, "Lord and Lady Penthorpe, madam."

"Mama!" Melissa flung herself into the arms of the tall, slender blond woman who entered the room. "Oh, Mama, you came, you came!"

Susan, Viscountess Penthorpe, said as she hugged her, "But of course we did, darling, just as fast as we could manage the journey. Indeed, I feel as if I had been running this past sennight and more, so do let me sit down and catch my breath. How do you do, Aunt Ophelia? Here we are, you see, just as you commanded."

"I'd nearly given you up," Lady Ophelia said. "Thought

maybe Penthorpe's tendency to procrastinate had delayed you," she added, smiling at the lanky, red-haired gentleman who followed in Susan's wake. Despite the words, she spoke in a more approving manner than she generally accorded to members of his sex. When he grinned at her, she said, "Sit down, the pair of you. You're looking well, Penthorpe."

"Thank you, ma'am," he said, making a bow. "You are looking mighty stout yourself. Don't mind telling you, I'm not altogether convinced that this notion was one of your knackier ones."

"As well to face things now as later, don't you agree?"

"Aye, perhaps, but I'm glad we left the twins at home."

Melissa looked from one to the other, settling at last on her stepfather in hopes of some enlightenment, but he only beamed and gave her a hug. "Damme, but you're looking fine as fivepence," he said. "What a thing, eh? Never would have thought even Seacourt could serve you such a dashed scurvy trick. Is it true he tried to auction you to the highest bidder?"

"Only in part, sir," she said. "Do sit down. I am so happy to see you both. I just pray that you are not dreadfully vexed with me."

"Good Lord, why should we be vexed?" Penthorpe demanded. "Not your fault your father's a damned scoundrel. Knew that before this happened, didn't we? Only wish your Uncle Gideon were here. He'd sort him out, dashed if he wouldn't. If it ain't just like him to be in France when he's needed here! Don't suppose, ma'am, that you thought to write to him and Daintry as well as to us, did you?"

Lady Ophelia shook her head. "I have no notion where they are at the moment. Daintry's last letter came from Paris, but Charlotte's parents had joined them, and she mentioned that they might be traveling south. I did not believe a letter could catch them, and it would only distress them to learn that they couldn't get home in time. I didn't notify your parents either, Susan. Thought you'd like to do that."

"Who is this fellow Vexford?" Penthorpe demanded, turning back to Melissa. "Don't know the name."

Melissa said, "He is the Earl of Ulcombe's elder son, sir."

"Ulcombe, Ulcombe . . ." Penthorpe frowned. "Dash it, name sounds familiar, but I don't immediately call to mind . . ." He looked at Lady Ophelia in clear expectation of an enlightenment.

She said, "Your uncle has most likely mentioned him to you in his correspondence. It was Ulcombe who founded that experimental village near Tattersall Green some years ago."

"By Jove, yes, of course," Penthorpe said with a laugh. "My uncle don't get about so well these days, or take pen in hand, for all that—rheumatism, you know—but I do recall his reaction to that village. Some nonsense about everyone living together as equal partners. Lasted less than a year before they were all at each other's throats. That was Ulcombe's notion, was it? Hope his son ain't cut from the same bolt of cloth." He arched an eyebrow at Melissa.

She tried to imagine Vexford organizing an experimental village, and had to smile. "I don't think he can be, sir, for he prefers gaming and horse racing to doing good works."

"Stout fellow, but nothing good about that particular work of Ulcombe's. Just told you, didn't I, that they nearly murdered one another. Seems to me, they called the place Harmony, though as I recall the matter, they'd have been a sight more accurate to have named it Unholy Discord."

The clock on the mantelpiece struck noon, and Lady Ophelia exclaimed, "Melissa, you must go up and get ready. Take your mama with you, and you can enjoy a comfortable coze whilst you bathe and dress, but do hurry, child. You don't want to begin your marriage by keeping the groom waiting. Be sure to wear the nice diamond earrings he sent you, too. Time enough to teach him his proper place later."

"Yes, darling," Susan said, "do let me help you. I want to hear everything that happened. I can't begin to describe how distressed I was to learn your father had abducted you, or how dreadfully frightened the children were by your sudden disappearance. It must have been horrid for you, but are you absolutely certain you want this marriage? I am persuaded that you need not—"

"Don't talk fustian to the child," Lady Ophelia said curtly. "As I took pains to explain in my letter to you, there is every chance that some fribble or other will take it upon himself to describe to the world what took place in Newmarket. Though I'm convinced most folks wouldn't believe it, you'd be foolish even to suggest that she delay. Once she's safely married to Vexford, no one will dare gossip about her, believe me. Am I likely to have helped her into a marriage that was not necessary?"

Susan flushed, and said hastily, "Of course not, ma'am. I beg your pardon. I simply wasn't thinking. We'll go up at once. Come, darling."

Melissa went without another word.

Nick, too, was preparing for the wedding. Dressed except for his coat, he sat at his dressing table, allowing Lisset to pare his nails while he watched Oliver pace impatiently from window to window.

"Looking for one with sunshine outside instead of rain, Ollie?"

Oliver looked startled, then smiled ruefully. "This ain't my sort of thing, Nick. Dash it, just look at me, all rigged out in knee breeches and this plain yaller waistcoat."

"Lady Ophelia ordained what we must wear. She called it a suggestion, but—"

"I know," Oliver said with a sigh. "What a dragon that woman is! She don't look like she's nearly a hundred, does she, Nick?"

"No, and for goodness' sake, don't suggest in her hearing

that you imagine she can be anywhere near the century mark."

"As if I could. Look here, do you—"

"Ready, my lads?" Lord Thomas Minley asked, entering without ceremony. He raised the quizzing glass he wore on a long black ribbon around his neck and peered at Oliver through it. "That you, my boy? Dashed if I wouldn't have overlooked you in a crowd. Those your togs, or did you borrow them from a Member of Parliament?"

"Don't provoke him, Tommy," Nick said. "He's as near as can be to abandoning me at the altar, even though I've promised him he need not stir a finger once the ceremony begins."

Oliver said with great dignity, "I'll leave you two to talk. I daresay you don't want me anyway, and I promised Rigger I'd drive to Berkeley Square with him."

Nick said calmly, "I did not know he was to be one of the guests. I hope you are not shabbing off, Ollie."

"I wouldn't do such a thing. Dash it, you're my brother! But of course, Rigger's going. Dashed well everyone's going, by what I can tell."

Tommy waited only until the door had shut behind the younger man before saying bluntly, "Who the devil is this Rigger?"

Nick flicked a glance at Lisset and said, "Ollie's friend from school. You've seen him about. Same height as Ollie, brown hair combed straight back, a similar, unrestrained taste in waistcoats but a much shrewder cast to his countenance."

"Yes, yes, I know the one you mean. One sees Oliver with him everywhere, especially at the Billingsgate. I just never paid much heed. Don't mix much with the yearling set. Seems friendly enough, I suppose, but what sort of name is Rigger?"

"A school nickname, apparently, but now that you mention it, I've never thought to inquire into his antecedents. In truth, I'm not interested, and I daresay my father has looked into them. If he hasn't, he will when he finds cause to do so."

Catching his gaze in the mirror when Lisset finished buffing his nails and had moved away to fetch his coat, Tommy said in an undertone, "Will he find cause, Nick?"

Nick shrugged. "Oliver has spent nearly every minute since he arrived in London with the fellow, that's all. No, I'm exaggerating," he said with a rueful grimace. "I don't think Rigger arrived till last Saturday or Sunday, but Ollie quotes him at every opportunity, and seems to think him a dab hand, particularly at card-play."

"Jealous, Nick?"

"Not in the least. The fellow seems to encourage those of Ollie's habits that my father seeks to discourage, that's all. It's a pity, but neither of his sons seems inclined to follow his excellent example of philanthropy. On the other hand, I don't make it a practice to give away as much money to the gaming houses as my father does to his charities. Oliver appears to be doing just that."

"And you believe this Rigger might be pressing him. Could he be a flat-catcher, Nick, or a Captain Sharp?"

Again Nick shrugged. "You always suspect the worst, Tommy. You could be right in this case, but I neither know nor care. Oliver must make his own mistakes and learn his own lessons. I am not his keeper. Let's talk of something else."

"Very well," Tommy said obligingly, "but speaking of being one's brother's keeper, let me tell you the latest about Dory. He's still dodging his predatory widow, of course, but do you recall that ridiculous tale he told us at Newmarket—the one about the mysterious chess player and his invisible opponent, playing in the Devil's Dyke?"

"I remember. Don't tell me he's encountered that lunatic again."

"But he has. I received a letter from him today, and I laughed so hard, I well nigh popped the button on my smalls. The fellow's a damned shamster, Nick. I ought to let Dory tell you himself, for he's coming down in a fortnight for the Derby—if the widow don't catch him first—but the tale's too rich to keep to myself."

"What happened?"

"Apparently, Dory went back to the Dyke on Friday. You recall that most of us returned to London after the last race, so scarcely anyone else was about by then, but he's got that female yearning to get her claws into him, so he skipped out and went for another walk. He don't say so, but it's plain as a pikestaff he did it to avoid her. At all events, he stumbled bang onto the fellow again, engaged as before."

"And did the vicar receive more money for the poor?"

"Not exactly." Tommy grinned. "He asked the fellow how the luck had stood since last they met. 'Sometimes with me; sometimes against me,' the fellow replied. So Dory asked if he was at play just then, to which the fellow replied, 'Yes, sir. My opponent and I have played several times today.' "

"Who did he say had taken the advantage?" Nick asked, trying to imagine what game was really being played with the good vicar.

"That's just what Dory asked him," Tommy said, "and he replied that he had won more times than not, and that the present game was just over because, as Dory could see, he had an excellent move to make that would checkmate his opponent."

"How much had he won?"

"Five hundred guineas."

"And how did he expect to be paid?" Nick asked, beginning to see where the story must lead.

Chuckling, Tommy said, "Aye, that's the rub all right and tight. Dory asked him that very question, and the scoundrel replied, 'God always sends some good rich man when I win, and *you* are that person. Remarkably punctual he is on these occasions,' he said. Can you credit it, Nick?"

Nick laughed appreciably. "How did the lunatic react when the vicar told him to seek his winnings elsewhere?"

"He didn't. Dory gave him the money."

"Where the devil did he get that kind of money?"

"As it happened, he had won the exact sum demanded of

him on your horse Quiz not long before, and he had the money in his pocket. But even though he thought it might be a sign from God, like the fellow told him it was, he was by no means convinced. He knew, of course, that the chap might somehow have learned of his win, but when he would have discussed the matter, the scoundrel produced a pistol. He compelled Dory to hand over the money, Nick. Dory, of course, wrote that one way or another it was a lesson from God. He wrote, too, that though he told any number of persons about the first encounter, he won't tell anyone about this one. Only his conscience, he said, compelled him to tell me. Myself, I think he's hoping I'll enlist your aid to go look for that devil in the Dyke, but I ain't such a fool."

"You need not tell me so," Nick said. "I've explained my position on the subject of trying to act as one's brother's keeper. It is an impossible task. Let us attend to my wedding, instead. My coat, Lisset."

"You know, Nick," Tommy said, "I'm not one to stick my oar in where it don't belong, but do you think you're doing the right thing in marrying this wench?"

Nick repressed an unexpected surge of annoyance. "Do you think I am being compelled, Tommy—that someone has produced a pistol and is holding it to my head?"

"N-no, of course not. Didn't mean to intrude. No need to bristle up like an angry hedgehog. Not that you look like a hedgehog," he added hastily. "In point of fact, you look bang up to the knocker. That is, you've got a bit of lint on your lapel, but I daresay Lisset will nip—"

"Silence, rattle! Call for my carriage."

Twelve

The Winner Collects His Due

The drawing room and two adjoining salons, all of which faced the rain-soaked garden, had been thrown together to accommodate the wedding guests. When Melissa entered on her stepfather's arm, gowned in pale pink, with a lacy veil that trailed behind her to the floor, the crowd fell silent and parted to make passage for them. The first face she recognized was her father's, and although Sir Geoffrey gazed at her accusingly, she did not falter in her steps. For once she felt truly safe from him.

She had known he would be there, because Lady Ophelia had said she could think of no acceptable way to bar him from the ceremony. She knew, too, why he gazed at her so reproachfully. He had made it clear that he thought he ought to be at her side. However, when Lady Ophelia agreed with her that under the circumstances she need not feel obliged to accept Sir Geoffrey's arm, Melissa had chosen Penthorpe.

She saw Vexford beside the rector of St. George's Chapel, with Lord Thomas and Oliver to support him. All three gentlemen wore ceremonial dress and sported white roses from the St. Merryn garden in the top buttonholes of their coats. At the rector's other side stood Charley, Melissa's only attendant, looking unnaturally solemn.

Vexford, like everyone else in the crowded room, was

watching Melissa. When she caught his gaze and smiled, his countenance softened. Although he wore even his formal wedding clothes with his customary air of casual grace, she thought him the most elegantly dressed man in the room. When they knelt together on the silk-covered prie-dieu provided for them, his presence beside her seemed to dominate everything else. She could sense his breathing, could feel his arm touching hers, and she felt pleasantly enveloped in the aura of competence and strength that emanated from him. Yet again, he made her feel safe and protected.

When he spoke his vows, he did not sound like a man who was marrying against his better judgment. His tone was firm and decisive. She did not think her voice was nearly so steady, but in what seemed only moments, she had promised to love, honor, and obey him until death, and the rector presented them to the assembly as man and wife. Outside, the clouds parted briefly, and a splash of sunlight spilled across the floor nearby. Melissa realized her hands were trembling.

Charley hugged her, but the next hour passed in a daze. She followed where Vexford led, murmuring polite responses to congratulatory remarks, smiling, even laughing. All the while she felt as if she walked through a fog that echoed with faceless, murmuring voices. Had she been asked to repeat a single exchange of conversation, she could not have done so. Not until they sat down to dinner did she have any sense of reality, and then it was only in knowing how tired she was.

The meal passed swiftly. While servants cleared away the tables afterward, she snatched a few moments to go up to her room with Charley. When they entered the bedchamber, Melissa shut the door, stripped off her white gloves, dropped them onto the dressing table, and reached up to unpin the long veil attached to the back of her headdress. Casting it onto the bed, she said wearily, "They must have invited every member of the *beau monde* today, for every nook and cranny of the house is stuffed full of guests. Even Yarborne is here."

She also had seen the blond woman from Northumberland House again, talking with Yarborne and Sir Geoffrey, and once with Vexford, but she saw no reason to mention her and said only, "I'm almost surprised to find this room empty."

"Here, sit down," Charley said, "and I'll brush your hair. Aunt Ophelia says the house hasn't been this full since Aunt Daintry's ball nine years ago. She also said she hopes your father will behave better today than he did then, but I don't know what she meant by that. No one ever tells me anything of consequence."

"Well, I don't know, either," Melissa said, thinking that for someone who was never told anything, her cousin seemed to know a good deal. "I can tell you, though, the way Papa has been glaring at Penthorpe is setting my nerves all on end."

"I heard Uncle Geoffrey say Aunt Susan was a fool to show herself in London. He called her a bigamist, too, which I believe means she is married to two husbands, so that cannot be true. She divorced Uncle Geoffrey in Scotland, did she not?"

"Yes, but he told me he never divorced her here in England. This morning, when Penthorpe told Aunt Ophelia that *this* was not one of her knackier notions, I thought he meant my marriage, but perhaps they meant Mama's situation. To be sure, I didn't understand all Papa said about the law, but if he wants to make trouble for Mama, I hope Penthorpe takes her home again straightaway."

"Well, I don't think Uncle Geoffrey means to make trouble tonight. He is being as charming to everyone as if he were the one paying for this, which, of course, he is not. Aunt Ophelia didn't ask him to contribute a penny. I heard her tell Penthorpe this morning that, although she is allowing Vexford to repay her for your court dress since his mama will present you, she is paying the reckoning today simply because she does not want to be plagued by bickering over who else ought to do so. In any case, the only one looking down in the mouth at the moment is Oliver. I think he is rather droll, but he does seem to kick up his heels one moment and go right off his feed the next."

Smiling, Melissa said, "You should not flirt with Oliver, Charley, especially when Rockland is looking on. I think you do it merely to irritate him."

Charley shrugged. "So what if I do? Rockland teases me one minute, acts the jealous lover the next, and brings me flowers the next. The idiotish man refuses to believe I never intend to marry. It serves him right if just seeing me chat with Oliver makes him livid. Oliver, at least, is not hanging out for a wife."

Melissa shook her head. "You are cruel, Charley, but I won't argue with you now. We'd better go back downstairs before someone comes in search of us."

"Right," Charley agreed, smoothing a strand of her dark hair back into place and taking a last glance at herself in the glass. Her sapphire-blue gown matched her dark eyes, and the circlet of pink silk roses in her headdress emphasized her rosy cheeks. Standing beside her, Melissa felt like she had as a child, like a pale shadow in the sunshine of Charley's brilliance. Catching her gaze, Charley grinned and said, "That pink dress makes you look like a spun sugar angel, delicious enough to eat. I'm glad you've got someone at last who will know how to protect you properly."

Surprised by the compliment, Melissa smiled and said as she drew on her gloves again, "I daresay Vexford will protect me, but who will protect me from Vexford?"

Charley laughed, and as they left the room, she said, "Though I never intend to marry, I do confess, I'm curious to know just exactly what happens between a husband and a wife in the marriage bed. You must promise to tell me *everything.*"

"Melissa, there you are!" Susan hurried toward them.

"Everyone is waiting for you and Vexford to begin the dancing, darling, but no one could find you."

"I came up to take off my veil," Melissa said, glad to be spared the necessity of replying to her cousin's outrageous demand. She would have liked to ask if any real danger existed that Susan could be taken up by the law for bigamy, but neither the time nor place seemed favorable for that discussion.

Not looking at all burdened or distressed, Susan gave her a hug and said, "I do like your husband, darling. I think he will be kind to you."

Other questions occurred to Melissa then that she would have liked to ask her mother, but there was no more time for talk. They hurried downstairs, and no sooner did they appear than a general cry went up for the bride and groom to lead the dancing. Melissa found her hand in Vexford's, heard stately music begin for the minuet Lady Ophelia had decreed suitable for the first dance, and stepped onto the floor.

Her husband danced with the same careless grace that she had come to expect in all he did, adjusting his steps to hers with the ease of long practice. His conversation—what there was of it—was casual, too, more as if they were simple acquaintances at a ball than man and wife. When the music ended, Lord Thomas stepped up to take Vexford's place, and Vexford asked Susan to dance.

The dancing soon grew more lively, and before the bride and groom bade everyone farewell, Melissa had danced not only with her new father-in-law and Oliver but with her stepfather, Sir Geoffrey—who behaved charmingly—Yarborne, Rockland, and later even with Yarborne's son, a man two or three years older than Oliver. Robert Yarborne, who clearly shared Oliver's taste in waistcoats, had Yarborne's brown hair, but his eyes were darker than his father's. He laughed frequently and danced energetically, but Melissa was relieved when Vexford claimed her hand again.

"Would you like to rest?" he said quietly. "We can get a glass of punch, if you like. Do you know who the coxcomb is, by the bye, who engaged you for that last waltz?"

"Robert Yarborne," she said. "Is he a coxcomb?"

He frowned. "Young fool was pulling you around as if it were a May dance. You look tired," he added. "I've spoken to Lady Ophelia, so we can leave whenever we like."

She was tired, but not knowing exactly what lay ahead, she received the news with mixed feelings and was not certain what she ought to say. They passed Sir Geoffrey just then, dancing with the bejeweled blond lady and evidently enjoying a flirtation with her. Melissa said, "Who is that lady with my father, sir?"

Vexford's gaze followed hers, and a wry smile touched his lips. "That, my dear, is Lady Hawthorne."

"I do not know her, but I saw her earlier, dancing with Yarborne."

"Clara always has an eye to the main chance," he murmured.

"What chance? She seems very flirtatious. What must her husband think?"

"Clara is not encumbered with a husband. She is a widow, and I think we will now talk of something else." They had reached the punchbowl, and he poured her a cup, then poured one for himself. She wanted to know more about Lady Hawthorne, but even as she searched her mind for a way to phrase another question, he caught her gaze and said firmly, "Drink your punch, Melissa."

"How did you know what I was going to say?"

"Women always want to know more about a man than he wants to reveal. It is human nature, I suppose. Nonetheless, we will not discuss Clara."

Noting that he called Lady Hawthorne by her given name, Melissa smiled and said, "I must do as you request, sir, naturally."

"See that you don't forget it." He smiled, too, as if he

meant to take the sting from the comment, but as he gazed at her, his expression warmed. He said abruptly, "It is time to go, I think. I'll have someone call for my carriage."

"I-I must get my things," she said hastily.

"That has all been done," he said. "The clothes you have purchased in London, and those your mama brought from Scotland, have all been transported to Barrington House." Turning to catch a passing footman by the sleeve, he said, "Have someone fetch Lady Vexford's cloak at once."

"Yes, my lord."

As they made their way to the hall, they were accompanied by a flurry of mild objections, complaints, and loudly expressed wishes for their future happiness. Once Melissa had donned her cloak, Vexford put an arm around her, and thus protected, she found herself swept past hovering family and guests, out to the still-damp pavement, and into his family's well-sprung carriage. Fifteen minutes later, they drew up in front of Barrington House, and five minutes after that, she found herself in a pretty bedchamber adjoining his lordship's, with orders to prepare herself for bed.

"C-could you ring for a maid to help me, sir?" she asked as he stepped through the connecting doorway into his own room.

"Yes, of course. I'd forgotten you've none of your own."

Lucy, the same girl who had helped her that first night in London, came to the room moments later. When she had helped Melissa undress and put on her white lawn nightdress and a soft gray wool dressing gown, she said, "I'll just put these clothes away, my lady. His lordship said you're to use the next room as a dressing room, but it requires some re-arrangement before it will be really suitable. In the meantime, we can make do here. I've ordered hot water for you."

"Thank you, Lucy." Melissa put her watch-bracelet and earrings away, thinking that once again her life was moving at top speed. She wished she had time to think. She could not imagine telling Vexford she really did not want to consummate her marriage just yet. When her hot water arrived, she washed her face and hands, scrubbed her teeth with water and salt, and carefully folded the towel she had used. Turning from the basin, she saw that Lucy was unpacking one of her cases and putting things into a chest of drawers. As the maid lifted a pile of kerchiefs from the case, a pack of cards fell to the carpet.

"Beg pardon, my lady," Lucy said, bending to retrieve them.

"You may give them to me," Melissa said. "I shall indulge myself in a game of patience while you finish putting those things away."

Pulling a side table and chair away from the wall, Melissa sat down and laid out a nearly forgotten pattern that she had played in her childhood. The game absorbed her well enough until the rattle of the latch on the connecting door startled her.

Vexford stood on the threshold, wearing his elaborate green and gold dressing gown, tied at the waist with its twisted golden cord. Warmth flooded her cheeks, and she glanced at the maid, wondering what she must be thinking.

Vexford said, "You may leave the rest of that, Lucy."

"I'm finished, my lord. The rest of her ladyship's boxes are in the next room."

"Well, leave it all for tonight. You can finish tomorrow."

"Yes, my lord."

Melissa, gathering the cards, heard with some misgiving the snap of the closing door. When she looked up, she saw Vexford regarding her with amusement.

"Do you often play cards before retiring?"

"No," she said, "it was an impulse. Lucy found the pack amongst my things. Charley and I played frequently on rainy days when I was small, and my parents enjoy piquet, as well as whist and commerce." The pack was the one Oliver had given her. She had no intention of trying to make use of anything he had taught her, but a game of cards seemed nevertheless like an excellent idea just then. She said, "Perhaps you would like to play a hand of piquet, sir. It is still early for bed, don't you think?"

He looked at her long enough to bring the warmth flooding into her cheeks again, but although she expected him to tell her she was being foolish, he said, "Why not? I ought to discover what manner of gamester I have married."

She knew herself to have been well taught, but she believed Vexford to be a superior player. When he pulled up a chair, she held out the cards to him.

He said, "You deal while I fetch a piquet marker."

His confidence made her wish she had the courage to try just one of the tricks Oliver had taught her. Even had her principles not deterred her, however, fear of what Vexford would do if he caught her cheating certainly did. Swiftly, she discarded the twenty cards that were not used in piquet, and by the time he returned from his room with the marker, she had dealt out twelve cards to each of them. She fanned out the remaining eight on the table between them.

As he took his seat, she opened her hand, astonished to find that she had dealt herself a veritable bouquet of aces and court cards. She hardly dared look at Vexford, lest she give away the excellence of her hand, but the clink of glass against glass drew her attention, and she looked up to see that he was pouring them each a glass of what looked like deep golden sherry.

"I-I'm not really thirsty, sir."

"It's very good," he said, setting one glass down before her. Then, smiling warmly, he added, "Sip slowly. I think you will like it."

While he took his seat and examined his hand, she obeyed, realizing that it was not sherry but something stronger that warmed her all the way down.

"I take five," Vexford said, doing so.

She took another sip. "What is this?"

"An excellent cognac. Does the dealer take cards?"

"No cards," Melissa said, "and I choose to leave the stock face down."

"Very well. Point of four."

"No good. Six."

Vexford marked six points for her. "Sequence of three?"

"No good. Five."

"Three tens?"

"Denied." Before the declarations were ended, she had scored a repique, giving her a bonus of sixty points, and by the end of play, she had scored over a hundred, giving her not only the hand but the first game as well. "Another game, my lord?" she asked sweetly.

He grinned at her as he gathered up the cards. "Pleased with yourself, aren't you? Yes, I think we've time for another." He shuffled expertly several times, and began to deal out the cards. Suddenly he stopped, picked up the one he had just dealt to her, examined it carefully, thumbed the end of the pack, then looked directly into her eyes and said in a harder tone than any she had yet heard from him, "So I've married a member of the Greek banditti, have I?"

Wetting her lips and watching him warily, she said, "I-I don't know what that means, sir, but—"

"The devil you don't! Where did you get these cards? From your scoundrel of a father, or from someone else?" Without giving her a chance to reply, he leaned menacingly across the table and went on, "By God, you fooled me, woman, and that's a fact. I never saw you do a thing out of the way, but I ought to have known you never drew that hand of yours in the normal way."

"But I did! I swear to you, I did nothing wrong. I don't deny that those cards are fuzzed, but I promise you, I did not cheat you. Even if I had been tempted to do so, I'm not nearly skilled enough to have fooled you. I dealt your hand and my own just as they came from the pack. Truly, I did!"

He was watching her narrowly. Gruffly, he said, "You lie even better than you cheat, my dear. I might believe you if

I hadn't been out of the room when you dealt. I'm inclined to acquit Penthorpe of teaching you such stuff, which means Seacourt must have begun very early, and taught you well enough to make the lessons stick."

Gathering her dignity, Melissa pushed her chair back and stood up. She wanted desperately to make him believe her, and she knew that if she let him intimidate her, she would never succeed. For a moment she was afraid he meant to stand too, that he might reach across the table and grab her, even shake her. Her courage nearly deserted her, but knowledge that she had done no wrong steadied her. She said, "I do not lie."

"All women lie."

"Does your mother lie to you?" she asked, surprised.

"We'll leave my mother out of this." He had put the cards down and was watching her, the hard glint still in his eyes.

"Do you think Aunt Ophelia would lie?"

"Melissa, where did you get these cards?"

"I did not get them from my father, nor have I ever used them to cheat anyone." She looked him in the eye, daring him to call her a liar again, although she was not angry. She could not blame him for what he believed. Quietly, she said, "Had I thought for a moment that you would recognize those cards for what they are, I would not have suggested playing piquet. I realize now that I ought to have known that a man of your experience would know a fuzzed pack when he encountered one, and would leap to the most natural conclusion. It is only because I lack the skills of which you accuse me that the thought never crossed my mind. Indeed, sir, a man of your vast experience ought to see quite clearly that I am no practiced cheat."

He was silent for a long moment, gazing steadily at her, and much as she wanted to look away from that stern gaze, she did not. At last he said, "If you did not get these cards from Seacourt, who did give them to you?"

"I would very much prefer not to say."

"I believe you, but you will nevertheless tell me who gave them to you. If Seacourt did not, then the only one left is Penthorpe."

"It was no one in *my* family, sir." She realized only after she spoke that she had given unintended emphasis, but it was too late to alter the fact. She saw at once, and with no little dismay, that his eyes had narrowed ominously.

The expression vanished at once, however. Giving himself a little shake, as if to clear his thoughts, he stood up and said ruefully, "What a way for a husband to behave on his wedding night! You must forgive me, my dear. I believe you did not cheat, and I beg your pardon for having doubted you."

The apology sounded sincere, and was most welcome, but she did not know what to make of the sudden change in his demeanor. "You really do believe me?"

He moved nearer, putting his hands lightly on her shoulders. When, involuntarily, she stiffened, he said quietly, "I did not mean to frighten you. I'm told that my temper can be formidable, and I was surprised to find such cards in your possession, but I do believe you. We will not speak of the matter again. Drink your cognac, and we will go to bed."

"I-I am a little tired," she said, making no move to pick up her glass.

He did so, pressing it gently into her hand and saying, "I agreed to play cards because you seemed nervous, and I thought it would relax you. The last thing I intended was to frighten you."

"I was not afraid," she said. Sipping the cognac obediently, she welcomed the warmth and the gentle tingling that spread through her body.

"Didn't you just tell me that you never lie, Melissa?" The words were low in his throat. Standing very close now, he raised a hand to stroke her hair.

She swallowed, unable to reply, thinking only of the way he touched her, of the strength in the body so close to her own. She could think of no way to tell him that it was not his temper she feared so much as the power he wielded as her husband. Such thoughts had not entered her mind in many years. With Penthorpe as one's nearest example, one simply did not think of the power of the position. But old memories and instincts had sprung to life from the moment she found herself in Sir Geoffrey's power again, and talking with Charley and Lady Ophelia of olden days, and of the unfair advantages men held over women, had renewed many of her childhood fears.

Suddenly, the way Vexford was stroking her reminded her of the way she gentled a nervous horse, and a chuckle bubbled up into her throat. His hands stilled. She looked up to find him regarding her with curiosity. Impulsively, she said, "I ought not to laugh, I know, but it just occurred to me that you have had vast experience with nervous fillies, have you not, sir?"

Appreciative amusement gleamed in his eyes. He said, "I suppose that is exactly what I've been doing, isn't it—both with the cognac and now with my hands?"

"I don't require gentling, sir. My duty requires me to submit to you."

"We'll hope it becomes more than merely a duty," he said dryly, "but I won't expect more tonight. I have no experience with virgins, but I'm told the first time is usually painful for a woman, so I daresay the quicker we get this over, the better it will be for us both." Gently he took the now empty glass from her and set it on the table. Then he reached for the tie on her robe, loosening it and pushing the robe from her shoulders. His fingers dealt swiftly with the ties of her nightdress, and it soon followed the robe. A log shifted on the grate. A candle guttered. He stood gazing at her body for a long, tantalizing moment before he murmured, "Get into bed, Melissa."

Silently she obeyed, watching solemnly while he took off the elaborate dressing gown. Reflections of firelight danced in its wild pattern then glowed in golden highlights on his bare skin. He wore nothing under the dressing gown.

Nick saw her eyes widen and wondered if she had never seen a naked man before. Knowing she had experience with horses, he was sure she understood basic details of the act itself, but she was so gentle and shy that she made him feel overlarge, in more ways than one, and unusually clumsy.

Moving to snuff the candles, he remembered how she had stood up to him, literally, and found himself thinking that she was not, perhaps, as timid or shy as he had first thought. Still, she was no brazen card sharp either, and he had been a fool to name her one. Climbing into bed beside her, he pushed the covers away so he could enjoy the sight of her slender body with the firelight playing on it, then moved over her to begin the process of consummating his marriage.

When she wriggled uncomfortably as he shifted himself to enter her, it occurred to him that he was being too hasty. A single whiff of her lavender scent stirred his sexual appetite more than any of the lures cast by women he had known before, but he held himself back, knowing that to rush things now would be a grave mistake.

Her skin was soft, her pink-tipped breasts plump and firm to his touch, and reflecting firelight made her gray eyes gleam like silver. Her lips parted invitingly. When his mouth touched hers, he felt a nearly overwhelming urge to hear her moan with pleasure beneath him. He wanted to master her, to make her squirm with desire for him. As his hands played over her body, seeking out the softest, most sensitive areas, he needed every ounce of his willpower to hold himself in check.

She was delightfully responsive and clearly exerted herself to please him. Every instinct pleaded with him to give free rein to the fire in his veins, but one niggling voice deep within him warned him to play this hand with care. More than anything else, the fear that he might hurt her made him heed that single voice.

He caressed her, and teased her a little, hoping to tempt her to a passion matching his own. But the time soon came when he knew that if he tried to restrain himself any longer, he would either end by losing his control altogether or by losing the ability to do what he had to do. Hoping he had prepared her enough so that he would not subject her to any more pain than necessary, he eased himself into her, wincing when an involuntary cry escaped her soft lips. He pressed on, knowing he would accomplish no good by stopping.

There were tears in her eyes when he finished. As he withdrew, he said ruefully, "Are you hurt very much?"

"The ache will pass," she murmured, looking up at him with her solemn eyes. "I think we've made rather a mess of the bed, though. I'm quite sure I'm bleeding."

"That happens, I'm told. I'll ring for Lucy to attend you."

Even in the firelight he could see the deep flush sweep into her cheeks. "Please, sir, don't call her. I scarcely know her, and I'd rather attend to myself. There is water in the ewer on the washstand."

"Very well," he said, "but do you mean to make the bed as well?"

"Do you think I cannot?"

He grinned at her indignant tone, and got out of bed. "I'll send Lisset for clean sheets and bring them in here to you myself."

"Thank you. Will you sleep here tonight?"

"No, the night is young yet, and I've something I want to attend to. I daresay you'll be glad to have your bed to yourself tonight."

She looked doubtful, but he put it down to natural feminine uncertainty and gave it little thought. Taking up his dressing gown, he slung it over one shoulder. Then, scooping the pack of cards from the table, he strode into his bedchamber to ring for Lisset and attend to his own needs. While the valet fetched clean sheets, he dressed for a normal evening out, and when Lisset returned, Nick took the sheets to Melissa. He found her sitting at her dressing table in her nightdress, plaiting her beautiful hair.

Catching his eye in the glass, she said, "May I ask where you are going?"

"Out and about."

"I see. Well, I hope you have a pleasant evening."

He kissed her and left the house, not bothering to call for his tilbury. The rain had stopped, the night air was fresh, and the Billingsgate Club was but a short distance away. Arriving there, he went swiftly upstairs to the card room, paying no heed to a friend who demanded to know what he was doing there on his wedding night.

There were more such remarks, but Nick made his way directly to Oliver's table, noticing only when he reached it that one of the four players was the man Melissa had identified earlier as Yarborne's son, Robert.

Oliver, clearly the worse for drink, looked up with bleary eyes and said, "That you, Nick? What the devil have you done with your bride? Just look at him, Rigger. Never know him for a man who'd got married only a few hours ago, would you?"

Robert Yarborne raised his eyebrows and looked as if he would respond in kind, but Nick caught his eye, and the younger man looked quickly back at his cards. Nick shifted his gaze to Oliver. "I want a word with you."

"What, now? This is becoming a dashed annoying habit, brother mine. We're in the middle of a game here."

"Put down your cards, Oliver."

Oliver reddened, glanced at the others, then threw down his hand and said, "I'm out. Rigger, cover my losses, will you? I make it four hundred. I'll send you a draft in the morning. Damn it, Nick," he added as he followed him from the room, "your timing couldn't be worse. I'm down as far as I've been all night, and what with Father cutting up stiff over my losses, you could at least have given me time to recover."

"You should be grateful I stopped you," Nick snapped. "If your luck's out, it's out, Ollie, and tonight it's out more than you know. I want an explanation for these, my lad, and it had better be a damned good one." He tossed him the pack of cards he had taken from Melissa.

Oliver nearly dropped them, but that he knew what they were was obvious from the look of mischief he threw at Nick when he said, "I wondered what the devil you were doing here. Any other man would be enjoying his bride. Don't tell me you've deemed her unacceptable to be your wife because she routed you at cards."

Grabbing him by his shirt, Nick put his face close and said furiously, "You'd be well served if I taught you a lesson tonight, Oliver, so don't tempt me. When you speak of my wife, do so with respect and civility. Is that clear?"

Sputtering a hasty apology, Oliver added, "I didn't mean any offense, Nick."

"Good, but that's not all I want to say to you. Come in here." Glaring at a servant trimming candle wicks, until the man left the room, Nick shut the door. Then he spoke harshly and to the point for several minutes, favoring Oliver with a description of his character guaranteed to leave him shaking in his boots. When he had finished, he said, "Now, take that resentful look off your face, admit you deserved to hear every word I said, and tell me where the devil you came by those damned cards."

"That's none of your affair," Oliver retorted. "Anyone who wants to avoid being cheated ought to know such stuff, which is exactly what I told Melissa. The more one knows, the less likely one is to be caught in a sharp's trap, that's all. You should be glad I taught her how to identify fuzzed cards. Did she use them to beat you?"

"No, she has more scruples than you do. How much did you lose tonight?"

"To Rigger and the others? Not above a thousand, if it's any of your business. I daresay you've lost more than that in a single hand, and more than once, at that."

"Go on home, Ollie," Nick said, "before I lose my temper altogether."

At first, Oliver looked as if he meant to refuse, but when Nick moved toward him, he stepped back and put up his hands defensively, saying, "Oh, very well, if you insist, but I think you're making a great piece of work about nothing."

When Oliver had gone, Nick went back upstairs, his demeanor now apparently calm and relaxed. To the next person demanding to know what he meant by leaving his bride on their wedding night, he said with a laugh, "I begin as I mean to go on, my friend, in marriage as in all other things."

Thirteen

A New Game Begins

Melissa had watched her husband's departure with mixed emotions, feeling abandoned but relieved. Their consummation had not only gone more smoothly than she had anticipated but in the impassioned moments before Vexford possessed her, her desire for him had grown to such a peak that she had feared she might somehow explode. He was a skilled and gentle lover. His touch seemed magical, stirring sensations she hadn't known lay within her body. Paying close attention, wanting to learn what would please him, she had quickly realized that he, too, could be aroused by a touch. She had discovered places on his body where the lightest pressure of her fingertip could make him gasp with pleasure, and the knowledge that she had this power over him both intrigued and delighted her. The power was a small one, though, since he had so easily left her afterward to join his friends.

She found out the next day where he had gone.

When Oliver emerged from his bedchamber and came downstairs to the green salon shortly before a light midday meal was to be served, she noted that he was looking dispirited and said, "Are you feeling unwell, sir?"

"If I am," he said curtly, "it's as much your fault as anyone's."

"Good heavens, how can that be?"

"Because you told Nick where you got that pack of cards, that's how. I can't think how you came to be so crack-brained as to show them to him on your wedding night! He came looking for me at the Billingsgate Club, and he was as near as he's been in years to tearing off my limbs and beating me to a pulp with them."

The mental image his words created was almost too much for her sense of the ridiculous, but knowing that he blamed her for his brother's fit of temper was enough to stifle any urge to laugh. "I didn't tell him where I got them, Oliver, but something I said may have led him to guess. I'm sorry if he was angry with you."

"Well, he was. Where is he now?"

"I don't know. We accompanied your papa and mama to St. James's Church this morning, but afterward he said he had business to attend to. Your mama told the servants not to wait luncheon for him, because she and your papa mean to go out of town again this afternoon."

"Do they?" His tone was indifferent, but then, as if he realized he was being uncivil, he added, "Where are they off to now?"

"I don't know precisely," she said, not wanting to confide to him her suspicion that Lord and Lady Ulcombe were leaving out of a tactful desire to give the newlyweds some time to themselves. When Ulcombe suggested at the table that Oliver might like to accompany them, she was sure of it.

"We mean to look in at Fairleigh, just overnight, you know," Ulcombe said when Oliver asked where they were going.

"Well, I'm surprised you're going on a Sunday, but I've no wish to visit my aunt and uncle, or to entertain their scruffy brats," Oliver said. "I've business of my own here in town. Oh, and that reminds me, sir, I've a small matter to discuss with you privately before you leave, if you don't mind."

"Dipped again, Ollie?"

"Aye, I could use an extra five or six hundred, right enough," Oliver replied, reaching to help himself from a dish of broccoli the footman held for him.

Ulcombe said nothing until the servants had departed. Then he said evenly, "I believe we have already had this conversation, Oliver."

"Well, I know I promised to go easy, sir, but you know how it is, and last night being Nick's wedding night and all, I expect I just drank too much to know what I was doing. I've promised someone a bank draft for four hundred to cover my losses, but I'll need the extra to keep me out of dun territory for a while."

"I see. Very well, I'll write a draft on my bank for you and put an additional hundred to your account, but that will have to suffice until Quarter Day."

"Quarter Day! But that's nearly six weeks away."

"So it is. How gratifying to learn that you are acquainted with the date. I might just remind you that one hundred pounds is more than a year's wages to most people. I fear, Oliver, that I have somehow led you to believe I am cut from the same bolt of cloth as the late Lord Chesterfield, who claimed that young men should be supported in all their worst excesses. His own son kept secret from him a wife and two children, and while I acquit you of any such deception, my boy, there are better ways to spend your money—and mine—than on mere pleasure. You must study to learn economy."

"You don't preach such stuff to Nick," Oliver said resentfully.

"I trust I do not preach to anyone, but if you mean that I do not recommend to Nicholas that he study to learn economy, allow me to point out to you that he is not dependent upon me for every groat he spends."

The object of their discussion chose that moment to enter the dining room, and Melissa, for one, was glad to see him because the exchange between Ulcombe and Oliver had rendered her acutely uncomfortable. Apologizing for his tardiness, Vexford glanced from his father to his brother, but although Melissa was sure he must have overheard at least the end of their exchange, he did not comment on it. He greeted her politely and bent to kiss his mother's cheek.

Beyond casting him a look of resentment, Oliver paid the interruption no heed, saying petulantly when Vexford had seated himself beside Melissa, "It's not my fault that I am dependent on you, Father. I'd enjoy high water just as Nick always does if you'd provide me with an income equal to his."

"Nicholas enjoys the income from the Vexford estate because it is his by right of birth, Oliver, but it is not as great as you seem to imagine. The difference between you is that he contrives to live within his means. I'll say no more about that, however. I proceeded with this conversation despite your request for private speech with me, and I have no wish to embarrass you further. Nevertheless, you will do well to remember my words. Not another penny will you get before Midsummer Day."

"Then I wish I'd asked for a thousand instead of just a monkey."

"You would not have received it," Ulcombe said.

Lady Ulcombe said cheerfully, "How very much nicer the weather is today than yesterday. I believe we will enjoy a most pleasant journey to Fairleigh, my dear sir."

Ulcombe replied in kind, and Vexford supported their effort to turn the conversation into more comfortable channels, but Oliver did not respond. Melissa noted in the next few days that he spent most of his time away from home. Even when his parents returned from Fairleigh, the Barrington household saw little of him. Not, she observed with increasing resignation, that it saw much of his elder brother either.

Vexford seemed content to continue living as she supposed he had before his marriage, apparently feeling no obligation to exert himself on his wife's behalf. His attitude toward her was friendly but scarcely that of a loving husband. Though he visited her bedchamber Sunday night, and the following night as well, when she pleaded exhaustion on the first occasion and a headache on the second, he did not press her but took himself off to Brooks's without complaint.

He clearly assumed that she had engagements of her own to amuse her, and indeed, cards of invitation appeared daily, beginning with Monday's early post. On Tuesday she received her first bride visits, the ladies of the *ton* apparently thinking that two days were sufficient time for her to settle into her new home.

Amongst the first callers were her mother, her outspoken cousin, and Lady Ophelia. Lady Ulcombe received the visitors with her, and Melissa was glad that Charley expressed none of her stronger opinions before the countess rose and said that she knew Melissa would enjoy some moments of privacy with her family. "I'll just go and tell the servants to deny you to anyone else until they leave, my dear," she said, getting up and going out of the room without further ado.

The moment the door had shut behind her, Charley said frankly, "I'm glad that she's gone. She is perfectly charming and very kind, of course, but I simply must know— How does marriage suit you, Lissa? What's it like? Do tell us everything."

"It suits me well, thank you," Melissa said, smiling at her but turning at once to Lady Susan to ask, "How much longer do you mean to stay in London, Mama? I must tell you, I have been in a worry, because Charley told me that Papa—"

"Charlotte talks a great deal too much," Susan interjected quickly, casting her niece a look of affectionate disapproval.

Melissa said, "He told me himself that you are not divorced from him here in England, so when Charley said that he had accused you of bigamy . . ." In the face of her mother's quick frown, she fell reluctantly silent.

Susan said, "If I must be truthful, your father has made

some ridiculous threats, but dearest Penthorpe assures me that he has already spoken to people who can arrange everything to our satisfaction, so you are not to trouble your head about it, Melissa."

"Lissa, do you go with us Wednesday to Yarborne's supper," Charley demanded, "or will Vexford refuse to allow it?"

"He does not sit in my pocket," Melissa said, "nor does he keep me in his. Indeed," she added with what she hoped was the right tone of modern self-confidence, "he expects me to choose my own engagements and leave him to choose his. In any event, nothing in Yarborne's invitation could displease him. The ladies' supper is in aid of a most worthy cause, is it not?"

Charley chuckled. "Rockland says it's nonsensical for a man of Yarborne's stamp to be holding suppers for ladies, but I think he's just curious to know what will go on there, and irritated because he was not invited."

Lady Susan said, "You should not talk that way about Lord Rockland, Charlotte. He is a most eligible suitor for you, and not only does he seem to haunt Berkeley Square, but from what I've seen of him, he is very kind to you."

"Sometimes he is," Charley agreed with a twinkle in her eyes, "though I am not going to marry anyone, thank you, and I think he was rude to say that I shall lose all my pin money at Yarborne's supper. I don't mean to do any such thing, and if widows and orphans suffer as a result, well, that will just show that gaming suppers really are not a good way to raise money for charity."

Lady Susan frowned. "I still don't think it's wise for you girls to attend such a function. I cannot like the fact that Yarborne was in any way connected with that dreadful auction, Melissa, and although Aunt Ophelia seems to have been right, and no one is talking about that, I did hear that he has been known to lend money at interest. That is not an activity that any gentleman ought to pursue."

"Oh, Aunt Susan, please—"

"Mama, it was Papa who dragged me to Yarborne, after all, and I'm a married lady now. If my husband does not object to my attending Yarborne's supper—"

Susan made a gesture of surrender and said, "Very well. I daresay I ought not to credit something I merely overheard. I shall not attend the supper myself, because dear Penthorpe has expressed a desire to attend the play at Drury Lane that Charley saw last week, but I'll not stand in the way of your pleasure—especially," she added with a smile, "since Aunt Ophelia means to accompany you."

Melissa knew there was more to her mother's decision not to go with them than Penthorpe's wish to see a play. Divorced women were not received in society, and even without Seacourt's threat to charge her with bigamy, Melissa knew that her mother feared ostracism. In any event, she and Charley would not require Susan's escort to Yarborne House even if Lady Ophelia were not going with them, for Melissa, now a married lady, could properly act as her cousin's chaperone.

The thought of trying to curb Charley's impulsive nature was daunting, and the next evening when they entered the first-floor drawing room of Yarborne's Bedford Square mansion in the wake of a bevy of other ladies, Melissa was glad Lady Ophelia had accepted that responsibility. Yarborne's invitation had suggested something on the order of a silver loo party, but most of the furniture that must ordinarily have filled the large room had been removed to make way for gaming tables, and even Lady Ophelia paused with an audible gasp at the sight. An unwelcome memory of Newmarket's Little Hell flitted through Melissa's mind, giving her a strong urge to turn tail and run.

When a woman behind them dryly suggested that they step aside to make way for newcomers, Charley laughed and gave Melissa a nudge, exclaiming, "Only look at this place! It's just as I've always imagined a gentlemen's club must look."

A masculine voice behind them said, "My intention exactly, Miss Tarrant. Does the sight amuse you?"

They turned to find Yarborne at their heels, and Charley said with another laugh, "Indeed, sir, what a treat this is! They told us at the door when we received our rouleaux and markers that supper will be served all evening upstairs, but I'm not the least bit hungry now. Is this the way all gentlemen's clubs look? It does seem such a pity that they will never allow us inside their most sacred haunts."

"That's what I thought when I arranged this little entertainment," he said, turning to Lady Ophelia with a smile to add, "Good evening, ma'am. May I ask Fenton here to find you a chair?" He gestured toward the liveried servant at his side.

"Thank you, but I believe I'll stroll about a bit first," Lady Ophelia said. "I am not decrepit, you know, just old. I'd no idea you meant to do this affair on such a grand scale, Yarborne."

"I never do anything by half measures, ma'am. I daresay many of my guests expected to find nothing more than a silver loo party tonight, but I see that Miss Tarrant, at least, appreciates my little surprise. I hope you brought vast sums of money to lose to my cause, all of you. If you did not exchange it all for rouleaux and markers at the front door, any servant can attend to the matter for you at any time."

Melissa said, "Are we destined to lose all we brought with us, then, my lord? Surely, these games of chance of yours will be fairly played."

She saw with discomfort that his gaze flitted from her countenance down over her figure, as if he were assessing her worth again as he had done in Newmarket. The look was gone in a trice, however. Although she saw approval in her eyes when his gaze met hers again, he said as if the moment had never occurred, "The games, Miss— Ah; but it's Lady Vexford now. Forgive me. I assure you, the games will be played just as they are at White's, at Brooks's, or at the Billingsgate Club. I've placed footmen and groom-porters at each table to instruct you in the rules of play and to see that all runs smoothly. If you win, you take your winnings home. If you lose, you contribute to my orphans. An amiable prospect in either case, I'm sure you'll agree."

Charley tossed her head. "Will you think me heartless if I declare that I hope to win a great deal of money, my lord?"

He shook his head, smiling at her. "No, indeed, my dear. That is why anyone plays. Just remember that many who go out for wool come home shorn, and the more you hope to win, the more likely you are to lose to my worthy cause."

"He talks as if he thinks us fools," Charley muttered when they left him with his servant still in close attendance, exchanging greetings with other newcomers.

"Men generally do take women for fools," Lady Ophelia said, using the handle of her cane to fend off a woman who nearly backed into her. "Just do not give him more cause to think you one by contriving to lose all your money at his tables. I'd advise you both to play a little whist, as I intend to do if I can find a suitable partner."

"Whist!" Charley's tone was scornful. "I never heard of anyone winning a fortune at whist. I mean to break his faro bank."

Melissa smiled at her cousin's energy and said, "Which is the faro table? I'm utterly at a loss here, Charley. Do you know how to play any of these games?"

"No, but don't be a goose, Lissa. This is the best chance we'll ever have to see just what fascinates gentlemen so much that they become addicted to their gaming."

Watching Charley approach one of the footmen to ask where the faro table was situated, Melissa decided that her cousin was right. Gaining made up a large part of Vexford's life, and if she was ever to understand him, she must understand something of the world in which he spent so much time. The opportunity Yarborne provided was the best she was likely to get. She just hoped she wouldn't lose all her money.

On Monday Vexford had given her ten pounds and told her to tell him when she needed more for such trifling items as she did not care to charge to his name. After the discussion between his father and brother, she had not felt comfortable reminding him what sort of evening this was, and asking for more. Thus, she was grateful when Lady Ophelia had demanded bluntly to know how much she had with her, and had given her twenty pounds more. Urged by her cousin to exchange the entire amount for rouleaux of sovereigns when they had first entered the house, she had done so, though their weight strained the seams of her reticule. Even in such a good cause, she did not want to lose it all, and she resolved to be frugal.

Charley caught her arm, urging her through the growing crowd of gaily dressed and heavily scented women to a table covered with green velvet and surrounded by players already enjoying the game. Melissa thought at first that cards had been laid out face up on the table, but she saw that they were only pictures enameled onto the velvet. Only the spade suit was represented, but as Yarborne had promised, she quickly caught on to the rules.

"Perfectly simple," Charley said, leaning out to place a sovereign on the king and setting her marker atop the coin. "One bets which card will next be turned up."

"Won't be kings," the lady beside her said quickly. "Two have turned up already, as you can see if you note the little markers." She pointed to the king on the table, two corners of which bore round red markers. "Each time the porter turns a card, the footman marks its rank that way. Choose one that has not yet been marked."

As Charley shifted her coin and marker to the queen, Melissa recognized their adviser as Lady Hawthorne. The blond woman smiled, fingered a fine emerald brooch on her gown, and said, "Good evening, Lady Vexford. I was present at your wedding, though I daresay you don't remember seeing me in that crush. I am Clara Hawthorne."

"Good evening, ma'am," Melissa said, introducing Charley before she added, "Do you have any advice for me? On which card might win," she added hastily when the older woman gave her an odd, measuring look.

"Good heavens, my dear, how should I know? I placed my own marker on the ace, but I daresay I shall lose my money. Indeed, I *must* lose a respectable amount before I leave here tonight, since I would not offend Yarborne for the world, and I'd as lief do it quickly. I've got another engagement at half past nine, you see."

Seeing that the groom-porter was about to turn the next card, Melissa swiftly placed a coin and her marker on the nine. When he turned up the nine of hearts and set it atop the pile at his right, she stared in astonishment.

Charley exclaimed, "You've won, Melissa! You've tripled your stake! Winners get two for one!"

"Leave it where it is and copper it," Yarborne said, appearing beside her.

When she looked at him in bewilderment, he smiled reassuringly. "Trust me, and I'll share a secret of gaming success with you. If you look at what's left of the pack from which Horton is drawing, you will see that very few cards remain. From the counters on the table, you can see that your nine of hearts is the first nine he's drawn. With three left and so few cards remaining in the pack, the odds are increased that the next will also be a nine. Since the next goes to the left-hand pile as the house card, you must bet to lose, by placing a penny atop your marker. If you leave your stake where it is, and your winnings as well, your money could be increased sevenfold."

"Oh, do it, Lissa!"

Charley's advice being echoed by a number of others, Melissa did as she was advised and exclaimed nearly as loudly as her cousin did when the porter turned over the nine of clubs.

"Do it again," Charley said, but Melissa shook her head, scanned the table to see what cards remained, and placed a single marker on the seven. She lost. After two more turns, only three cards remained, and Yarborne, still standing beside her, said, "Four to one now, ladies, to anyone who guesses the order of the last three cards. There are six possibilities. Who wants to wager?"

"I will," Charley said instantly.

Melissa, feeling lucky and very wealthy, had begun to think of the coins as mere game pieces. She put five sovereigns down as her wager, and she won.

Lady Hawthorne said wryly, "With your luck, you ought to be playing hazard."

"Indeed, you should," Yarborne said with a laugh, "for it's the only game in which my orphans gain from winners as well as losers. Since we're playing English hazard, one plays against other players rather than against the house, so tonight the house keeps not only the money lost on nicks—which is when a throw goes against all players—but we also keep ten percent of the winnings, as well."

"Do let's try it," Charley urged. "I daresay hazard may not be as easy to play as faro, but I expect someone will explain it to us, and I want to win a lot of money."

"Well, you can do that at hazard, all right and tight," Yarborne said. "I'll take you over myself, and explain the rules of play to you. Fenton," he added, turning to his ubiquitous servant, "fetch Lady Vexford and Miss Tarrant each a glass of champagne."

Melissa allowed herself to be persuaded, feeling quite rich now with more than forty pounds of her own, and curious to understand more about the game so many gentlemen enjoyed. She was aware, too, however, that although great amounts might be won, as Charley hoped, men had lost entire fortunes at the hazard table.

The table was a large round one with a deeply beveled edge, which she saw at once was meant to prevent the dice from shooting to the floor when they were thrown. Yarborne began to explain the rules, saying, "The only throws that win are *main* and *chance*. One begins by calling a main and casting the dice. If the caster throws her main, she wins. If she doesn't, the number that turns up becomes chance. Chance is then the caster's winning throw. If she casts her main after that, she must pay each of those playing against her a sum equal to their stake. Any player can demand a change of the dice at any time during the game, and the demand must instantly be honored. Here is your champagne, my dear. Thank you, Fenton."

Taking the glass offered her and sipping slowly, enjoying the sensations of bubbles tickling her nose, Melissa watched the play for some time before joining in. Though the game was complicated, she caught on quickly, and soon discovered that her luck was still in. Several turns at casting the dice showed her that she was singularly fortunate. She found the game not only more fun than faro but also addicting. Yarborne left to mingle with his other guests, and as play progressed, she won more, lost some, and began to think herself a natural gamester. Charley soon wandered off, but though she suggested that Melissa accompany her, Melissa shook her head, sipping her second glass of champagne, keeping her attention focused on the table.

When Yarborne, who had gone to mingle with other guests, returned and asked how she was faring, she looked up with a grin and said, "I've thrown chance six times running, sir. Just look at my winnings!" She indicated what seemed to her to be a vast quantity of sovereigns and markers on the table. "I'm going to throw one more time."

"More champagne, Fenton. Her ladyship's glass is nearly empty again. I take it the main is seven," he added, "if chance is five."

She nodded, shaking the leather cup, her mind already on

the pair of dice rattling inside. As she threw, a feminine voice called, "Dice!"

Seeing the ivory cubes turn up a four and a one, Melissa scarcely heeded the interruption. Grinning, she reached to scoop up her winnings.

"One moment, my dear," Yarborne said. "You must throw again, I'm afraid."

"But I've won." She looked up at him, not understanding.

He said in a kindly tone, "The dice were called. That means you must change them and cast again."

"But I'd already thrown!"

"Nevertheless, that's the rule, I'm afraid. If you recall, we play by the same rules as Brooks's." He signed to the groom-porter, who scooped the dice off the table with his rake and dropped new ones into Melissa's cup.

"I don't know," she said, hesitating, finding it hard to think clearly. "Perhaps I had better stop now."

"Oh, but you cannot," he said. "You have already placed your wager and nearly everyone else has covered it, but have faith. I myself am so confident of your extreme good luck tonight that I will wager my own money on you, and agree to double your winnings if you will give half of the excess to my orphans."

"Done," she said, giving the dice cup a shake, shutting her eyes, and casting.

A collective gasp from around the table alerted her to disaster before she opened her eyes, and when she did, she stared at the two wayward cubes, one showing a six, the other an ace, and sighed with disappointment. Taking the refilled glass of champagne that Fenton produced just then, she turned to Yarborne and said, "I'm sorry not to live up to your faith in me, sir, but at least there's a satisfactory amount of money there for your orphans. I'm going to find my aunt now, I think. I've only twenty pounds left, and I mean to keep it."

"I'm afraid you won't do that, my dear," he said gently.

She stared at him. "What do you mean?"

"You didn't just throw out, Lady Vexford. You threw your main." A new note entered his voice, one that recalled instantly the man who had agreed to her auction at Newmarket. He turned to the groom-porter, who had not yet raked in the money on the table, and said, "Pay them all, and make an accurate reckoning of the total."

Only then did Melissa recall that throwing the main after the first cast meant paying everyone who played against the caster. She had won small amounts before when others had cast an unlucky main, but she had not thrown one before, and no one else had faced such an enormous number of markers on the table. Having dared to leave her winnings in place, just as Yarborne had encouraged her to do at the faro table, she had been delighted to see how well the strategy served her. Now, owing money to everyone else at the table, she saw how fortunes were lost to a single cast of the dice.

She realized, too, and with chagrin, that she had been carried away by good fortune and champagne. Worse than that, she had wanted to stun Charley with her winnings, and she had wanted to show her husband how well she could succeed in his world. Setting down her glass, and waiting with a sinking heart to learn the sum she had to pay, she wished desperately that she had left the table when her cousin had.

Yarborne, having finished conferring with the groom-porter, drew her aside and said, "Only a hundred twenty pounds, my dear. Not so bad, after all, especially when you consider that twelve pounds of that goes to the orphans."

"One hundred and twenty pounds!" She had been feeling dizzy from the shock of losing, and the champagne, but the appalling amount sobered her instantly. "You must be mistaken, sir. I have only twenty pounds. I cannot pay such a large sum. Indeed, I must not."

He frowned and said, "I know you ladies don't set as much store by debts of honor as gentlemen do, but I'm afraid I'm not willing to pay your losses for you, Lady Vexford. It's only because I feel some responsibility in having urged you to go forward that I'm willing to cover them until you can repay me. You say you have twenty pounds? Then I need only apply to your husband for—"

"No," Melissa said, opening her reticule and lowering her voice to add urgently, "you must not. Indeed, sir, here are the twenty, and I will repay you the rest somehow. It might take me some time, though. I-I cannot do so at this moment, I'm afraid."

"Am I simply to take your word that you will pay?"

"I can write you a-a promise—"

"A vowel?" He chuckled. "I think I would rather have surety. Though you are reluctant to have word of this get to Vexford, which I perfectly understand, I must point out that he might well refuse to believe you had written a promise to pay if you were to deny it later."

"But I would never do that!"

"Nonetheless, I think I would rather keep those pretty earrings of yours until you can redeem them," he said gently.

"I cannot give them to you. Not only are they worth much more than I owe you, but Vexford gave them to me as a wedding gift and would instantly notice their loss."

"Then I'll take that bracelet."

Reluctantly she unclasped her watch-bracelet, saying, "This was a gift from my favorite aunt, sir. As you can see, it's got a small watch set into the band. I don't know what it's worth, but I assure you, I would redeem it at any cost."

"Excellent." He took it, and patted her paternally on the shoulder. "Don't trouble your head about this, my dear. I daresay we can make things right very soon."

"Melissa!"

Hearing Vexford's voice made her jump as if she had been shot, for it was the last voice she had expected to hear in that house. When she turned, she saw that he was frowning heavily. She stammered, "G-good evening, sir. My, what a surprise!"

"I can see that. Where is Lady Ophelia?"

Relieved to see Yarborne slip the bracelet into his pocket and turn away to speak to his servant, she tucked her hand in the crook of Vexford's arm and smiled up at him, saying, "How did you get into the house, sir? We were told that no gentlemen other than Yarborne himself would be allowed on the premises tonight."

"They could scarcely object when I said I had come to collect my wife," he said, adding curtly, "What the devil are you doing at such an affair, and flirting with that scoundrel Yarborne? And why did he have his hand on your shoulder?"

"Goodness me, sir, I was not flirting. He is our host, and he just patted my shoulder in a fatherly way to console me for losing my money to his charities."

"So you lost it all, did you? I learned at Brooks's what manner of entertainment this was, which is why I came to fetch you, but you cannot have had much to lose."

"I had what you gave me Monday," she said, "and Aunt Ophelia gave me twenty pounds more." She hoped devoutly that he would never learn she had lost another hundred pounds above that. She had already cost him far too much money.

"Where is Lady Ophelia?" he asked her again.

They found her at a whist table, and when Melissa asked if she had seen Charley, she said, "Not for an hour or more, but don't concern yourself. She cannot get into trouble here amongst all these women. Just how did you get in, young man?"

He explained, adding, "I came to save you a journey to Barrington House, ma'am, and to repay the twenty pounds you lent my wife."

Lady Ophelia took the money with an appreciative chuckle. "Thank you. If my cards don't improve, I shall need it."

Outside, Melissa discovered that he had driven his tilbury. Artemus held the horses' heads while Vexford lifted her to

the front seat. Once he had swung himself up and taken up
the reins, Artemus climbed up behind, but no one spoke until
they reached Barrington House. Vexford's expression was so
forbidding that Melissa hesitated to initiate conversation, but
as he reached to help her down she said, "Thank you for
coming to fetch me, sir. It was a delightful surprise."

"Well, it was a surprise, clear enough. Take them round
to the stables, Artemus. I'll not need you again tonight."

Inside, as they went upstairs together, Melissa said coax-
ingly, "Are you vexed with me, sir?"

He looked down at her ruefully and put an arm around
her shoulders, giving her a hug. "No, my dear, just possessive
of my belongings. I've been that way since childhood. Just
ask Oliver."

No female relative of Lady Ophelia's would like to hear
herself referred to as a man's possession, but Melissa was
too relieved to hear apology in his tone to take exception.
In her experience, an apologetic man was much more easily
dealt with than an angry one. She said lightly, "I have
scarcely laid eyes on Oliver of late, sir, so I'll simply have
to take your word for that. My, but I'm tired. I'll be very
glad to lay my head on my pillow, I can tell you."

"Not at once, I hope," he said, giving her another hug. "A
man who goes out of his way to look after his wife deserves
some reward, don't you think?" His smile said he was teasing, but she felt herself stiffen and did not blame him when
the smile faded.

Hastily, she said, "I will do my best to stay awake."

"Don't put yourself out," he said, looking at her more narrowly. "I must say I don't understand you, Melissa. One minute, you act as if you want to seduce me, the next you're
tired or have a headache. I'm beginning to think you might
benefit from some quiet time at Owlcastle."

"Owlcastle?"

"My family's home in Hampshire," he reminded her.

Biting her lip, Melissa resolved to do her best to please

him at once, in order to keep him from sending her out of town. Not only did she not want people to think her husband had sent her away in disgrace but she was determined to go nowhere until she had managed to redeem her watch-bracelet from Yarborne. She smiled seductively and said, "I'm sorry if I vexed you, sir. What can I do to make it up to you?"

Fourteen

Charley's Point Is Good

Lucy opened the curtains to let in the sunlight, and the first thought that stirred in Melissa's head was a depressing awareness that she had failed in her resolution to please her husband the previous night. She was alone in her bed.

Lucy said, " 'Tis a fine bright day, my lady, perfect for the King's Drawing Room. Not a cloud in the sky. My lady and Lord Vexford are in the breakfast parlor, and my lady said she hopes you will join them, so I didn't bring your chocolate, but if—"

"Of course, Lucy, I'll dress at once and go downstairs."

She was surprised to find her husband breakfasting with his mama, for she had not seen him do so before. The blame was not all his, however. Lady Ulcombe rarely showed her face before eleven.

Vexford rose politely when she entered, but Melissa was quick to notice that, although his mama greeted her, he said nothing.

"I hope you slept well, my dear," Lady Ulcombe said.

She had not slept much at all, but avoiding her husband's eye, she said, "I slept very well indeed, ma'am, thank you."

"Well, you've a busy day ahead," Lady Ulcombe said, "so do get your plate and sit down. We've certain matters to discuss. We ought to have talked them over before, I expect, but it is the nature of things that one remembers last-minute details at the last minute. Now, I have arranged it with Ophelia that she and Charlotte are to come here at noon so we can go in train to St. James's Palace. Your court dress was delivered last evening after you had gone, and it looks perfectly splendid, but of course, you must try it on to be sure it fits properly, and to practice your court curtsy. If there is anything amiss, don't trust your Lucy to adjust it but send for my woman instead."

Vexford said, "Considering the enormous cost of that gown, I should expect it to fit her as well as her skin does."

"Now, Nicholas, don't be difficult," his mother said. "You could not in good conscience allow Ophelia to pay for your wife's court dress, after all, and you would not be at all pleased to have a dowdy at your side at the Drawing Room."

"At my side? Whatever gave you the notion that I would be present, ma'am? Royal Drawing Rooms are petticoat affairs."

"They are no such thing." Lady Ulcombe stared at him. "My dear Nicholas, you cannot think we are going without you."

"But, surely, my father—"

"Don't be vexatious. Your father will go much earlier than we shall, for he's been asked to be at hand when His Majesty receives the French ambassador. Moreover, Melissa is being presented on the occasion of her marriage, so you must certainly be with her to present your compliments. For goodness' sake, even if she were not being presented, your father would expect you to go. Would you offend His Majesty by making it appear that you support the opposition? And for goodness' sake, do not neglect to wear knee breeches, Nicholas, and a smallsword. Remember, His Majesty has a veritable obsession with propriety of dress and appearance."

It being clear from Vexford's expression that he had not considered His Majesty at all, or his own wife, for that matter, Melissa tried to think of something to say to ease the tension of the moment. He glanced at her. The look was ambiguous, but it stilled the words half-formed on her tongue.

The previous night, stimulated by fear that he might send her out of London at any moment, she had intended to respond to his lovemaking not just as she knew wifely duty demanded but by exerting herself to please him. Her own stirring passion had led her to believe that the task would be easy, but when he moved to enter her, she had stiffened involuntarily. Before long, she had begun to experience again that odd sensation of floating above the bed, watching. Nicholas left shortly afterward, and she was sadly certain now that he was annoyed with her if not downright angry. She was annoyed with herself, but she had been unable to overcome that strange sense of being a watcher rather than a participant.

She had no time now to fret about their relationship, however, for Lucy and the countess's woman both awaited her in her bedchamber. Fortunately, her court dress, an elegant confection with a cerulean-blue bodice over a white petticoat edged in green and trimmed with gold lace, fitted her perfectly and required not a single stitch or tuck. After she had practiced her deep, formal curtsy, the women whisked it off again, and the countess's dresser left her with Lucy, to bathe and arrange her hair.

Though she did not linger over her preparations, she was the last to join the group in the green salon. Pausing on the threshold, she looked at Nicholas, willing him to turn toward her so that she could judge if her appearance pleased him.

Before he turned, Charley, wearing an undergown of her favorite sapphire blue with a white gauze overdress, exclaimed, "How pretty you look, even with white and gold plumes sprouting out of your head! Aren't they ridiculous? And our lappets look more like hounds' ears than apparel for ladies of fashion. I loathe mine, but at least the hoops required for court dresses are smaller this year. You ought to have seen the one I had to manage two years ago!"

"Stop chattering, Charlotte," Lady Ophelia said testily. "I declare, child, you've been rattling like a tin full of gravel from the moment we left Berkeley Square. Come closer, Melissa, and let me look at you. Do not forget to carry your train over your arm until just before you are presented, and then—"

"Aunt Ophelia, she knows all that. We've all told her time and again that she must let the royal page arrange it for her just before she approaches His Majesty. Have you got your cards, Melissa?"

Melissa nodded, still watching Nicholas. He had not spoken, and she did not think he had really paid her entrance much heed. He looked splendid in his court dress and smallsword. His dark coat fit snugly over his shoulders, and the cream-colored knee breeches and white silk stockings hugged his muscular thighs and calves. He carried his chapeau bras and white gloves, giving her the impression that he was impatient to be gone.

"If we are all ready," Lady Ulcombe said in her placid way, "I am persuaded that the carriages must be at the door by now."

"Oh, yes," Charley said, "for yours was already drawn up when we arrived, and indeed, we ought to go, ma'am. The guns at the Tower have been thundering for more than an hour now. Trumpets are blaring in the streets, and all London is a sea of traffic. We saw a magnificent cavalry unit parading along Piccadilly—all jet black horses rigged out in grand style—and a squadron of foot soldiers, too. Everything is much more magnificent than it was when I was presented."

Lady Ophelia said, "That is only to be expected. Not only is this the first Drawing Room His Majesty has held in two years but St. James's Palace has been repaired at last, nearly a decade and a half after the great fire burned down the southeast corner, and everyone wants to be there today to see the alterations."

Melissa said, "It seems a pity that we can't simply walk to the palace. It's only a few steps along Pall Mall, after all."

Charley grinned at her, and even Nicholas smiled. The countess said, "It does seem foolish, especially since we must drive all around through King Street and Duke Street, then into Piccadilly, in order to fall into a long line of vehicles at the top of St. James's Street. One could so much more easily at least *drive* up Pall Mall."

Nicholas said, "Console yourself, ma'am, with the thought that the return journey will be shorter." Picking up the fan she had dropped when she stood up, he handed it to her and moved to assist Lady Ophelia from her chair.

As they all emerged from the house, Charley said to him, "I know you intended to ride with Lissa in the smaller carriage, sir, but I've something I particularly want to talk to her about. Would you mind dreadfully, exchanging places with me and riding with your mama and Aunt Ophelia in the larger one?"

Lady Ophelia clicked her tongue, but Nicholas agreed to the request, and as Melissa entered the smaller carriage with Charley, she was not certain whether to be grateful or irritated. She wanted to clear the air with Nicholas, but she had no wish to stir his temper, and feared that she might. When the two carriages passed from the square into King Street only to find themselves halted in a line of traffic, she decided she was grateful. She was even more so when Charley, surveying the vast assemblage of vehicles, said, "If we reach the palace in under an hour, I will be astonished."

Settling back against the crimson plush squabs, Melissa watched the people lining the pavements. Every man, woman, and child in London seemed to have turned out to watch the procession to St. James's Palace, and there was much to see— even old-fashioned sedan chairs. A particularly elaborate one passed them, with uniformed guards to clear the way and six liveried footmen to carry the chair. Recognizing the occupant as the Duchess of Northumberland, Melissa returned her stately nod.

Charley said, "Lissa, there's something you ought to know."

Turning her head with care, since her plumes brushed the ceiling of the carriage, Melissa said, "Has something happened? Did Papa do as he threatened and—"

"No, no! At least, Aunt Susan has not been arrested, if that's what you fear. Indeed, I don't know what your papa might be up to. We have not seen him, and Penthorpe said he's got his eye on another woman at last, which may be all to the good. The thing is, I think your mama thinks Penthorpe has, too."

"I don't understand. Penthorpe has what?"

"Another woman."

"Nonsense. He wouldn't. Never."

"Well, you will recall Aunt Susan said they meant to go to a play last night, but they didn't. She was dressed and ready to go when Aunt Ophelia and I left to fetch you for Yarborne's supper, but Penthorpe had gone out earlier, and he never came to get her. She's all hollow-eyed and sad this morning, not talking much to anyone."

"What did Penthorpe say?"

"Just that he forgot, that something else occurred that knocked the dashed silly play right out of his head."

"You sound just like him," Melissa said with a smile, "but maybe he just put off going home till he realized it was too late to go to the play, and then feared to face Mama's disappointment. Procrastination is his most besetting sin, you know."

"Perhaps," Charley said, "but he looked guilty, Lissa, and when I asked him what occurred to make him forget, he colored up and said it was none of my affair. But I could see that he hadn't told Aunt Susan either, and it is certainly her affair. She didn't cross-question him, of course. She never does."

"No, but nonetheless he's right, I expect, to insist that it's none of our business. What happens between married people should be private, Charley."

"I suppose so, but that reminds me— What *does* happen between married people?" Charley demanded. "I've been meaning to ask you that, and having seen the way you looked at Vexford today, as if your every dependence lay with him, and—"

"I never looked at him like that. I wouldn't!"

"Oh, yes, you did. You had the old look in your eye, the one you were used to get as a child when you feared you had displeased someone like Grandpapa or Uncle Geoffrey. You were very quiet, too. You aren't afraid of him, are you?"

"Oh, no, not in the least!"

"Well, I don't know that I believe you," Charley said frankly, "for you have that haunted look in your eyes even now. I know that men generally treat women badly, and that husbands can be dreadful creatures—only consider Henry VIII, or your papa—but I confess, I had a better opinion of Vexford than of most."

"He is very kind to me," Melissa said, twisting the cords of her fan. "Indeed, he scarcely heeds what I do and makes no effort to assert his authority over me, which is what makes it so—" She broke off, looking straight ahead at the red-silk-covered panel opposite them, not wanting to confide the rest of that thought to her perceptive cousin.

For once, Charley did not rush into speech. She was silent for so long that Melissa could not resist turning to look at her again. She saw with surprise that her cousin was blushing.

Meeting her gaze, Charley said in a rush, "Do you mean to say he doesn't . . . that is, that he didn't—" She broke off, took a deep breath, and said, "Just listen to me, will you? I never thought I was the least bit missish, and here I am stammering over a perfectly simple question. Have you done it or not?"

Feeling fire in her cheeks, and struggling at the same time to repress a bubble of laughter, Melissa said primly, "That, miss, is none of your affair."

"Oh, pooh, how else is a person to learn if she does not ask questions?" Charley shot her a shrewd look before adding swiftly, "If it's not that, what is it? It's you, isn't it? You've done something he won't like, and you're worried about angering him."

Melissa nearly gasped. She had said nothing about her dreadful losses at the hazard table the night before, and she had no wish to confess them now, so she said quickly, "No, it was nothing that I *did*. Indeed, it wasn't!"

"So you didn't do anything," Charley repeated in a musing tone. Then, with another of those penetrating looks, she said, "And that's the difficulty, isn't it?"

Melissa was silent.

"You might just as well tell me the whole, you know. We've at least another quarter hour before we'll get there, so I'll winkle it out of you one way or another."

"I know." They were turning into St. James's Street. The traffic was moving more rapidly than she had expected, but there was still the full length of the street to go before they would reach the palace. Having been told that ladies of quality did not enter St. James's Street, ever, she looked curiously out the window but could see nothing of interest, only ordinary buildings. She knew that some of them, at least, were famous gentlemen's clubs, but there was nothing to tell her which ones they were.

Charley cleared her throat impatiently.

Turning back, Melissa said sadly, "It *is* me, and he is very near to sending me into Hampshire, to Owlcastle—his family's seat, you know—and I don't want to go, Charley. I can't!"

"But why would he?"

Feeling heat sweep into her cheeks again, Melissa said, "I daresay I ought not to be talking to you about this. You are not a married lady, after all, so——"

"Oh, for goodness' sake, Lissa, I breed horses. Do you think I don't know how children are bred? I thought men just covered their wives when they wished to, but you said he does not exert his authority. Do you mean you don't let him touch you?"

"No. Well, not precisely. Indeed, I . . . I like him to touch me. My insides seem to melt like warm syrup when he enters the room, and when he touches me, it's . . . it's the most provocative sensation, like nothing I've ever felt before. The first night he made me feel for a time as if my nerves might explode, like fireworks, and I wanted the feeling to go on and on."

"Really?" Charley said. "I've never experienced anything like what you're describing, certainly not in the company of dolts like Rockland and his ilk, but I'll take your word for it. Still, if Vexford makes you feel like that, where's the rub?"

"I don't know," Melissa said with a heartfelt sigh. "It begins well, and then suddenly all the good feelings are gone, and I have the oddest sense of not being in my own body anymore. He said once that one minute I act as if I want to seduce him—and, indeed, I do—but the next I behave quite differently. He said that just before he said that maybe I'd benefit from some time in Hampshire. And, Charley, he's right."

"Well, you've not been married a full sennight yet," Charley said practically. "Maybe he means to take you into Hampshire himself, to get to know you better."

"No, for he's scarcely paid me any heed at all but goes on as he did before the wedding. I-I'm merely a newly acquired possession."

"I see. So he does think you've behaved badly." Charley was silent, thinking, before she said slowly, "You know, Lissa, some mares are particularly skittish, and some stallions particularly masterful. In order to breed out the fidgets in the mare, it is sometimes advisable to match them. However," she added thoughtfully, "one doesn't generally leave such a pair alone to attend to the matter all by themselves."

Melissa stared at her, then burst into laughter, laughing harder than she had in a fortnight. "Are you offering to oversee our conjugal unions, Charley?"

"Melissa, for heaven's sake!" But she chuckled, too, adding, "I like to hear you laugh like that. I was just thinking aloud, but though I don't mean to oversee your union, I do mean to speak my piece. I know exactly what Vexford meant when he said you act as if you want to seduce him. You have always behaved that way."

"I haven't! What a thing to say."

"Don't argue. You were always used to employ a flirtatious manner when you thought your papa was displeased with you. Aunt Susan did the same thing in the same circumstance. You both exerted yourselves to gratify him, and with good cause, too, considering his habits when he was displeased. But if Vexford has given you no cause to fear him, then you're just being a coward."

"But I'm not . . ." Melissa nibbled her lower lip. "Well, maybe I am, a little. He's very large, after all, and since husbands, by their very nature—"

"Fiddlesticks. You think Vexford large only because you still think of yourself as small and helpless. One's perception of any opponent, in my opinion, derives directly from one's perception of oneself. That always affects one's ability to deal with another person. What you are describing to me is more than mere fidgets, Lissa, and you know it. Either that, or you are being both deceitful and sinful in your marriage."

"How dare you!"

Charley said wryly, "It's no use flying into the boughs with me, as you know very well. Since you agreed to marry Vexford, you owe him honesty and plain dealing. I don't believe in half measures, so if you take my advice, you must make up your mind to be a proper wife to him, and first you must stop teasing him. I've seen good mares well bitten for playing the coquette and then trying to draw away. Moreover, since I believe that somehow episodes from your past are still haunting you, you simply must resolve to put them behind you. Inflicting rubbish left from your childhood on your unsuspecting husband is just not fair."

The carriage turned then, and she glanced out the window, adding, "Here we are. Just think, tomorrow you will see your name with all the other presentations in the *Times*—'Lady Vexford on the occasion of her marriage, by the Countess of Ulcombe.' "

Melissa greeted the abrupt change of subject with relief, for Charley's frank advice had sorely tried her composure. Her throat had begun to ache, and she wanted to cry, but as they passed through the huge iron gates of St. James's Palace, into the palace yard, she drew a steadying breath and fixed her attention on what lay ahead.

The carriage drew up beside a colonnade. A liveried footman opened the door and let down the step, and both young ladies, taking care to manage their hoops and trains, accepted his help to step down. Nicholas, his mama, and Lady Ophelia awaited them, and no sooner did Melissa's feet touch the pavement than the man put up the step again, shut the door, and the carriage rolled off to make way for others behind it. Hundreds of people milled about, chatting as they took their places in line, and hundreds more stood waiting to leave. Empty carriages returned for them in the steadily moving circle of vehicles in and out of the yard.

The line ahead moved slowly, so, despite having to hold her train over her arm, Melissa was able to smooth her long white kid gloves and untwist the tangled strings of her gilded fan. Friend greeted friend, and in the general din, private conversation was impossible. Nicholas, Lady Ulcombe, and Lady Ophelia nodded to acquaintances, and Charley chat-

tered to all and sundry in her usual manner, leaving Melissa
to compose her thoughts in solitude.

Not until they had passed through the vast guard hall and
up the grand staircase did she comprehend the enormous
size of the company. Looking down from the upper landing,
she saw a sea of waving white and gold plumes. People
pressed together, and more than one gentleman, including
her husband, skillfully avoided stabbing someone with his
dress sword. A similar crush lay ahead, and a solid mass of
humanity descended the stairway on the opposite side of the
hall. Melissa was grateful for Nicholas's solid presence at
her side. He did not speak, but his presence was soothing.

When they entered the first room, Lady Ulcombe leaned
near her and said, "This is the old presence chamber. The
Mortlake tapestry yonder on the wall was lost in the reign
of Charles I, then found and replaced by His present Majesty's grandfather."

A huge looking glass ahead of them seemed to double the
size of the enormous crowd as they passed into the next
room, where the King's page approached them. Each lady
handed him a card with her name written on it, and gave a
second, similar card to the Lord in Waiting just inside the
new presence chamber.

Here the crowd melted away. The King stood with his back
to a window, in front of a chair. Lady Ophelia explained in
an undertone that the persons to his left were his royal relatives
and cabinet ministers, arranged according to their rank.
Melissa could think of nothing but how enormously fat he
was.

The Lord in Waiting announced, "Lady Ophelia Balterley
and Miss Charlotte Tarrant," and Melissa watched them approach, curtsy, and move away. Having been warned that,
while compliments and curtsies were made in a string, one
after another, like the receiving line at a ball, presentations
were another matter, she was not surprised when the Lord
in Waiting paused. He waited until Lady Ophelia and Charley

had moved on before he announced Lady Ulcombe and Lord Vexford.

Melissa began to walk forward with them, remembering only after two or three steps to release her train. She scarcely noticed the page who leapt to arrange it behind her, for Lady Ulcombe was already saying to the King, "May I present my new daughter-in-law, Lady Vexford, Your Majesty."

Melissa made her deep curtsy, hoping she wouldn't topple over and disgrace both herself and Nicholas. When she lifted her gaze from the floor to the enormous but nonetheless magnificently attired man before her, she saw that he had extended a hand to assist her to rise. He smiled and said affably, "Well met, Lady Vexford. How do you like our new-modeled palace, ma'am?"

"Very well, Your Majesty. It is a most magnificent residence."

"We were born here, you know, and so the place has always been a prime favorite. And since we fancy ourselves a dab hand at building, we could do no less than our very best. It delights us to find you well-pleased with our efforts."

That he spoke of himself in the plural seemed, in view of his girth, perfectly reasonable. He was a gentleman, however, and despite the fact that he was already nodding to someone behind her—Nicholas, no doubt—he had made her feel for a few brief moments as if he might, ten minutes hence, even recall having met her. Remembering that she was to back away, Melissa hoped fervently that the page had a good sense of timing, and would not allow her to trip over her train.

She need not have worried. She and Lady Ulcombe returned to Charley and Lady Ophelia without incident, and once Nicholas had caught up with them, rejoined the flow of company. They moved along a passageway leading directly to the grand staircase, without passing through any rooms they had seen before, and came to a ground-floor chamber with places to sit until their carriages returned.

With the initial excitement of her presentation over,

Melissa turned her thoughts back to what Charley had said. Over the years since her childhood, especially since leaving Cornwall, she had formed the habit, whenever she wanted to accomplish something, of thinking about how Charley would do it. Having had such faith in her for so long, she knew that to ignore her advice now would be absurd.

Waiting only until Nicholas stepped across the room to tell the porter they required their carriages and then to speak to Lord Thomas Minley, she drew Charley away from Lady Ulcombe and Lady Ophelia and said, "I'm sorry I flew into a miff. You were right, of course, and I shall do what I can to become a better wife."

"Excellent. You just need to learn to put your thoughts forward, rather than back, and all will be well. You'll see. You must put the memories of Uncle Geoffrey's dreadful behavior out of your head, and concentrate on your feelings for Vexford instead. Good Lord, there's Rockland," she said, looking past Melissa. "Am I never to have any peace from that man? He insists that I am destined to bear his children."

"Charley!"

"Oh, properly married, of course. He simply cannot conceive of how any sensible female can want to avoid matrimony. You won't want to be a party to the discussion, so I shall just intercept him before he can bore you to tears with his absurd thoughts on the matter. I only wish I may convince him that his hopes are futile."

Lady Ulcombe and Lady Ophelia had evidently found seats, and for a moment Melissa found herself alone in the milling crowd. She recognized many people, but despite an unceasing din of conversation, no one spoke to her. Then a hand touched her arm and she turned to find herself face-to-face with Yarborne.

"Good afternoon, my dear Lady Vexford," he said warmly. "I must say, you look utterly delectable in all your court finery."

"Thank you, sir. Can you see where Lady Ophelia or Lady Ulcombe have got to? I seem to have misplaced them."

"Yonder, talking with Ulcombe," he said. "I daresay he is collecting his wife so she can accompany him to the little dinner His Majesty means to serve in the new banquet room for the many august persons who have the entrée. I am not one of them yet, I'm sorry to say, but doubtless my turn will come. No, no, don't run away just yet," he added, catching her arm when she turned to look for Vexford's parents. "You and I still have a small matter of business to discuss, my dear."

"Not here, surely! I carry only a fan, sir. You cannot have expected me to tuck such a sum into my bodice."

"A delightfully appealing thought, my dear, but do not toy with me. You will very soon catch cold at that, I assure you. Vauxhall Gardens opens Tuesday night with a gala masquerade. Everyone will go, I expect, so it will be a simple matter for you to arrange to meet me—say, near the statue of Milton at half past eleven—with a hundred pounds tucked into your bodice, or elsewhere, to redeem your pretty watch-bracelet."

"But how could I possibly—?"

"Don't fail me," he said sternly, looking past her, "or I shall be forced to apply to your husband for the money you owe, and since everyone will be leaving town for Epsom on Wednesday or Thursday— Well, surely I need say no more."

Involuntarily, she glanced toward the spot where she had last seen Nicholas, only to encounter a smile and a wave from Lady Hawthorne, dressed all in gold with three towering golden ostrich plumes in her headdress, and diamonds everywhere. When Melissa looked back, Yarborne had vanished and Nicholas stood in his place.

"The carriages have entered the yard," he said. "The others are waiting."

He looked grim, and she felt an instant urge to placate him, but remembering Charley's words, she resisted it, saying only, "I am quite ready to leave, sir."

Fifteen

Cards on the Table

Shaken by Yarborne's threat to apply to her husband for payment of her debt, Melissa could think of nothing to say to Nicholas during their return to St. James's Square. They had scarcely spoken to each other in twenty-four hours, and now he sat beside her in the carriage, staring out his window, looking relaxed if rather bored. She wished Lady Ulcombe had not remained at the palace, because she could at least have chatted with her about the Drawing Room.

Exerting herself to put Yarborne's threat out of her mind, she decided to concentrate on her husband and begin, as she had promised Charley she would, to try harder to be a more admirable wife. With that end in mind, she reached a hand toward him, only to draw it back before she touched him.

Glancing at him to see if he had noticed, she saw with relief that he was still staring idly out the window at the crowded flagway. Drawing a long breath and letting it out slowly, she placed her left hand gently on his right thigh, but when the hard muscles beneath her palm tensed, she nearly snatched it back again.

He turned and said, "Did you enjoy your first Drawing Room?"

"Y-yes, thank you," she replied, adding hastily, "No one told me how old the King is, or how very fat he is." Her hand quivered on his thigh. What on earth was wrong with her?

Nicholas seemed not to notice anything amiss. He said, "His Majesty eats too many rich foods, and drinks too much, and this last episode of the gout has pulled him about a good deal. He is sixty-one, I believe, but he does look much older."

When he put a hand on hers and gave it a gentle squeeze, she felt another foolish urge to snatch hers away. Suppressing the urge, forcing herself to leave it where it was, she blurted, "Nicholas, I . . . I talked to Charley."

He said lightly, "Yes, I know—in the carriage, earlier. I observed that you talked to several people at the palace, as well."

"Yes, of course, I did. One does. But that's not the same. I . . . I talked to her about what you said last night. About sending me to Owlcastle," she finished in a rush.

His eyes narrowed. "You ought not to discuss our affairs, Melissa, not even with your cousin." He seemed suddenly overlarge for the carriage.

She reminded herself that she had no cause to fear him, that a mere awareness of the fact that he took up more space than she did was no reason to feel overpowered by him. Remembering that Charley had suggested that her perception of his size was no more than an extension of the way she perceived herself, she wondered suddenly if that could be true.

"Do I seem small to you, sir?" she asked.

He looked confused by the change of subject—as well he might, she thought—but his stern expression relaxed and he said, "Your size is just right. 'Tis I who am large, not you who are small."

"I was just curious," she said, forcing herself to meet his gaze. "Charley said she believes I think of you as large only because I think of myself as small."

"Well, I am large. Is that all she said?"

"No." She wanted to tell him all that Charley had said, to

say that she believed her cousin had been right about many things. She wanted to admit that she had not been a proper wife, that she had even been teasing him, just as he had said she did. She wanted to tell him that somehow things from her past were disturbing her, disturbing their relationship, but her throat closed, trapping the words inside. She began to pull her hand away, but he held it. She knew he still watched her, but she avoided his gaze. Charley was right about another thing, she decided grimly. She was a coward.

When he drew her hand to rest upon his other thigh and shifted his body so she could rest her head in the hollow of his right shoulder, she did so. The position made her feel safe and protected. When he began to stroke her arm with his right hand, however, the motion both teasing and seductive, she stiffened, hoping he would not begin something right here in the carriage in broad daylight.

He sensed her resistance, for his hand stilled and his arm lay quiet for the rest of their short journey. When they reached Barrington House, he opened the carriage door before the lackey could do so, and kicked the step down, barely touching it when he got out and turned to assist her. Inside the house, she said, "I must go up and change, sir. My headdress is making my head ache, and this hoop is too cumbersome to wear a moment longer than necessary."

"Shall I play tirewoman?" he asked, his gaze intent.

"After the fuss you made about the cost of this gown, I should say not. I'd never hear the end of it if it got torn by my so-called 'tirewoman.' You'd conveniently forget that you were the one who had done the damage."

"You must think me very clumsy," he said. The intensity in his eyes increased.

She smiled quickly, lowering her lashes, and said, "Really, sir, it is nearly time for dinner, and I am famished. You may enjoy standing about for hours making idle conversation, but I am quite exhausted and will be no fit companion until after I have got out of this gown and been properly fed. Perhaps . . . perhaps later . . ." She looked up then, right into his eyes, and slowly, invitingly, ran her tongue over her bottom lip.

The intense expression eased, and he said, "I'll expect you to keep that promise, sweetheart. Run away to change your gown, and I'll order dinner moved ahead a bit. My parents are dining at the palace, and we needn't wait to accommodate Oliver, for I doubt that he means to burden us with his presence tonight."

Moving dinner ahead was not at all what she had wanted him to do, but she was determined this time to honor the vow she had made to herself. He was her husband, and Charley had been right to say she had been behaving badly. She smiled again, and when he bent to kiss her, she met him halfway.

As a result, Nicholas put his arms around her and pulled her close, his kiss deepening with a promise of delights to come. Responding was not difficult, and for a glorious moment, passion ruled instinct and she submitted willingly, experiencing a sharp surge of disappointment when he released her.

He stood for a moment, looking down into her eyes again, before he turned her around toward the stairway and gave her a pat on the backside. "Hurry, sweetheart, or you'll not get any dinner."

Her laughter came easily, and warm thoughts engendered by the exchange remained with her while she changed her gown. She began to think her resolution would not be hard to honor, after all. She looked forward to dinner, to seeing the warmth rekindle in his eyes, even to feeling his hands on her body again.

At the table, he was in an exceptionally good mood, and she found herself responding to it. She twinkled and laughed with him, flirting and responding enthusiastically to every conversational gambit. Not since their wedding night had she felt so easy and comfortable with him. She decided that Charley's plain speaking had been good for her.

When she stood, intending to let him enjoy his port in solitude, he unnerved her a bit when he said to the butler, "Nothing more, Preston. I'm going upstairs with her ladyship. We mean to make it an early night."

"It's not even seven o'clock," she murmured when he urged her toward the stairs. "The servants will think you ill if you take to your bed at such an hour."

"Let them think what they like."

"But you cannot want to go to bed so early. Would you not rather play piquet until it's time for the tea tray to be brought in? We can use your cards if you like," she added with a demure smile, twinkling at him from under her lashes.

"I don't want to play cards, and I don't want to drink tea. I want to enjoy some time with my wife."

"But—"

"Are you changing your mind again, sweetheart?"

"No! No, of course not. It's just . . . Well, it just seemed rather unbecoming for us to be in such a hurry."

"I thought all you needed was enough sustenance to regain your strength."

An edge had entered his voice, and she said hastily, "You must think my brain quite addled, sir. Y-you are quite right. Let us go up at once."

Upstairs when he would have drawn her directly into his bedchamber, she demurred, but she had collected her wits enough to say with a chuckle, "I think we would both do better to prepare properly for the night, in our usual fashion."

"Melissa . . ."

"No, no, don't scold me for using good sense, sir, unless," she added archly, "you mean to ring for Lisset and warn him that we are in your bedchamber and that he should not come in. He generally does, you know, to assure himself that all is in order for you. Indeed, I'd not be surprised to find him there now, expecting you to refresh yourself before going out to Brooks's or to the Billingsgate Club."

Seeing acknowledgment that she was right dawn in his eyes, she breathed a sigh of relief.

He said, "Go then, and let Lucy do whatever she must do for you, but I warn you, I'll not be patient longer than it takes me to get rid of Lisset."

"I'll hurry."

"See that you do."

Hastening to her bedchamber, she rang for Lucy, busying herself with various unimportant tasks while she waited, one moment anticipating what lay ahead, the next, trying to keep her mind off it. When Lucy entered, Melissa asked her to light the fire. She gave other orders in her usual manner, but with each passing minute her tension increased. Knowing she was succumbing to nerves, she exerted herself to relax, and before Lucy had finished brushing out her hair, she had succeeded in convincing herself that she was completely calm again.

That illusion lasted only until the connecting door opened. When she turned to face him, she could feel her heart thumping like a hammer in her chest.

Nicholas wore his elaborate dressing gown, tied firmly at the waist with its twisted cord sash. Hearing Lucy's indrawn breath at the sight of him, she smiled and said lightly, "I am not quite ready to bid you good-night yet, sir."

"You look ready to me. Good night, Lucy."

"Good night, my lord," Lucy said, dropping a hasty curtsy and leaving the room without another glance at Melissa.

Vexed, Melissa said, "I wish she had at least awaited a proper dismissal."

"I dismissed her," he pointed out, adding as he moved toward her, "Moreover, like any good servant, the wench knows when she's not wanted. These candles and the firelight make your hair gleam like silver gilt, sweetheart."

She stood, vividly aware of the thinness of her lawn nightdress beneath the soft lamb's wool shawl Lucy had wrapped round her shoulders when she had sat down to have her hair brushed.

He moved nearer, the lust in his eyes as unmistakable to her as the much more physical evidence she could see for herself distending the folds of his robe.

Moistening suddenly dry lips, Melissa said, "Do you want to stay here or shall we go to your room?"

"We can stay here," he said. "Why delay our pleasure merely to go elsewhere?"

"The fire is a trifle too warm, I think."

"Then take off your shawl," he said, reaching for her.

Stepping back, trying to make the move seem natural rather than evasive, she slipped off the shawl and turned to fold it, intending to place it on the dressing stool.

Reaching over her shoulder, Nicholas took it away, and tossed it over the stool. Then he put his hands on her shoulders and bent nearer to murmur into her ear, "Still shy, sweetheart?"

"Oh, no, not anymore."

His silence disturbed her.

Looking into his eyes, she saw skepticism, and added ruefully, "A little nervous, perhaps."

"Do I frighten you?"

"N-no, sir." He didn't. What she feared was not him but herself.

Gently he turned her and drew her toward him, slowly lowering his head to kiss her. The kiss was weightless, a mere brushing of his lips against hers, but Melissa felt its effect all the way to her toes and fingertips. Nerves stirred uneasily, but desire overpowered them, leaping like tinder to a flame. Telling herself again that he was her husband and could not be denied, she placed her hands at his waist and pressed her lips hard against his, determined to let lust rule the night.

His mouth softened, opened slightly, and when his tongue

touched her lips, teasing her, challenging her to play, she responded at once, feeling the flames rise in her body. Reminded of the explosive emotions he had awakened on their wedding night, she thought this must be the way marriage was meant to be.

"Loosen my robe," Nicholas murmured. "Touch me."

Obeying without thinking about anything beyond her growing desire for him and her hope that he would not stop kissing her, Melissa opened his robe and moved her hands across his hard stomach and around his sides to the small of his back.

His arms slipped around her, and he pulled her closer, kissing her with more authority. Again, she responded, hardly noticing when his right hand slipped between their bodies and moved to the lacing at the front of her bodice.

Her attention was riveted to his kisses, to his tongue plunging into her mouth, teasing hers, exploring the soft interior. Boldly, she dared to do the same to him.

When his right hand touched the bare skin of her breast, she started, but he held her, kissing her more passionately, the hand at her back sliding up to caress her neck beneath her hair, then to cup her head.

Fingers at her breast teased its nipple, and she moaned softly. He straightened, smiling, and said, "Your gown is in my way, sweetheart."

The breath caught in her throat when he eased the gown from her shoulders, but in less than the time it took to begin breathing again, the soft lawn slipped from her body to the floor.

Nicholas reached for her, murmuring, "My robe comes off too, sweetheart, just as easily. And this time, when you caress me, move your hands lower. I would have you caress me, even kiss me, where my desire for you is plainest."

Stiffening, Melissa found all sensible thought suspended. He seemed too large, too domineering, almost as if he had changed before her eyes to someone far more threatening.

She stood motionless, aware of an odd buzzing in her ears, a sense of separation, followed by the strange sensation of watching herself from a distance and a vague awareness that there were things in her past that even Charley did not know.

Only when Nicholas shook her did she realize he was speaking to her. "Answer me," he said sharply. "What's wrong?"

"N-nothing."

"Then why didn't you answer me? I spoke to you several times."

"I-I didn't hear you."

"Nonsense, Melissa, you are standing right here in front of me. You must have heard me. I want to know why the devil you're playing the tease again. You pretend to want my attentions, then reject them when they are offered. That is not how this game is honestly played, madam."

"This is not a game!"

"You make it one," he said flatly, "and you cheat."

"I don't!"

"You do. When one plays by one's own rules, that's cheating, plain enough. I have certain expectations as your husband, my dear, just as I would expect certain things of my partner in a game of whist. It is not acceptable in either case to begin play when you have no intention of finishing the hand."

"Everything in this world is not comparable to a game, Nicholas. *People* are not cards to play one against another."

"No, of course not," he said, "but don't pretend not to understand the elements of this game, because I saw you with Yarborne at St. James's, and I saw the way he looked at you. If you are thinking of complicating my hand by continuing to flirt with that fellow, you'll soon wish you hadn't. I am not a man you can safely cuckold."

Shocked to learn he would think such a thing but well aware that she dared not explain the real meaning of what he had seen, she said quickly, "It is not what you think.

Yarborne is naught to me but a nuisance, like a fly. And I can manage him, so you need not look murderous when I call him a nuisance. If I am polite to him, it's only because I'm afraid that if I am not, he might tell others about what transpired in Newmarket. You said that no one would dare speak after you had warned them not to, and I know Great-Aunt Ophelia agrees that I needn't worry now that I am married to you, but do you really exert such a powerful influence over Yarborne?"

He grimaced, and she saw that she had made a point. He said, "So that's it. Well, you are right in that I don't know him well enough to speak for him, or to be certain that my reputation will keep him silent. I daresay he believes his age would protect him from me. On the other hand, he is said to care deeply about his reputation, and those events don't redound to his credit. Has he threatened to speak of that night?"

"No," she admitted, "and perhaps I am foolish to worry. You are my husband, after all, and far more important to me, so if it distresses you to see me speak to him, I won't. I truly don't mean to tease you, sir, in any way. That is why I talked to Charley today. She agrees that I tease you, and says I have not been fair to you."

"Do you mean to say you spoke of such private matters with your cousin?"

"I did. I daresay I ought to apologize, but I won't. She told me to my face that I've been unfair, and when I'd thought about it, I knew that she was right. The trouble is, I don't know how to mend matters." Tears clouded her vision, and her throat tightened. "I don't mean to tease you, Nicholas. It just happens. Even when I think all is going well, and I'm stirred to . . . to ecstasy by your touch and your kisses, something happens to spoil it. I can't explain. I just know that when it happens, I feel as if I were another person, standing apart, watching us. That's what occurred just now. Truly, I didn't hear one word you said before you shook me. You must think I'm demented!"

His expression softened and his hands were gentle when he touched her shoulders again and drew her into his arms. "You are quite sane," he said. "That sensation of standing apart sounds unusual, I admit, but presumably it arises from no more than a crisis of nerves. In Newmarket, I wondered how you could expect me to believe you didn't recall that damned auction. Did the same thing happen then?"

She nodded.

He was silent for a long moment. Then he said, "Perhaps I have expected too much too soon," he said. "Though I've little experience with young, innocent females, I assumed that you'd take the same pleasure from sexual activity that I do. However, if your previous lack of exposure renders you uncomfortable, expecting you to respond with enthusiasm is as unreasonable of me as it would be to expect you to play whist well without ever having played it before. I've heard it said that many women of gentle birth never learn to yield easily in bed, let alone to enjoy themselves. I don't want that, sweetheart. Now that you've explained your feelings, perhaps I can help."

"How?"

He began to show her, but although he was patient and gentle, and although she tried to relax and enjoy his caresses, her earlier passion had abandoned her. Lying wide-awake beside him, long after he had fallen asleep, she decided that following Charley's advice was going to prove much more difficult than she had anticipated.

Nick was dreaming of Newmarket, of standing in the enclosure, watching his horses win race after race, when the scene abruptly switched and he found himself in bed with Clara. Not really in a bed, he decided, but floating on a soft cloud while Clara, ludicrously attired in the flowing white gown and gilded halo of an angel, caressed him. While her steady gaze held his, her hands, light as thistle down, slid over his chest, touching each nipple lightly, then moving downward, barely stirring the hair on his chest, or farther down. Her fingers felt like a butterfly's wings, skimming over the taut bare skin of his stomach, moving lower and lower. They slowed tantalizingly as they neared his awakening sex. Still, she watched him, her eyes fixed on his.

Her hands stopped, and her head dipped toward his chest. He closed his eyes when her lips captured one nipple. Her tongue stroked gently at first, then nibbled, stirring an awareness of danger within him that teased his libido and drew a moan from deep in his throat. Her little white teeth gripped harder, then released him, baring the nipple to a kiss from the chilly air. He stopped breathing, waiting, his desire increasing with each passing second until he felt her soft lips at the other one, teasing him again, tantalizing him, stirring his lust to unbearable heights. First came a soft caress, then the nibble, then a new caress. When she stopped, letting the air chill him again, he opened his eyes, intending to pull her back, to demand full satisfaction from the saucy wench.

Her face changed, and the white gown and halo no longer seemed ludicrous. The face was Melissa's, the halo a silvery glint of pale light on her hair. Perhaps, he thought dreamily, this was an omen, a sign that the Lord meant to guide his wife in a more proper direction. Nick smiled, thinking of what Melissa's outspoken cousin, or Melissa herself, would think of an Almighty with such profound consideration for manly needs. The Melissa of his dream did not see his smile. Her attention was focused elsewhere as she bent to kiss the straining nerve center of his needs.

At the touch of her lips, Nick realized he was no longer floating on a cloud, or even in his own bed. He was in Melissa's bed. He realized, too, that she was real and was really bent over him. The hands caressing his naked thighs and stomach were her hands. Her soft mouth enclosed the exact same part of him that Clara's mouth had enclosed in his dream.

Believing she was trying to make up to him for the night before, and not wanting to startle her, he kept still, slitting his eyes just enough to watch her through his lashes. Subdued light filtered into the bedchamber. Either fog still hid the sunlight or a bit of the dawn had slipped through a crack in the curtains. Most likely the latter, he thought. Knowing his habits nearly as well as her mistress did, Lucy would not expect him to have remained with Melissa until morning. He wondered if Melissa had thought of Lucy. Lucy would not knock.

Melissa's tongue glided over a particularly sensitive area just then, and thoughts of time and place slipped away as he closed his eyes in ecstasy. When he could think again, he realized he had been within aim's ace of begging her not to stop. To maintain the passive role was hard, nearly impossible, because such behavior simply was not in his nature. He suspected, however, that allowing her to take the lead would better serve his interests in the end, though it would not be long before she knew he was awake. At that very moment, she stopped what she was doing. Peeping through his lashes again, he saw that she was watching him.

He opened his eyes, hoping his smile appeared lazier than he felt. "Don't stop," he murmured. "That's wonderful."

"Is it?" She watched him, her curiosity open, like a child's. "Do you like that?"

"Don't talk, sweetheart." He could hear the strain in his voice. "Please, just go on doing what you were doing before."

Her expression turned impish. "What will you give me, Nicholas?" Teasing him, clearly enjoying herself now, she touched him with her tongue, lightly.

"Anything." He tried to make his reply playful, but to him, it sounded desperate. He refused to say more and lay still, struggling with himself, delighting in her renewed attention but wanting to touch her, to become actively involved in what was happening. He had never played a passive role in love-making. He preferred to take the lead. She stopped again, and he groaned. "Melissa, don't stop, for God's sake. Not now."

"But I want to stop for a moment," she said, her voice sounding sultry now. "My tongue is tired. Moreover, I like feeling as if I have some power over you. When you said a moment ago that you would give me anything if I would continue, I believed you. I've no doubt, sir, that I could ask for the moon, and you would at least promise to try to get it for me. Is that not so? Tell me." This time her tongue began at the base and moved in one long, sweeping stroke to the tip. "Say something nice."

He shuddered in a wave of pleasure. "My God, Melissa, don't stop again. You're driving me mad!"

But instead of continuing as he had begged her to, she slid upward, moving her hands and breasts tantalizingly over his belly and chest, while she continued to kiss him, her lips teasing him until he couldn't take any more. When she drew back, her eyes twinkling as if she were measuring his response, he reached up and caught her, pulling her down to him, capturing her mouth with his and thrusting his tongue inside. Giving her no time to react, he rolled her beneath him, holding her squirming body with one hand while he explored gently with the other to see if she was ready for him.

Finding her slick and wet, he positioned himself to take her but paused in that last moment before thrusting himself inside to savor her expression. To his shock, he saw that she was not writhing with passion as he had thought, but was struggling like a madwoman, her arms flailing wildly.

His lust disappeared in a blink and he rolled off, still holding her, seeing clearly what his passion had blinded him to before, that her eyes were wide with terror.

Her body strained almost to the point of arching, as if she

had frozen in place. Nick kept perfectly still, just holding her, but the look of terror did not fade and she did not relax. Remembering her description of feeling as if she stood apart from her body and watched, he said gently, impulsively, "Come back to me, sweetheart. You are safe now." He spoke in the same soft murmur he would have used with a trembling young racehorse. "You stirred the beast, Melissa, but he is tamed and quiet now."

He knew he was talking nonsense, and he wasn't by any means certain she heard him, but all his instincts told him to keep talking to her. He would never remember what he said in the next few moments, for he felt almost as if he were playing a musical instrument, watching her eyes and attuning his voice and his words to her slightest response. A new emotion stirred within him as he lay there holding her, an emotion deeper and more consuming than any he had ever felt before. At last, her body relaxed and her eyes focused, but he was not prepared for the first words she spoke.

"That's what he did."

Shocked, he struggled to keep his voice calm. "Who?"

"Papa."

A chill of rage raced from his groin through his midsection and upward till he feared he would burst, but despite an overwhelming, furious desire to murder Seacourt, he remembered that Melissa had been a virgin both when they met and on their wedding night. Keeping himself under rigid control, he said, "What did he do?"

"What you just did."

"I was moving to possess my wife, sweetheart, because she had enticed me beyond all bearing. Whatever else your father may have done, I know from my own explorations of your body that he never did that."

"Not as a husband does, no, for he said it would diminish my value on the marriage mart, but he did other things, horrid things, from the time I was small."

"Come here," he said gently, knowing just as he would

have known in dealing with a nervous thoroughbred that he must conceal his fury if he was to steady her and learn what he wanted to know. The gentle tone was not enough, however, for she pulled back when he tried to embrace her.

"You're safe, Melissa," he said in the same tone, forcing the rage away to a distant part of him, certain she would sense it otherwise and misunderstand its origin. "You will catch cold, sweetheart. Come closer, so you can get warm. I'll hold you."

This time she obeyed, lying stiffly beside him with her head in the hollow of his shoulder. He drew the bedclothes over them, gathering his thoughts.

She said in a small voice, "Are you angry with me?"

"I'm angry, but not at you. You've done nothing wrong. Why did you wake me as you did?"

"Because you asked me to last night, and I knew from Papa that men like it," she said, her voice so low now that he could scarcely hear her. "When he was angry, he would make me do that, and he would call me his magic girl, his sorceress, who could change him from a beast to putty in a child's hands. You liked it too, Nicholas, but when you said I had stirred the beast . . . Papa said that once, too, when he tried to enter me. I screamed, and it must have frightened him because he stopped and he promised it would never happen again. It didn't, but are all men beasts inside?"

He felt sick, but he said evenly, "No, they are not. Many of us are idiots, however, and some are knaves." He wanted to know more, but he was not sure if he should press her now or force himself to let it all slide into oblivion for her sake.

"It was my fault for stirring the beast," she said. "I-I had only to look at Papa in a certain way, and he would not thrash me. The other was horrid, but it was easier and less painful to withstand than a beating. It would happen anyway afterward, because he would apologize to me and then begin to stroke and caress me to show how much he loved me. I think that was when I first began to go into another place and watch."

Not certain how much longer he could restrain the urge to find Seacourt and beat him to a bloody pulp, it was with unmixed relief that Nick heard the sound of the door latch. "Come in, Lucy, come in," he said heartily when the little maid put her head round the door and stared in astonishment at them. "Before you bring our chocolate, throw open the curtains, and let's have some more light in this room."

She obeyed at once. He had not noticed a change in the light, but when the curtains were opened, sunlight poured in, spilling paths of gold across the carpet.

Sixteen

Nick Plays His High Card

Melissa, too, had welcomed Lucy's interruption, albeit not with the same unmixed relief as Nicholas. Though she had sensed his anger and frustration, and had recognized at least one moment of pure rage, his anger had not frightened her. She knew it was not directed at her.

Still, she was grateful when he did not demand more detailed explanations after Lucy left them with their chocolate. When she expected him to return to the subject of Sir Geoffrey, he asked instead if she would like to visit the menagerie at the Tower of London that day. Surprised but not displeased, she agreed with alacrity. On Saturday, he took her driving in Richmond Park, and on Sunday after attending church with his parents and Oliver, he hired a boat to take her to Hampton Court Palace.

Each night, he slept with her and held her in his arms, but he made no attempt to do more than caress her. He was gentle and kind, and she saw new sensitivity and tenderness in the way he looked at her, but she sensed a barrier between them and knew she was as much to blame for it as Nicholas was. More than once he seemed to hover on the brink of reopening the fateful subject, but he did not. They talked of many things, but most were commonplace, as if, like the barge that carried them to Hampton Court, their conversation skimmed the surface, unready to explore the depths.

She wished Nicholas would put his feelings into words. She thought he was being kind, and wished she knew him better, but each time she was tempted to generate more intimate conversation, the knowledge that she had no way to repay Yarborne stilled the impulse. Twice, she nearly confessed the whole, but she was afraid to spoil the growing bond between them. She believed now that she had loved Nicholas from the moment he took her away from the Little Hell, and she hoped his growing tenderness toward her might someday blossom into love. She would not spoil that chance by telling him what she had done and asking him to pay yet another hundred pounds on her account. There was only one thing she could think to do that might yet prevent him from learning what a fool she had been.

"Thank God you're here," Charley said, meeting Melissa in the entrance hall of St. Merryn House Monday afternoon, and dragging her into the nearest parlor. Melissa's mind was still fixed on her troubles, but she made no effort to resist. As she laid her whip on a nearby table and began to remove the wash-leather gloves that matched her pale yellow riding habit, Charley exclaimed, "They are driving me mad, the pair of them. If I don't end by murdering one or the other, I shall be extremely surprised. You've simply got to do something."

"What are you talking about?" Melissa had paid little heed to her cousin's words, and now, as she dropped her gloves onto the table beside her whip and turned toward the pier glass to remove her hat, she evaded Charley's sharp gaze.

"You came because of my message, didn't you?"

"No, I . . . I've been out riding." She could not explain that, after a long night and morning of wretchedness, she had come to St. Merryn House in hopes of begging a hundred pounds from Lady Ophelia, or that she had slipped out of the house and ridden for two hours in Hyde Park with only a groom for company, thinking. She had watched other riders, and people strolling on the green, until the clouds that had been gathering since late morning became truly threatening. Smoothing her hair now, she kept an eye on her cousin but continued to avoid meeting her gaze.

Charley said suspiciously. "You are not yourself today. Have you had a tiff with Vexford?"

"No, of course not."

"I don't see any *of course* about it. I've scarcely seen you to talk to since the Drawing Room on Thursday. Now that the Season is in full course, what with four and five engagements each night, one never has time for a comfortable coze. And it won't be any better this week, since Vauxhall opens tomorrow, and the Derby is Thursday, but I've scarcely seen you for days!"

Melissa was well aware of that. Having taken great care to evade her perceptive cousin even at the few evening affairs she and Nicholas had attended since Thursday, lest Charley demand a new report on the state of her marriage, it was all she could do now to say casually, "We have been amazingly busy, have we not? But you said that you had sent for me. What's amiss?"

Charley gave her another sharp look but said in a tone of pure exasperation, "Your father is up to mischief again, that's what, and he's been making Aunt Susan miserable, because she doesn't know if or when he means to charge her with bigamy. I don't believe he will, myself, for he abhors scandal as much as the next person does. Still, in the midst of it all, what must your step-papa do but set up a flirtation with some other woman. I daresay he is merely feeling his oats, but—"

"He is doing no such thing," Melissa said indignantly, looking directly at her at last. "You must be all about in your head to suspect such a thing of Penthorpe. He is mad about Mama. He would never—"

"Don't be a ninnyhammer, Lissa. All men do such things, and it must be rather flat for him always to leave Aunt Susan home when he goes out and about, which he does nearly every night."

"She would be snubbed if she did go with him," Melissa said. "People do not approve of divorced women, and they can be very cruel."

"Oh, yes, that must be it," Charley said sarcastically. "In fact, Penthorpe is so protective that he refuses even to take her to the opening of Vauxhall Gardens tomorrow evening. Everyone will be masked, Lissa. No one would slight her, for no one would recognize her so long as she left before the unmasking. It is, in fact, the first chance she has had to do anything that is the least bit of fun, since he has not made the slightest push even to take her to the theater again."

"Do you mean to go to Vauxhall?" Melissa asked, hoping her expression did not reveal her fear that Charley might somehow discover her assignation with Yarborne.

"No, for Aunt Ophelia means to play cards, and so I've cozened Rockland into making up a party to visit Astley's Amphitheater. I have never seen the equestriennes there, and since he is so determined to fling himself at me, it seemed an excellent opportunity to make use of him and do something I've really wanted to do."

"I'm sure you will enjoy Astley's," Melissa said, profoundly relieved. She could not even be sorry that Susan would not attend the gala opening of Vauxhall Gardens. Certain as she was that her mother would enjoy the outing, Melissa knew she would find it even harder to avoid Susan's eye than to avoid Charley's. It was going to be difficult enough—without their presence—to elude Nicholas, even for the short time she would require to meet with Yarborne. Even so, she said thoughtfully, "It does seem odd that Penthorpe refuses to take Mama to Vauxhall."

"He makes it sound utterly noble," Charley said. "He says he means to see her wholly out of danger of being incriminated, or of being cut by old friends, before he will let her be seen in company. Of course, I'll wager that he does not mean to miss the Vauxhall opening himself. Indeed, I think he must be going with you, for he mentioned being engaged with Vexford for the evening. It's all part and parcel of the way men have everything their own way in this world. No one casts aspersions on Penthorpe for marrying Aunt Susan after her divorce, only on her for being divorced from beastly Uncle Geoffrey. And Uncle Geoffrey is received everywhere! If Aunt Susan were widowed, heaven knows, she could do as she pleased. She could even take a married man as her lover, as long as she was discreet about it. But then, of course, if Uncle Geoffrey can be believed—which one takes leave to doubt—Aunt Susan is not a divorced woman at all, since she is still married to him under English law."

"But if she is not divorced, then she is guilty of bigamy," Melissa pointed out, "so her situation would be worse, and she still would not be received anywhere."

"Yes, and isn't that the maddest thing? Why on earth England should see fit to recognize a Scottish marriage—even if it is only a matter of a man and woman saying before witnesses that they are husband and wife—but refuse to recognize a Scottish divorce that was properly decided in a court of law, I shall never understand if I live to be a hundred."

"No, it does seem odd, but even Vexford's papa says that is the way things are. He says it will continue that way until a great many more members of Parliament demand that the laws be made equitable. In the meantime, I do wish Penthorpe would take Mama home before Sir Geoffrey can make real mischief for her."

"Yes, so do I," Charley said, "for I can tell you, I grow weary of their problems. I do sympathize, but what with Aunt Susan wearing a Friday face and refusing to speak to anyone when Penthorpe goes out for an evening, my patience is at an end. He looks guilty whenever one asks where he has been, or when he means to return to Scotland—or when he means to begin making all tidy for Aunt Susan, for that matter. His habit of procrastination and his casual air of doing exactly as he pleases quite make one want to shake him. The servants gossip, you know, and I'm certain Aunt Susan has heard things, for I have heard more than one rumor myself."

"What sort of rumor?"

"Oh, just things, mostly about his flirting. I'm sure the man cannot help himself. Most of them do it, and of course, since she cannot be with him all the time, and refuses to insist that he stay home with her instead of going out, she imagines the worst. He tells her not to worry her pretty head—that sort of thing." Charley's scowl made her opinion of Penthorpe's manner very clear.

"What about Aunt Ophelia?" Melissa asked. "What does she say about all this?"

"That your mama ought to make Penthorpe behave himself," Charley said, grinning. "Oh, you needn't tell me it's useless to give Aunt Susan such advice. Even Aunt Ophelia knows that, but she says your mama must rise above her weaknesses if she means to keep her husband and sort out her life. Personally, I think Penthorpe should just challenge Uncle Geoffrey to a duel and put an end to the whole mess."

"But duels are against the law!"

"Nonetheless, men fight them. Why, only last week I read that there was a meeting between the Marquess of Londonderry and a man named Battier."

"Well, yes, but nothing came of that. They both fired their pistols in the air. I assumed it was some sort of mad gesture, not meant to be real."

"They say that Mr. Battier's pistol misfired," Charley said. "He did not fire into the air on purpose, and if Penthorpe ever calls your papa out, his pistol won't misfire. Penthorpe was a soldier, after all, and fought at the Battle of Waterloo. I think it would be a good thing for everyone if he *would* shoot Uncle Geoffrey."

"Excuse me, Miss Charlotte," a footman said from the doorway, startling them both. "Lady Ophelia sent me to ask Lady Vexford to step up to the drawing room."

"Yes, of course," Melissa said, flicking a warning look at Charley. "We'll come at once." As they mounted the stairs together, she said in a casual undertone, "If Mama is sitting with Great-Aunt Ophelia, will you see what you can do to draw her away for a short time? I-I want to speak privately to our aunt."

"Of course," Charley said with a sympathetic smile. "I'll be grateful if you can help resolve this business, Lissa. I can't tell you what it's like, living in the same house with them. If only they would explain themselves to each other, I'm sure things would be more comfortable. But don't run away after you talk with Great-Aunt Ophelia. I want to enjoy some normal conversation with you."

Melissa made no promises, nor did she explain that her desire to have a private word with Lady Ophelia had nothing to do with her mother or Penthorpe. They did find Susan sitting with Lady Ophelia, but although Melissa greeted her with a hug, she was not sorry to see her go with Charley a few minutes later to look over the outfit the latter intended to wear to Astley's the next evening. When they were gone, she turned to Lady Ophelia, only to discover that elderly dame gazing fixedly at her. Summoning up a smile, she said, "Have I got smut on my face, ma'am?"

"More likely, it's apprehension on your mind, my dear. What's amiss?"

"Oh, dear, is it that obvious? I hope Mama didn't notice."

"She didn't. Susan's thinking only of her own troubles these days. If she would only . . ." With a gesture that looked as if she had waved the rest of the sentence away, Lady Ophelia let her words trail to silence, then said briskly, "I daresay Charlotte took her away on purpose. Since Charlotte saw your arrival from the window and ran downstairs at once, we'd been wondering what kept you below. I daresay now that you were concocting a way for her to draw your mama off. Can't say I think much of her solution to the problem. Don't think she's asked anyone's opinion of a dress since she came out of leading strings."

Realizing that her mission was not going to get any easier, Melissa blurted out, "Ma'am, I-I need a hundred pounds."

Lady Ophelia was silent for a moment, but her direct gaze did not falter. Melissa waited for the inevitable question, her heart pounding, her cheeks hot, still not knowing what on earth she could say to express her desperation without revealing the whole tale. To her shock, Lady Ophelia said calmly, "Yes, very well. Is that all?"

Scarcely daring to breathe, Melissa said, "Th-thank you, ma'am. I-I daresay you must want—"

"I cannot give it to you now," Lady Ophelia said, "for I do not keep such a large sum in the house, but if you will return tomorrow morning after eleven, I shall have it for you then."

"But don't you want to know—?"

"Do you want to tell me any more?"

Melissa bit her lip.

"Then you need not, my dear. Someday you may tell me, if you wish to do so. In the meantime, I choose to assume that you know what you are doing."

"I-I hope I do, ma'am. Thank you." Her throat ached, and she felt a nearly irresistible urge to burst into tears and cast herself down to lay her head in the old woman's lap. Instead, she collected herself and said quietly, "I won't stay, ma'am. Please tell Mama I will visit with her tomorrow."

Scarcely waiting for Lady Ophelia's dignified nod, Melissa slipped quickly down the stairs, through the empty hall, to the parlor, where she collected her hat, gloves, and riding whip. Then, casting a wary eye toward the stairs, half expecting to see her cousin lean over the railing to demand to know why she was leaving so soon, she let herself out of the house.

Somewhat to her consternation, she discovered that it had begun to rain. It was still little more than a heavy mist, but her stylish hat gave her no protection, and she knew she would be soaked before they reached St. James's Square. She said apologetically to her groom, "We are going to get very wet, I'm afraid."

"As to that, my lady," the man said, flicking a glance toward a pair of carriages drawn up on the opposite side of the street near the entrance to the square's central garden, "I were already told to get on home, but since I takes my orders from you—"

"Who told you to leave?"

"Ah, there you are, Melissa," Sir Geoffrey called, appearing from the far side of the front carriage and striding toward her.

Stiffening, Melissa felt an impulse to run back into the house. She repressed it, squared her shoulders, and said calmly, "Good afternoon, sir."

The front carriage began to draw away, and for just a moment, she saw a blond head framed in the window. An ornament on the figure's hat sparkled even in the gloom of the afternoon, and she was certain the occupant was Lady Hawthorne.

Sir Geoffrey said, "I recognized the Barrington livery on your man and knew you must be visiting here, my darling. I didn't want to intrude, but with it coming on to rain, as it is, you certainly ought not to ride home. I'll take you in my carriage."

Her hand tightened on her riding whip. "Oh, no! That is, if I require a coach, I can ask Great-Aunt Ophelia for hers, but I don't think—"

"Don't be nonsensical, Melissa. You will come with me. I've some things I want to say to you." He smiled warmly and shook his head at her, his expression one of fond understanding. "I know I've blotted my copybook, darling, but you won't deny your old papa the chance to mend things, will you?" When she hesitated, he said gently, "Tell him to go home, darling. You don't want the man to catch his death."

Making up her mind, she said to the groom, "Sir Geoffrey will see me home."

"Yes, my lady."

Watching him mount and ride away, leading her horse, she calmed her remaining unease with the thought that since the groom would tell anyone who asked that she had gone with her father, Sir Geoffrey would not do anything horrid.

He helped her into the carriage, gave the direction to the coachman, and climbed in beside her. "I like that habit," he said. "Soft colors always did become you best."

"Thank you," she said quietly.

Silence fell between them for several moments before he said in a conversational tone, "I hope you are happy, my dear."

"Yes, thank you."

"Vexford is not the man I would have chosen for you."

"I have met the man you chose."

He chuckled. "I daresay you will hold that against me till your dying breath, but indeed, I was desperate, darling. Yarborne likes to pretend to be a gentleman, but at heart he's a banker, and an unforgiving one at that. Recollect, too, that I scarcely knew my little daughter anymore. Is it any wonder that I thought of you as an asset first and as a daughter second? Would it help if I admit that what I did was unconscionable and that I know I have no reason to hope you might one day forgive me?"

"You've apologized before, only to do the same things again," she said, looking at her gloved hands, folded tightly around the whip in her lap. She felt uncomfortable, and wished she had not come. She certainly did not want to admit that she, too, now owed a debt to Yarborne. Oddly, however, she no longer feared her father.

He sighed. "You are right, of course, darling. I wish I could explain my behavior, but I cannot. When rage overcomes me, I become quite another person inside, one who hurts the people I love the best. If you believe nothing else, Melissa, you must believe that I love you." An odd break in his voice made her look at him. His eyes glittered, as if with unshed tears.

She wanted to touch him, to comfort him, to tell him she believed him. To her surprise, however, the feeling quickly disappeared. She said evenly, "Was that what you wanted to tell me, sir?"

He straightened abruptly, glancing out the window as if he did not want her to note his temporary weakness. His voice was controlled when he said, "That and to find out if you are happy. I hope Vexford treats you well."

"He does."

"Excellent. Are you enjoying your first London Season?"

"Yes, thank you."

He turned to face her again. "What have you enjoyed most?"

She found herself telling him about places she had gone and people she had met, talking more easily than she had thought she could with him. When she told him she thought the King was very fat, he said, "I recall once in Brighton, they had to use a hoist to put him on his horse. Nearly broke the hoist then, and he's much fatter now."

She laughed. "The poor horse!"

He smiled. "You and your cousin Charlotte always did care more about horses than people. Do you go to the opening of Vauxhall Gardens tomorrow night?"

"Oh, yes," she said. "I'm told they are quite spectacular."

"Yes, indeed. You will go with Lady Ophelia and Charlotte, of course."

"Why, no, sir. I believe Vexford means to take me."

"Does he, by God?"

His frown and the note of surprise in his voice made her realize that she had just assumed Nicholas meant to take her. He had not definitely said he would, but when one of his friends had said he would see him there, Nicholas had agreed that he would. Melissa realized that Charley's assumption that he meant to take her had reinforced her own belief that he would. Wondering now if she could have misunderstood him, she realized he might only have meant that he was going, alone. The past four days had been very unlike him. No doubt he longed to return to his normal pastimes.

Speaking carefully, so as not to reveal her uncertainty to Sir Geoffrey, she said, "You seem surprised, sir. Did you think Nicholas would not take me?"

"I think he shows damned cheek if he does."

"But why? I'm sure any number of ladies go to Vauxhall."

"Yes, but not— That is, there are circumstances of which I am aware that perhaps . . ." He grimaced, then looked at her ruefully. "I must ask you again to forgive me. I'd just assumed that he did not mean to take you. The fact that he does puts me in something of a quandary."

"Why?"

"My darling, one gentleman simply does not . . . uh, squeak beef, as they say, on another. That is to say—"

"I know what the phrase means, sir. Gentlemen don't reveal each other's misdeeds. But what tales could you tell of my husband?"

When he hesitated, she remembered the face in the carriage window. She was as certain as she could be that the face had been Lady Hawthorne's. Well aware now that her ladyship had enjoyed a certain relationship with Nicholas before his marriage, and remembering Charley's words about discreet widows but determined to ask no question that would betray either her knowledge or her uncertainty, Melissa waited to hear what Sir Geoffrey would say.

He seemed strangely unsure of himself, glancing at her, then away again, before he said, "Dash it, my daughter's happiness must come before any schoolboy notion of honor. I have it on excellent authority, my darling, that Vexford's attention might be—shall we say?—divided tomorrow night.

I don't know how to put it more plainly without sullying your tender ears, but I have been told that at a certain hour . . ." He let his words trail meaningfully to silence, watching her, looking very uncomfortable.

"I believe I understand you, sir," she said. She realized that if Nicholas had arranged an assignation, she would not have nearly as much difficulty as she had expected in slipping away from him long enough to conclude her transaction with Yarborne, but the knowledge provided no comfort. She wondered how, when the knowledge ought to bring relief, she could be so uncharitable as to want to strangle her husband for his unfaithfulness.

Sir Geoffrey turned the topic deftly to the weather, apparently feeling that her nerves required soothing, and she followed his lead gladly, having no wish to discuss the matter further. The drizzle had turned to a downpour by the time they arrived in St. James's Square, and the lackey who emerged from the areaway carried an umbrella. He ran to open the carriage door and put down the step, and Melissa said, "Do not get out, sir. You will only get wet to no purpose. The boy can see me to the door."

"Very well, my darling, but I hope we will see more of each other. I should be very sad if my past behavior has created an unbridgeable gap between us."

To her surprise, she was able to be frank with him. "Truthfully, sir, I'm still a bit wary, but I promise I won't offer the cut direct if you choose to speak to me."

He chuckled, reminding her again of his innate charm, and when he reached to squeeze her hand, she smiled at him. A moment later, ducking beneath the umbrella the lackey held, she ran with him up the steps and into the front hall, only to come face to face with her husband.

Nicholas looked stern. "Where the devil have you been?" he demanded.

Aware of the porter, the butler, and a maid dusting the silver salver that generally held the post before it went out,

Melissa said calmly, "Were you anxious, sir? I was gone a bit longer than I intended to be."

"A *bit* longer? You left this house hours ago without so much as a word to anyone about where you were going. You did not take a carriage, only your horse and a groom. I damned well want to know—" He broke off when she put a hand on his arm and shot an oblique, warning look toward the servants.

She said calmly, "Is the library free, Preston?"

"Yes, my lady."

Reddening slightly, Nicholas said, "Pour her ladyship a glass of sherry, Preston. She looks chilled."

"Yes, my lord." The butler signed to a footman who appeared just then from the nether regions to open the double doors to the library, and Melissa and Nicholas went in. Preston, entering behind them, went to a side table where several bottles, decanters, and glasses lay ready to hand.

A fire crackled on the hearth. Heavy dark-blue-velvet curtains hid the gloom outside, and candles flickered warmly in sconces set at intervals between the book shelves lining three walls of the room. The huge overhead luster remained dark except for dancing reflections of candlelight. While Preston poured Melissa's sherry and a glass of wine for Nicholas, she removed her hat and gloves, and gave them, along with her riding whip, to the footman. A moment later she and Nicholas were alone.

Eyeing him warily and hoping he would not press her for details, she said, "I am sorry you were concerned about me. You were up before I was, and I did not think you were at home when I left the house."

"I went riding with Tommy, then had breakfast with him. Where have you been?"

She set down her glass and moved to warm her hands at the fire, saying, "I rode in the park for a time, then visited Mama and Great-Aunt Ophelia."

"If that's all, why the devil didn't you tell someone where you were going?"

"I didn't know I was expected to. You usually don't tell me where you go or what you do, and if you give that information to anyone else, I never knew of it."

"That's different."

She glanced at him. "Why?"

"Because I can take care of myself."

"I see. You don't think that I can."

"I know damned well you can't, and don't change the subject. The plain fact is that you generally do explain your plans to someone, but today you did not. You slipped out of the house without a word to a soul."

Drawing a deep breath, she turned toward him and said, "I don't understand you, sir. You told me at the outset that you prefer women who look after themselves, who understand the rules of your game, and who don't need to be constantly coddled. Yet whenever I attempt to act independently, you become vexed with me."

He said flatly, "You misunderstood what I said. Though I may once have been attracted to certain qualities in certain women, I am not attracted to those same qualities in my wife. Your independence, as you call it, has so far led you to flirt with other men, to attend a gambling party, and to disappear for hours without a word to anyone. None of those actions is particularly sensible or safe. I protect my own, Melissa. You are not to disappear like this again. I won't say that you may not go out when you like, but I will insist that you tell someone where you are going when you do. And I hope I need not add that you are never to go out all alone."

"No, sir. I will try not to vex you again. Now," she added, moving toward the door, "If you will excuse me—"

"Just a moment."

She stopped, stiffening at the note of command in his voice. "Look at me."

She did, aware that her heart was beating faster. She said

carefully, "I would like to change out of my habit. I'm a trifle damp."

"In a minute. I collect from the fact that your habit is not soaked that Lady Ophelia must have sent you home in her carriage."

"No, but——" She broke off, wondering how much to tell him. He would most likely think her an idiot even to have gotten into a carriage with her father, and because of the need to take care not to reveal what Sir Geoffrey had said about Vauxhall, or to reveal her debt to Yarborne, it was hard to think what to say.

After a few tense moments of silence, he said with a grim look, "Never mind, Melissa, I will refrain yet again from pressing you to explain things you do not want to explain. But don't mistake my self-restraint for anything more. I am aware that you have misunderstood me in the past, so let me make myself plain now. You are my wife, and I expect you to be faithful. Don't give me cause to doubt your fidelity, or I will make you very sorry."

Fine words, she thought, from a man who had made an assignation with his ex-mistress for the following evening. The thought gave her courage to say sweetly, "In that case, sir, I will take care not to take so much as a step from your side tomorrow night without your express permission."

He looked at her blankly. "Tomorrow night?"

"We are going to the opening of Vauxhall Gardens together, are we not?"

"Oh, that. Yes, if you like, although I did assume that you had already made plans to go with Lady Ophelia and Charley."

"But I thought, from something you said before, that you meant to take me."

"Then I will do so, of course."

She escaped then, satisfied that although she had inadvertently stirred certain unfortunate suspicions, she had managed to lay them to rest again.

Her sense of well-being lasted only until her return from Berkeley Square the next day. Strongly aware of the presence of one hundred pounds in her reticule, it was with no little dismay that she encountered her husband halfway up the swooping main stairway. He was coming down, and he clearly saw her distress, for he demanded in much the same tone as the day before to know where she had been.

"Only t-to Berkeley Square again," she said quickly.

"Why?"

Her cheeks flashed fire, and she stumbled over her words. "Just v-visiting Mama and Aunt Ophelia. I must go, Nicholas. I'm already late for an appointment." She moved to pass him, but he blocked her way.

"What appointment?"

"Your mama's dressmaker is to measure the length of my domino for Vauxhall. I promised to be back here to try it on for her thirty minutes ago."

He said, "Well, as to Vauxhall, the reason I've been on the watch for you is that Drax will be in town tonight on his way to Epsom, so I can't take you, after all."

She had looked away, but she looked back at once, dismayed, and without thinking of anything but that he would cause her to miss meeting Yarborne, she exclaimed, "But you must, Nicholas! I must go, and there is no one else who—" Catching his gaze then, she broke off, silenced by the flash of anger in his eyes. Forgetting where she was, she stepped back, and would have fallen down the stairs had he not caught her. His grip was like iron.

"Please," she gasped with a familiar sense of rising panic, "oh, please don't!"

He released her instantly, saying in a tone much more gentle than any she had expected, "I won't hurt you, Melissa. You need never again fear that from me."

She breathed more easily. "A-and Vauxhall, Nicholas? Surely, you said that about meeting Drax just to tease me. Everyone we know will be going tonight."

"You won't, unless you mean to explain this sudden urgency of yours to go. Drax *is* moving my horses to Epsom, and he will be in town tonight, just as I said. So although I'll admit I mentioned it only as a wild cast to see what would turn up, I will meet him, and you will stay home, if I don't get an explanation." He waited, watching her. Then, sternly, he said, "Well?"

Much as she would have liked to demand a few explanations herself, she knew she could not, but neither could she do as he commanded. When she remained silent, he said, "Well then, that's that, isn't it?"

Seventeen

Pique, Repique, and an Opening Gambit

Nick dined that evening at Brooks's. He had hoped to find Tommy there, but when he did not, he dined with only his thoughts for company. They were not pleasant companions. A feeling had seized him, that he had overreacted to Melissa's reluctance to confide in him, and it would not be assuaged. Her behavior had been evasive for some time, but so had his own, he knew. From the moment she had told him about Seacourt, whenever he thought about what the villain had done, the rage surged up again and threatened to choke him. He could not even ask her to talk about it, fearing that if he opened the doors to his rage, he would no longer be able to contain it. Still he knew that she had been distressed for some time. Having learned about Seacourt, he thought he had learned the worst. Now he was not so sure.

He wanted to be with her constantly, to protect her. He knew he could not hover over her without making matters worse, but it galled him to think that the minute he had left her to her own devices, she had done something she did not want to discuss.

"Thought you might be here."

Looking up from his plate, Nick found his wife's stepfather

standing by his table, gazing pensively down at him. "Hello, Penthorpe. Looking for me?"

"Yes," Viscount Penthorpe said, glancing around. "Kept up my membership all these years because most of my friends are members, but dashed if Brooks's don't still feel just like a duke's house with the duke lying dead upstairs. Mind if I join you?"

"Pull up a chair. Footman, another bottle!"

Penthorpe lowered his lanky body into a chair, waited until the footman had poured his wine, then said casually, "You'll be going to Vauxhall tonight, I daresay."

"Sorry," Nick said, "but my trainer is moving my racers to Epsom by easy stages for the Derby Thursday, and he will be in town tonight. I've sent for him to meet me here at seven. You find me dining early because I've decided to go with him to Clapham afterward to have a look at them. They'll be stabled there overnight."

"Dash it," Penthorpe said, "I'm sure Susan and Charley told me you meant to take Melissa to Vauxhall tonight." Then, brightening, he added, "Look here, you didn't forget, did you? I'd understand that. Done it myself, frequently. The case is, you see, I told them I'd be spending the evening with you, and I've got to go to Vauxhall."

Deciding he was under no obligation to explain, Nick said only, "I didn't forget. I am definitely not taking Melissa tonight, but that needn't stop you from going."

"Well, it won't," Penthorpe said, adding with an engaging air of confidence, "Tell you the truth, I'm just as glad the lass ain't going. She'd be bound to tell her mama about seeing me there, and Susan's already out of reason cross with me because I won't take *her.* Said everyone would be masked, so no one would recognize her; but I ask you, don't you recognize nearly everyone you know, mask or no mask?"

"I do, and I take your point, but aside from the possibility that someone might insult her, don't you think your wife would be altogether safer back in Scotland? I can understand her wanting to come to London for our wedding, but now—"

"She misses the twins, but she don't want to look like she's running away," Penthorpe said with a sigh. "You know the whole tale by now, I expect. Fact is, we never thought much about Seacourt once we'd got settled in Scotland. It was on the trip down that I chanced to remember we'd never received word of an English divorce. Susan never knew it could make a difference, but I'd meant to look into it years ago. From some cause or other, I forgot about it before I ever got round to doing it. Never thought he could cause such a ruckus, though."

"How much of a ruckus?"

Penthorpe grimaced. "Fact is, he seems to enjoy tormenting Susan. Sends her little notes, or messages by way of so-called friends paying calls. Hints one day that he means to sue her for adultery or have her clapped up for bigamy. The next day he sends a charming letter, or a friend assures her he don't mean her any harm. Even tried to get me to pay him to leave her alone. I'd have done it, too, if I'd thought I could trust his word. Man's a beast. Ought to be put down, and that's a fact."

Looking at him just then, Nick thought perhaps Seacourt ought to give thanks for Penthorpe's habit of procrastination. He said, "I've some cause to dislike him, myself."

"I don't doubt that," Penthorpe said with a penetrating look. "I daresay young Melissa remembers a good deal about the way that brute treated her mother."

"Yes, she does." Nick did not know if Penthorpe knew about anything beyond Seacourt's brutality, but he had no intention of adding to his knowledge.

Penthorpe leaned forward, saying, "Look here, Vexford—no, dash it! You're my son-in-law now, or as near as makes no difference. Look here, Nicholas—"

"Nick."

"Right. Fact is, I'd be extremely grateful if you'd toddle

along to Vauxhall with me tonight. Don't want to make myself conspicuous, don't you know."

"No, I don't know. They say fifteen or sixteen thousand people will be there tonight. How could you be conspicuous?"

Penthorpe grimaced. "Well, you see, the fact is, Susan already suspects I've been . . . I haven't! Damme, I wouldn't, but I'm to meet with a magistrate, and—"

"A magistrate at Vauxhall?" Amused but skeptical, Nick raised his eyebrows. "Does this magistrate wear skirts, sir?"

"Now, dash it, you sound just like Susan—or you would if she knew anything about the magistrate. Thing is, a lady's going to present me to this fellow. She says he can grant Susan a judicial decree, protecting her against a charge of bigamy or adultery. Says a whole lot of people have told her it can be done, and she named I don't know how many magistrates who would see to it after a lot of rigmarole, but she says this fellow will grant it solely on the basis of our Scottish divorce. Must say it's the most sensible thing I've heard about the law since we came into England."

Suspicion stirring, Nick said gently, "I believe you mentioned a lady, sir."

"I did, and dashed if that ain't why I'd be grateful if you could see your way clear to going with me. I don't want to have to explain the matter to anyone outside the family, you see, and you're the only one in it who's in town, who ain't female."

"Forgive me for pressing you, sir, but just who is this lady of yours?"

"Dash it, haven't I just told you she's not mine? Closer to being yours, for that matter, from what I've heard, for it's Lady Hawthorne. Now, what have I said to make you look gimlet-eyed all of a sudden? I know your name ain't been linked with hers since you married Melissa or, by God, I'd have had a thing or two to say to you. Don't you believe she knows a magistrate who would be willing to help us?"

"Oh, I believe Clara knows all sorts of magistrates," Nick said. "I just don't know why she would exert herself to help anyone, let alone you. She is not, by and large, responsive to other people's troubles."

"Well, she's been most kind to me," Penthorpe said stiffly. "We've met several times this past fortnight, at different houses but always in the best company, don't you know. Still, I don't mind confessing, I'd as lief not be seen by some gossiping biddy whilst I'm traipsing around Vauxhall arm in arm with her, looking for her tame magistrate. Much better if I were seen with you, my son."

Better for whom, Nick wondered, trying to imagine how Melissa would react to learning that he had gone to Vauxhall without her. In truth, however, there were few people likely to bear tales of him to her, and there were clearly many who delighted in carrying tales about Penthorpe to Lady Ophelia or Susan. The *beau monde* was already talking about Susan, and he had heard tales about Penthorpe's flirting, too. Making up his mind, he said, "You'll have to wait until I've spoken with my trainer."

"I don't mind," Penthorpe said, heaving a sigh of relief. "Said I'd meet her between nine and ten, and there's bound to be a crush till long after eight, what with everyone lined up, wanting to see the new illuminations the moment the gates open."

Melissa sat alone in the countess's pleasant sitting room, gloomily looking forward to a solitary dinner. Nicholas had left almost immediately after refusing to take her to Vauxhall, saying he would dine at his club. Lord and Lady Ulcombe were dining with friends in Grosvenor Square, and Oliver had not put in an appearance for dinner in days. Unhappily suspecting that Nicholas was not dining at his club at all but was somewhere else with Lady Hawthorne, she had just reached the depressing conclusion that she would be more comfortable ordering a solitary tray served to her in her bed-chamber, when the door to the sitting room opened, and Oliver looked in.

"You alone?" he asked with a grimace of annoyance.

"Yes, and I am very glad to see you. I was just going to order a tray in my room, but if you mean to dine here, I'd much rather dine with you."

"Of course I mean to dine here," he said, stepping into the room and leaving the door ajar. "I must say, I think it's the outside of enough that everyone has gone out."

"Not everyone, Oliver. I am still here."

"Well, yes," he said, moving aimlessly about, "but you're not one who's been complaining that I never show my face around here anymore. My parents are leaving for Wimbledon Park tomorrow, then to Epsom for the Derby—and where the devil's Nick? Not that I really want him, mind you. I do much better without him, in general."

"He went out earlier," Melissa said, trying to sound matter-of-fact.

Oliver looked at her. "I say, are you moped? What are you doing here if everyone else has gone out? Ain't you going to Vauxhall? I thought someone said—"

"I did think we were going," Melissa said in a small, dignified voice, "but I was mistaken."

"I see." His expression sharpened. "Are you at outs with Nick? You can tell me. I'm frequently out of charity with him myself, but I always come about."

"Do you, Oliver?" She was not accustomed to confiding her troubles to anyone else, with the exception of Charley, who ruthlessly dragged confidences out of her. Something in the way Oliver looked at her led her to say, "In truth, sir, I'd welcome your advice. I'm afraid I did something foolish, and Nicholas is displeased."

"You might as well tell me all about it," Oliver said, taking a seat on a nearby sofa, taking care not to wrinkle his coat or pantaloons. "Since I've taken the trouble to dine here, someone might as well benefit from my presence."

"Well, I don't really want to relate any of the details, but—"

"Dash it, how can I help if I don't know what the devil you've done?"

"That's true. Have you really resolved your troubles? I know your papa—"

"We'll leave my papa out of this," Oliver said stiffly.

"That's just like a man," Melissa said. "You want me to reveal a lot of uncomfortable details about what I've done, but you don't mean to tell me anything about yourself. You're just like your brother, Oliver."

"No, I'm not," Oliver retorted. "What the devil do you mean by that, anyway?"

"I don't understand either of you, that's all," Melissa said with a sigh, "and I don't think I want to tell you my troubles, after all."

"You'll have to tell me if you want my help. For that matter, I'm a dashed sight easier to understand than Nick is. I'm a simple creature with simple habits."

"Expensive habits," she said, smiling at him.

He lifted his chin and said, "Didn't I just tell you, I've taken care of that. I won't go begging to my father again, that's certain, and I've never gone to Nick."

"You had enormous gaming debts, did you not?" Melissa asked.

"Not so enormous, and they're no concern of yours." When she did not respond, his eyes narrowed. "Look here, don't go telling me you're burdened by debts of honor. I know that females occasionally wager more than they should on silver loo and that sort of nonsense, but you can't have lost so much as all that."

"Well, if you must know, I did lose some money," Melissa said, "but it wasn't on silver loo, and that's not why Nicholas is vexed. I went out without saying where I was going yesterday, and was gone longer than I'd intended."

"You said it was foolish. That's just heedless."

"I know, but when it came on to rain, I let Sir Geoffrey bring me home, and I didn't want to explain that to Nicholas, because I didn't understand myself how it came about, but somehow he got a notion I was hiding something, and practically accused me of trying to cuckold him."

"What, Nick jealous?" Oliver laughed. "I wish I may see that. But tell me about this money you lost. I can't see why that would put him in a pucker. He's had a few debts of his own in his time, after all. You must not have explained—"

"It's not the money, anyway, because—" She broke off, certain she would be unwise to say more to him when she did not know if he could be trusted to keep silent.

Oliver regarded her shrewdly. "I see how it is."

"You don't! You can't possibly!"

"Plain as print. You've got a problem you're afraid to tell him about because you've stirred that damned temper of his by flirting or some such thing. Well, I fixed my problem, but I don't know how the devil to fix yours, if that's what it is. I certainly can't pay your debts. Mine are paid, but I ain't exactly rolling in lucre."

Seeing no point in gratifying him by telling him how close to the mark he had come, she said only, "How did you pay yours?"

"That, my dear, is none of your affair," he said loftily.

"Oh, Oliver, you didn't go to the moneylenders!"

"I did not," he snapped. "I've no intention of discussing it further. I resolved my problem, that's all." After another long look, he said, "Maybe you should speak to my father. He'll give you a scold if you were foolish, I expect, but he won't eat you, and like as not, he'll pay your debt without splitting on you to Nick."

"No, I'd rather tell Nicholas the truth than do that. Besides, I don't really need money. You're wrong about that part." Though she certainly meant to repay Lady Ophelia, the need was not urgent. To repay Yarborne was essential.

"Then tell Nick the whole," Oliver recommended. "I can't say how he'll react without knowing more about it—perhaps not even then. He's a deep one, is Nick."

"In everything," Melissa agreed with a sigh. "I never know what he's thinking, about me or anything else, and I don't know how to ask him about his feelings or thoughts, yet I'm nearly certain that he's . . ."

"You'll know what he's thinking if he ever loses that temper of his with you," Oliver said when she hesitated. "Lord, the way he's been squiring you about lately, not to mention this crazy jealousy you speak of, I'd have said he was nutty on you, myself. But if you can't be plain-spoken with your own husband—"

"Do you really think so, Oliver? That he's . . . that he cares about me?"

"He married you, didn't he?"

"Well, yes, but—" Unwilling to reveal her deeper concerns or feelings to Oliver, she said instead, "I find it hard to talk to him for the very reason you mentioned. He keeps his feelings deep. I suppose I must just try harder, but before I try to sort that all out, I'd like to attend to this one problem of mine. You say you resolved your trouble on your own, and I believe I could resolve mine if I were a man, but a female cannot go out and about by herself, and I dare not take my maid, or—" She broke off again when a thought struck her. The solution seemed too obvious to have missed. She looked at Oliver, wondering what he would say.

"What?" he demanded.

"You could take me," she said. "Oh, Oliver, will you take me to Vauxhall? I've been racking my brain, trying to think how to get there tonight. Nicholas h-had other plans, but if I am to resolve my problem, I must go to the opening. I promise I won't do anything horrid, and he won't know a thing about it. He's meeting Drax and doesn't mean to go to Vauxhall himself, and no one who sees me with you will think the least little thing about it, so no one will tell him. Oh, do say you will take me!"

"To Vauxhall?" He shook his head. "Don't think I can do that. Not afraid of Nick, even if we should meet him, but I promised to meet Rigger and some others at the Billingsgate at ten."

"But—"

"No, really, Melissa, everyone will be leaving town Thursday, if not tomorrow, for the Derby. I'm promised tonight."

"But not until ten," Melissa said. "Oh, please, Oliver, you could take me to Vauxhall and go straight on to join your party. I-I don't want to arrive before half past nine or ten, myself, and everyone will be masked, so no one will pay me any heed once I'm inside the gates. I'm bound to find someone who can escort me home later, or perhaps we can arrange for a coach and driver to collect me."

"Can't do that," Oliver said. "The road's bound to be jammed full of coaches for hours. Water's the only way to get there without being stuck in a line of traffic. You could pay a waterman to row you back, I expect, and that would be safe enough if our coachman awaited you at Westminster stairs. Of course, he'd be bound to say something to Nick or my father unless we slip him a few yellow boys to keep mum."

"Yellow boys?"

"Guineas. Pay him for his silence."

"I couldn't. That would be worse than anything. I'll hire a hack if I must, but truly, Oliver, someone will look after me. In point of fact, I'm mee—" She stopped.

"Meeting someone, are you? Look here, Melissa, if you are thinking of cuckolding Nick, I dashed well won't help you. For one thing, it ain't the thing to help my brother's wife give him a slip on the shoulder. For another, he'd murder me. Come to think of it, if he said you weren't to go tonight— Did he?"

"He said he wouldn't take me himself, but there is no one

else. Aunt Ophelia is going to a card party, Charley went to Astley's, and my mother does not go out in public. I'm not doing anything horrid. Oh, please, Oliver, don't say no."

"Very well, I'll take you, but if Nick cuts up rough, you've got to tell him you made me do it and that you would have gone alone if I hadn't agreed to help you."

"Oh, I will, I promise. I know his temper frightens people witless, and I wouldn't want him angry with you for this."

"Well, his temper don't trouble me for I don't heed it," Oliver said unconvincingly, "but I've certain important matters of my own to attend to over the next few days. I don't want to be distracted by one of Nick's little tantrums."

She repeated her promise, and dinner being announced shortly thereafter, they repaired to the dining room in complete charity with each other. After the meal, they retired to the green salon to pass the intervening time, and Oliver most obligingly taught her a few more ways to avoid being cheated at cards. The only discord between them arose briefly when he suggested that his friend Rigger might provide her with advice on how she might better understand her husband.

"Rigger's as sharp as he can stare," Oliver assured her. "He pays heed to how people think, you see, which is what makes him such a dashed fine gamester that *he's* never in debt. He'd understand how Nick thinks, if anyone can, and he'd have good advice on how to manage him, too. He's a knowing one, is Rigger. Only one he has trouble reading is his father. Does something he thinks will please the old fellow, and sure as check finds out he was wrong. He's always putting his foot in it with Yarborne. Of course there's nothing odd about that. Don't understand my own father from day to day. But Rigger is a knowing one, so—"

"If you please, Oliver, I'd as lief you did not discuss me with him."

"Well, I think you're missing an excellent opportunity." He said no more about Rigger, however, and Melissa was glad, for her opinion of his friend was not high.

Shortly after nine, Oliver drove her to Westminster Bridge in his curricle, leaving it in the care of his groom at the landing, to await his return. A slight hitch arose as they prepared to hire one of the twenty-foot water taxis, when he discovered that she expected him to pay the fare.

"Look here," he muttered indignantly, "you might have told me before you let me request a second oarsman."

She chuckled. "Oh, Oliver, gentlemen always pay for such things, so it never occurred to me that you would not wish to. Moreover, I heard the man tell you what the rates are. The extra oarsman will cost you only a shilling."

"That's a shilling each way, I'll have you know, which means two each for the oarsmen, plus another for the sculler. I wish I'd thought to drive to Lambeth Bridge, but we always go from Westminster. Have you no money with you?"

She thought of the hundred pounds in her reticule. Lady Ophelia had given her bank notes, and she could almost hear them rustle, but there was no reason to tell Oliver about them. Not only had she carefully secured her reticule to the sash of her gown beneath her voluminous pink domino, as a precaution against thieves, but that money was useless for the purpose at hand. Therefore, she said, "I have a few shillings, I think, but I might need them to get home again, so you will have to frank me now. Does one pay to get into the gardens, by the bye?"

"One certainly does," Oliver said with a groan. "Three and six if I remember correctly. Seems to me, they raised the rates a couple of years back."

"You seem very concerned about money," she said. "I thought you said——"

"You need not repeat what I said for all the world to hear," he told her, flicking a warning glance toward the nearest waterman. "It's just that I've better use for my blunt than to waste it on wherries and tickets of admission. Look here," he added, his gaze sweeping over the crowded river, "are you sure you can manage by yourself in that place? All London seems to have turned out for this dashed opening of yours."

Determined to see the matter through now that she had come this far, Melissa suppressed her own alarm at the size of the crowd, put up her loo mask, and said, "No one will know me from any other female. However, you can stay with me if you like."

"Not if you don't wish it," Oliver said. "If there were some way to warn Rigger and the others not to expect me . . . But there ain't. It's just that . . ." His voice trailed off again, and she could see that he was peering into the distance. He said, "I say, isn't that Lady Caroline Fiske and her mama?"

Following his gaze to a passing boat, Melissa saw a young woman whom she had met several times before, and agreed that it was certainly Lady Caroline.

"Well, that makes it all right then," Oliver said, relaxing. "They will have got through the water-gate before you pay for your ticket, but you'll catch them up quickly enough. I needn't worry about your safety if you're with them."

"No, certainly not," Melissa said, settling herself beside him in the wherry.

When the oarsmen maneuvered their craft alongside Vauxhall Stairs, she restrained Oliver when he would have disembarked and escorted her to the gate, saying firmly, "You will lose your wherry, sir. I'll be quite all right now. Thank you very much for bringing me."

He still looked doubtful, so she slipped quickly into the crowd, keeping a wary eye out for Lady Caroline and her mama. She felt oddly safe in the bustling crowd, but put up her hood and kept her loo mask in place even while she purchased her ticket.

Passing through the water-gate, she moved with the crowd along the lighted walkway past a colonnade and the entrance to the Rotunda, trying to imagine how she was going to find the statue of Milton by half past eleven. She could see that the gardens were larger than she had expected, because far ahead, beyond two temples marking the distant corners of the rectangular green, she could see more lighted walks and shrubbery. Water spouted high in the air from a large, circular fountain nearby, reflecting light from a myriad of lanterns. An orchestra played beneath a gilded cockleshell in the center of the green. Semicircular rows of patrons' boxes, filled with masked and costumed merrymakers, surrounded the orchestra, facing the green.

The music was stimulating, the laughter and merry chatter of the crowd around her were contagious, and suddenly she wished she were not alone. The night was meant to be shared with a friend, or a lover. She wished she were with Nicholas.

Since Yarborne had her watch, she had no easy way to know the time. She had hoped to find a clock tower, but not seeing one, she decided that she had better stop enjoying the sights and find Milton. Perhaps Yarborne would be early. She prayed that he wouldn't be late and that, if people unmasked at midnight, like they generally did at costume balls, she would be away from Vauxhall long before then.

Hoping the garden was not littered with statues, she decided to follow each walkway until she found Milton, and lengthened her stride to do so as quickly as possible. She was just passing the huge fountain when the sight of a tall, broad-shouldered figure some distance ahead, approaching the nearside temple, stopped her in her tracks. Even from the back, she recognized Nicholas easily, but not until that moment did she realize she had not believed for a moment that he really would be there.

Someone bumped into her from behind. "Take care," a feminine voice said sharply, "you're blocking the way."

Melissa had already begun to move forward, but as the woman pushed between her and the fountain's low rim, she caught a glimpse of sparkling jewelry and tendrils of blond hair beneath the hood of a domino almost the same shade of pink as her own. Impulsively, she said, "Lady Hawthorne?"

Starting, the woman turned, her features behind her lace-trimmed loo mask already composing themselves into polite curiosity. She said, "Do I know you? I'm dreadfully sorry if I seemed rude, but I'm in a tearing hurry to catch up with my party, you see. Won't you excuse—" She broke off, recognition dawning. "Why, hello, my dear. Have you misplaced your escort?" Her mouth twisted with wry amusement. "I must say, I didn't expect to see you here. Indeed, I was quite sure that Nicky— That is," she added in a more polite tone, "I've heard a vast deal about you of late, and I'd just love to become better acquainted with you, but I simply cannot stop now. I've a gentleman waiting for me, you see." Her smile broadened smugly, and as she turned away, Melissa saw unmistakable triumph in her eyes.

The look was too much. Melissa had always been quiet and reserved, and had never before in her life responded with violence toward another human being. But at that moment, in the face of Lady Hawthorne's smug look of victory, feelings she had never known she could possess rose up and consumed her. Without a single thought for the consequences, completely ignoring the crowd that milled around both of them, she put both hands out and shoved. Lady Hawthorne stumbled, caught her foot against the side of the fountain, and tumbled in with a mighty splash as a veritable cloud of pink satin billowed up around her.

Gasps and shrieks from people nearby brought Melissa to her senses. Aghast at what she had done, she waited for someone to accuse her but soon realized that in the swirl of nearly matching pink dominoes, no one had seen her push the woman. People exclaimed in dismay, and as several moved to help the dripping Lady Hawthorne from the fountain, Melissa melted into the crowd, wanting to disappear as quickly as possible, and wondering at her own effrontery. Remembering all the warnings she had received about her husband's temper, she knew she had not yet seen the worst of it. She wondered how long it would be before Lady Hawthorne carried this tale to his ears, and decided she had better find Yarborne before that happened.

Walking quickly past the temple, she kept a wary eye out for the tall, broad-shouldered figure she had seen earlier, but saw only men of average height ahead. She reached a broad walk lighted by hundreds of Chinese lanterns, and paused, unsure which way to go. Like the rest of Vauxhall, the walk was crowded, but most people were turning right. She went with the crowd, pausing a moment later for what she promised herself would be only a second, to watch a rope dancer.

"Clara?" His voice came from so close behind her that Melissa nearly jumped out of her skin. As she turned, she remembered that Lady Hawthorne's domino had been the same color as her own, and held her mask firmly in place. Knowing she was of a height with the woman, that the lantern light changed the color of her hair, and that her own, less buxom figure was concealed by voluminous folds of pink satin, she was not surprised when Nicholas went right on talking. "Where the devil have you been? We've well nigh turned this damned place upside down looking for you!"

Without looking right at him, hoping she sounded sultry rather than angry, she murmured, "Have you really, *Nicky?*"

"Yes, by God. Now— Melissa! Why the devil are you pretending to be—?"

She lowered her mask. "Pretending to be whom, Nicholas?"

"Never mind that. What in the name of all that's holy are you doing here?"

"I wanted to come."

"That's beside the point. I told you to stay home." When she glanced at an interested bystander, he added, "Come with me. I've a number of things to say to you."

"I know you came to meet Lady Hawthorne," Melissa said as he grabbed her hand and pulled her out of the thickest part of the crowd, "so you needn't pretend that I'm the only one who did anything wrong, Nicholas."

"I did not come to meet Lady Hawthorne," he muttered in an angry undertone, urging her back the way she had come.

"Yes, you did. I know you did. W-we don't need to discuss that, however."

He bent nearer and said with menace in his voice, "Oh, we will discuss it, but you won't say another word, little wife, until we are out of earshot of this crowd, or you will regret it. I don't intend to make everyone here a gift of my private affairs."

She shivered at his tone, but although she felt stimulated rather than terrified, she held her tongue. They walked past the intersection leading back to the fountain, and Nicholas guided her toward a less-populated, darker section of the gardens. When they came to the end of the broad walk, he turned to enter a walkway guarded by a looming, shadowed statue of a seated man. The path ahead disappeared in blackness.

Melissa stopped and dug in her heels. "Nicholas, no, wait!"

Eighteen

Black Knight Takes Pawn

Nick's anger vanished. He caught Melissa's shoulders in a strong grip, keeping his voice calm when he said, "You are safe with me, I promise. I told you before, I won't ever hurt you. We are only going to talk, and I don't know another place in this garden where we can have the smallest degree of privacy. I'd take you home at once, but I came with your stepfather and I seem to have mislaid him. I won't deny that we intended to meet Clara, but it was not for the reason you think."

"I'm not afraid of you," she said quietly. "When you're angry, at least I know what you are thinking." With a crooked smile, she added, "You won't deny that you *are* angry with me."

"No, I won't deny that. I'd like to shake you till your teeth rattle. What the devil do you mean by coming here alone? Or are you alone? By God, if I discover—"

"What's that statue?" she asked, staring at a point behind him.

He glanced impatiently over his shoulder at the large lead figure that guarded the entrance to the Dark Walk, and said, "Milton, supposedly listening to music. Never mind that. Did you hear what I said to you?"

"Yes, you'd like to shake me. I can understand that, but I

hope you won't. This place does give me the jitters, Nicholas. Couldn't we please go into the light again?"

"Yes, very well. I suppose we ought to look for your step-father. I can't think where he's got to." They began walking back toward the Chinese entrance.

She wrinkled her nose thoughtfully, then said, "If you came with Penthorpe, and you were not meeting Lady Haw-thorne yourself, he must have been the one meeting her. Charley said he was setting up a flirt, but I told her she was wrong."

"She *was* wrong. Clara beguiled Penthorpe into believing she can introduce him to a magistrate who can make every-thing tidy for your mother with the law. He hasn't told Susan about it, because he doesn't want to get her hopes up until he's arranged the whole business, or so he says. It's just as likely, of course, that he simply hasn't got round to explain-ing it to her yet."

"But Mama thinks— That is, Charley said that Mama sus-pects—"

"Your cousin is a great deal too busy, if you ask me," Nick said roundly. "She probably carried those tales to your mother in the first place."

"She wouldn't!"

"Well, I don't know that I agree with that, but we are not going to argue about Charley. I'm still waiting for an expla-nation of how you got here, and with whom."

"Th-there's Lord Yarborne," Melissa said.

"Don't change the subject," Nick said sternly, nodding to the older man, who walked past them unmasked and unac-companied. With a flicker of amusement, Nick saw Melissa raise her mask, then lower it again. He said, "Would you like me to carry that for you? I'd just as lief let everyone know that I'm here with my wife."

"Would you?" She looked up at him as if the answer were important to her.

"Certainly. Why not?" He took the mask, and dangled it

by its stick as he walked. "You continue to evade the subject, sweetheart. How did you get here? I seem to recall making it clear that you were never to leave the house alone."

"I didn't."

"Then where is your escort?"

She seemed reluctant to reply, so he stopped her and turned her to face him, ignoring the people passing them on both sides. Putting a hand under her chin, he made her look up at him, so he could watch her expression. "I want to know, Melissa."

"I know you do, but in fact, I have no escort now. I did have one, but I insisted upon entering the gardens alone. I-I had my reasons, Nicholas, truly I did."

"Yes, I know your reasons," he said, releasing her chin.

She seemed surprised. "You do?"

"Of course. You haven't made much of a secret of the fact that you came looking for me in a belief that I'd arranged an assignation with Lady Hawthorne."

"Oh." She paused, evidently trying to think what to say next.

"I have never thought well of jealous women," Nick said, still watching her.

"You . . . you haven't?"

"No."

She looked away. "I never seem to be much like the ladies you prefer."

He wanted to tell her that he liked her just fine, that despite his general distaste for jealous women, her jealousy stimulated him. In some odd, unfamiliar way it made her feel different from the way any of the others had made him feel, but he didn't know how to say that to her without sounding either odiously arrogant about his conquests or ridiculously maudlin. He was not a man who spoke easily of his emotions, and just the thought of trying to put his rapidly changing feelings for her into stark, ordinary words made him uncomfortable.

He said, "I can't think where the devil your stepfather's got to. We were looking for Clara, right enough, so she could introduce him to her magistrate, but Penthorpe said he would keep returning to the Chinese Walk so we wouldn't lose each other. I haven't seen him once since we parted company. Nor, I might add, have I seen Clara."

Melissa looked self-conscious, but she didn't say anything.

Believing that she felt remorseful for having wrongly accused him of arranging an assignation—as well she should, he thought virtuously—he held out his arm to her and said matter-of-factly, "We'll stroll back and forth until he finds us again."

She tucked her hand in his arm, but said nothing, and as they walked, she seemed to be considering some weighty matter. He realized he still had not received an answer to his question about how she had got there, and wondered if she was dreaming up something acceptable to tell him. Deciding she would speak in her own good time, he did not press her, and was rewarded a few moments later.

Looking up at him, she said, "There's something I ought to tell you."

"I thought so."

"It's about Lady Hawthorne. Most likely she will tell you herself, but I'd prefer to make a clean breast of it even if she does not."

She had his attention now. They had reached an intersection with the walk leading to the fireworks tower, and a crowd surged around them in anticipation of the midnight display. Finding a relatively private space near one of the tall hedges that separated the areas of the garden, Nick put Melissa between himself and the hedge, sheltering her from the others with his body. "What is it?" he said. "Tell me."

She hesitated, then squared her shoulders, looked up at him, and said, "You are going to be furious, I know, and indeed, I don't know what overcame me at the time. I just did it without thinking, because she made me angry."

"Clara?"

"Yes. She called you Nicky, for one thing."

He remembered then that earlier, in the brief few seconds when he had mistaken her identity, Melissa had addressed him in Clara's usual manner, a fact that he had not recalled until that moment. "Then you met her here! Whereabouts?"

"N-near the big fountain. Oh, Nicholas, I'm most terribly sorry, but I'm afraid I pushed her in!"

He stared at her. "You did what?"

"I pushed her. It was awful. No one even saw me do it. It happened very fast, so even though there were people all around us, they were all looking elsewhere, I suppose, and we both had pink dominoes on, and we were standing quite close, so it would have been difficult for anyone not looking right at us to tell what—"

"Whoa," he said, "pull up there, sweetheart."

"You sound like Charley," she said with a wan smile. "She always talks as if people were horses."

"Melissa."

She bit her lower lip, then said, "It's a dreadful thing to have done, I know, and I daresay you will demand that I apologize to her, but indeed, sir, I don't know if I can."

He couldn't help it. The laughter that had been threatening to burst from him ever since she mentioned pushing Clara into Vauxhall's famous fountain could not be contained any longer. "I don't believe it," he gasped when he could speak again.

She gaped at him in disbelief. "You aren't angry?"

He chuckled, the vision of the haughty Clara sprawled in the fountain as clear to him as if he had seen her himself. "Don't make a habit of it, sweetheart, but if I know Clara, she deserved it. I can imagine her tumbling into the water. I just can't picture my sweet, gentle Melissa pushing her. Oh, Lord!"

Her cheeks grew pink. She said, "Must we keep looking for my step-papa?"

He grinned. "I think I'd rather enjoy the fireworks with my wife. Besides, if he found Clara soaking wet, it probably never occurred to him to come find me before taking her home. Have you seen the Cave of Fingal yet, or the Chinese ballet?" When she shook her head, he said, "There is also a wonderful mechanical theater and something called a Cosmorama. Before we go a-wandering, however, we must watch the fireworks. They say an intrepid American gentleman is to make an ascent on a rope to the top of the Moorish tower. I'm sure you will enjoy seeing that."

They watched the American's ascent, which climaxed amid leaping flames of blue light and a volley of rockets, augmenting the constant din of fireworks and cheers. After the last blue light flickered out, Nick took Melissa to look inside the Rotunda, and then to the mirror-lined supper room and the picture room. Afterward they wandered along the South Walk, listening to the orchestra. When they reached the far end of the Dark Walk, near Fingal's Cave, and he drew her into the darkness again, she did not protest. He pulled her into his arms. Then, taking advantage of the fact that the crowd had thinned and the walk was temporarily deserted, he kissed her.

She responded instantly and enthusiastically.

A moment later, Nick murmured, "I think I'd like to go home now."

"Yes."

She snuggled against him in the wherry, and in the hack he hired at Westminster, when she rested her head in the hollow of his shoulder, he felt at peace with her, and comfortable. Despite what she had admitted doing to Clara—the thought of which brought another smile to his lips—his Melissa remained a gentle soul, a dove among the more predatory birds of the *beau monde*. Inhaling her lavender scent, recalling the way she had faced him, the way she had trusted him not to hurt her despite his anger, he recognized what he was feeling as an overwhelming desire to protect her from harm.

Inside the house, she did not protest when he picked her up and carried her to his bedchamber. Not a murmur about sending for Lucy, or warning Lisset. The latter had left a lamp burning low on the dressing table, and the bed turned down. Nick put Melissa down, untied the pink ribbon at her throat, and pushed the domino to the floor.

"Goodness me, I forgot!" Her hand clamped against something at her side, and for a moment he thought he had hurt her.

"What's wrong?"

"Oh— Oh, nothing, really," she said. "I-I forgot I had my reticule, that's all. I tied it inside my domino so I wouldn't attract a cut-purse. I needed it because of the admission cost, you know, and . . . and to get home again, if necessary."

He did not think she was being completely frank with him, but at that moment, he did not care a whit. "You've tied it to your sash. Shall I help you untie it?"

"Oh, no, I can manage." She untied it at once, and set it casually on a side table.

He thought she looked reluctant to leave it there, but she turned to him while the thought was still half-formed in his mind, and tilted her face up, silently inviting him to kiss her. He did. His fingers made quick work of the rest of her clothing, and his own. To his delight, she responded as she never had before, relaxing, allowing him to explore her body with his hands and lips, then following his guidance without the slightest sign that she was not fully enjoying herself, until they both were exhausted.

They lay for some moments in silence. At last he said in a teasing tone, "Don't think I've forgotten that you never revealed the name of your companion tonight, sweetheart. If you tell me it was Oliver who escorted you to Vauxhall and then left you at the gate, I swear I'll throttle him."

"Then I certainly won't tell you it was Oliver," she murmured sleepily.

When Melissa awoke the following day, she was astonished to learn from the clock on Nicholas's dressing table that she had slept into the afternoon. She was alone. Not only had Lisset not disturbed her, no one had. Wondering where her husband was, she glanced uneasily at the reticule sitting where she had put it the night before. It looked as if it had not been moved, and she did not think Nicholas had looked inside. Surely, he would have wakened her and demanded to know what she thought she was doing, carrying a hundred pounds to the Vauxhall opening.

She had missed her opportunity to redeem her bracelet-watch, but Yarborne knew that Nicholas had prevented the meeting, and thus—she hoped—would not immediately reveal her debts to him and demand payment.

Thinking about the previous night, she wondered if her fear that Nicholas would look in her reticule had motivated her determination to please him. Fear of one sort or another had inspired her behavior before now, she knew, but she did not think her actions the previous night fell into that category. She had never guessed that intimate relations could be so pleasant, so enjoyable. Thinking of Sir Geoffrey, she realized that she had known, both from her disbelieving reaction at seeing Nicholas and from his assurances later, that her father had lied to her about an assignation, but she felt no anger. Sir Geoffrey Seacourt had lost all power to control her thoughts or feelings.

Suddenly, she wanted to find her husband, just to be with him. She hoped he had not gone out. Going into her bed-chamber, she rang for Lucy, who arrived a few moments later, bearing a tray with bread, cheese, and a pot of tea.

"His lordship said you was to eat something, my lady," Lucy said. "Lady Ulcombe wanted to rouse you when she ordered luncheon, but his lordship—my Lord Vexford, that is—said you was to sleep till you woke natural. Still, he said you weren't to starve, and it's my head as will be on the platter if you don't eat this, ma'am."

"I'm perfectly willing to eat, Lucy, thank you." Munching and sipping from time to time while Lucy arranged her hair, Melissa then chose an afternoon frock of azure muslin and dressed with care but without wasting time. As soon as she was fit to be seen, she draped a light shawl around herself and went downstairs.

Finding only servants in the drawing room, the green salon, and the hall, she walked into the library through the open door to discover her husband, talking with his father. A footman hovered nearby, as if awaiting orders.

"Oh, I beg your pardon," she said. "I didn't know—"

"Come in, Melissa," Nicholas said, his tone so grave that she thought instantly that he must have looked into her reticule, after all. Ulcombe, too, was looking unnaturally solemn. Only her habit of silence in the face of danger kept her from bursting into explanation. "Sit down," Nicholas said, drawing a chair forward for her.

"I-I think I'd prefer to stand, sir," she said.

Ulcombe said, "Look here, Nick, you're frightening her witless, and we've no reason to think there's any cause for that. Not yet, at all events."

Melissa looked at the earl, all thought of the evidence in her reticule dissipating like smoke. "What is it? Not Mama! Aunt Ophelia? Oh, please, tell me, Nicholas. Don't try to spare me. I can't stand the wondering!"

"Penthorpe didn't get home last night," he said flatly.

"What?"

"A runner just brought word to us from St. Merryn House." He gestured toward the footman. "I was about to send Silas to have Lucy waken you. We'll send him up to fetch a cloak for you instead."

"I don't need a cloak," she said. "I have my shawl. Oh, can we go at once?"

He looked as if he would insist upon the cloak, but Ulcombe said, "I've ordered you a carriage, my dear. I can't go along, because my chaise is at the door and I'm just waiting for her ladyship to attend to some last-minute details before we leave for Wimbledon Park. Nicholas will look after you, of course, and Wimbledon is only six miles from London, so we can return in a trice if you need us. Not that there can be any cause for alarm yet. For all we know, Penthorpe just—" He broke off, as if he realized that what he was about to say was tactless.

Melissa said, "You think perhaps he overslept like I did, sir—only in someone else's bed? I can assure you that he didn't. As I keep telling everyone, Penthorpe adores Mama. He would never do what you suspect."

To her astonishment, however, she learned soon after she and Nicholas arrived in Berkeley Square that Susan was not nearly so confident of Penthorpe's fidelity.

They found the three ladies in the drawing room, and although Susan greeted Melissa with a hug, tears clung to her lashes. She said, "He has behaved so oddly since we came to London that there's no telling what he has done, and you don't know the whole. That dreadful woman has disappeared, as well."

Melissa stared at her. "What dreadful woman?"

Charley turned from greeting Nicholas and said, "I told you how it was, Lissa. It's that glitter and gilt woman. What's her name?"

Melissa said only, "How can you know she's disappeared, ma'am?"

Susan turned bright red, but after a pause during which she visibly struggled with her sensibilities, she said, "I awoke soon after midnight, you see, and couldn't sleep. I waited and waited, and when he still had not returned by ten this morning, I was frightened. I had to know he was safe, so I-I sent a message to that woman to ask if she had seen him. But the footman returned without delivering it. He said he could not do so, because her ladyship is out of town. Oh, Melissa!"

"But, Mama, Penthorpe is not having an affair with her!" She explained about the magistrate and the writ, whereupon Susan burst into tears.

Lady Ophelia, who had been listening to them from her favorite chair, banged the tip of her cane on the floor and said, "Now, Susan, that will do. You did what you could, and surprised me mightily, I might add, by showing such unaccustomed spirit. Don't spoil it now by flying into alt. The man most likely just didn't get around to coming home. Put it off, like he does, and now he thinks he might just as well visit his tailor or his bootmaker first. He'll turn up, you'll see."

Susan was not consoled, but less than an hour later, as they sat discussing various courses of action, the drawing room door opened with a snap. Penthorpe stood on the threshold, looking rather the worse for wear.

"Hallo, ducky," he said to Susan. "Miss me?"

She flew into his arms. "Oh, where have you been? I've been sick with worry!"

"There, there," he said, patting her and stepping into the room.

Melissa, staring at his tattered clothing, said, "What happened to you, sir?"

"Yes," Charley exclaimed, "what on earth happened? You look as if you'd been dragged through a bush backward. And where's La—"

"Charlotte, hold your tongue," Lady Ophelia interjected sternly. "Penthorpe will answer our questions in his own good time. At the moment, I'll wager, he'd like a glass of something to restore him, and a chance to make himself more presentable."

"Damme, so I would," the viscount said, "and I'll take the

glass of something first if you don't mind. You, there," he added to the footman standing solemnly in the doorway, "stop your gaping and fetch me some good Scotch whisky. My throat's as dry as dust. If you won't take offense at my appearance, ma'am," he said to Lady Ophelia, "I'll explain what happened before I go up to change." When she nodded regally, he said bluntly, "I was abducted, that's what happened."

Everyone exclaimed in dismay, but Melissa saw that Nicholas was eyeing her stepfather narrowly. She could not blame him. Penthorpe's explanation seemed preposterous. However, once he had sat down and accepted a glass of whisky from the footman, he began to tell his tale. Soon everyone, including Nicholas, was spellbound.

"I got separated from Nick at Vauxhall," Penthorpe began glibly, avoiding his wife's gaze. "Stepped outside the gate for a moment, to see if he'd gone looking for me, don't you see, and dashed if someone didn't cosh me over the head and fling me into a carriage. By the time I came to my senses, I was miles from London—somewhere between Baldock and Newmarket, I think."

"Not simple robbery, then?" Nicholas asked.

Penthorpe shot him a look but said only, "No, didn't even search me. I can tell you, I wished more than once that I had my pistol by me. It was lying useless in my bedchamber, but I'll wager most men don't carry pistols around London nowadays."

"They don't," Nicholas agreed. "I keep mine in my bedchamber, too, when I'm in town, or locked in my gun room, but your villains might well have found your pistol if you'd had one."

"I doubt it. They didn't even take my purse, which was a dashed fortunate circumstance, although I believe they just didn't think to take it before I got away."

Melissa said, "But how did you manage that, sir?"

At the same time, Charley said, "I want to know about Lady—"

Lady Ophelia snapped, "Be silent, Charlotte. If you cannot sit quietly and listen, then we will be happy to excuse you from the room."

"Damme, but that's an excellent notion," Penthorpe said, glaring at Charley.

"Please, sir," Melissa said gently, "tell us what happened next."

"Employed a ruse," he said, smiling at her. "Dashed clever one, too, if I do say so, although I admit those fellows— common ruffians, they were—weren't the sharpest pair in the world. They must have counted on their size and intimidating nature to ensure my silence, for when they got hungry, they decided to take their meal at a common roadside tavern. Afraid to leave me, so they threatened to murder me if I gave them grief, and took me right in with them. The place was not any sort of place that caters to the gentry. Filled with tough-looking scoundrels, by and large."

With a visible shiver, Susan moved to sit on a stool at his feet. Tucking her hand in his, she said, "It is a wonder they didn't murder you."

"Aye, it is," he agreed, smiling at her and squeezing her hand, "but as you know from experience, my pet, it's not as easy as some think to put a period to my life."

Seeing Charley open her mouth to speak again, Melissa said quickly, "But what was the ruse, sir?"

Penthorpe grinned. "Told you the place was filled with rough sorts," he said. "Two louts sitting at a corner table looked over at my little group, and were clearly talking about us. Doubtless they were astonished to see a gentleman in company with that sorry pair, but I nodded at them and smiled. When the larger of my two oafs demanded to know what I was about, I said I had just given a signal to my friends that they were not to spare my captors." He chuckled. "Told them the other pair were my bodyguards and had been following us, according to orders. Those orders, I added ever so casually, included not just rescuing me at the first opportune moment, but dispatching my captors as soon as such action became expedient."

Nicholas raised his eyebrows. "Expedient?"

Penthorpe chuckled again. "Had to explain to them what it meant. To their credit, they did not require more than the barest definition. I said if they left at once, leaving me unharmed, my men would merely see to it that they did not try to capture me again. When they left the inn—at some speed, I might add—I went over to the other table and dropped two yellow boys on the table. When they demanded to know what I was about, I said I was working for the Bow Street magistrate. Said I was tracking thieves, and that the pair I'd been with were likely to lead me to a nice reward, which I would share with them if they were able to tell me where the lads went next."

"Well done," Lady Ophelia said, nodding. "Very clever of you, indeed."

Susan's eyes widened. "Those men won't come here, will they?"

"No, ducky. I told them to seek me at Bow Street. Since they looked like a pair of thieves themselves, however, I think they'll avoid that place like the plague. Still, I'll trot round this afternoon and have a talk with the folks there, just in case they do learn something about my captors. Since they are likely to duck into the first bolt-hole they come to and stay there, I doubt they'll trouble us." He drained his glass and stood up, adding, "I'd best get tidied up. Then I can take my beautiful wife for a drive in the park, and put some color back in her cheeks. Why don't you come along upstairs with me, Nick, my boy. Like to apologize properly for abandoning you last night."

Nicholas got up at once, and Melissa, seeing that Susan intended to go with them, said, "Mama, if you are going to drive in the park, you'll want to fetch a pelisse or a cloak, and put on your bonnet. I'll go with you to your bedchamber, shall I? I've seen much too little of you since you came to London."

Susan hesitated, then smiled and said, "Oh, yes, darling, do come with me."

"I'll come, too," Charley said, getting to her feet.

"Oh, no, you will not," Lady Ophelia said. "You will remain here with me, miss. I've got a thing or two to say to you."

Going upstairs with her mother, Melissa felt a twinge of sympathy for Charley. She was not the only one who wanted to learn what Penthorpe knew about Lady Hawthorne's disappearance, but Lady Ophelia was unlikely to spare her a peppery rebuke for so small a reason as that.

Alone with Penthorpe in the little room he used for his dressing room, Nick said, "What the devil really happened? You weren't just wandering aimlessly about."

Just as bluntly, Penthorpe replied, "The only bit I left out was Clara. Met the wench looking as if she'd tried to swim the Thames in her gown and domino. She was drenched, but she wouldn't tell me how it happened. My guess is she fell into that damned fountain. Ought to know better than to put such a thing so near the walkway."

"But what had Clara to do with your adventure?"

"Asked me to find her a hack, so she could go home at once. Told her she'd get home quicker with the watermen, but she said she'd catch her death on the river and insisted on a hack. Either way, of course, she wanted to go in the opposite direction from where I'd left you. Couldn't see dragging her along to find you, so I did as she asked. Only trouble was, we no sooner got out to the road than she said she saw a friend's carriage. Before I could stop her, she scuttled over to the darker part of the road, and that's the last I remember till I came to in a carriage that smelled too much of onions and other less palatable things to have belonged to any friend of Clara's. The rest happened as I described it. I don't mind telling you that if my made-up bodyguard does happen to track those villains to their principal, I won't be sorry."

"Do you have any idea who that might be?" Nick kept his tone casual, but he watched the other man closely.

Penthorpe grimaced. "I didn't have a clue at first," he said, "but when I came to my senses, I did expect Clara to be there with me. When she wasn't, and the louts insisted they didn't know any gentry mort like her, I began to think she must have had something to do with it. Later, I realized that she might have been hurt when they abducted me. Either way, once I'd returned to town and collected my rig from the stable near Lambeth Stairs where we left it last night, I decided I'd best look in on her. You needn't mention that to Susan, however."

"I won't. She knows about Clara."

"That Charley wants thrashing," Penthorpe said sourly, "but if Susan already knows about Clara and the magistrate, I'll have less to explain now, won't I?"

"It was your own fault, not Charley's, that she suspected a flirtation between you and Clara," Nick said brutally, "and Melissa told her about the magistrate. There's one more thing you won't like, too. Susan sent a message to Clarges Street earlier today."

"Did she, by God?"

"Yes, and they told her messenger that Lady Hawthorne had gone out of town."

"Well, if she did, then that damned Seacourt has free run of her house."

"Would you care to explain that?"

"Saw him myself as I drove into Clarges Street. He was on the stoop, the door opened, and he walked right in. Saw him as plain as day. Decided Clara was fine and healthy, and came straight here. Now, need I say what I suspect?"

"No, for it's what I suspected myself. Not that she had arranged an abduction, but that she was involved in your disappearance, and that somehow Seacourt was behind the whole affair. I own, I'm surprised to see Clara mixed up in something like this. Seacourt may be able to charm women, but I'd not have expected him to sway someone as wily as Clara."

"Well, I don't know about that," Penthorpe said. "Like I said before, the man's dangerous and ought to be put down."

Nick nodded vaguely. He found it hard to believe that he had underestimated Clara. His perception of other players was not generally so misguided.

When Penthorpe had changed his clothes, they rejoined the others downstairs. Susan seemed much happier, but Charley looked chastened, and Melissa said at once that she was ready to return to St. James's Square. They made their farewells and went down to the street.

In the carriage, Nick braced himself for questions, but when Melissa remained silent, he turned his thoughts back to what Penthorpe had told him. Remembering how angry Clara had been when he had first broken with her, he began to think it more likely that she might have joined league with Seacourt. Though he exchanged a few comments with Melissa along the way, his thoughts continued to return to potential ramifications of such a partnership until the carriage drew up before Barrington House.

When they entered the hall, a footman handed Melissa a note, and Nick saw that she looked startled to receive it. Although he wanted to ask her about it, he would not do so in the servant's presence, and when Preston spoke to him, he turned to reply. When he turned back, she was hurrying up the stairs. Tempted though he was to follow her, it occurred to him that although he could question her any time about her message, it might be a good idea to ask someone else a few home questions before that person had time to concoct a tale more palatable than the simple truth.

Nineteen

White Queen in Jeopardy

Melissa stared at the note the footman, Silas, had handed to her. The bold, black, masculine script seemed to leap out at her, the stiff expensive paper to burn her fingers. Realizing that Silas waited patiently for her instructions, no doubt wondering why she hesitated to open her message, she glanced over her shoulder and saw with relief that Nicholas was talking with Preston.

Smiling at the footman, she said quietly, "There will be no reply, Silas. I'll just take this upstairs with me." As heat surged into her cheeks, she decided she was making a bad situation worse and hoped he would not suspect her of having taken a lover. Remembering how casually Oliver had suggested telling his friend Rigger about her difficulty understanding Nicholas, and putting no faith in her young brother-in-law's discretion, she realized that rumors could easily get back to her husband that would seem to support any unfortunate suspicions stirring within the household.

Silas seemed to notice nothing amiss, however, for he merely bowed and murmured, "Yes, my lady."

Glad to escape her husband's sharp eyes, Melissa took advantage of his conversation with the butler to hurry up the stairs, waiting only until she had reached the privacy of her bedchamber before breaking the seal and opening the letter.

Her heart thumped wildly even before she saw the scrawled initial *Y* at the bottom. She had known from the moment Silas handed it to her who the sender must be.

"Madam," the note began, *"you have disappointed me once. That must not happen again. If you do not come to my flat at Number 37 Jermyn Street, directly opposite the rear of St. James's Church, this afternoon at four o'clock, you will leave me no choice but to present your vowels to your husband at five for payment. I cannot think you want that to happen. I shall post a servant at the street door to await your arrival, so that you need speak to no one else. Four o'clock, madam. No later."*

Yarborne had been very sure of her, she thought, to sign the message with no more than his initial, but she could not doubt that he had sent it. The situation terrified her. Her relationship with Nicholas had grown so delightfully friendly, and showed every sign of running smoothly at last, but Yarborne could ruin everything. Any chance was worth taking to avoid that, even the chance of meeting him privately. Moreover, he left her no choice.

Glancing hastily at the small ormolu clock on her dressing table, she saw that its gilded hands indicated some minutes after three. Jermyn Street was but a short distance away, and she had been to more than one service at St. James's Church. Though the church faced Piccadilly, they had generally entered through the churchyard from the rear, on Jermyn Street, but she was by no means certain she would find Number 37 as easily as Yarborne expected. Reaching to ring the bell, intending to summon Lucy, she paused when her hand touched the cord, then drew it back, realizing that if she did not want to stir gossip, she could trust no one.

Turning back to examine her reflection in the cheval glass, she decided that the azure muslin dress she had worn with her light shawl to St. Merryn House was insufficient for a visit to Yarborne. The neckline was too low, for one thing. Remembering that Lucy kept kerchiefs in one of the lavender-scented drawers of the dressing table, she quickly found one with a deep, falling frill that would leave no bare skin showing. When she had tidied her hair, she donned a Pomona green pelisse and a black hat with a Mary Stuart brim, trimmed with pink roses and greenery to match the pelisse. Drawing on a clean pair of white kid gloves, she took a last look in the glass.

Plate armor, she decided, would be more practical for such a visit. Picking up her reticule, she looked inside to be sure the money Lady Ophelia had given her was safe. The sight of it reminded her of the precautions she had taken when she carried the money to Vauxhall. Walking along the street, she could conceal her reticule as she had the previous night, under her pelisse. What concerned her was the private flat that Yarborne apparently kept, despite owning the large house in Bedford Square. Given such a setting, she had a strong notion that Yarborne might prove much more dangerous to her than any common thief.

Hastening into Nicholas's room, praying that since he had not followed her upstairs at once, he would not come up at all, she began quickly to search through his drawers until she found what she had hoped to find. She did not know if the little pistol was loaded, and concealing it was not as easy as it had been to conceal the reticule beneath her domino the previous night. In the end, she was forced to exchange the pretty reticule that matched her pelisse for a larger, less attractive one that would accommodate the weapon, but she did so without the smallest twinge of regret. She had not used the larger bag since coming to London, and it still contained several of the lavender sachets she habitually put amidst her clothing, but although the thought of a lavender-scented pistol made her smile, she did not take the time to turn them out.

Not until she was hurrying toward the main stairs did she realize that leaving the house without being hindered might prove difficult. She could not order a hackney carriage because, with no fewer than six town carriages at her disposal, the servants would think her mad. If she were to declare her intention to walk, Silas, Preston, or the porter would insist upon providing her with proper escort, and more daunting than all the rest was the possibility that she might still encounter Nicholas downstairs. In effect, she decided, she could not leave by the front door if she wished to go alone.

Hoping no servant would have cause to use the northeast service stairs at such an hour, she whisked herself across the main stair hall, through the countess's sitting room to the anteroom behind it. Pausing there to listen carefully, and hearing no sound, she tiptoed down the stairs to the side door that led into an area between the rear of the house and the archway to the square. Keeping watch for any link boy or stable lad who might betray her, she hurried to the north end of the square, but not until she had turned into the narrow confines of York Street did she believe her escape had been successful.

Nick paced impatiently in the narrow entrance hall of Clara's house, where her butler had left him to kick his heels while he went to discover if her ladyship would receive him. When Nick had protested, assuring the man that she would, and demanding to know where she could be found so he could go straight up to her, the butler said firmly that her ladyship had been indisposed for several days and was not receiving anyone. "It is only because it is your lordship that I dare even to inquire if her ladyship will see you," he added.

Nick decided that since he had cut the more intimate connection between them, Clara did have some cause to insist that she behave like a ordinary visitor, but that reasonable decision made it no less irritating to be kept waiting. He glanced up sharply when the butler returned ten minutes later, looking harried.

"Well, man? If you dare to tell me that she will not receive me, believe me—"

"I should not so demean myself, my lord. Her ladyship has agreed to see you, but she did ask that I inform your lordship of her indisposition and request that you take more than ordinary care not to distress her."

"Where is she?"

"Her ladyship is in her boudoir, sir."

"Not completely bedridden then?" Nick knew his tone was sarcastic, but he did not much care. He was certain now that Clara was reluctant to see him, and almost as certain that he knew why.

His tone apparently had no effect on the butler, who said with his customary dignity, "No, my lord, she is not bedridden. If you will just come this way."

"Never mind showing me the way," Nick said, his patience snapping. "Find me something to drink, and be quick about it." Leaving the butler to attend to this important matter, he took the stairs two at a time and found Clara lounging on a claw-footed sofa in front of the window in her boudoir with warm western sunlight glowing behind her, and a rose-colored silk coverlet draped artistically over her legs and feet. She made no effort to rise or even to look at him. With the sun in his eyes he could not see her clearly, but he sensed her wariness.

"Good afternoon, my dear," he said, approaching the sofa and looking down at her. "I am sorry to find you unwell."

Without turning her head, she said, "Sit down, Nicky, for goodness' sake. You tower over me, and Greaves must have told you I've been dreadfully ill."

"Ill? From a tumble into a pond?" He made no move to sit. Spotting a large damp patch on the carpet, he chuckled. "Looks like you dumped your clothes right there by the fireplace. Very untidy."

She still did not look directly at him, but he could see her left profile clearly. She bit her lower lip, then muttered, "I spilled a vase of flowers." Abruptly, she added, "So the little vixen told you what she did to me. Your wife is neither well-behaved nor obedient to her husband, darling. I'm quite sure, knowing you as I do, that you did not expect her to show up at Vauxhall last night."

"I did not come here to discuss my wife."

"Did you not?"

"No, Clara. I came to discover what the devil became of you last night. I collect, from Greaves's saying that your indisposition has troubled you for several days, that you intended to spin me a Banbury tale of some sort and say you were never there, but I've neither the time nor the patience for such nonsense, so I decided to nip that in the bud. I suspect that first you attempted to seduce Penthorpe. When that proved unsuccessful—as I'm quite sure it did, despite your undeniable charms and all the wild rumors flying round about his having set up a flirt—you decided to try another gambit to compromise him. I know about last night. There is, therefore, no reason to pretend that you have been lying here on your sofa all day, nursing some imaginary complaint. I won't believe you."

She lifted her chin, clearly striving to look innocent while still giving him no more than her left profile, and said, "You won't, darling? What *will* you believe?"

"I don't believe you intended to run off with Penthorpe, or he with you. Is that what you hoped people would believe when he disappeared? Don't try that innocent look again, Clara. The role has never suited you, and it won't avail you now. I believe Penthorpe told me the truth about where he's been, and I know, in any case, that he was not with you last night for more than a few minutes. He went to Vauxhall because you promised to get him a writ of some sort to help Susan, but he found you alone instead, all agitated and dripping wet. I shall pass generously over your unfortunate misjudgment of my wife's gentle nature, and leap right to your meeting with Penthorpe. You took advantage of your bedraggled condition to implore him to help you get home, but the pair of you no sooner emerged from the gardens than he was struck down by a pair of ruffians who carried him off to Baldock."

"Dear me, is that what happened to the poor man? I did hear that he had gone missing, but an abduction?"

"I told you before that your innocent look is wasted on me," he said sternly. "You were with him, Clara. You did not raise an alarm. You did not report his disappearance to anyone who might have helped him. You had to know that I was with him, yet you did not send anyone to find me. Now, in fact, I find myself wondering why you don't even seem surprised by how much I know. Can it be that you already knew he had escaped his captors? Such knowledge on your part would certainly arouse my suspicion, were it not aroused already, since he came straight back to Berkeley Square, stopping only to collect his rig from the stable where we left it last night." Nick knew he was misstating the truth, but he did not see any advantage to be gained by mentioning that Penthorpe had seen Seacourt enter Clara's house.

She did not speak at once, but she was watching him warily through the one eye he could see, and he knew her well enough to be certain now that she had taken a full and knowing part in Penthorpe's ordeal. He shifted his position slightly, trying to get a clear look at her face, but she turned away again, saying with near childish defiance, "You make no sense at all, Nicky. Surely you cannot believe that I was party to such a dastardly prank as you have described!"

He said softly, "Are you trying to make me angry, Clara?"

"No." She licked her lips, then straightened and slowly pushed the coverlet to one side. Bringing her feet to the floor, she looked directly up at him at last and said in a small voice. "I don't want to make anyone angry ever again, Nicky."

Nick stared at her face in shock. Despite the late afternoon sunlight streaming through the window, he could see that the side she had kept turned away from him was deeply bruised and swollen. Reaching for her, his anger forgotten, he pulled her upright to peer more closely at her face, exclaiming, "My God, Clara, who struck you?"

She cried out when he grabbed her, and he saw her swallow now and blink quickly, as if to hold back tears. Looking, at that moment, more vulnerable than he had believed she could be, she opened her mouth to speak, closed it again, and flung herself, weeping, into his arms.

Holding her, he muttered, "Seacourt. By God, that man wants strangling!"

"It was my own fault," she whispered.

"Only if you count your idiocy in taking up with him in the first place," Nick said, struggling to contain his temper.

"You'd better let me go," she said. "My ribs are bruised, too."

Reminded all too strongly of the way Seacourt had treated Melissa and Susan, Nick felt murderous, but he released Clara at once. He had reacted impulsively when she flung herself at him, embracing her as he would anyone who had been badly hurt. Though he was still angry with her for her part in the plot against Penthorpe, he was more angry with Seacourt. Still, he knew that if he was going to get any information about what the villain was up to, he needed to keep a tight rein on his temper.

Clara would tell him more. He was certain of that, but it would not do to frighten her more than he already had. "Has he done this before?" he demanded. When she shivered and stepped away again, he made a stronger effort to control his tone, saying, "I want to know, Clara, and not just because of what he's done to you."

"He was terribly angry," she said, her voice sounding rough in her throat. "It was all his doing, just as you suspected. I met him some time ago, Nicky, and when you were so cruel to me . . . He was kind, and charming. But he was unreasonable about Penthorpe. He hated him, Nicky. At first it was just a lark for me, then something of a challenge when

Penthorpe didn't respond. I . . . I didn't know then that Geoffrey thought that if he could be rid of Penthorpe, the courts would force Susan to return to him. The magistrate was all his notion, too, only there was no magistrate and Geoffrey blamed me when he learned that Penthorpe had got away. He said I must have warned him, even that I must have sent someone to help him escape, but I didn't, Nicky, I didn't! All I did was follow orders. That's all I have ever done."

"Seacourt's orders? Just how long *have* you known him?"

She looked wary again, but she said, "Yarborne introduced us in Newmarket. Geoffrey's a charming man when he wants to be, Nicky. You know he is. And you'd been unkind, so I was vulnerable. He is seductive, and . . . and—"

"Never mind all that. You know—you must know—that his wife ran away with Penthorpe years ago because of the way Seacourt had treated her. He is a violent man where women are concerned, Clara, especially when his wishes are thwarted. You should have nothing more to do with him."

"I . . . I won't. You need not worry about that," she added more firmly. "I promise, I won't ever see him again."

"Well, you can scarcely be certain of that—"

"Oh, yes, I can," she snapped. Then, turning away again, she added in a calmer voice, "I-I'm going to Paris for a time, I think. Don't be fierce with me, Nicky. It wasn't my fault that he got such a hold over me. He made it all seem so reasonable. Men do, you know, when they want a woman to obey them. Or they take advantage, and then hold what they know about her over her head to make her do what they want. Seacourt was like that, always. So are most other men, I've found."

"What the devil do you mean, other men? If you mean me, Clara, by God—"

"I don't! Never! Just . . . just others." She gave him a sidelong, measuring look, then added quickly, "If you knew the whole, Nicky, you wouldn't be so angry with me, truly."

"Then tell me the whole, damn it!"

"You don't really want to hear it." Sitting back down on the sofa and arranging her skirt, she murmured provocatively, "It involves your precious little wife, you see."

"Melissa?"

"Unless you have more than one wife," she said with a mocking little smile.

"So help me, Clara, if you don't want me to haul you back up off that sofa and give you the shaking of your life——"

"Just like a man," she snapped. "When you can't get your way with a woman by seducing her or coercing her, you take to brute violence, every blessed one of you!"

"Don't tempt me," he said, standing over her and looking down. He didn't care now how much his temper frightened her. Briefly, he wanted to shake her, even to slap her. But his eye fell again on her swollen face, and the latter thought made him feel sick to his stomach. He said much more gently than he had intended, "Tell me, Clara. I won't strike you, I promise, but you must tell me what you know about Melissa. I am her husband. If someone is taking advantage of her, I want to know."

"Truthfully, Nicky, I don't know who's taken advantage of whom, but I have it on unimpeachable authority that your precious Melissa is meeting with Yarborne right now, as we speak, in a little hideaway flat that he keeps in Jermyn Street."

"Nonsense. You're mad. Or else you're lying through your teeth."

Had she argued with him in her usual fashion, glibly offering a myriad of supposed witnesses or evidence, he might never have believed her, but she did not. She only shrugged and said, "You know how he is, so protective of his reputation. Only the most devoted of his servants even knows the place exists." When he turned on his heel to leave, she added petulantly, "I said I'm going away, Nicky, and you never gave me the gold bracelet you promised."

He looked back. "You'll have to consider that a forfeit, my dear."

* * *

Melissa paused at the corner of York and Jermyn Streets and stared at St. James's Church, almost directly opposite, not sure whether to turn right or left. Even as the question crossed her mind, however, she glanced right and saw the manservant who had attended Yarborne at the ladies' supper.

He approached, his manner properly obsequious, and when he was near enough, he said, "I am Fenton, madam. You might recall me from a previous occasion."

She nodded.

"His lordship expects you. My orders are to see you safely to the door of the flat, and then to take myself off again. There is no one else with the master."

She nodded again, not certain whether she was glad or frightened to learn she would be alone with Yarborne. Clearly, the servant knew who she was, despite his failure to use her title, and she was grateful that he had not used it there on the street. She wanted no listening ears, no tongues to prattle of her visit, no peeping eyes to see what passed between them. Yet she was by no means certain she wanted to be alone with Yarborne. Deciding it was too late to quibble over details of their meeting, she drew a deep breath and nodded to indicate that she would follow him.

Fenton turned and walked swiftly to the second building from the corner, a four-story edifice of brick with white stone belt courses. Stone steps led up between the wrought-iron areaway railings to a plain wooden door beneath an ordinary glass fanlight. Melissa noted each of these details as if they mattered and were of interest, firmly keeping her mind off the scene that lay ahead.

The manservant pushed open the door and held it for her. Inside, he led the way again, up plain wooden stairs arranged in half flights around the well, to the next floor. Her footsteps and his echoed hollowly upward through the stairwell. At the first full landing, he gestured toward a dark wood door at the end of a narrow corridor, and said, "Shall I knock for you, madam?"

The thought occurred to her that if she sent him away at once, and if she should then happen to shoot Yarborne, Fenton would never be able to tell anyone that he had seen her enter the flat. Repressing a nearly overwhelming and quite ridiculous urge to chuckle at the wicked thought, and wondering if she were perhaps losing her mind after all, she gathered her wits and made a dignified gesture of dismissal. Whether or not his absence could make any difference in a court of law, it made a difference to her. She did not want anyone to see her groveling to Yarborne.

Waiting until she heard Fenton's footsteps fade away and the door below open and shut again, Melissa rapped lightly on the one in front of her. It opened at once.

"Engaging in second thoughts, my dear?" Yarborne stood solidly in front of her, smiling. "It took you rather an age to knock. Come in, come in."

"I brought your money," she said bluntly. "There is no need whatsoever for me to step inside your flat."

"Oh, but there is. Doing business on doorsteps is for street vendors and their ilk, certainly not for a lady of quality doing business with a gentleman."

Tempted though she was to tell him she did not consider him any sort of a gentleman, let alone a man of quality, Melissa obeyed his unspoken gesture to enter. She remained by the door, however, moving at once to open her reticule.

"Pray, do not be in such a hurry, my dear. Fenton has left us a pot of tea, and while it may not still be quite as hot as you like it, he has left some excellent biscuits, as well, to eat with it."

"I did not come for tea, Yarborne," she said crisply, removing Lady Ophelia's bank notes from her reticule in a near cloud of lavender. "If you will just take this money and return my bracelet to me, I shall be much obliged to you."

"Will you, by God? I shall hold you to that." He sniffed appreciatively. "Even your money is scented. I find such attention to detail quite admirable in a woman. Indeed, my dear, you grow lovelier and more attractive by the day. I know now that I made a grave mistake in agreeing to that auction. Sir Geoffrey Seacourt was wiser than we knew, for I believe that you would have made me a excellent wife had I accepted his proposition that I marry you."

Repressing a shudder at the thought, she said grimly, "You would never have got the money he owed you."

"Ah, but I've come to believe that the rewards of marriage to you would have outweighed any monetary loss."

"You flatter me, sir." Pointedly, she held out the bank notes. Yarborne ignored them. "Sit down, Melissa."

"I have not given you leave to use my name," she said. "I would prefer that you continue to address me by my title."

"No doubt you would, but I can't think why I should cater to your preferences just yet. Now, sit down and be civil, or I shall make certain that your husband very soon learns of this meeting and everything that preceded it."

"You promised not to tell him, if I repaid you!"

"So I did, but I am certain I can think of a good reason to break that promise if you are foolish enough to put me to the trouble of doing so."

Turning toward the window, she began to put the money back into her reticule. Though she moved slowly, her thoughts were racing. Her fingertips touched the cool metal pistol barrel, then the handle, but although she gripped the handle longingly, she did not take the pistol out. To threaten Yarborne with it would do no good. Even if the gun proved to be loaded, not only was she certain she would be unable to shoot him but the best she could hope for would be to make an escape. That would scarcely solve her greatest problem, since he would merely wait until she had gone, then tell Nicholas at his first opportunity that she had been there. His man would support that claim, and no reason she could offer Nicholas would mitigate his anger with her for visiting Yarborne's flat. She would do better by far to calm Yarborne now.

How she would calm him, she could not imagine. He seemed bigger than life at that moment, and quite terrifying. Recalling Charley's observation in response to a similar complaint about Nicholas, Melissa realized she was letting her perception of Yarborne's power over her frighten her more than the man did. She tried to imagine what his perception of her must be. His attitude having consistently given her to believe that he thought all women were foolish, she began to wonder how she might use that erroneous assumption against him.

As the thought crossed her mind, he came up behind her and grasped her left arm, turning her toward him, his purpose all too clear. "You are very beautiful, my dear. Since you seem reluctant to sit down, perhaps you will not deny one tender kiss to the man who nearly became your husband." Both his hands rested on her shoulders.

Her right hand was still in her reticule. Looking up into his face, she said steadily, "Release me at once, my lord. I am holding a loaded pistol aimed directly at your stomach. I can scarcely miss my mark at such close range as this."

He went very still, his grip on her arm loosening instantly. Melissa stepped back and withdrew the pistol from her reticule.

"I see that I have made you angry, my lord, but you have not played this game fairly, have you? Cheaters must expect to lose in the end. I trust that you have my bracelet near at hand."

"Yonder on the table," he said with a small movement of his head.

She had not noticed the watch-bracelet before, but she saw it now and moved carefully past him to pick it up.

He said scornfully, "So now you turn thief, madam. Very pretty behavior."

"I am no thief," she snapped, stung by the accusation. "I brought your money, and I will leave it with you, but I will not allow you to take further advantage of me."

"By heaven, you are a woman truly worthy of me," he said with a sigh. "I can see now that I was very much mistaken to allow Vexford to win you."

A sudden clatter of footsteps in the stairwell ended with a loud pounding at Yarborne's door. "Yarborne, open up! I know you're in there. I must talk to you. Open this door at once, damn you!"

Frozen in place by the sound of her husband's furious voice, Melissa stared at the vibrating door, expecting it to burst open. Only when the doorknob rattled ineffectively did she realize Yarborne had locked the door behind her. She turned to him and saw that he looked as dismayed as she was.

"Please, sir," she said urgently, "do not give me away. He will murder the pair of us if he finds me here."

"I am well aware of that," he muttered. "This is most unfair, I must say. To have him threatening mayhem, as I make no doubt he will, only because I have been generous enough to assist you—"

"Don't talk fustian! Where can I hide?" The pounding on the door had not ceased, and she knew it would be only seconds before Nicholas broke down the door.

Yarborne clearly shared that opinion. "In there," he said, indicating a door right behind her. "Hurry, for God's sake, and take that damned bracelet with you."

"Here's your money," she said, thrusting it at him.

"I don't want it, "he snapped. "Go! Hurry!"

But when she threw down the money in place of the brace-let, he snatched it up, thrusting it hastily inside his coat as he hurried to the door. "Silence, Vexford, I'm coming as fast as I can. Good Lord, man, can't you let a chap get his coat on?"

"You'd better have a damned good reason to have taken it off," Nicholas shouted through the door.

Hearing him, her heart pounding in her throat, Melissa slipped into the room Yarborne had indicated, shut the door, and pressed her ear hard against it.

Twenty

Black Forfeits a Knight

Nick shifted impatiently from foot to foot. He had heard nothing from inside the flat except Yarborne's voice, and only the sound of firm footsteps approaching the door had kept him from battering the door down. All the way from Clara's house, he had been imagining what he might discover. One moment he imagined Melissa helplessly struggling in the villain's clutches, the next writhing in his embrace. Fuming by the time he reached Jermyn Street, he had not been able to think what might draw her to Yarborne's flat, but he was certain the attraction was nothing good.

His hands had managed the reins by reflex while his mind flashed images ranging from Yarborne's having tricked her into meeting him, to an idiotic one of Melissa deciding she would have done better to have married Yarborne. No single idea followed logically upon another. Disjointed half-thoughts tumbled through his mind, replacing sensible reflection with dazed emotion. Drawing up before Yarborne's building, he had tossed the ribbons to Artemus and leapt down, urged on by an increasing fear of greater magnitude than any he had experienced before.

Only as he raced up the stairs to Yarborne's flat had he realized that he ought to have demanded a more detailed explanation from Clara. He had been foolish to leave without learning more, and it occurred to him that despite his saying she could not have her bracelet, she had made no effort to call him back. What had possessed him, he wondered as the sound reached his ears of a hand on the latch, to believe so easily the outrageous charge she had laid against Melissa?

The door opened, and Yarborne stood before him. In that instant, Nick knew that Clara had spoken the truth, for despite the note of heartiness in the words shouted through the door, the man did not look at all pleased to see him. That single look was enough to make Nick shove the door wide and brush past Yarborne into the room.

The words, *"Where is she?"* leapt to his lips, but he managed to quell them. Looking quickly around, he noted a tea tray laid with two cups and a plate of biscuits, and said grimly, "I trust I have not interrupted a tête-à-tête."

"Nonsense, nonsense," Yarborne said bluffly. "My man merely set out refreshment for me before taking himself off for the afternoon. Meeting his sister or some such thing, I daresay. Don't precisely recall just what his plans were."

"No, nor would you have cared a jot had they not marched with your own," Nick snapped. "You begin to sound like someone else I know, offering detailed explanation before I have requested any."

"Did you not request one? Dear me, I thought you had. But won't you sit down?" He made a sweeping gesture toward a chair near the window embrasure, and as he did, a crumpled bank note slipped from beneath his coat to the floor.

Bending swiftly to pick it up, Nick said, "Rather careless with your money, Yarborne. Never would have thought that of you." As he straightened, he saw that Yarborne's eyes had widened with alarm. The man turned away quickly, as though he realized his expression had been too revealing, and Nick, catching a slight but familiar scent, lifted the bank note to his nose, sniffing delicately. "Lavender, Yarborne? Do you perfume your money, sir?"

Something in his tone must have warned Yarborne, for he went very still. He did not turn, nor did he reply.

"Look at me, you scoundrel."

Visibly drawing a deep breath, Yarborne turned. Though his face showed none of his thoughts, he was not wholly intimidated, for his eyes narrowed slightly and he said in a stern tone, "You forget yourself, Vexford."

"Where is she, damn you?"

Yarborne's eyebrows rose. "My dear boy, do you accuse me of employing this flat for romantic assignations?"

"By God, Yarborne, if you won't answer me, I'll—"

"You'll what? I have heard much about your temper, young man, but I cannot believe that any gentleman raised and schooled as you were would lift a hand to one old enough to be his father. Do I misjudge you, sir?"

"Will you allow me to search this flat?"

"I will not."

"Then you do indeed underestimate me, for if what I believe is true, and I find the one I expect to find here, no man in England would judge me guilty of assault, or even of murder, by God." He reached for Yarborne, who stepped quickly back, saying warily, "Now, Nicholas, I must protest. Really, my lord. Nick, no!"

"Nicholas, no!"

The feminine cry joined Yarborne's as Nick grabbed him by the throat, and Nick saw that a door had opened across the room.

His wife stood framed in the doorway, her face white with shock. Her voice was perfectly calm, however, when she said, "Let him go at once, Nicholas."

Seeing cold fury leap to her husband's eyes, Melissa realized with a shiver of fear that although she had thought him angry enough to commit murder, his emotions where Yarborne was concerned paled by comparison to what he felt when his gaze met hers. A brief, tense pause followed. She was not certain Nicholas even remembered that he held Yarborne by the throat in what was doubtless a painful grip. She dared not speak again, however, until he spoke.

"Is that this villain's bedchamber?" he demanded.

"I-I don't know." She did not have any notion what room it was, for she had not taken even a moment to look, nor did she want to look now. Her full attention was riveted upon her husband, just as it had been from the moment he arrived at the flat.

A gurgling sound from Yarborne apparently reminded Nicholas that he still held the man, for although his eyes remained fixed on her, he abruptly released Yarborne.

Rubbing his throat, Yarborne said hoarsely, "That is the dining room, Vexford. I am not a fool. Even in my haste to aid the lady, I was not so lost to my senses as to send her into the bedchamber."

"Not so heedless of your safety is what I'd call it," Nicholas said.

"If you prefer to describe it that way, certainly."

"What I prefer seems to have had no influence whatsoever on this little farce. What the devil goes on here, Yarborne?"

Straightening his cravat, Yarborne glanced at Melissa.

Unsure of just what he would choose to tell Nicholas, she said quickly, "Say what you will. I mean to tell him the truth."

"Then, pray, madam, take him away from here before you do. I have had a surfeit of his temper for one day, and since I doubt that I can rely on you to put the matter in the kindly light that my patience and generosity deserve, and since a gentleman must hesitate to contradict a lady, even when his safety is at stake—"

"Shut your damned mouth, Yarborne," Nicholas snapped. "If I learn that you have harmed her, there won't be anything you can say to save yourself."

"Then I must most urgently implore her to speak the truth, for in point of fact, the only one threatened here today—"

"You need say no more, Lord Yarborne," Melissa interjected hastily "I promise you, I shall tell him the truth." Forcing herself to meet her husband's stern gaze, she said, "I am ready to go home now, sir, if you please."

"Are you, indeed?"

His voice was gentle, so she was not sure what there was in the tone to send shivers shooting up her spine again, but so it was. She had all she could do to keep her voice steady long enough to say, "Yes, Nicholas."

His eyes were like chips of steel, his mouth drawn into a hard straight line with lips pressed together tightly, as if he did not trust himself to speak. She dreaded what he would say to her when he was able to control his tongue again, but she hoped he would restrain himself at least until they reached the street. The thought of having her character shredded before Yarborne was almost more than she could bear. She did not look away, but neither did she attempt to speak again, lest an unintended word turn the ice in his expression to fire, and set him off like one of the skyrockets at Vauxhall.

The silence grew heavy, almost tactile. At a point somewhere beneath the heavy cloud of her husband's anger, she sensed that Yarborne's wariness was as strong as her own, but he, too, seemed to recognize the wisdom of not speaking. At last Nicholas stepped aside and gestured toward the door. "After you, my dear."

The shivery sensation increased to a prickling when she passed him, as if the very hairs on her body stood up in awareness of his wrath. She could hear his breath rasping in his throat, and could feel the tension emanating from him.

Yarborne moved, as if he had been released from a spell, stepping hastily past her to the door. He opened it for her, then stood beside it, looking for all the world like a gentleman seeing afternoon callers on their way. Not for a single moment, however, did Melissa consider bidding him fare-well.

She swept past him, conscious only of the large man be-hind her, whose presence loomed over her all the way down the twisting flights of steps to the ground floor. Not waiting for him to open the outer door, she pulled it open herself and stepped to the pavement, looking for the carriage.

"My tilbury is yonder," he said curtly.

She saw it then, and saw too that Artemus stood beside it. For a moment she was grateful, certain that Nicholas would not scold her with his groom perched up behind them. When they reached the carriage, however, he caught her by the waist and tossed her onto the front seat, taking the reins from Artemus and saying grimly, "You may walk home from here. I'll leave the rig with a lad at the door."

"Very good, my lord."

Melissa swallowed hard when Nicholas swung up onto the seat beside her, but he did not speak other than to give his horses the office to start. There being little traffic, he set them trotting as soon as he turned the corner into York Street, and in less than five minutes, without having spoken a single word to her, he drew up before Barrington House. Jumping to the ground, be handed the reins to the boy who ran up the areaway steps to meet them. "Artemus will be along shortly to collect them," he snapped over his shoulder as he reached to help Melissa down.

His hands, warm at her waist, belied the chill in his eyes, and she almost hoped something else would intervene to pre-vent the scene she knew was coming. Telling herself she was being foolish beyond permission to think of putting it off, since his wrath was likely only to increase if he were denied the relief of venting it, she went silently beside him into the house.

"Good afternoon, my lord," Preston said, approaching from the stairway. His kindly gaze shifted to Melissa, and reading surprise in his expression, she held her breath. He said, "Good afternoon, my lady. I was not aware that you had gone out."

"Were you not, Preston?" she said.

"No, madam. Nor did Silas or the porter know that you had left the house."

Unable to think of a thing to say that would not make matters worse, she held her tongue.

Nicholas said quietly, "Thank you, Preston. We require nothing further."

"Yes, my lord, though you might perhaps find a glass of wine refreshing, if I might be so bold as to suggest it."

"Not now. I'll ring if I want you."

"Yes, my lord." And with a sympathetic glance at Melissa, the butler turned on his heel and returned to the nether regions.

Melissa hesitated, but when Nick's firm hand on her elbow urged her toward the library, she went without a word, remaining silent even when he shut the door behind them and moved past her to lean against the huge desk, facing her. No fire had yet been lighted in the room, but the chilly air was not what made her shiver again.

After another moment's silence, he said, "Now you may tell me the truth. Don't leave out a single word of it."

She did not know where to begin, but she knew his patience would not long endure silence, so she said in a rush, "I made a foolish wager at the ladies' supper that I could not make good, and Yarborne lent me money to cover my losses. Later he said he would collect what I owed from you if I did not repay him. I know I ought never to have accepted his money, Nicholas, but at the time, I could think of no other recourse. You were not there, and I did not think to borrow from anyone else because he just told the groom-porter to pay everyone off. He seemed so kind and thoughtful, so . . ." His glare stopped the words in her throat. After another long pause during which he seemed to be measuring the truth of her tale, she said, "I suppose you think me a fool."

"You don't want to know what I think. Good God, borrowing money from him does not explain sneaking out of this house today, which must be what you did if no one saw you leave. Nor does it explain your presence in that damned flat of his."

"But it does. I went there to repay him. I could scarcely take my maid or a footman on such an errand."

"Why the devil not? Just what did he demand in payment, Melissa? That's what I want to know."

Every impulse cried out to tell him he was wrong, but she could not lie to him. Facts were facts, and Yarborne had expected exactly what Nicholas had inferred. "He did think I might be willing to do what you imply, sir," she said quietly. "I am sorry to find that you believe I might willingly submit to such horrid demands, however."

"Don't throw idiotic sanctimony at me! He had every right to expect just that, once you'd agreed to meet him privately."

"You say that as if you believe he gave me a choice in the matter."

"Of course you had a choice. You need only have said no. You could also have brought the matter to me, you know. I'd have dealt very speedily with Yarborne."

"Would you?" She kept her voice under control, but her lips were dry. A familiar instinct stirred her, and she wanted to lick them, to look at him from under her lashes, to move in the sensuous way she had long since learned would divert a man's thoughts from his temper. Even as her mind sought wildly for those words least likely to infuriate him again, she realized she was behaving just as she had years before when faced with her father's wrath. The thought brought tears to her eyes, which she dashed away with the back of her hand. Strenuously, she fought her instincts. Even more than she wanted to soothe Nicholas did she want to retain what little dignity she had left.

"I'm afraid tears will not move me," he said. "You have behaved badly, Melissa. It is of no use to pretend remorse now in hope of lessening your punishment."

"I'm not remorseful," Melissa snapped, surprising herself. "I'm becoming angry, Nicholas! I am trying to tell you what happened and how I came to find myself caught in such a predicament, but when you stand there glowering at me, all I can think about is the way my father used to look before he punished me."

"Damn it, don't fling that in my teeth! I've not lifted a finger to you, nor will I, but you lied to me. You went to another man's flat, and I found you alone with him. Don't blame me if I'm angry about that, and don't dare to imply that my anger puts me in a class with that damned father of yours."

"But you blame me for being afraid to tell you what happened," she retorted. When he looked about to protest, she added quickly, "Yes, Nicholas, that's just what you are doing. You tell me I ought to have come to you. You say I should have known that you would deal with him, but how could I know *what* you would do? I thought you would be angry, and when you get angry, you frighten people, even those who care about you. I do care, and I care what you think of me. Don't you understand? Things had been going well for us, and Yarborne threatened to spoil it. I wanted to make it right by myself, so you would never know how foolish I had been." She took the pistol from her reticule and held it out to him. "I would never have let him touch me. Once I'd got the money from Great-Aunt Ophelia—"

"How much?" He took the pistol, staring at it in bemusement.

"A hundred pounds," she said reluctantly, "and before you demand to know why I didn't ask you for it, I couldn't. I had already cost you far too much, and the sum seemed enormous, but Great-Aunt Ophelia didn't even blink or ask any questions. She certainly trusted me more than Yarborne did, for he demanded surety in case I denied later that I owed him the money. That's why he made me give him my bracelet."

"What bracelet?" he demanded grimly.

She explained, adding, "I know now that I was foolish to trust him, especially since he demanded such surety, but somehow he made it seem like the most sensible thing to do. I wasn't thinking altogether clearly, either. I'd been drinking champagne. You weren't there, and there was no one else to advise me, because Aunt Ophelia was in the card room and Charley had wandered off. What should I have done?"

"Leave the damned supper and come home," he retorted ruthlessly. "Only a idiot compounds his wagers at the hazard table."

"Had you explained that before Yarborne told me my luck was bound to hold, I would no doubt have taken your advice rather than his," she said, spreading her hands. "Yes, and furthermore, as I look back on that night, I think he enticed me to play the way I did from the very first. Furthermore," she added without thinking, "your precious Lady Hawthorne helped him. I hadn't realized that before, but if she was not helping him on purpose, she certainly was at hand, both at the faro table, and later, at the hazard table. I think she was the one who demanded a change of dice."

He glared at her but did not reply. He had put the pistol down on the desk, and to her surprise, he seemed to be thinking.

She looked steadily at him.

He straightened, looked at her intently, then said in a more normal tone of voice, "Just how good was your luck that night?"

"I won several times at faro," she said, "and then Lady Hawthorne suggested I try hazard. Yarborne taught us the rules, but Charley soon left to do something else. Once I began casting, Nicholas, I seemed to throw only chance—six times running! Yarborne wandered off about the same time

Charley did, but once I began winning, he came back. I told him I was going to throw once more. When I did, someone called the dice. I rolled chance again, but he said the throw didn't count. Is that true?"

"It is," he said, but she saw that he was looking more intent than ever. "What happened when you threw the new dice?"

"I threw my main. I had to pay everyone at the table."

"Uphills and downhills," he murmured, "or— No, by God, Fulhams!"

"What?"

"The dice were weighted, both sets, the one to turn up only what would win for you, the other only what would lose. They set you up for a dupe," he said, shoving a hand through his hair. Then he frowned and looked at her thoughtfully. He said, "I've just remembered that we encountered Yarborne at Vauxhall."

Melissa stopped breathing.

"I see how it was," he said slowly. "You weren't looking for me. You were looking for him, and I'll wager a year's income that your disappearing escort was my idiot brother. I was wrong to think you stopped at the Dark Walk because you were afraid of me, wasn't I? You stopped because you had expected to meet Yarborne there to pay him. That's why you asked me about that damned statue, isn't it, Melissa?"

Before she could reply, the door opened with a bang and Charley burst into the room with Preston right behind her.

"Lissa, Uncle Geoffrey has been found in Hyde Park— dead! Someone bashed him over the head and robbed him, and they say it was footpads. Isn't it dreadful? Uncle Geoffrey was a terrible man, but even I never wished him such a fate as that. And we can't find Penthorpe," she added, in what was apparently an afterthought.

Melissa felt dizzy. Nick said to Charley, "I thought Penthorpe took your Aunt Susan for a drive in the park."

"Yes, he did, but they returned some time ago, and he

went out again. He said he was going to find some friends of his and tell them he meant to stay in London with Aunt Susan, and not go to the Derby tomorrow, but he neglected to say where he was meeting them, and you know how he is. We could have sent servants running all over town, of course, but I thought you might know—"

Interrupting her, Nick said, "I'll find him. Preston send someone to the stables and tell them to hitch a fresh pair to my tilbury. And take Miss Charlotte to the—"

Charley said indignantly, "I'm not going anywhere. I came to lend Melissa my support and comfort. Not that she ought to require much, because she didn't even like him, but he was her father, after all, and my uncle, and I don't intend to leave her alone at such a time as this. You men always think—"

"Preston, take her away. No, Charley, I won't listen to you. Chalk it up to masculine arrogance if you must, but go."

"I won't! You can't order me around, Nick. I'm not—"

"Oh, stop, both of you!" Melissa's head was spinning. When Nick touched her arm, she turned and looked blindly at him, saying, "He's really dead?"

"So it appears." He glanced at the butler. "Preston, take Miss Charlotte to the green salon. If she protests any more, put her out of the house. If she behaves herself, order tea for two to be served in the salon."

He looked at Charley, daring her to oppose him further, but Melissa saw without much surprise that her cousin had been silenced.

When Charley and Preston had gone, Nicholas said quietly, "I agree with Charley that Penthorpe must be run to ground as soon as possible, so I must go, but I want you to stay right here. Don't leave the house for any reason."

"But I must! Mama will be terribly distressed. I must go to her at once."

"Lady Ophelia will look after her. I mean this, Melissa. Don't defy me again."

"But why?"

"It's the only way I know to protect you until I can find out more about this."

"To protect me, or control me?"

"Now, look—"

"No, Nicholas, you look! From the first night you brought me to this house, you have reacted to every unexpected turn of events by trying to lock me up—like a dog guarding his bone, or," she added bitterly, "like a gambler guarding his winnings!"

"It isn't like that."

"Then tell me how it is. You expect me to anticipate your thoughts and your wishes—like a good servant—and to assume that your reasons are wise. You can't explain feelings, Nicholas, but you can certainly declare commands. Am I wrong?"

He opened his mouth, shut it, then said, "Just do as I tell you. Until I know more, I can't be expected to explain myself."

"But you never—"

"Look, Melissa, I just want to protect you. Rumors will be flying. I believe Yarborne's concern for his reputation will keep him quiet about this afternoon, but I can't guarantee that. As to your father's death, I have some ideas of my own on that subject, but I need the answers to some questions, and since everyone who hasn't already left town will certainly do so for the Derby tomorrow, I mean to go to Epsom, just as I'd planned, in the morning. I know you won't like that, but—"

"You would go to a horse race at such a time as this?"

"Some answers to this puzzle may be found there. Moreover, I've got horses running. People expect me to go, my parents will be there, and none of my friends or family will expect me to shed tears over your father's death."

"People might expect you to support me while I do so. What will they think?"

"That I'm the same man today that I was yesterday," he

said ruthlessly. "As soon as I get back from Epsom, however, I'll take you to Owlcastle."

"Owlcastle! You're just angry about today. I won't go!"

"It isn't that. I want you away from the gossips. I'll make it clear to everyone that our visit to Owlcastle is planned and quite ordinary, even understandable in view of your father's murder. But until I get back, you will stay in this house. Don't leave for any reason. Do you understand me?"

She glared at him. "Perfectly."

He returned the look steadily, and she saw that the fires of his earlier anger were only banked. The silence lengthened uncomfortably before he said quietly, "If you defy me again, you will be sorry. And there is one more thing. You would be wise to say nothing about your visit to Yarborne, even to Charley."

"On that issue, sir, you may certainly have my word. I've no wish to reveal my stupidity to anyone else."

"Good." He gave her another measuring look. "I'll say nothing more now, but we'll have another talk when I've found Penthorpe and learned all I can about your father's death. I'll take this with me," he added, picking up the pistol.

When he had gone, Melissa found Charley awaiting her in the green salon, looking subdued for once. She did not instantly censure Nicholas's behavior, as Melissa expected. Instead, she said, "This is all dreadful, I know, but isn't it just like Uncle Geoffrey to cause as many difficulties with his passing as when he was alive?"

"What difficulties? Nicholas will soon find Penthorpe, if that is what you mean. And as to causing difficulties, I should say that his death resolves at least a few. Mama can no longer be accused of adultery or bigamy, for one thing."

"But that's exactly my point."

"What are you saying?" Melissa demanded. "Not that Mama—"

"Don't be a goose," Charley said, getting up to hug her.

"I meant only that some mean-spirited person might suggest Penthorpe had reason to murder Uncle Geoffrey."

"Good gracious, Charley, I just remembered that you said the other day, that Penthorpe *ought* to kill him." But she thought of someone else who might have had even better cause to murder Seacourt, and found herself suddenly glad that Nicholas had come after her at Yarborne's.

Charley said, "Penthorpe didn't do it, of course, and despite the fact that there must be hundreds of other persons in this world with cause to kill Uncle Geoffrey, I'm quite sure the authorities are right to suspect footpads. Look here, are you being driven to distraction by all this? I must say, you look as if you've been utterly torn apart."

"In a manner of speaking, I have," Melissa said, "but don't ask me to explain, for I won't. I gave Nicholas my word."

"Well, I saw his face when I burst in upon you. He had obviously been scolding you, for he looked ready to eat you. I can't think how you manage to infuriate men so. You were always such a quiet, obedient little thing, but he is a typical man, of course, always bullying and carping. Dreadful creatures, all of them."

"He is not dreadful," Melissa snapped, adding instantly, "Forgive me, Charley. I must be more distressed than I thought. I am just a little angry, too. He is taking me to Owlcastle, you see, just as soon as he returns from the Epsom races."

"Well, you might be wise to leave town for a time," Charley said frankly. "If a hue and cry is raised over Uncle Geoffrey's death, it could become very unpleasant."

"If I should *choose* to go out of town," Melissa said tartly, "be sure I will do so for my own good reasons and not because of any unpleasantness arising from Papa's death."

Twenty-one

Bishop Challenges Rook

Two hours later, when Nick entered the Billingsgate Club, he had already been to St. Merryn House in the hope that Penthorpe might have returned. He had found only Lady Ophelia and Susan, the latter worrying herself to the bone over where her husband might have gone after their return from the park. Nick went on to Brooks's, White's, and Boodle's without finding Penthorpe. When he did find him, he decided, he would tie him up like a parcel, take him straight back to St. Merryn House, and throw him down at Susan's feet.

The thought made him smile as he passed into the high-ceilinged entrance hall. A man approaching him smiled back and said bluffly, "Evening, Vexford. Expected you to be down at Epsom by now. Didn't you have nags running in today's heats?"

Jolted out of his brown study, Nick shook the hand held out to him and said, "I do have horses running, but not till tomorrow and Friday. I'll go down early in the morning." He excused himself after some brief conversation, and moved toward the stairs, his thoughts returning to his ever-increasing responsibilities. He realized when they did, however, that he was not irked by his obligations. He was certainly no longer bored. In fact, he decided as he approached the subscription room, one thing he could say for a certainty was that his boredom with the game of life had ceased the night he met Melissa in the Newmarket stable. That he had even ceased to think of life as a game occurred to him now with some force.

A footman leapt to open the double doors leading to the subscription room, and a low hum of voices punctuated by terse announcements of odds by the groom-porters greeted Nick. His gaze swept the room, searching for Penthorpe's red hair. Seeing his brother at the faro table with Yarborne's brat, he made a mental note to have another stern chat with Oliver just as soon as he had time for it. He spotted his quarry at the hazard table and moved toward him, not noticing until he had nearly reached them that Penthorpe was standing with Tommy Minley.

Both gentlemen greeted him cheerfully when he stepped between them. Minley added, "Amberley's thrown in four times now. Bound to throw out soon, dashed if he ain't. Dig out your blunt, Nick."

"Not tonight, Tommy. May I have a word with you, sir?"

"Got markers on the table," Penthorpe said, turning back to watch the cast, then sighing loudly and reaching to retrieve his markers when he lost. The groom-porter raked in the losing wagers. Watching, Penthorpe said with exasperation, "Damme, but it seems I've only to put a sovereign down to lose it. Been out of vein all evening."

"Then you won't mind coming away," Nick said. "I've unpleasant news for you."

"If it's about that damned Seacourt, I've heard it," Penthorpe said bluntly, "and I don't think it's unpleasant at all. Footpads did us all a public service, if you ask me."

"All the same, sir," Nick said patiently, concealing his annoyance at the unthinking response, "I'd appreciate a private word. You'll excuse us, Tommy."

"I'll come with you," Minley said. "My luck's no better than Penthorpe's, and I want the pair of you to dine with me. They put an elegant dinner on the table here, and Dory's in

town. Said he wants to see the place. Don't mean to let him
throw his blunt away, mind you, just to give him a good
meal."

"I'll dine with you," Nick said, adding to Penthorpe as the
three men moved away from the hazard table, "See here, sir,
don't you think you ought to go home? I don't mind telling
you I've turned the town upside down, looking for you."

"Looking for me? Why?"

"Because your wife desires your presence at home," Nick
said flatly, urging him toward the nearest doorway. When
Penthorpe looked at him in surprise, he added, "Surely, that's
not odd, under the circumstances."

"What circumstances? Look here, lad, you ain't going to
try to convince me that Susan's crying her eyes out over that
scoundrel's death, because I know for a fact she won't do
any such thing. I daresay Melissa ain't weeping much either."

Glancing around, Nick saw several men looking their way.
He said in an adamant undertone that left no room for discussion, "Come with me into that next room. I think you do
not quite understand the situation."

Penthorpe did not argue, nor did he object to Minley's
presence. When they entered the small, empty anteroom that
Nick had used in a previous conversation with Oliver, he
shut the door and said bluntly, "Don't you realize half of
London must be speculating on whether you murdered Seacourt?"

To his surprise, Penthorpe grinned. "Are they, by God?
Well, I must say, I'm flattered. Didn't think anyone would
mistake me for a man of action. Been a long time since
Waterloo, you know, and folks tend to forget I was there.
But, look here," he added when Nick remained grimly silent,
"I was driving Susan in Hyde Park just shortly before they
found him. Do you honestly imagine anyone will think I
asked her to hold the reins while I jumped down and nipped
behind a bush to murder Seacourt?"

Not mincing words, Nick said, "You don't know when he

was killed. Many who don't know of your disappearance do know that Seacourt has been making your wife's life miserable, and the fact that she's led a quiet life since coming to London hasn't stopped rumors from sprouting. In fact, it's probably added to them. Moreover, sir, those who do know of your disappearance believe Seacourt was responsible for it."

"So do I," Penthorpe said. "Damme, so do you. It can't have been anyone else. The man did everything he could to frighten Susan. One moment he wanted her back, claiming to love her; the next he tormented her just for the fun he got out of it. I've no doubt at all that he arranged my abduction to frighten her out of her wits. Don't think I haven't realized I was the only thing standing between him and Susan. With me in the picture, he'd have had to apply to a court to get at her, in full view of the entire *beau monde*. With me out of the way, no one would have contested his authority over her. He could just have stepped in and taken her home with him."

Nick sighed. "The fact that you realize that does not help your cause. I'd suggest you go home before you're foolish enough, or become drunk enough, to say that to anyone who might repeat it in a court of law."

Minley said, "He's right, Penthorpe. You won't like hearing that from me when we scarcely know each other, but the fact is I've heard talk myself. Didn't realize this was a family chat, however, so I'll just skip along now. Must keep an eye out for Dory, at all events. Will you still join us for dinner, Nick?"

Nick nodded. Watching Penthorpe, he saw that the older man had not dismissed their warnings out of hand, but he was not certain that Penthorpe understood his peril. Quietly, he said, "Tommy's right about the rumors, you know. I looked for you in several clubs before this one, and while no one said anything to my face—they know better—I could see their suspicions in the way they looked at me."

"But, damme, Nick, that's most likely because they think *you* murdered him, not me," Penthorpe snapped.

"I agree that a number of them might think I had cause if they know how I met Melissa," Nick said calmly. "I haven't heard a whisper about that night, but few would dare repeat to me what they'd heard about it. In any case, I'd guess you and Susan are more vulnerable to rumor just now than I am. You ought to go home to your wife, sir."

"But, damme, she won't have heard—"

"She didn't have to. She and Lady Ophelia thought of the possibility of your being accused the moment they learned of Seacourt's death. That's why they were so anxious for me to find you. I don't think they shared their fears with Charley, however. If they did, she had the sense, for once, not to blurt them out to Melissa."

"I'd not count on her continued silence," Penthorpe said. "That chit's as sharp as she can stare. Even if no one pointed it out to her, I'd wager she'll soon figure it out on her own— aye, and that you might have done it, too—and I've never yet known her to keep her tongue hidden behind her teeth."

"Well, I've done what I can to protect Melissa from all the rumors that will be flying if the men who killed Seacourt are not quickly apprehended. For a start, I told her to stay home till I return from Epsom, so I hope you'll explain to Susan that that's why she did not go at once to see her."

"Maybe you should take her to Epsom with you. She ain't as horse mad as her cousin, but she'd enjoy the races."

"I'd have to look after her," Nick said, "and it would be difficult to keep an eye on her and still look into things. Even though my parents will be there on Derby day, I don't know when they will arrive or how long they mean to stay, and I've learned over the years not to try to divide my attention at such times. I'm too apt to get caught up in the business of racing. Better by far that she stay safe in London, and better, too, that I look as if I'm behaving normally. That will do more than anything else to scotch any rumors directed toward me—or toward you, for that matter." He realized that he was beginning to offer as many excuses as Clara did when she was lying, and cut himself off, saying abruptly, "I don't want Melissa worried about this."

Penthorpe smiled. "I hope that means this marriage of yours is working out better than we all expected at the outset."

"I've no complaints," Nick said, though his thoughts flicked to Yarborne. "Will you go home now, sir?"

"Oh, I'm off," Penthorpe said, adding with a grin, "but mark my words, this riot and rumpus will die out just as soon as they catch the footpads that killed that blasted scoundrel. You'll see."

Nick walked with him to the stairs, where they found Minley waiting on the landing. He was peering down over the railing at the entrance hall, but he straightened and joined Nick in bidding farewell to Penthorpe. As they watched him descend, Nick smiled and said, "Waiting here to catch me in case I forgot about dinner, Tommy?"

Minley shook his head and said, "Just been telling one of the footmen to keep an eye out for Dory. Ought to be along soon. Had a word with that brother of yours, too."

"Where is Oliver? I want a word with him myself."

"He left. That's why I was talking to him, as a matter of fact. Told him you were here. Even asked him to stay and dine with us. Very large-minded of me, I thought, considering that brat still gives me a pain. Most uncivil, he was tonight, too. Said he'd no wish to take his mutton with two sour faces and a parson. I tell you, that lad wants a lesson in manners, and I told him so, too."

"Did you, Tommy? I hope he listened to you. He's been avoiding me these past two days, but I've got a good notion why."

"Yes, so do I," Minley said roundly. "The lad's been dipping deep, Nick. Heard about it from more than one chap, and saw a bit of it tonight for myself. Tried to put a useful word in his ear, don't you know, but got rudeness in return."

"He resents advice generally," Nick said. "He's long overdue for that lesson you mentioned."

"Know what I think?"

"I know you will tell me."

"What I think is that young Oliver's not as smart as he thinks he is. If that sprout of Yarborne's ain't setting him up as a dupe, I've never seen a rig run before."

"You've seen more of the pair of them than I have," Nick said. "I've seen very little of Robert Yarborne. However," he added, thinking of what he had learned from Melissa, "I've reason to believe Yarborne himself may be no stranger to duping."

Minley's eyebrows shot upward. "You don't say so! I always did think there was something wrong with that fellow. Said so any number of times."

"I know you did, but then you suspect everyone of something, so if I didn't pay you the attention you deserved, you must forgive me. What makes you think Robert Yarborne is setting Oliver up for plucking."

"For one thing, they call him Rigger, don't they? I'd say that derives from thimble-rig, if anyone were to ask me. I can just see that chap picking up a pretty living with a quick hand, a rattling tongue, a deal board, three thimbles, and a peppercorn. Did you know he'd paid young Oliver's debts for him?"

"No, I did not."

"Well, he did. Won't tell you where I had that. Promised not to name names, but someone thought you should know. No telling what Robert will want as interest on that loan, of course, but I'd guess he just wants young Oliver nicely under his thumb. That's the general reason for plucking a minor, ain't it? M' friend said he heard Ulcombe had refused to keep paying the piper, and told Oliver he'd got to learn economy. Surprised to hear that, myself, but of course, if they present him with a lot of Oliver's vowels, Ulcombe's bound to pay them. Very expensive, your brother is."

"Nearly as expensive as I am," Nick said gently.

"Now, don't take a pet! Would you rather I'd kept the news to myself? Don't mind telling you I nearly did. Ain't one to split on a fellow, dashed if I am, but— Well, when all's said and done, I don't want to see your brother rolled up."

Nick reached out and squeezed his arm. "I'm not angry, Tommy. Not with you. I'll agree that Oliver's got some warm moments coming to him, but I want to see which way the wind's blowing where Seacourt's death is concerned first. If he was truly murdered by footpads, I hope they catch them quickly."

Minley looked sharply at him. "You say that as if you ain't sure, Nick. You think someone else did him in?"

"I don't know," Nick admitted, "but I've any number of thoughts on the subject. One thing Penthorpe said is true. Few people will mourn Seacourt, and there are many who might have wished him dead."

He was thinking of one person in particular when he saw Robert Yarborne cross the lower hall toward the exit. Taking a quick step toward the stairs, meaning to speak to him, Nick stopped when, below him, the outer door opened and Lord Dorian Minley entered. Robert brushed quickly past him and out to the street.

The vicar turned abruptly toward the closing door, then turned back to speak to the porter before he looked up and saw them. Handing his cloak to the porter, he gestured toward Nick and Tommy. Less than a minute later, he joined them at the railing.

"Did you see that young man push past me?"

"The young have no manners, Vicar," Nick said, putting out his hand.

The vicar shook it warmly, smiled at him, but did not speak. Looking at Tommy, then back at Nick, he seemed momentarily at a loss for words.

Tommy said, "Hope you're hungry, Dory. They offer a dashed fine meal here."

The vicar glanced back down at the hall, saying vaguely, "That sounds quite nice. I say, do you know who that young man was, the one who pushed past me?"

Nick was watching him closely. He said, "I begin to think I do, Vicar."

Tommy looked from one to the other in astonishment. "Well, of all the absurd things to say, Nick! You know Robert Yarborne as well as I do. By Jupiter, we were just talking about him, and now all you can say is that you begin to think you know who he is. Have you got windmills in your head?"

"Not windmills, Tommy, castles—and pawns." When Lord Dorian looked at him, his cheeks growing pink, Nick said softly, "Your chess player, Vicar?"

Tommy exclaimed, "Now, dash it all, Nick, how can you—?"

"He's right, Thomas." The vicar grimaced, looked ruefully at Nick, and said, "You're very astute. You always were, of course. I must suppose that Thomas told you about my second encounter with the fellow."

"Tommy's a sad rattle, "Nick said, smiling at his friend.

But Tommy was staring at the vicar. "Dory, do you really mean to tell us your unscrupulous chess player was Robert Yarborne?"

"I never knew his name, but if that fellow is Robert Yarborne—"

"He is, damn his impudence."

Nick gently suggested that they ought to continue their conversation in the dining room. Once they were seated at a corner table, where they had some privacy—and a bottle of wine to fortify them until their meal was served—Tommy said pensively, "I've been thinking, you know. It makes no sense. You must be wrong."

Nick said, "You said you could imagine Robert with three thimbles and a peppercorn, and it was you who suspected that he's been setting Oliver up as a dupe."

"Suspicions, Nick, that's all—no more than hypothetical examples of what I see when I look at him. Dash it, I expected you to say straight off that I'd suspect a nun of being the devil with a good habit. Still, if he ain't a flat-catcher, he's an egger. That's a chap who encourages flats and pigeons to bet more than they should," he added in an aside to the vicar. "What I can't figure is what's really in it for young Robert. He can't want to put himself in Ulcombe's black books. Dash it, Lord Yarborne's tried for the past year to cultivate your father, even to emulate him."

Nick said thoughtfully, "Maybe that is the plan, Tommy. Robert Yarborne, in the little I've seen of him, has not shown great intelligence. He's clever, and he's an opportunist, but his chess scheme had to have been impulsive at best. He must have known his victim could identify him, and might charge him with robbery."

The vicar cleared his throat. "If it's all the same to you, Nicholas, I don't want to do either one. No one wants to advertise being made to look foolish. Had it been the church's money, it would be different, of course, but—"

"That's probably what he counted on," Nick said.

"All the same . . ."

Tommy had been thinking. He said, "I still can't fathom his motive."

"Power, perhaps," Nick said. "Yarborne—Lord Yarborne, that is—seems to have used duping at least once before now to exert pressure on someone to submit to his will. At the very least, if Robert lent money to pay Oliver's debts, he's a gull-groper."

"But what's he get from it?" Tommy demanded. "If he's charging interest, my source hadn't heard of it, and he's no Captain Sharp, for I've never heard of him bullying anyone. If he's a cheat, he's a dashed good one. He don't palm cards or dice, and no one's ever caught him with uphills or downhills, let alone Fulhams. Why, if they did, he'd have to resign from his clubs—at least from the Billingsgate. Don't know that he belongs to any others. Not a member of Brooks's, is he?"

"No," Nick said. Seeing the vicar's bewilderment, he added, "Your little brother is revealing his vast knowledge of the business of Greeking, Vicar. I'd be ashamed that he knows so much, if I were you, but there it is. Uphills are false dice that throw consistently high. Downhills are the reverse. Fulhams, on the other hand, are weighted dice that consistently turn up the same numbers."

"And gull-gropers?" the vicar asked, raising his eyebrows.

Nick chuckled. "Men who lend money to gamesters at exorbitant interest, or in order to entwine them in activities they might otherwise avoid. You'll be interested to know, Tommy, that Oliver was kind enough to give my wife a pack of fuzzed cards as a gift, and to teach her how to use them. Fuzzed cards, Vicar, are cards marked or shaved in such a manner that one player knows where the court cards and aces are located."

The vicar seemed distressed. "You say Oliver gave such a pack to Lady Vexford? Good gracious, Nicholas—"

"He said he did so—indeed, that he had them himself—because it is to one's benefit to understand Greeking in order to avoid falling victim to it," Nick said blandly.

"Poppycock." Tommy snorted.

"Precisely," Nick agreed. "There is one more little bit of information I might give you. I'm fairly certain that Melissa encountered Fulhams at that ladies' supper Yarborne gave to benefit his charities."

"Then, by Jupiter, the fellow's a crook," Tommy said.

"In fairness," Nick said, "I've no evidence that Yarborne was to blame. I merely suspect him, because if the twig is tainted, most likely the tree is, too."

"We'll keep our eyes open," Tommy said. Then, grinning at his brother, he said, "How's your predatory widow, Dory?"

The vicar blushed rosily and said self-consciously, "As a matter of fact, I'm rather hopeful that she has begun to look elsewhere. A new gentleman in the parish has begun paying court to her, you see."

"She's jilted you," Tommy declared dramatically, clapping a hand to his chest in the general vicinity of his heart. "Poor Dory!" Then, looking beyond Nick, he added in quite a different tone, "But enough chat for now, gentlemen. Our dinner arrives."

Conscious of hovering footmen, they talked of other matters while they dined, but when the dishes had been cleared and replaced by two bottles of excellent port, a board of cheddar, and a dish of nuts, they returned to the subject of Greeking.

Cracking a walnut, Tommy said, "I still say that if Robert Yarborne is hunting bubbles and pigeons, his methods don't fit Vincent's Law, Nick. To acquire termage—that's velvet to you, Dory—one requires both a booty and gripe to do the Vincent."

"That's *all* Greek to me," Lord Dorian said, smiling again.

"Exactly," Tommy said, carefully picking the nut meats from the cracked shell.

Catching Lord Dorian's eye, Nick said, "I think the vicar was making a joke."

Tommy looked up from his task. "A joke? Dory? Don't be daft."

Pausing with his wineglass at his lips, Lord Dorian said, "Well, I did mean to be humorous, but the fact is that I don't know velvet from— What were the others?"

Seeing Tommy about to explain, Nick said, "Put simply, Vincent's Law is that cheating at cards or dice requires a banker, a gamester associated with the banker, and a victim. In this case, there is certainly no evidence that Robert Yarborne is the banker, even if he did lend Ollie money to pay his debts."

"Then none of it makes sense," Tommy said flatly, "unless someone else is paying Robert to shepherd lambs to some hell where they can be fleeced. As far as I know, he generally plays here at the Billingsgate, so that's out."

"He's clearly up to no good," Nick said. "Vicar, you really ought to challenge him over that chess-player business."

Lord Dorian flushed and looked away, then collecting himself, he looked back, straight into Nick's eyes. "I ought to do so, I know."

Nick shrugged. "Of course, he's bound to deny it."

Tommy said hotly, "No one would believe him over Dory!"

The vicar grimaced. "Such tawdry stuff. I should cut a pretty figure when all is said and done."

Nick smiled at him. "Learned a lesson, Vicar?"

"I certainly have."

"Then forget what I said. Chalk it up to experience, and be done."

"Dash it, Nick, he can't do that. That damned scoundrel—begging your pardon, Dory— He threatened him with a pistol, Nick!"

"Without witnesses," Nick explained patiently, "it is Dorian's word against his."

"But still—"

"No, Thomas," Lord Dorian said firmly, "As I said before, had it been the church's money, I would feel differently about it, but it was doubtless meant to be a lesson to me, and I've no wish to pursue it further. I'm very much afraid," he added with a self-conscious look, "that the main reason I returned to the Devil's Dyke—how aptly named it is, to be sure— The main reason—indeed, perhaps the sole reason—is that I'd hoped to meet that chess player again and perhaps obtain more money for the poor box. Greed, even on behalf of the church, is not a sin to which one wants to admit."

Tommy said, "But that fellow ought to be clapped up."

"Don't fret, Tommy," Nick said gently, "if I find that Oliver is meant to be the next dupe, being clapped up is the least that will happen to Robert Yarborne."

"If you're taking a hand in the game, that's all right then," Tommy said.

"I am rapidly ceasing to look upon these matters as moves in a game," Nick told him. "If you have both finished your wine, I suggest we adjourn to Brooks's. I prefer the atmosphere there, I think."

They left soon afterward, and when Lord Dorian expressed an interest in finding someone who would indulge him in a little whist, Nick surprised both of his companions by saying that he was in the mood for a game of whist himself.

"Now, dash it, Nick," Tommy demanded, "when's the last time you sat down in a foursome? I was sure you'd want to play hazard."

"You were wrong. I'm sure my luck would be out tonight. Moreover, I'm enjoying the vicar's company. Shall we find a fourth?"

The game broke up shortly before midnight, and Nick went home only to be told that his wife had retired early with a headache. He remembered then that he had promised to continue their conversation after he had found Penthorpe. He had certainly hoped to have a word with her before he left London. However, when he looked in on her, she was sleeping soundly, and he decided not to wake her. Instead, he left one hundred pounds on her dressing table so she could repay Lady Ophelia when next they met, and went in search of his brother.

Here again his intent was denied. One of Oliver's servants glibly informed him that Master Oliver was spending the night with friends on the road to Epsom, in order to arrive before the first heats on the following day.

Deciding he would do well to get to bed, since the road would be jammed long before nine o'clock with vehicles traveling the fifteen-mile distance just for the day, Nick rang for Lisset, and gave orders to be wakened before dawn.

Twenty-two

Pawn Threatened En Passant

The following morning, Oliver strolled into the breakfast parlor as Melissa was finishing her meal, and bade her a cheerful good-morning.

She regarded him with surprise. "Why, I thought you had gone to Epsom! I'm quite sure Lucy told me you spent last night with friends on the road."

He grinned at her. "Dashed clever, don't you think? Told my people to put it about that I'd gone already, because when I saw Nick last night, he was looking like he'd like to murder someone. Oh, sorry," he added. "Forgot about your father. I suppose I ought to offer my condolences, but I never thought you cared a button for him. Don't look at me as if you're seeing a ghost, Silas," he added when the footman entered. "Since you've cleared everything away, you'll have to stir your stumps to get me breakfast, but some beef and bread will do, and coffee. My head wants clearing."

Melissa waited until the footman had gone to do Oliver's bidding before she said, "The whole business about Sir Geoffrey is distressing, of course. One never wants another person to die, let alone to die violently, but I'd scarcely set eyes on him in nine years before he brought me to England, and I own that I'd come to care much more deeply for my stepfather than for him. But, Oliver, you should not have lied to Nicholas.

Not only will he be displeased but one ought never to tell lies."

"I didn't lie to him," Oliver said in a virtuous tone as he took a seat opposite her. "I never said a single word to him. Took dashed good care not to, for that matter."

"Well, it is much the same thing, I think."

He shot a look at her from under his brows. "You look pale. Has Nick been riding roughshod over you again? The minute I learned you had run into him at Vauxhall, I knew I'd best stay out of his way for a spell, but it occurs to me now that he must have cut up pretty rough over that business."

Remembering Vauxhall brought a smile to her lips. She said softly, "He was not angry, only a little vexed to find me wandering around the gardens by myself."

"Then you didn't catch up with Lady Caroline and her mama?"

"I didn't try to find them," Melissa admitted, "but now that I come to think of it, not having seen you since Tuesday night, Oliver, I never thought to warn you that I'd met him. How did you know?"

He shrugged. "People talk. I think it was Rigger who told me. Yes, that's right. He said his father had met the pair of you there, but I daresay you're wrong about Nick not being angry, and in any event, if he's learned that I'm in debt again—"

"Oh, Oliver, not again!"

"Don't say *not again* as if it were some dreadful fate. One hundred pounds don't last a fellow a single night if his luck's out, so my father ought to have known better than to think it would serve me till Quarter Day. I've tradesmen's bills, as well, which I didn't even think to tell him about at the time. Dash it, everyone is in debt to some extent or another, but I'll come about shortly. You just see if I don't."

"But how?"

"I put my money on Nick's horses for the Epsom races,

that's how. And if that don't work— But never you mind about that," he added, flushing.

"How can you have money to bet on races if you cannot even pay your debts?"

He waved airily. "One arranges these matters, that's all. Ah, there you are, Silas, and about time, too. I'm famished." As the footman set a platter of beef and a loaf of bread on the table and poured his coffee, Oliver said casually, "What are you going to do these next few days, Melissa? I thought Nick would take you to Epsom, but perhaps you don't care for horse racing."

She flicked a warning glance toward Silas, waiting until the footman departed again before she said, "You keep forgetting that my father was murdered. It would not be seemly for me to dash off to the Derby, especially since I did not like him much. People will be watching to see what I do, and although I am not certain exactly what I ought to do in such a case, I am persuaded that Nicholas is right to say I should stay home."

"Then he ought to have stayed, too," Oliver said, piling beef on his plate and tearing a large chunk from the loaf of bread. He chuckled. "Daresay that notion didn't suit him though, not after he'd missed all the best heats at Newmarket."

She hesitated, not wanting to tell him about her encounter with Yarborne, or to try to explain Nicholas's behavior when she really did not understand it herself. Although her headache had disappeared overnight, a certain dullness lingered, making it difficult for her to think, but she longed to confide in someone who knew him well. Meeting his brother's curious gaze with difficulty, she said, "There is a little more to the matter of my staying here than I led you to believe, I'm afraid."

"Well, I know Nick's in a temper again. What is it, if it ain't Vauxhall?"

She grimaced. "Some of it is private, Oliver, but when I said before that he had ordered me to stay here, I meant here in this house, not just here in London. He says he's worried about rumors arising from Papa's death, but I know he's angry with me, too, and he's got good cause to be, so I don't know how much about the rumors is true. But I'm not a child, after all, and I think I could deal with the sort of gossip he's talking about as well as anyone else can."

"Well, if he's angry, I can dashed well believe he rang a peal over you," Oliver said, grimacing. "The way he talks when he's in a fury makes most folks shiver in their shoes and fear he might do more to them than talk, but no matter how angry he is with you, you certainly can't believe he'd harm you."

"Oh, no," Melissa said quickly. "I am not afraid of him, but I never seem able to please him, either, and oh, how I'd like to please him, Oliver, if only to repay him for saving me. You don't know the whole tale about that, I daresay, and I don't propose to tell you now, but he did save me, and it cost him a great deal of money. Perhaps, now that Sir Geoffrey has died, I'll inherit enough to repay him, but indeed, I am sure he must wish by now that he had never married me. He only did so, after all, because he felt obliged to protect me from Sir Geoffrey, and now that reason no longer exists."

"Are you sorry he married you?" Oliver asked bluntly.

"Oh, no, I—" Tears choked her, and she turned away so he would not see her distress. When she could control her voice, she said quietly, "I know I've been talking wildly, and most of what I've said must seem foolish, but I want only to do what would be best for Nicholas. I just don't know what that is."

"You love him, in fact."

Melissa did not answer, but to her surprise, Oliver made no effort to pursue the point. Instead, he said, "You know, I've been thinking, and I wouldn't be surprised if Nick wasn't right about protecting you from the rumors. There's bound to be a lot of dashed unpleasant talk, you know, and it's his duty to protect you."

"But his notion of protecting me is to lock me up till he

makes it safe for me to show my face again," she protested. "I don't want that, and in this case, it's silly. I know Charley said people might think ridiculous things about who killed Papa, but the villains must have been footpads, and the authorities are bound to—"

"Dash it, Melissa, if Nick didn't explain, I daresay I oughtn't to either, but you must have thought about who's most likely to have wanted your father dead."

His words and the way he looked at her sent an icy chill racing through her. "Nicholas? I thought about that before, because of how angry he was about all that Papa did to me, but Nicholas was with me, Oliver."

Oliver stared at her. "What a dashed ridiculous notion! I can't believe I've heard such nonsense from two people I'd have expected to know better, and all in less than a day. I never meant that at all, and that's exactly what I told Rigger, too. It's Penthorpe, not Nick, who had reason to kill Sir Geoffrey Seacourt."

She realized Oliver did not know what she had meant, that he was unaware of all that Nicholas knew about what Sir Geoffrey had done. No one knew as much as Nicholas did, not even her mother or Charley, and no one else had seen the look of rage on his face when he learned about the dreadful things in her past. But even as the thought crossed her mind, she rejected any notion that Nicholas might have killed Sir Geoffrey. Not only had he been with her at Yarborne's, but it was as absurd to suspect Nicholas as it was to suspect Penthorpe. "Oliver, do you really think anyone could believe Penthorpe killed Papa to keep him from charging Mama with bigamy?"

"Not *could*. People *are* believing it."

"Good gracious, how very odd. Penthorpe is the gentlest of creatures. Although he was in the army and even fought at Waterloo, I don't think he would murder anyone. Moreover, he was not in town when it happened, and Nicholas was with me."

"But we don't know when Seacourt was murdered. We know only when he was found. Moreover, though I've heard that tale about Penthorpe's dashed odd abduction, you've only his word for it, and he's got the most to gain from Seacourt's death. As for this crazy notion that anyone could think Nick might have murdered him—"

"Robert Yarborne thought so. You said as much."

"Oh, Rigger was just out of sorts because Yarborne's been a bit short with him of late, but he says he can set that to rights again in a trice. In any case, I'll tell you like I told him, you can just put that notion out of your head. I don't deny Nick's got a fearsome temper. I won't even deny, between these four walls, that I've taken good care to keep out of his way since Tuesday because, whatever you say about his being only a trifle vexed, I don't trust him not to tear me limb from limb for taking you to Vauxhall and dashed well abandoning you there."

"But that was my fault, not yours. After all, you thought at the time—"

"It don't matter what you cozened me into thinking, Melissa. I knew then, and I know now, that I was wrong to take you there when I couldn't stay and wrong to leave once I'd taken you there. Whether you've noticed it or not, Nick is devilish protective of you. Good Lord, he's been so ever since you first met, if half what I've heard about that night is correct."

She felt the blood rushing from her head. "Then you *do* know! But I've not heard a soul speak of that awful night. Oh, Oliver, pray don't tell me that talk about that night is running through all the gentlemen's clubs!"

"Nothing of the sort. Nick would soon put a stop to it if that were the case. I chanced to hear about it from—"

"Robert Yarborne! But he was not there, was he? I don't recall much about that night, but I do think I would remember him."

"He wasn't at the Little Hell, but he was in Newmarket,

and since you were being delivered as a bride to his father, of course he heard most of the tale. You needn't worry that he'll tell anyone else, though. He agrees that it wouldn't help his father's reputation to have it noised about all over London that he was willing to take you in exchange for Seacourt's debts. And if Yarborne—Lord Yarborne, that is—cares about anything, he cares about guarding his reputation."

"I do wish you wouldn't discuss me with Mr. Robert Yarborne," Melissa said gently. "It makes me feel very uncomfortable to know that you have done so, especially since I particularly asked you not to."

"Well, it needn't," Oliver said, "and Rigger's had some dashed good notions. I told him you never know from one minute to the next what Nick is thinking—like you told me—and he said it's no doubt dashed uncomfortable for a wife not to know, but that it's likely Nick just ain't accustomed to letting his emotions show. He's a gamester first and foremost, Rigger said, and he's trained himself not to wear his emotions on his sleeve. In many card games, after all, to do so would be to betray to his opponents whenever he had a winning hand."

"But I am not his opponent," Melissa said.

"True, but Nick treats everyone the same. He believes, like any good gamester does, that the only time a man talks about his feelings is when he expresses satisfaction at winning the game. He don't gloat, of course, and he don't keep talking about what a good thing he did, but all the same," Oliver added with a smile, "I don't think he's sorry that he married you, you know."

"Because he won their stupid game that night? It cost him a great deal."

"I know it did, but he won more than he expected, after all. In gaming, that's called velvet, and it's a very good thing."

"He may have won more than he expected," she said with

a sigh, "but I don't think Nicholas thinks of it as a good thing right now."

"You *are* in the mopes, but Rigger did suggest that there is one way to learn the truth about Nick's feelings." Oliver pushed away his plate and refilled his cup from the coffeepot Silas had left at his elbow.

"How?"

"Leave him. Now, don't look so amazed. I reacted the same way, but as I told you before, Rigger's a dashed clever chap, and I think it will serve. First, if you go, it will show Nick you don't mean to knuckle under each time he tries to hide you away from trouble, and secondly, he'll follow you like a shot. Of course, I can't say what he'll do when he catches you, but at least you'll know he don't want you to leave."

Seeing the glint of mischief in his eyes, she opened her mouth to tell him he must be mad to suggest such a thing. But her own words to Charley echoed in her memory: *If I should choose to go out of town, be sure I will do so for my own good reasons.* She said, "Where would I go?"

His eyes twinkled. "Why not home to Scotland? Now don't bite off my head. You can't just go wandering hither and yon, after all. That would be foolish. And if you imagine Nick won't follow you that far, you've mistaken your man. Moreover, if you ask Penthorpe and your mama to take you, you'll accomplish two ends in one."

"Because it would remove Penthorpe from harm's way?"

"Well, it would."

She did not argue. The malaise that had settled over her since waking to discover that Nicholas had left the house without so much as bidding her farewell—although he had taken time to leave money on her dressing table for Lady Ophelia—began to lift. Charley thought she ought to go away. Clearly, Oliver did, too. Perhaps they were right. Nicholas had not really wanted to marry her. She was not certain he even had intended to rescue her. Now that she had come to know him better, she knew it was quite possible that he had outbid the others that night in Newmarket simply because he could not bear to lose.

No doubt some similar passion was to blame for the impulsive declaration that had led to their marriage. Having feared that Sir Geoffrey might win that hand if not the entire game, Nicholas had played his only trump card and taken the prize again.

She did not really care what his reasons had been then, but she wanted passionately to know what he felt now. She had seen signs that he cared for her, but he had never said so, and in truth, she had vexed and exasperated him more than she had pleased him. Their evening together at Vauxhall had been wonderful, and things might well have improved afterward, but that was before he caught her at Yarborne's flat, and before Sir Geoffrey's death had changed everything. Now, she feared that Nicholas might be relieved to let her go, and indeed, that it might be better for him if she did.

Oliver could dismiss the notion that people might suspect his brother of the murder, but now that she realized his presence at Yarborne's flat would not protect him, Melissa was not reassured. If they could believe Penthorpe had killed Sir Geoffrey, they could certainly suspect Nicholas. Robert Yarborne might even have started such a rumor. She had learned enough about the *beau monde* to realize people might believe anything if it were sufficiently scandalous, and her husband's temper was legendary. But if he let her return to Scotland, no one could seriously believe he had committed murder for her. One thing she would not do was ask Susan or Penthorpe to go with her, for despite Oliver's assumption that they would, she knew they would refuse to leave London so long as the smallest cloud of suspicion lingered over them. They would also insist that her proper place was with her husband.

"You going to do it?"

Soberly returning Oliver's mischievous gaze, she said, "He may not follow, you know. He is more likely to divorce me. I would certainly be giving him cause."

"Aye, abandonment. Of course, you'd have to stay away for quite a time before he could make Parliament swallow that, but since the circumstance won't arise . . ." He grinned, clearly seeing no reason to finish the sentence.

"He won't have to wait. Thanks to Mama's experience, I know something about Scottish divorce, you see. All I need do is suggest to the Commissary Court in Edinburgh that Nicholas has enjoyed sexual congress with another woman."

Oliver stared at her. "Look here, what do you know about such things?"

"Lady Hawthorne made no secret of their connection, nor has he."

"By Jupiter, I'll warrant neither of them claimed any such connection since your marriage. Well, Clara might have," he amended. "I don't trust that wench. Shouldn't even mention her name to you, of course, but dash it, Melissa, you can't go about saying Nick has committed adultery when he wouldn't do any such thing!"

"I don't know that," Melissa said, though her conscience pricked her. She went on steadily, "If I do say it, no one here needs to know, and if I divorce him in Scotland, he can easily obtain a divorce here. He will then be free to play his games any way he chooses. I suspect he might say no more than that I've put down my cards and left the table, having no wish to risk more of my stake on the outcome."

Oliver smiled wryly and said, "No, he won't. If you do go through with this, Melissa, I just hope you never tell him I had anything to do with it."

"You need not trouble your head about that," she said, lifting her chin. "Since I'm growing more and more certain that he won't pursue me, the question won't arise."

"Now I wish I'd never suggested this," he said, grimacing, "because if Nick ever does find out I had anything to do with it, he'll murder me. Still, I'm sure Rigger's right, and he'll be after you in a flash. Then you'll know exactly how he feels about you." He paused with another frown, then said, "Look here, how do you mean him to learn that you've gone? I hope you don't want me to tell him."

"No, I don't," she said.

"Well, I'm glad of that, although if I were to tell him straight off when I reach Epsom, it might serve to send him dashing back to London. That would suit me down to the ground, under the circumstances. Are you sure he ain't vexed about Vauxhall?"

"He did once say that if he learned you had taken me he'd throttle you, but I daresay he didn't mean it, and in any case, I never actually told him that you did. Even so, Oliver, don't say anything about this. I'll go, because the more I think about it, the more I'm sure it's the best thing to do, but I don't want you to spoil the races for him. It would, you know, since other people might think he ought to follow me, and—" She broke off, unable to think of any other reason.

"Well, I won't. It wouldn't do you any good to be caught before you'd left London, and you'll need time to talk Penthorpe and your mama around, I'll wager."

"No, for I don't mean to ask them," she said. "I could never persuade them to go like that, and they would either send me back here or keep me at St. Merryn House until Nicholas returns from Epsom. If I do go, I mean to go alone."

"But, dash it, you can't do that!"

"I'll take Lucy," Melissa said hastily.

"That's all right then," Oliver said, grinning at her. "I daresay you can be ready to leave by tomorrow, but you'd do better to wait until Friday. Nick's bound to get back that evening, so he can be hot on your trail at once or early Saturday morning. I'll wager he catches you before you get to York."

In that case, Melissa decided, she would leave at once, because if she was to do the thing at all, she would do it thoroughly. She would probably learn more than she wanted to know about Nicholas's feelings, but if people began wondering if he might be guilty of murder, the sooner she took the wind out of their sails, the better it would be. She hoped the authorities found the footpads quickly, and that Nicholas's horses won their races. He deserved to win something after all the trouble she had given him.

When Nick arrived at Epsom Downs shortly before nine that morning, he learned that, as usual, the company the previous day had been small, consisting mostly of families from nearby country houses, and a few gentlemen of the turf with their friends.

"A good many more will come today," Drax said, greeting him. "Speculation's running high for the Derby, my lord."

"Wagers are running high, too, I hope," Nick said.

"Aye, sir. Odds are best on Reformer to take the Derby, but to my mind, it's near impossible to say which of the seventeen running is the best. No one names the same favorite for two hours together, but most agree that the Prince ain't even in the running. Odds against him are twenty to one right now."

"Good," Nick said, smiling at him. "I'm putting my blunt on Shelley's Cedric to win, and on the Prince to place second. He'll gain only a hundred pounds from the subscription stakes, but I'll do much better than that in private wagers. Can Quiz take the Oaks tomorrow, do you think?"

Drax was noncommittal, so Nick decided not to put more than his subscription stake of ten sovereigns into that race. He was not disturbed, for the winning horse was to be sold on demand for one hundred fifty pounds, and he was not ready to sell Quiz. The three-year-old would be worth much more in another year.

After looking over his horses, he strolled about the grounds looking for friends and acquaintances. The number of private tents had increased this year, he noted, and, as he discovered for himself by walking to the top of the hill, a commodious stand, newly erected there, commanded an excellent view of the greater part of the course.

Epsom racecourse resembled a great amphitheater nestled

in woodland at the bottom of the hill. By ten o'clock the hill was covered from top to bottom with carriages, many filled with females of elegant appearance. Customarily, Nick would have paused to flirt with more than one of them, but no such urge overcame him today.

Despite an overcast sky, people continued to arrive in droves, and from the hilltop he could see the road to the Downs, thronged with vehicles of every description. Curricles and four-in-hands, pony-chaises and humble market carts formed an unbroken line as far as he could see.

He was glad he had left London at dawn, for although there had been traffic on the Epsom road, he had maintained his usual fast pace. Now, in the creeping sea of vehicles, he was able to pick out a number of friends, including Tommy and the vicar. He did not see his parents, however, and not until it was nearly time for the running of the Derby did he catch sight of his brother.

He had joined the Minley brothers before he saw Oliver. Since Lord Dorian was nearly certain that he had spied his predatory widow in the surging crowd, Nick had been helping them keep watch for her, but he did not hesitate to excuse himself. Striding toward Oliver, he caught his gaze and waved.

For a moment, Oliver looked as if he meant to turn tail and disappear in the crowd, but he evidently thought better of it.

"I want to speak to you," Nick said when he was close enough.

"I'm looking for my friends," Oliver said airily. "Just got here, you know. Lord, what a crush! Like this all the way from London—-a damned snail's pace."

"All the way from London? I thought you came part way last night."

"Oh, did you? Well, I didn't. I decided to come down with Rigger, but at the last minute, he changed his mind."

"Which last minute," Nick asked gently. "Last night, when you were supposedly already on the road, or this morning, when you actually left London?"

"This morning, not that it makes any difference," Oliver said. "I know you don't like him much—"

"I don't know him well enough to like or dislike him," Nick pointed out. "I'll admit, however, that what I do know of him, I don't much like."

"Well, dash it, that's just what I mean. You say you don't know him, then you insist you don't think much of him, and I suppose you've said as much to Father. I'll tell you to your head, Nick, Rigger's been more help to me than anyone in my family."

"By paying your debts, in fact," Nick said evenly.

"I don't know where you heard that, but it's perfectly true. My own father said he wouldn't help me when I got into dun territory—and through cursed bad luck, too—and I didn't even ask you. I knew that would be futile."

"Yes, it would. You must learn not to wager money you can't afford to lose."

"Easy for you to say. You're as rich as Midas."

"No, I merely take care to win more than I lose, and when my luck is out of vein, I don't bet. Witness the fact that I'm risking only my stakes money tomorrow on Quiz. He's outclassed in the Oaks, I'm afraid."

"Well, you might have told me that before now. I bet on him to win."

"I haven't seen you since Sunday. If you want to hedge those bets today, put a bit on Shelley's Cedric to win the Derby. He's paying four and a half to one, and if the sun doesn't come out, he should win. I've watched him for months. He always runs best when there is no glare on the track. He should take this field easily."

Oliver looked shocked. "You're betting against Prince in the Derby?"

"Oh, I've my subscription stake of fifty guineas on him, of course, but half of that is forfeit, no matter who wins. He's at twenty to one, Ollie, with the same odds against his placing, so my real money's on him to take second."

"Dash it, I put money on him to win, too."

"Well, I'm sorry about that, but you might have asked me what his chances were, you know. If the sun were shining, I'd back him to take Cedric, odds or no odds, but as it is . . ." Abruptly, he added, "You've been avoiding me, Ollie. Why?"

Oliver looked away, saying gruffly, "Thought you'd be angry about Vauxhall."

"I ought to be."

Flushing, Oliver looked back at him. "I know I shouldn't have taken her there."

"No, but I've a notion she would have gone anyway, so I'm glad that you were with her on the river at least. What I really wanted to talk to you about is these new debts of yours. You know Father is not going to be happy—"

"My debts are my concern," Oliver said, his voice low and tightly controlled. "They are none of yours."

"You won't say they are not Father's concern, however," Nick said gently.

"Well, they're not!"

"Yes, they are. Who do you think will be expected to pay if you cannot?"

"I'll pay them. It's all arranged, damn you!"

"Keep your voice down," Nick said sternly. "No one is paying heed to us now, but they will soon enough if you begin shouting at me. I collect that Robert Yarborne has helped you arrange some way to pay your debts. Are you aware that his code of conduct is not of such a high standard as your own ought to be?"

"I don't know what you mean." His tone was sullen, and he looked away.

Nick told him about Robert Yarborne's duping of Lord Dorian, but if he had hoped to change Oliver's opinion of his friend, he was disappointed.

"A prank, that's all that was," Oliver said, laughing. "I'm sure I've done the same sort of thing to Tommy, although nothing as clever as that. If Dory was taken in, it was his own fault. Don't tell me he didn't hope to get more money from the chess player for his precious church. He'd never have gone back if he didn't."

"No, that's true, as he will admit himself. But it doesn't make Robert Yarborne's behavior any more admirable. He threatened him with a pistol, Oliver, like a highway robber. Is that what you admire? I'd thought better of you."

"Well, I don't believe Rigger used a gun, and if he did, I'll wager it wasn't loaded. As to my so-called code of conduct, it's the first time you've given me credit for having one," Oliver muttered.

"You are fast proving me wrong," Nick said brutally. "First you introduce two innocent young women to the art of card sharping, then you incur debts you cannot afford to pay and lie about your whereabouts in order—"

"I didn't lie!"

"Did you not?" Nick spoke coldly. "You must forgive me, Oliver. In my book, encouraging one's servants to lie is much worse than doing so oneself. You ought to be setting a good example, not encouraging immoral behavior. How can you trust them to speak the truth to you if you've encouraged them to lie to others?"

"Dash it, they wouldn't lie to me, and I don't need lectures from you, my Lord Vexford, to know how to deal with my affairs. I'll tell you how it is, Nick. Melissa's right. You can't be content with playing your own cards. You want to play everyone else's hand as well. At least, she didn't say it that way, but my debts are none of your damned business, and my servants even less so. Just stay out of my life!"

"Very well," Nick said, keeping his temper with difficulty. "I'd intended to offer to stake you to a more likely wager on the Prince, but as it is your wish to deal with your affairs alone, I won't interfere."

"Don't then! I won't conceal from you that I'd hoped your nags would win their races, but I've already set a plan in motion to take care of things if they don't. You are not the only one with a brain, I'll have you know. My other plan *can't* miss."

"What other plan?" Nick demanded.

"I won't tell you, because it was Rigger's notion, and you're bound to say something cutting, but you'll see how he looks after me. I'll be making my fortune, Nick. In fact, I won't be around tomorrow, because I'm going back to London tonight. I've an important engagement at the Billingsgate," he added loftily, turning on his heel.

Nick made no attempt to call him back, knowing it would be useless. He was well aware that he had handled Oliver badly. Nonetheless, much as it went against the grain, he decided to open the budget to Ulcombe when he found him. He did not doubt that the earl could speedily rein Oliver in, but that was not why he knew he must bring the matter to his attention. Certain now that someone intended Oliver to play the pigeon, Nick knew it was Ulcombe, not Oliver, who would bear the plucking if the plot succeeded.

Deciding he had better return to town that evening himself, he was surprised at how much the decision buoyed his spirits. Not until that moment did he realize he had been feeling increasingly uncomfortable about the way he had left things with Melissa.

He wished that he could leave at once, but he decided that to do so would betray his hand to his brother if to no one else. He would talk with Ulcombe, and as the day progressed he would give the appearance of a gentleman enjoying the races. Once Oliver had departed, he would follow, not on his heels but soon enough. He would get Tommy to go with him as a precaution, but heaven help any man who got in his way, especially if his name proved to be Yarborne.

Twenty-three

Rook Captures Queen

Melissa departed from London with less effort than she had expected. Despite having assured Oliver that she would take Lucy, however, she did not mention her plan to the maid. She was certain that Lucy would feel, and rightly, that her allegiance was to the Barrington family, not to its newest member. Soon after Oliver left, just before ten o'clock, she packed a change of clothing into a bandbox, donned her blue hooded cloak, slipped the money Nicholas had left her to repay Lady Ophelia into her reticule, and slipped out of the house without a word to a soul.

In Pall Mall, after allowing several hackney carriages to pass by, she waved at last to an older jarvey who she thought looked less larcenous than the others. When he drew his vehicle up beside the flagway, she paused before getting in to say, "I wonder if you can help me find a post chaise to hire for a journey to York, or possibly farther?"

The burly, grizzled man regarded her thoughtfully before he said, "You running away from home, missy? Because if you are, I won't help you a jot. Wouldn't like someone helping one o' my lasses if she took it into her head to bolt. Which none of them wouldn't," he added, "knowing what's good for them."

Taking Lady Ophelia as her model, Melissa drew herself

to her full height, looked the man in the eye, and said, "My good sir, I am, in fact, attempting to return to my home, and I am in a considerable hurry. If you won't assist me, I shall simply find another man who will. I have plenty of money, so someone will certainly oblige me."

The jarvey looked swiftly both ways along the pavement, then said, "If you've half a brain in your cockloft, miss, you won't go announcing to the world around us that you're carrying a bagful of money. Now, before, I'd have said you was needful only to get yourself to the Black Bear in Piccadilly to hire yourself a job-chaise, but knowing you now for an innocent wench without much sense in your noodle, seems to me the best thing would be for me to take you to Barnet, where I've a brother-in-law working at the Green Man. He can be trusted to see you safe on your way."

"Barnet? Isn't that too far for a hackney to take me?"

"Bless you, miss, if you was to pay my fees, and if I was of a mind to be out of town for a fortnight or more, I could take you all the way to York without a-breaking of a single rule of law."

"Well, how much will you charge to take me to Barnet then?"

He frowned. "Regular fee be nine and six, I'd guess, for it's all of eleven miles, and the rate be sixpence for each half mile, plus an additional sixpence for each two miles completed. Law says I ought to charge you for my return, as well, but I shan't, for I can get a passing fine dinner from my sister, you see, and visit with her and her family. Just saw her at Easter, but I warrant she won't say I've worn out my welcome."

Realizing that he was making a joke, Melissa smiled. "You are very kind, sir. I'd be most grateful if you would take me to Barnet."

Not only did he do so but his brother-in-law arranged for her to hire a yellow-and-white job-chaise and a pair of fine looking bays, and the jarvey's sister packed a lunch basket for her to take along. The postilion, wearing the green livery of the posting house, was young but seemed much in awe of the jarvey's brother-in-law, and Melissa knew she would feel perfectly safe with him.

The jarvey seemed to think that she ought to hire a full team of four and a second postilion, but when she asked the cost, the sum astonished her, and she firmly rejected the suggestion. Even more than the cost, she worried about the attention she would be likely to draw with such an equipage. A single female alone in a job-chaise drawn by an ordinary pair would not be nearly so likely to be remarked.

The postilion would not accompany her all the way, of course, but would remain with his horses when the change was made. Nonetheless, the jarvey assured her that since she had hired the chaise, she would have Green Man postilions all the way to York. She had paid for the chaise only for the first day's travel, but the men assured her that although it was past noon, she ought to make Wandsford or even Stamford before day's end if she was willing to endure the long hours in the chaise, and travel after dark. She assured them that the more distance she could cover the better she would like it.

Just north of Barnet, she saw the first in a series of unusual signs, a banner stretched between two poles at the side of the road with painted black lettering that read *M, forgive me.* The second one, a poster at Hadley Green, said *M, I've been a fool.* The third was a large placard fastened to a wall of the Duke of York Inn at Ganwick Corner. It read, *M, please, darling, I need you,* and was signed, amazingly, with the initial *N.* Melissa had thought the first one no more than an amusing example of the lengths to which someone might go to express his feelings, if he were the sort to express them. Seeing the second, she thought that whatever the fellow had done he was certainly exerting himself to make things right again. The third made her smile and pretend to herself that she was the mysterious *M* and that Nicholas had put up the signs. She opened the basket and took out a sandwich. Munching thoughtfully, she began to watch for the next one, wishing the postilion's steady but slow pace were faster.

A boulder by the side of the road outside Hatfield displayed the message, *You are my only love.* By the time the postilion drew up for the first change, in Welwyn, she had been on the road for nearly three and a half hours and had seen at least ten signs. She wished she had written down the messages. They seemed to indicate that the sorrowful and clearly repentant *N* had done something to make his *M* believe him unfaithful, or—at the least—to think he did not love her. He was doing everything in his power to correct that misconception, and Melissa was convinced of his sincerity. She hoped the unknown *M* would be convinced, too, and wondered if the signs would continue all the way to York, or if *N* would win his point long before that.

At Woolmer Green, the sign said, *If you must leave London, at least don't leave me.* The next, at the Swan in Broadwater, said, *I'm waiting for you, darling.* But at Stevenage, she got a shock: *Melissa, I love you.* When the letters leapt at her from the large white placard fixed somehow or other to the brick wall of the White Lion Inn, she felt dizzy. Surely, the painter could not be Nicholas. It crossed her mind then that Oliver might have set her up for a prank, but at first she dismissed the notion out of hand, believing he would not—despite his insistence that he did not fear Nicholas—make mischief of a sort guaranteed to bring that gentleman's wrath down upon him. But if not Oliver, who? Nicholas could not possibly have done it. Her imagination, which had made her feel increasingly guilty and uncomfortable with each passing mile, boggled when she tried to imagine him with a paintbrush in one hand, a pail of black paint in the other, lettering the signs she had seen along the road.

Then it occurred to her that Oliver might have had a more devious plan in mind. He had told her he believed Nick cared for her, and he had deduced for himself that she loved Nick.

What if he had decided to bring them together, to make them see that each cared for the other? What if he not only had set her up for his latest, but had set Nicholas up as well?

At Graveley, she nearly shouted at the postilion to turn back when she saw *Melissa, I want to make things right between us. I love you, my darling—N.* Two thoughts stopped her. The first, that the messages might be meant for another Melissa, made her fear she would make a fool of herself if she assumed Oliver had written them. The second thought, that Nicholas might already be waiting for her somewhere on the road to the north, made her peer ahead, eager to read the next sign. She found it at Baldock: *Melissa, come to me where we first met. We'll begin again. Nick.*

Lingering doubt vanished, and she knew that from the moment Oliver had suggested leaving, she had hoped and prayed, despite her insistence that Nicholas would not follow and demand her return, that he would do precisely that. Now, persuaded that Oliver had somehow managed to arrange it all, and that Nicholas might have learned of her absence within minutes of her departure, she felt profound relief that he had not caught her in Pall Mall, chatting with the jarvey. Even now, thought of his temper gave her pause, but hoping Oliver knew his brother as well as he thought he did, she let down the window and shouted at the postilion to stop.

When he drew up and looked over his shoulder, she said, "I've changed my mind. I want to go to Newmarket instead of York."

"Newmarket!"

"Yes, can there be any objection?"

He scratched his head, frowning, then said, "That'll mean Royston to Cambridge, that will. Aye, mistress, we've got arrangements with the Green Man in Royston and the Birdbolt in Cambridge, so you can keep the chaise and make your change at Cambridge. I've never been to Newmarket, myself, so I dunno where you'll fetch up there, but I daresay something of a sort can be done there, too."

"The Rutland Arms Inn is where I want to go," Melissa said firmly, "but you need not trouble your head about where I'll find horses or a postilion, for I won't want the job-chaise any longer after that. It can be taken back with the Cambridge horses. Is that not what should be done when I've no more use for it?"

"Aye, mistress. It will get back to London from Cambridge as easy as from York or Edinburgh."

"Need we change horses before . . . you said Royston, did you not?"

"Aye, I did, and we don't, for this pair be good till Biggleswade which is much of a muchness with Royston, as I recall."

"Can you spring them? I'm in a hurry."

"Not from here to Royston, I daren't," he said. "That be a mighty slow road, ma'am, but from Royston to Cambridge be a fine one. Like as not, if you pay extra, the Royston lad will make as much haste as you like."

"Then I'll want four horses hitched up in Royston." She could not think why she was in such a hurry, for she knew Nicholas would be displeased that she had left London, even if it was all part of Oliver's scheme. She wasn't even sure she wanted to give Oliver the satisfaction of knowing how easily he had influenced her to do as he wanted. But, if he was right about Nicholas, the prize would be worth the cost.

The road from Baldock to Royston was as poor as the boy had predicted, taking them two full hours, though he told her it was only a bit more than eight miles. She saw no more signs, and shortly before they rolled into the yard of the Green Man in Royston—which looked nothing at all like its counterpart in Barnet—she had begun to wonder if she might be mistaken. Surely, Oliver—or whoever had acted for him— would have put up at least one sign to show he really wanted her to go this way.

Doubts continued to assail her on the Cambridge road. What if she were mistaken? What if Nicholas was at Epsom, just as he had said he would be? What if she were making an utter fool of herself? However, her doubts vanished again east of Cambridge when she saw, *The inn garden, darling. I'll be expecting you.*

Just as well that she had doubled the number of her horses and postilions, she thought, smiling in anticipation. The day had been gloomy, with the sun never putting in so much as a brief appearance, but the gray light was fading rapidly, and she was sure the sun must have set some time before. After the slow pace she had been forced to endure before Royston, she might well have missed that last sign in darkness.

The closer the chaise drew to Newmarket, the more clearly she remembered her first visit. How much had happened since that dreadful night. Less traffic traveled the road to-night than she and Sir Geoffrey had encountered then. Not only were there no races being held now, but nearly everyone in town associated with racing had undoubtedly gone to Ep-som for the Derby.

Darkness had fallen some time before the job-chaise rolled through the arched gateway into the torchlit inn yard. A middle-aged groom came running to let down the steps and open the door of the chaise. Melissa thanked him but said, "One moment, please. I must speak with the postilions." Moving to the nearside wheeler, she said to the man mounted on it, "I hope you don't mind returning to Cambridge tonight. I shan't need this chaise any longer."

"No, ma'am, that's what we were told when we left Cambridge."

She had paid extra posting charges in Royston and Cambridge, but she gave both postilions generous gratuities and thanked them for delivering her safely. The man on the wheeler tipped his hat when the foremost one gave his leader the office. As she watched them deftly turn the chaise in the narrow confines of the yard, she became conscious of a presence behind her. Turning, she saw that the groom was still there. He held her bandbox, which she had forgotten until that moment.

"Oh, thank you for retrieving that," she said. "I'd have left it in the chaise and never given it another thought till I required something from it."

"I've a message for ye, ma'am. The party what you're meeting tonight be yonder in the garden behind the stables."

"Oh, good, then he *is* here!" Since her mind was occupied with wondering what Nicholas would have to say to her, it was not until she had moved past the stable into the garden that it occurred to her to wonder how the man could have known she was the one to whom he was meant to give the message. She turned back to ask him, but when she did, he gestured, and she turned again to see a cloaked figure standing a short distance ahead of her in an area shadowed from the torchlight. He stepped further back into the darkness, and Melissa hurried forward, exclaiming, "You don't know how close I was to turning tail once I realized what Oliver had done, but now that I see you here, if you dare to be angry with me for allowing myself to be gulled—"

Her last words, and the scream that followed, were muffled by the heavy cloth thrown over her before she was scooped up into a pair of strong arms and carried swiftly away. She saw nothing more before she heard the eldritch screech of a door opening and found herself dumped onto a hard floor. Though the cloth was removed, she was quickly blindfolded, bound, and gagged, all without once having clapped eyes on her captor. The door screeched again. Then all was silent.

Nick reached London shortly before ten that night, driving his phaeton, with the Minley brothers following in Tommy's curricle. Leaving Tommy to deposit Lord Dorian at his house, and believing Melissa to be safely at home, where he could speak with her later at length, Nick drove straight to the Billingsgate Club. He had taken care not to follow Oliver too closely, for he wanted to discover exactly what mischief his brother had become embroiled in, and he fancied that if Oliver knew he was looking into it, he would elude him. In any event, Nick was convinced that Oliver would be allowed to win for a time at least, so there could be no need to make haste.

As he entered the main subscription room, he wondered if Robert Yarborne might be in league with one of the groomporters there. He supposed it would be possible to suborn one of these men. Since the Billingsgate apparently encouraged young men like Oliver to wager stakes they could not afford, the standards set for their servants could not be too high. He saw Lord Yarborne talking with another gentleman, but he did not see Robert or Oliver. Moving from table to table, he made no attempt to place bets but was twice delayed by friends anxious to commiserate with him over the results of the Derby, which they had learned not long after the race, thanks to the excellent services of the carrier pigeons. Since Prince Florizel had placed second, just as he had hoped, these conversations did not divert Nick long from his purpose.

He made his way at last to the card room. Here, play was quieter, and he quickly spied Oliver on the far side of the room, near the opposite door, at a table with a second man. The room was large, most gentlemen were absorbed in their cards, and no one called out to him. Not recognizing the man with Oliver, Nick took a seat at a table as far removed from the pair as possible and signaled to a footman, asking him to bring wine and a pack of cards.

"Are you expecting someone else to join you, my lord?"

"Yes, shortly," Nick said. "I'll amuse myself until he arrives, but bring us a piquet marker, will you?"

Tommy arrived fifteen minutes later. He, too, slipped into the room quietly, drawing no attention to himself. "Who the devil's he playing with?" he muttered, reaching for the wine decanter and glass the servant had brought for him.

"I've never seen the fellow before. Oliver's winning, I

think, but not enough to make him do more than smile occasionally. He's been letting him win, I'd guess, but if a move's to be made, the fellow ought to make it soon."

"Thought you expected to see Robert Yarborne here."

"I did. Yarborne senior is in the main subscription room, but the younger one's nowhere to be seen."

"Think his lordship is in it, too?"

"I don't know," Nick said, "but I wouldn't be surprised. I spoke to my father at Epsom. Well, I could hardly keep this to myself," he added with a sardonic smile when Tommy raised his eyebrows. "It's his money they're after."

"All the same, you might have made a push to settle this without telling him."

"Not without knowing whether they have already approached him in some way. They haven't, but he's returning tonight. He's leaving this to me, however, so stop bristling, Tommy. I thought you wanted Oliver to learn a sharp lesson."

"I did. He deserves one. Be a good thing for Ulcombe to know what queer stirrups he's got himself into, too. Can't deny that."

Nick grinned at him. "But you'd like to, Tommy. You complain about Oliver all the time, but you wouldn't split on him any more than I wanted to."

Tommy grimaced. "You think you know everything." He sat up straighter. "Don't look now, Nick, but Yarborne's come in—not the youngster, his lordship."

Nick began to deal cards for a hand of piquet. "What's he doing?"

"Just wandering about, speaking now and again to someone. He looks like a host, chatting up his guests at a ball, if you ask me."

Nick said evenly, "He's a cold-blooded man, Tommy. The only reason it hasn't become apparent before now is that whenever anyone notices one of his vices, he seems adept at opposing them with proof of a contrary virtue."

"You never seemed to care about him one way or the other before," Tommy said. "What's happened, Nick?"

Nick was watching Oliver's table and did not answer, for Oliver was clearly losing now. Quietly, he said, "Do me a favor, Tommy. Find out who that fellow is."

"I'll get us another bottle of wine," Tommy said in a normal tone of voice.

Nick noticed that he was careful to keep his back to the table where Oliver sat with the stranger, but he thought it would not have mattered if Tommy had turned toward them, because both men were absorbed by their cards. Oliver was frowning, but before Tommy returned, he had begun smiling again.

Tommy said, "You won't credit this, Nick. He's a dashed Belgian count."

"You're right, I don't credit it. A Captain Hackum, perhaps, but that fellow is no nobleman, Belgian or otherwise. I wonder who introduced him to the Billingsgate?"

"Seems a bit nearsighted, the way he keeps peering at his cards," Tommy said.

"So he does," Nick agreed, still watching the pair. There could be no doubt now that Oliver was winning again, and winning a considerable amount by the look of it. Moreover, Nick soon realized just how he was winning. No one else, as far as he could see, was showing any interest in that particular table, which was a good thing. Oliver was not very accomplished yet in his cheating. Evidently, he, like Tommy, believed that the "count" was exceedingly nearsighted.

When the hand was done, Oliver's opponent smiled and said something. Oliver nodded, put down the cards he had been about to deal, and stood up, stretching a little.

"Looks like they're stopping," Tommy said.

"Just to have supper, I think. Don't watch so openly, for God's sake. I want to keep an eye on them, but if you keep looking that way, too, they're bound to notice us."

"Give me the cards then," Tommy said. "I'll deal the next

hand. Shame I ain't betting on this game though. I'd be sure to take you for a monkey at least."

Nick smiled, but he did not look at Tommy, for Oliver had turned away from the table, and in that instant, the Belgian "count" exchanged the two packs of cards on their table for two others. If Nick had not been looking at him, half expecting such a move, he would not have seen it. As it was, the exchange was so practiced, so smoothly and confidently accomplished, that he nearly did not see it anyway.

"What is it?" Tommy demanded. "You're looking like thunder."

Nick picked up the hand Tommy had dealt him and began to sort his cards, muttering, "That rogue just switched packs while Oliver's back was turned."

"The devil he did!" Tommy put his hand down. "By Jupiter, let's go explain to him that, in England, that sort of thing just ain't done." He began to get up.

"Sit down," Nick growled. "Oliver's playing in water deep enough to drown in, but I want to see what rig's being run, and he deserves whatever is coming to him."

"Dash it, Nick, he don't deserve to be cheated!"

"I take three cards," Nick said flatly, doing so.

"Damn you," Tommy muttered, but he returned his attention to his hand, adding a moment later, "Dealer takes five."

"Point of five," Nick said.

They played idly for the next half hour, neither man keeping his mind on the game. The card room was quiet. Lord Yarborne had left some time before. Nick did not know whether the older man had seen them, but he was not surprised that Yarborne had not included them among the friends with whom he had stopped to speak.

A footman refilled the decanter on Oliver's table and put down fresh glasses. Otherwise, no one took any notice of that table. Forty minutes passed before the players returned, and Nick half expected Oliver to see him then. Doubtless believing Nick still at Epsom, Oliver was not keeping watch, but the fact that he clearly had no thought beyond his next hand spoke volumes to an experienced gamester.

Tommy apparently noticed Oliver's concentration, too. As Nick shuffled for the next deal, he said, "He didn't even glance around. By Jupiter, look at the way he's snatched up the cards to deal them. He's shuffling. Seems most intent, Nick."

"Yes. He wants the money, Tommy. He owes Robert Yarborne a considerable amount, I believe—more than he ever confessed to my father—and if I don't mistake the matter, he put borrowed money on my nags to win."

"Young lunatic, but you know, Nick, you ought to be flattered by his confidence in your horses, and by the fact that he tries to be like you."

"I'd be better pleased if he would try less to emulate me and act sensibly."

"You being such a pattern card of sense yourself."

Nick grimaced. Glancing at the other table, he saw that Oliver was looking in bewilderment at the hand he had just dealt himself. As play began, the look changed quickly to amazement, then fear. When the hand was played out, the "count" spoke first, but Oliver shook his head, gesturing in agitation. His opponent signaled to a footman, spoke to him, then leaned back in his chair, as if waiting for something.

Oliver's complexion had paled from fiery red to a bloodless white. Judging it time to intervene, Nick put down his cards, saying, "I believe I want a closer look at that game now, Tommy. You with me?"

Tommy got quickly to his feet. "By Jupiter, yes. Young Oliver looks as if he's swallowed a spider." He would have moved quickly, but Nick slowed him with a touch, then stopped him when Yarborne entered by the supper-room door and bent to speak to the "count." The latter spoke briefly, then gestured toward Oliver.

Oliver said something in agitation to Yarborne. Then, as Nick and Tommy strolled within earshot, Yarborne said, "I'm afraid the club cannot allow you to extend your credit further, Mr. Barrington. You will have to cover your losses at once. I believe the best thing, if the 'count' will agree to it, would be to sign your vowels over to me. Since he is leaving the country, I will cover what you owe him and then apply to your father for payment. I daresay that Ulcombe, grieved though he—"

"No," Oliver said. With his attention on Yarborne, he still had not seen Nick or Tommy. He said grimly, "I'll pay my own way, sir. I-I can't quite manage to put my hand to the money tonight, but I'll come about. I assure you, if you will be kind enough to cover what I owe, I'll repay you as soon as I'm able."

"Mon Dieu, milord Yarborne, but that will not serve," the "count" said haughtily. "This young man, you see, he tried to play me false. Those cards are shaved, as you will find if you but examine them. He is a cheat, but me, I was too skillful to be caught."

Flushing, Oliver straightened and drew a breath, but before he could speak, Nick said, "I'll guarantee my brother's losses, Yarborne, but I'd like an opportunity to win the money back." He looked steadily at the supposed "count." "Shall we say one game of piquet, sir, winner take all?"

The "count" bowed. "I would like to accept such an offer, sir, but how am I to know that you, too, will not attempt *un petit tour de fripon?"*

Yarborne said, "The man makes a point, Vexford. I'd never have suspected that Mr. Barrington would attempt such a knavish trick as to cheat an opponent, so how can I speak for you, sir?"

Nick said calmly, "I don't recall asking you to speak for me, Yarborne. Just what concern is this of yours?"

When Yarborne hesitated as if considering his answer, the "count" exclaimed in surprise, "But, *mon Dieu,* surely you know that milord *owns* this grand establishment!"

Making no attempt to hide his astonishment, Nick raised

his eyebrows and shot a sardonic look at Yarborne. "Is that a fact?" he said. "How very . . . commonplace."

Flushing, Yarborne said in a voice filled with meaning, "My honored friend spoke out of turn, but I feel sure I can rely on your discretion, Vexford. I admit I would not like it noised about that I hold an interest in this club—not any more, I feel sure, than you would like certain other matters talked about publicly."

Nick smiled, but there was no amusement in the expression. "It was not Oliver who switched the packs on the table before the two went down to supper," he said in a voice that he knew would carry to nearby tables. "I saw this fellow switch them, and I believe my brother was set up for duping. I'll wager you will find, if you examine these cards, Yarborne, that they are shaved just as your *honored friend* claimed they are, but I'll wager, too, that if both Oliver and the Belgian turn out their pockets, you will find the original packs with the Belgian."

Indignantly, the Belgian said, "He lies! Never would I so demean myself. However, if he desires to try to win his brother's money back, I shall oblige him. Me, I do not wish to make a scandal for so elegant a club. Sit down, monsieur."

"We'll have a fresh pack, if you don't mind," Nick said, taking Oliver's seat.

A servant approached and gave a folded message to Yarborne, saying, "I was told to hand this to you at midnight, my lord."

"Thank you. Fetch these gentlemen a fresh piquet pack, at once."

Nick said gently to the "count," "I'd be obliged to you if you would take off your ring, and put it in your pocket. I won't suggest that you have been using it to mark your cards. I'd just feel better if you were not wearing it while we play."

Without a word, the "count" took off the heavy signet he wore and slipped it into his pocket. Other players had left their tables to stand nearby and watch, but although the principals had apparently dropped the notion of turning out any-one's pockets, no one suggested doing so. Yarborne, having read his message, said curtly, "You will have to excuse me, gentlemen. I've business to attend to."

They played swiftly, and Nick's luck was in. In the second hand, the "count" found himself piqued, repiqued, and capot-ted.

"You play exceedingly well, monsieur," he said. "The stakes, they are even now. Would you like to play another game?"

"No," Nick said flatly, "I don't stay. Come along, Oliver."

Following obediently in his wake, with Tommy behind, Oliver was silent until they were outside on the pavement. Then, looking from one man to the other, he drew a deep breath, looked into Nick's eyes, and said wretchedly, "He was right, you know."

"I know."

"Then how the devil did you dare suggest to Yarborne that he look for any packs in that fellow's pocket? Did he really switch them on me?"

"He did. I saw him. A reverse pack, I'd wager. You dealt to him what you thought you had dealt yourself."

"That's it, exactly. I knew my tricks weren't working, but I couldn't think why."

"Those who set you up, Ollie, and taught you how to cheat, knew exactly what you'd do, but I gambled that your near-sighted Belgian wouldn't dare produce your cards to prove they'd been shaved. To do so, he'd have had to admit he'd cheated, too. But I've got a question for you," he added gen-tly. "You were clearly winning before dinner."

"I was. I began with a thousand that Rigger lent me, and by the time we stopped to eat, I was nearly three thousand ahead."

"Then how did you come to grief on a single hand after-ward?"

"He said he had an appointment, that he'd set himself a

limit of what he could lose before he'd have to quit, and that
if I was willing, he'd just bet the rest—five thousand pounds,
Nick!—on one game. I'd been winning so much, so quickly,
and I was absolutely confident that I'd win again." He had
the grace to look ashamed, adding, "I didn't cheat at first,
Nick, honestly. I was winning fair and square, but then when
I began losing, I got more and more desperate. Rigger had
arranged for us to get those packs to begin, you see. I thought
he must have bribed a porter, but I suppose, if Yarborne owns
the club, he didn't have to do any such thing. He's the one
you were talking about, I know, for he's the one who taught
me the tricks of the cards. Dashed if I'm not beginning to
think now that this is why it's always high tide with him."

"Yes," Nick said, "and with Yarborne, too. Now I think
we know how he amassed his wealth. They are sharps, plain
and simple. I won't be surprised to learn that even the title
is spurious."

"Probably the real name is Yard-born," Tommy said scornfully.

"I was a fool," Oliver said.

"Yes, but they set you up, first by teaching you how to
cheat and then by easing you into a position where you'd be
too desperate to do anything else. They depended on your
guilty conscience to keep you quiet while they extorted the
amount of your losses from Father. I have more to say to
you about all this, which you are not going to enjoy, but that
can wait. How did Rigger get you into the game with that
Belgian?"

"He lent me my stake, as I told you," Oliver said ruefully.
"He said I couldn't lose, that the fellow was so nearsighted
he couldn't tell one card from another, and so it was at first.
I swear I never meant to cheat, but Rigger had lent me so
much money, and I owed other creditors, and"—he drew a
deep breath—"and since I knew just how to do it, the temp-
tation grew until it became irresistible. If you hadn't come
along—" His voice broke on a sob. "God, I'd have been

ruined, and Father— What he would have said! I-I deserve whatever you do to me, Nick."

"I own I'd like to horsewhip you, Ollie," Nick said quietly, "but we'll talk about it all later. I think we can arrange something slightly less painful. You might as well know that Father knows about the duping. I won't tell him about your cheating though, and you are not to tell him yourself. It would disappoint him far too much."

Oliver licked his lips, shoved a hand through his hair, then looked at him again. "I'm grateful, Nick, but the devil of it is that I've served you a dashed backhanded trick in return. I don't deserve what you've done for me, and that's a fact. Melissa's gone."

"What the devil are you talking about?"

"She left, or if she hasn't gone, she's leaving. It was one of my fool pranks, because she thinks you don't care for her, that she's just a prize in a game you won. She said you were angry with her again, that she can never be what you want."

"She's wrong," Nick said, fighting to control his dismay.

"Lord, I know that. It's my belief you fell hard for her the moment you laid eyes on her, or you'd never have parted with your blunt like you did. It's why I told her to go. I knew you'd follow her and bring her back. Even Rigger agreed with me. Half of London must know you're nutty on her, the way you poker up if anyone so much as—"

"You say Robert Yarborne knew of this? What's his part in it?"

Oliver looked surprised. "Why, we just talked, the way friends do. There was Seacourt's body being found and all, and Rigger was saying how his father was a deep one, and how when Rigger thinks he wants someone to do a thing, it frequently turns out that Yarborne wanted them to do something else altogether. Well, he wasn't making much sense, I can tell you, but it struck a chord with me, so I told him Melissa had said something similar about you. Well, Rigger likes a prank as well as I do, and he said we ought to put it into her head to bolt so that you'd follow like— What?"

Nick looked at Tommy. "I'm thinking that more than one rig has been run today. I just wonder if one sharp is dealing the cards, or two."

Tommy frowned. "Are you thinking Seacourt's death is a part of this, Nick?"

"I'm thinking it was a miscalculation," Nick said. "I think we'd best get back to the house. If Melissa's already gone—"

"I told her not to go before tomorrow," Oliver said, "but I'll wager anything you like that she left the house soon after I did this morning."

"We'll soon find out," Nick said, "and if she's gone, my lad, you can forget what I said about painless remedies." He turned to Tommy. "It occurs to me that we might want to lay hands on our Belgian 'count' again, if for no other reason than to help shut down Yarborne's damned club. Will you attend to that? I'll leave it to your judgment how to manage him, but I'll support any promises you have to make."

"Leave him to me," Tommy said, "but are you sure you won't need me if you have to go out of town again tonight."

"I won't need you," Nick said, "but if anything happens to Melissa before I find her, Oliver is going to need someone to patch him up when I'm through with him."

"That just goes to show that you do love her," Oliver said shrewdly, "but you needn't worry about her coming to any harm, you know. She promised faithfully that she wouldn't go anywhere without her maid."

"You damned well better hope she didn't lie about that," Nick said grimly, striding forward to meet the phaeton before his groom had drawn it to a halt.

Twenty-four

Check and Counter-check

After Melissa's captors left her, she felt the blackness closing in, shutting off the very air she needed to breathe. By moving against the side wall, she managed after some moments to scrape the blindfold off, but even then she could not have seen a hand before her face had she been able to raise one. Since her captor had not spared an ounce of compassion in binding her, she feared the circulation in her wrists and ankles soon would be impeded. No use to hope she might somehow free herself, either. Even the gag was cruelly tight.

Tears welled in her eyes, and for a moment the urge to give way to them was nearly too much for her. But then anger replaced fear. Not for a moment did she believe Oliver responsible for her present position, and if he were not, then someone else had put up the road signs. But who could have done such a thing? Who could possibly have known she would respond as she had, that she would recognize their meaning and obey the final instruction to return to Newmarket, to the Rutland Arms? She realized then that Oliver could not have known so much. Surely no one but Nicholas himself knew her well enough for all that. But even if somehow Nicholas had aided Oliver, he had no motive for such a betrayal—no reason to have her captured, bound, gagged, and left to rot in this dank and dismal shed. Or had he?

Remembering some of the things he had said after finding her at Yarborne's, but remembering, too, that he had promised on his oath never to lift a finger against her in anger, she wondered if somehow this could be his way of keeping his promise while still teaching her a lesson he thought she deserved. He had commanded her to stay at Barrington House, and he had said he would make her sorry if she defied him. What better punishment than to show her the risk she had run? In her experience, for a man to believe he was keeping his word even when he was doing something hateful like locking his wife in a toolshed to teach her the error of her ways, would be entirely in keeping with the way men generally interpreted their authority over women. Moreover, Nicholas had shown a taste for locking her up from that first night when he had taken her clothes to keep her from leaving the house.

Somehow, though, it was hard to put such a deed in the context of what she knew about him now. She could not imagine him forgoing the Derby to commit such a vile act against her, no matter how errant he thought her behavior. To imagine him sacrificing Epsom to prove his affection for her had been easier, because it fit with his view of himself as a gamester through and through, a man answering a challenge in such a way as to win his point unconditionally.

The night was not cold, but the shed was nippy, and before long, despite her cloak and a pile of what she suspected were burlap sacks beneath her, she could no longer ignore the creeping chill. Wriggling to find a more comfortable position helped get blood moving in her veins again, but she became increasingly uncomfortable and began to fear that she would soon have no feeling left in her hands and feet.

Time passed slowly. She could hear occasional sounds from the inn yard, the clatter of horseshoes on cobbles when a single rider arrived, and the greater noise of iron wheels and a team when a carriage rolled into the yard. Shouts rang out from ostlers and grooms now and again, but the yard was not busy, certainly not so busy as it had been on her previous visit.

A rustling alerted her to the possibility of rats or mice, and she shivered, feeling colder than ever. Would her captor, whoever he was, leave her in this awful place much longer? She tried moaning, but the sounds did not even stop the rustling. Persuaded now that a mouse, if not a horrid rat, shared her quarters, she wriggled again, scraping her feet back and forth along the ground. The rustling stopped.

Knowing she would not sleep, she turned her thoughts to Nicholas again, and to the decision she had made to leave. She had been foolish then and even more foolish to dismiss her postilions before discovering who awaited her at the inn. She wondered how she had ever thought she was sensible enough to look after herself. Clearly, she required a keeper. If she ever got out of this mess, Nicholas would be the first to agree with that assessment, if he did not order her clapped into Bedlam.

A new rustling caught her attention. Realizing that the sound came from outside the shed this time, she struggled to sit upright, wincing at a streak of pain that shot up her arms from her bound wrists. Thumping followed by a metallic rattle and a muffled epithet told her that someone was coming. But even as the hope entered her mind that one of the inn servants had come to the shed to fetch some tool or other, and that freedom was at hand, the door swung open with a screech, two shadowy figures stepped hastily inside, and the door shut with only slightly less noise than before.

"Find some oil, for God's sake," muttered a masculine voice, "and slosh some on those damned hinges."

"Aye, sir, I'll have a look, but I'll be needing a bit o' light if I do, and someone will be bound to see it."

"Here, I've a tinderbox with brimstone matches. No one will notice a small flame, for it will be dawn soon. We didn't see a soul around, you'll recall."

"Nay, for who'd come to a shed at the back of a garden

when all's said and done? Still and all, it don't do to be lighting the place up too bright, I say."

"Nor to draw the attention of everyone for miles about by opening that damned door again without we muffle its screech," the other retorted sarcastically.

Melissa had not recognized their voices, but when, after the metallic scrape of flint against steel, a match flared to life, she was not surprised to see that her chief captor was Robert Yarborne, and his companion the man she had mistaken earlier for a stableboy. Wrinkling her nose against the sulfurous smell of the brimstone match, she remembered Oliver's saying that he had confided her troubles to his friend, and knew he must have also informed Robert of her intent to depart for Scotland. To imagine Robert Yarborne or the scoundrel with him scurrying about with a paintbrush and pail was certainly much easier than it had been to imagine Nicholas in that role. She could only wonder how they had managed it so quickly.

"I suppose you are surprised to see me," Robert said smugly as his henchman, finding a lantern, lighted it with a second match and quickly turned it as low as it would go. The soft golden glow set shadows dancing on the walls of the shed, but only after moments had passed without a reply from her did Robert notice the gag. He said in much the same tone as before, "I'll remove that thing but only if you promise not to shriek. Believe me, you don't want to be found here with me, for I shall say that we were running away together, and you'd have a dashed hard time, in the circumstances, to prove otherwise. Do you understand me?"

She nodded, wishing she could slap him, wishing she were Charley or, better yet, Lady Ophelia, either of whom would know better than she how to deal with Master Robert. But even as that thought crossed her mind, the name she had unconsciously given him presented a ludicrous image to her mind of Robert as a child, and she began to relax. Charley was right. Courage was all in how one perceived one's opponent. That, in turn, affected the way one perceived oneself and one's ability to cope with any situation. She looked directly at him as he leaned to untie the gag, wishing the lamp were not behind him so that she could read his expression and better gauge his mood.

He loosened the gag and untied her ankles, and she had all she could do not to cry out at the sudden pain caused by returning circulation in her cheeks, lips, and feet. Opening and shutting her mouth with care, several times, she licked dry lips and wiggled her toes, glaring at her captor.

"Cat got your tongue?"

"You told me not to shriek," she said hoarsely. "In any event, I've nothing to say to you that you want to hear."

"A wench ought to keep her mouth shut, in any case, and just do as she's told," Robert said, his grin so wide that even though she could scarcely make out his features, she could see his white teeth.

She held her tongue.

"See, Lakey," he said over his shoulder. "Females just need to be taught to know who's master, like I said before."

"I don't think much of this business," the man called Lakey muttered. "You shouldn't ought to be tyin' up a gentry mort like that 'un."

"I suppose you think I ought to turn her loose."

"Not sayin' that neither," the man muttered. "Just sayin' they'll be some-un coming to this shed before long, and then we'll find ourselves in the suds, certain."

"I don't intend to be here when they open the shed," Robert said. "I'm not daft, you know. I'm a proper guest of the establishment. What are you looking at, dear madam? Do you dare to laugh at me?"

"No," Melissa said, "but I must say, I cannot think how you intend to get away with this outrage. I am not entirely unprotected, after all."

"If you mean that husband of yours, I don't think you should expect to see him anytime soon," Robert said.

An icy tentacle of fear wrapped itself around her heart. "Why not? You didn't do anything horrid to Nicholas, did you?"

"No need for that. The Derby will keep him out of my hair for a time, and although Ollie seems to think he'll ride after you when the races are done, I take leave to doubt that. Stands to reason. No man would chase after a wife who made him look foolish, and Vexford ain't one you'd expect to chase after a petticoat of any kind."

"But when he learns what you've done—"

"Time enough to fret about that if it happens," Robert said. "Long before then, I'll have handed you over to the man who by rights ought to have had you from the outset. He'll know how to keep our Nick out of the business. For that matter, once you've been properly dealt with, Nick won't want you back. Some men are funny like that, and as I recall it, he was never much for taking another man's leavings. If you want my advice, you'll exert yourself to please your new protector."

Melissa straightened, trying to put aside warring emotions that threatened to prevent her from thinking properly. She did not doubt that Nicholas would shun a wife who had been used by another man. His own activities would mean nothing. Her actions, on the other hand, especially those that had brought her to this pass, would be as everything to him. And for that, she had no one to blame but herself.

"Master Robert, I be hearin' more activity in yon inn yard," Lakey said from his position near one of the cracks in the wall. "Can't see nothing, but sounds like more folk be up and about. I don't like this. Don't like it at all."

"Let me worry about it," Robert said with an edge to his voice. "There will be no trouble, not when she realizes she has no choice but to obey me."

"Are you my new master then?" Melissa asked. She tried to keep her voice even, but she seemed to be losing the knack of speaking submissively, and she saw from the way he stiffened that he disliked her tone.

He said grimly, "Do you think I cannot master you, madam?"

"I do not know," she said calmly. "You are bigger than I am, certainly, although you are not by any means as big as Nicholas."

He paused. She hoped he was visualizing her husband's formidable size and having second thoughts, but he said with a sneer in his voice, "I am not afraid of Vexford, madam, so I'd advise you not to be insolent."

"Considering the circumstance, I thought I had expressed myself in an extremely amiable fashion," she said. Really, she thought, she sounded less and less like the old Melissa. She began to wonder if her brain had been affected by the events of the past few days. Although she could not be certain one way or another, one thing had become clear to her, and before Robert had thought of a response to her admittedly provocative remark, she said quietly, "You captured me for your father, did you not?"

Seeing that he looked more like a sulky boy than a villain, she realized that more light had found its way into the shed. If she could keep him talking, perhaps someone would come who could protect her until she could get word of her plight to Nicholas.

Robert said, "It was bad enough when my father realized what he had lost to your husband in that auction, but if you had any notion of how angry he was at losing you a second time, you'd know why I've exerted myself to arrange this. He'd give anything now, I think, to have you in his power again."

"I paid the debt I owed him," she said.

He smiled. "Setting that little trap for you amused him, but it didn't get him what he wanted. He wants you, madam, and I mean to make him a present of you to do with as he pleases, as a bit of velvet added to what he's already gained today."

"Velvet? What do you mean?"

"Velvet means—"

"I know that it means a profit beyond what is expected," Melissa said, recalling that Oliver had told her as much, "but how can that pertain to me?"

"Only that first I gave him a fool, guaranteed to enrich the coffers at his club, and now he will have the woman he prizes above all to warm his bed."

"What club? What are you talking about?" Her mind swiftly calculated the points he had mentioned, and presented a shocking conclusion. "Good gracious me, you've duped Oliver, haven't you? That's what he meant when he said that he would make all tidy even if he didn't win any money at Epsom. It was you all along, wasn't it? You seduced him, teased him with the thought of riches, of being free of his family, free from his father's discipline and his brother's oversight. I know you taught him all those wicked card tricks, for he told us so. He said you told him a gentleman had to know the tricks in order to spot cheaters and sharps, but he never spotted you, did he?"

"I fancy I'm clever enough to befuddle a wiser man than Oliver Barrington."

"You even cozened him into suggesting that I leave London, and befuddled as *I* was, I let him persuade me. But you won't fool his brother," she added curtly.

"Oh, I don't know. Whose side does Ollie generally take, may I ask? Does he leap to believe what Vexford tells him? Did he believe I had anything but his best interest at heart? Ah, now you're looking a bit nohow, madam. The fact is that, even after the losses he suffered last night, I shall bring young Oliver round my thumb again. I'll simply say we were shocked to learn that a certain Belgian count is no more than a Captain Hackum of the first stare, that when Ollie began to cheat—as I'm certain he did because he was perfectly primed for it—his opponent caught on and only waited his chance to turn the tables. And Ulcombe will pay Ollie's debts, you know. Whatever he might have said to the contrary, these latest ones will be too large to refuse. That was the whole point of the exercise, that and giving him cause to be beholden to my father for not making a scandal of Oliver's naughty habits."

"I don't know what you are talking about," Melissa said, "but if you think you can continue to deceive Oliver—or to extort money from Lord Ulcombe—after I tell them what you have told me, you are all about in your head."

"But you will not tell anyone anything, madam. By the time my father tires of your company, you will not want to show your face in London, let alone to your husband or to Ulcombe."

She knew he was right. If she did indeed fall prey to Yarborne in such a manner, she would be less welcome in society than her mother was. The knowledge sent a wave of fear through her, but to her astonishment, it did not paralyze her thoughts as fear had done so often in the past. She had no sense of withdrawal or of watching herself from a distance. Instead the fear transformed itself into rage, burning deep inside but doing nothing to inhibit the workings of her mind. If anything, her thoughts grew clearer. One way or another she knew she would outsmart this man, and his precious father, too. She could do it, and she would. The only problem was how.

Lakey said, "Master, stir about, do. No time to be chit-chatting with the mort. We must be out of here in a pig's wink if we don't want to meet trouble."

Robert said, "First I mean to make it plain to our captive what will happen if she crosses me." Reaching for her, he yanked her to her feet and gave her a shake rough enough to elicit a cry of pain. "Be silent, damn you," he snapped, slapping her.

Her ears rang, but she said steadily, "I couldn't help it.

My wrists and ankles have been tied for hours, and they're afire with pins and needles now."

"Well, it will get a lot worse if you give me cause," he muttered. "I don't mean to be taken up by the law for this, so if it comes to a matter of your life or mine, guess which I'll choose."

She believed him. "I won't provoke you," she said quietly, "but I'd like to know how you think you'll get me away from here. People will want to know why you are dragging a woman about with her hands tied behind her and a gag in her mouth."

"But I'll be doing no such thing," he said. "I'll be walking arm in arm with my lady, who, if she values her hide, will not say a word. I know how that father of yours treated you, and I promise I'll do much worse. I've already set it about that my sister has run away from home and that I'm here in Newmarket hunting for her, so if you give me any trouble, dear madam, I'll slap you silly right in front of the person to whom you speak. Then I shall tell him—or her—that I am taking you upstairs to await our father's arrival, and that when he arrives, you will receive the beating you deserve. Do you think anyone will believe a tale of your telling after that?"

She didn't. Although his story conflicted with what he had said before—that if she screamed he would claim the two of them had run off together—she had no doubt that he was clever enough to talk his way through any circumstance, or that he had already planted information most skillfully. It was, after all, part of his trade as a seducer of innocents to be able to tell a lie with aplomb. Still, to one who had ceased to fear Sir Geoffrey even before his death, Robert Yarborne seemed a tame villain.

Sighing in what she hoped he would mistake for subdued resignation, she said, "I won't defy you. Where will you meet your father?"

He looked surprised. "Why, here of course. I wrote a message yesterday before I left London, and ordered it delivered to him at the stroke of midnight. We should see him by noon or thereabouts. In the meantime, I've taken the precaution of bespeaking a bedchamber and a private parlor. We'll go there as soon as I am convinced that you understand the folly—indeed, the grave danger to yourself—of making a scene of any kind."

"I understand," she said, "but you had better untie my hands now. My feet feel better, but it will take time to restore circulation to my hands."

"Oh, I'll untie you," he said, dealing quickly with the ropes at her wrists, "but I'll tell you right now"—he grabbed her chin and made her look into his face—"that you'd best mean what you say, dear madam. Not so much as a greeting to anyone inside the inn unless you want to be soundly slapped and thrown over my shoulder. There's not a man in the place who won't understand I'm just chastising an errant sister, and cheer me for it. And if you begin shrieking, I'll clap my hand over your mouth and tell them you've got a tongue like a fishwife's and that I'll not allow you to disgrace the family any further with your wickedness."

She didn't doubt any of his threats, but an idea had taken root. Hardly daring to hope that she might find an opportunity to put it into play, she rubbed her aching wrists, ignoring the tears that welled in her eyes. She forced herself to think only of the possibilities that lay ahead. Again, that odd sense of everything growing clear in her mind overcame her. She felt calm and collected. If there was a niggling fear at the back of her mind that she was in acute danger, that she ought to be terrified out of her wits and praying for Nick somehow to know of her plight and rush to her rescue—and forgive her for her foolishness—she drew on her increasing resolution to repress it.

When she could walk steadily again, she decided the light had improved enough for him to see the smudges on her face, the marks from the gag and ropes, and the state her hair was in. "I-I must look a fright," she said, hoping the sight would bring him to his senses.

"Aye, you do," he agreed, "but no one will expect you to resemble a fashion plate, will they? Not after your brother's been hunting high and low for you all night. Now, let me think. Where did I find you?" When she moved to shake out her skirts and straighten her cloak, he said sharply, "Keep your hands beneath the cloak. I don't want to hear any remarks on those rope burns, and I doubt they'll vanish soon."

She said, "My gloves are yonder, where you must have thrown them when you tied me. They are long enough to cover the marks, should the cloak swing open."

Gesturing for his man to fetch the gloves, he said approvingly, "That's a good notion. I'm glad to see you mean to be sensible."

Since that was the impression she had hoped to convey, she was satisfied. Praying that she did not look too much like a wench from the stews of London, she let him lead her to the door. Outside, she drew a welcome breath of fresh air, but she was not cheered by what she saw when they reached the stable yard. Ostlers hurried about, but not one looked at them. It was, she thought, as if people appeared in the garden at dawn every morning. The more likely reason, she knew, was that, since the gentry were known to be odd, an ostler did himself no good by questioning their actions. With that knowledge in mind, she was not surprised when their approach to a side entrance of the inn went unchallenged and unremarked. She would receive no help from the servants.

Robert's grip was tight enough to leave bruises on her arm. He kept a sharp eye on the men in the yard until they reached the door and Lakey leapt forward to open it. When he did, Robert clearly recalled the role he had chosen to play, for he gave Melissa's arm a sharp yank, propelling her through the doorway.

She had never entered the inn by that particular door, so she was surprised to find that they had entered the coffee room. Robert's grip on her arm warned her to keep silent, and she realized that he had expected the room to be empty. It was not. Two men sat at opposite ends of the long table near the fire, eating their breakfast. The distance between the pair showed that they were strangers who happened to be sharing a table. The one with his back to them did not take his attention from his plate. The other, however, looked up at their entrance.

Melissa saw his gaze shift quickly from Robert to her. His eyes widened, and she knew she must look as bad as she had feared. Nevertheless, keeping her head at an angle that she hoped Robert would mistake for humility, she shot a look at the stranger that would have earned her a sharp rebuke from either her husband or her great-aunt. Fluttering her lashes, she was amazed at the ease with which she seemed able to keep her ears cocked for the sound of Lakey's footsteps, her body limp and responsive to Robert's stern grasp, and her central mind focused on the man at the table. That she had caught the latter's interest was clear. His eyes widened more, and his lips twitched with the beginning of a grin.

Melissa batted her lashes again, then curved the corners of her mouth into a slow, responding smile, hoping that if she looked a mess, she looked a seductive mess. She straightened and glanced obliquely at Robert, assuring herself that his attention was on the opposite doorway, before she allowed herself a grimace of distaste for the benefit of the watching man. He stirred responsively, and just as it looked as if he might stand up, she tugged on the hand grasping her arm.

"Mr. Yarborne," she said quietly, "I ought to tell you that the man at that table is a friend of Vexford's. He knows me, and will not for a moment believe I am your sister. I should infinitely prefer to avoid making the sort of scene that might lead to gossip in London, but he does look as if he means to approach us. If you hustle me into the hall, I am sure he will follow, and he may well say something to the landlord that will lead to your discredit."

Robert glanced at the man in such a way that the stranger sat back down rather hurriedly. "He won't trouble us," he said in a grim undertone. "You just keep silent."

"Very well," she said docilely, "but it can do you no good to have him inquiring about Lady Vexford's whereabouts if you have bamboozled the landlord into believing I am your runaway sister. You might recall that Vexford frequently stays here when he is in Newmarket, so he is known to them. His temper is legendary in these parts, I believe."

"Then perhaps I had better call for a carriage at once."

"Well, you may certainly do that, but I should think it would be better to allay Mr. Amory's curiosity before it grows. If we were to sit down at that other table and order breakfast, instead of retiring to a private parlor, he may assume that I am traveling with relatives, and won't be stirred to ask the landlord any questions about us."

"And I am expected to believe that you will not speak to him, I suppose," he said in an undertone laced with irony.

"Certainly not, if he does not speak to me first. I am not so forward in my manner as that, and I scarcely know the man. He has been presented to me, but he is not of our class, of course, so if he does more than bow in passing, I shall be amazed. If I were to go straight into the inn, however, he would doubtless think Vexford himself is a guest here, and inquire after his whereabouts," she added, pleased with this excellent embellishment.

It convinced him, for he gestured toward a table near the window, saying, "Lakey, we want coffee and a proper breakfast. See to it."

"Aye, master," the man responded in a tone that revealed his deep disapproval of this change in plan.

Melissa took the seat nearest the window, arranging her skirts and trying surreptitiously to smooth her hair, all the while aware that the stranger was watching her. "Have I got smut on my face?" she asked in a voice that she knew would carry across the room.

"You have." To her astonishment, Robert chuckled and said in a carrying voice. "That will teach you to ride full speed at a gate, my dear, when you cannot see what lies on the other side."

So indignant at having her horsemanship mocked that she forgot her plan for a moment, she exclaimed, "As if I would ever do such a foolish thing!"

"Just bad luck then," he retorted in a tone that told anyone who was listening that he was humoring her.

Recollecting herself in an instant, Melissa looked down at her hands, then shot a furtive look at the stranger from beneath her lashes. He was still watching, clearly intrigued. The second stranger shoved his empty plate away and stood up, coffee mug in hand, to stride across the room toward the hallway, shouting for more coffee. Lakey had gone in the same direction, looking for a waiter.

Melissa flicked a come-hither look at her target, but this time Robert saw what she was about and reached across to grab her hand, his grip crushing her fingers together so sharply that she winced. Caressingly, he said, "Oh, my dear, I believe you did injure yourself. We'll find the landlord's wife, shall we? She will know just what to do for you." As he began to get to his feet, he leaned nearer, adding in a menacing tone that only she could hear, "If you know what's good for you, you'll come quietly, or you'll very soon get that scene you want to avoid."

Submissively, she got to her feet, murmuring, "Yes, sir." But when he reached to take her arm again, she leaned away as if to catch up her skirt with her other hand. Swiftly, she sent a beseeching look at the stranger, who got to his feet again and took a step toward them.

"Oh, Mr. Amory," she said, hurrying toward him before Robert could stop her, "I did not recognize you at first, sir. You must forgive me, but you know I've only met you a time or two with Nicholas." Turning back to Robert, she went on glibly, "You need not leave the table, sir. Mr. Amory will be more than pleased to take me to the landlord's wife whilst we exchange compliments and chat about Nicholas. Won't you, *dear* Mr. Amory?"

"To be sure, lass, I'd be pleased to do whatever you've a mind to."

"There, you see, Robert," she said, chuckling. "You have been complaining about what a charge I have been to you ever since Nicholas placed me in your care—first by falling off my horse, and now by finding that I require help simply to care for my arm. You must make me look after myself now, mustn't he, Mr. Amory?"

"Whatever you say, lass."

Robert looked eye to eye with the stranger, who was the same height and a few stones heavier. Melissa held her breath. "I'll look after her," Robert said.

"No need to stir yourself about, young man. I'll take the lady where she wants to go." His flat tone made it clear that he intended for Melissa to make the choice.

She placed her hand on his arm. "You are much too kind, sir, but I do promise you that I shall not be such a charge to you as I have been to Mr. Yarborne."

"No trouble at all, lass, and how is old Nick keeping himself these days?" He grinned, and Melissa grinned back at him, grateful to have such a willing conspirator but hoping he would not prove difficult to be rid of later.

"Oh, Nick is fine, sir. I'll tell you all about him."

Leaving Robert with his mouth open, she went with her newfound friend, wondering what on earth she would do next to keep from falling right back into Robert's clutches. A glance over her shoulder as she left the coffee room showed her that at least he was not going to challenge the man again, for he stood gaping. When they met Lakey just inside the corridor, and saw his surprise and then dawning awareness that she had got away, she hoped she had nothing more to worry about.

Lakey went past them into the coffee room, whereupon Melissa stopped and turned to her curious rescuer. "Thank you so much for helping me get away from those men," she said. "If you could just see me safely to the landlord now, I will ask him to order a chaise to take me back to London. I know you haven't the least notion of what you have done, but you have earned my eternal gratitude."

"Dramatic as ever, my dear Melissa," declared a hatefully familiar voice. Her rescuer, whose large person blocked her view of the coffee-room doorway, turned in surprise, then stepped away without a word, to reveal Lord Yarborne, looking extremely haughty and precise to a pin. He had apparently come through the coffee room almost immediately after they had left it. Inclining his head to the stranger, he said, "I understand that my darling daughter has been playing her tricks again. She has led us a merry dance, I promise you, but she will soon learn that she has run her course at last."

Twenty-five

Mate

Melissa drew herself up to her full height and faced Yarborne. "I think," she said, "that it is you who have run your course, not I."

"If you look about you, my dear," he said evenly, "you will see that your erstwhile knight errant has fled. He was scarcely worthy of you."

"He served his purpose," she said, ignoring her thumping heart. At the moment they were alone in the short corridor leading from the coffee room, past the foot of the stairs, to the entrance hall, but she was certain that Yarborne's reinforcements could not be far behind. Backing slowly toward the hall, she said, "I hope you don't think you can terrorize me here in the inn, sir, for I warn you, I am not so easily intimidated."

"No," he agreed, "you have altered a good deal from the wilted flower that Geoffrey Seacourt dragged into Little Hell a month ago, have you not? You are now more worthy of a good man, my dear."

"I am not yours, however."

"As to that, we have much to discuss, so if you will come upstairs quietly with me now, we will talk about what is to be done next. I cannot imagine that you want to have such a discussion here in the hall where anyone might hear us.

You must want as much as I do to avoid any scandal that might arise from this."

"I don't want to discuss anything with you," she said flatly, "and I certainly do not want to go anywhere with you. Much as I should dislike creating a scene, I will not hesitate to scream for the landlord, sir, so keep your hands off me."

He did not speak, and his expression remained wooden. She had just begun to hope she had confounded him when a hand clapped over her mouth and an arm clamped tightly around her waist, lifting her bodily from the floor.

Melissa opened her mouth and bit down hard.

Her captor gasped with pain, but struggled to hold her.

"Take her upstairs quickly," Yarborne snapped. "You've bungled badly, so the least you can do is to act with dispatch now. And you, Lakey, watch that rear door. We don't want to be interrupted."

"It is not the rear door you should fear, Yarborne. Your destiny lies before you." At the sound of Nick's quiet voice so near at hand, Melissa expelled a sigh of relief. "Put down my wife, you scurrilous piece of dung, and do it gently," he added in an even more gentle but much more terrifying tone.

She had felt Robert's arms stiffen—for surely they were his—but slowly he set her on her feet again and took his hand away from her mouth. Slipping quickly from between the Yarbornes, she stepped past Robert toward Nick, her anxious gaze meeting his as she did. She saw at once that he directed none of his anger at her. There was even a flash of warm relief in his eyes, and something else less easily defined. She observed that he had not come alone. Oliver and—to her astonishment—Ulcombe stood behind him, each looking nearly as grim as Nick did. Lakey was there, too, having evidently hurried through the inn yard from the coffee room with Robert, to trap her between themselves and Yarborne. But Lakey, like everyone else, watched Nick.

Nick looked back at Yarborne. "Shall we step outside?" he said in that same gentle tone. There was little expression on Yarborne's face, and he did not speak. He watched Nick warily, but his glance flicked more than once toward Ulcombe.

Robert said tauntingly, "You don't frighten us, Vexford."

"Then you are a bigger fool than I thought," Nick said, grabbing him by the front of his coat. Without appearing to exert himself in the least, he propelled him through the front door into the yard. A moment later, Robert lay flat on his back in the dirt, rubbing his jaw. Nick brushed his hands together and turned back toward Yarborne, who had followed him outside with the others.

Standing beside Ulcombe on the uppermost of the two steps leading to the front door, Yarborne held his ground. He fingered his cravat, looked haughtily down at Nick, and said, "Surely, my dear Vexford, you would never employ such rough and ready tactics against a man old enough to be your father."

"He wouldn't," Ulcombe muttered, and with a quickness almost equal to Nick's, and a single hard blow to the jaw, he sent Yarborne sprawling on his backside in the yard beside Robert.

"Oh, good show, Father," Oliver exclaimed. Standing over the fallen pair, he added, "Just try getting up, Rigger, if you want more of the same. I'd like nothing better than to give you a good taste of home-brewed, myself."

Robert looked daggers at him but made no attempt to get up. It was otherwise with Yarborne. He got shakily to his feet, brushed himself off, and looked ruefully at Ulcombe, saying, "I don't suppose it will serve any useful purpose at this point to assure you that I came here expressly to put an end to what was clearly a half-witted scheme, or to point out that Lady Vexford left London voluntarily."

"It would not," Nick snapped before Ulcombe could speak. "According to what we've learned from Oliver, your precious son did much to instigate her flight, Yarborne, and

I don't doubt for a minute that he got the notion to do so from you."

"I own I said certain things to him that may have led him to believe I wanted her. In view of an unfortunate habit he displays of acting without due preparation, that was unwise." Flicking a glare at his son, he added, "He deserved his punishment."

"Then you deserved yours as well, Yarborne, for you can scarcely deny that he learned his pretty maneuvering from you."

"But I do deny it. I am never so ham-handed. Moreover, I assure you, that having learned how resourceful your wife can be, I would never have depended upon her being so easily led by the nose that—"

"By God—"

"Wait, Nick," Ulcombe said quickly. He turned a harsh gaze upon Yarborne, and Melissa saw at once where Nick had inherited his temper. "Before you say more that you will regret, Yarborne, allow me to point out the very pertinent fact that your credibility has been severely damaged by this affair."

Yarborne flushed but said evenly, "I agree that my son acted with both haste and recklessness. He has not yet learned subtlety of manner or address, but what's done is done, and you can't want a noise made of it, so what do you propose to do?"

Ulcombe gestured toward Nick, who said, "That will depend on you, Yarborne. I won't pretend we would welcome scandal over this, but there will not be any if you are sensible. You have outworn your welcome in London. Since your talents, and those of your scurvy son, might be better appreciated on the Continent, I suggest that you remove there at once."

"But why should I want to conciliate you to such an extent?" Yarborne asked.

"Because your alternate choice is prison, sir. Your son is

guilty of abducting my wife, and if you did not aid him in that endeavor, you still had a part in it. Your other crimes are less easily proved. By using your great wealth to insinuate yourself into the uppermost ranks of London's *beau monde,* you succeeded where most would have failed, even to the extent of penetrating the hallowed precincts of Almack's. But it is clear now that your wealth derives entirely from the Billingsgate Club, and I need not tell you what will happen when word of that gets out. Nor need I mention how your reputation will suffer when it is suggested that your success is due to tactics like those employed at your ladies' supper. Yes, I see by your expression that I am right about that. Well, sir, add to all that the fact that both of you were in league to extort money from my father by entrapping Oliver in your schemes, and I think your race is run."

"You can prove none of it, however."

"Oh, I think we can persuade your Belgian 'count' to testify against you."

"You'll find that he has left England, I believe," Yarborne said less confidently.

"On the contrary, he is still in London. Lord Thomas Minley promised to look after him for me, you see, which brings to mind another charge we can lay against your son," he added, looking at Robert, who had begun to get to his feet.

Encountering that look, Robert sank to the ground again.

"Very wise," Nick said. "You don't want to tempt me to teach you the lesson you really deserve." Turning back to Yarborne, he said, "I'll acquit you of having any part of this, except insofar as you passed on a lack of integrity to your offspring, but I hope it serves to persuade you that there's no good to come of resisting our wishes. Robert not only duped an innocent clergyman with a hare-brained thimblerig, but robbed him at gunpoint when he refused to hand over the money. Oh, yes, I know all about it," he added when Robert started and looked astonished. "What will amaze you even more is that I can assure you, he would testify against you in court."

"Well, you know," Yarborne said, "I take leave to doubt that."

"Will you continue to doubt if I tell you the clergyman is Lord Dorian Minley? Keep in mind that the penalty for the crime is hanging."

Yarborne shrugged, and Robert said, "A nob ain't more likely than an ordinary pigeon to speak up about such stuff. I didn't know who he was, but it don't much matter. I never even dreamed the rig would work so well. Tried it on the first chap who came along, figuring once he got money, he'd come back to get more. Just dumb luck that I saw him win a monkey on the heat just before he returned. I had the devil's own time getting there ahead of him, but I knew it would be worth it. Even with a win of five hundred pounds, he was looking to get more, so he got what he deserved. It's greed that creates pigeons, my friend." He glanced at Oliver, who looked away.

"Very true," Nick said, "but it is the recognition of that greed in himself that will persuade Lord Dorian to give evidence if he is asked to do so. Generally, you and your ilk depend upon your pigeons to keep silent rather than admit what greedy fools they've been. I promise you, however, that if we take the pair of you before a magistrate's court, the vicar will look upon his testimony as a well-deserved penance. Do you want to put that to the test along with all the rest? If you are thinking it would be no more than his word against yours, let me point out that with the mass of other evidence to point out your various maneuverings . . ."

"You make your point," Yarborne said. "There may well be more scope for our talents in Paris than in London. We'll leave as soon as I can make the arrangements."

"Make them quickly," Ulcombe said. "I am not a patient man, and I can assure you that Nick is even less so."

Yarborne said quietly, "I am sorry we could not deal better, my lord. I have great admiration for you."

Ulcombe was silent.

Nick reached for Melissa then and drew her into the shelter of his arm. When she sighed and leaned against him, he murmured, "Did they harm you, sweetheart?"

The endearment warmed her considerably. Tempted though she was to tell him that Robert had bound her so tightly her circulation nearly stopped, that he had gagged her so tightly her lips still felt bruised, and that he had left her overnight in a rat-infested shed, she said only, "I am fine now, sir, truly."

Oliver was looking at her speculatively, and he said, "Your face is bruised. Did that damned scoundrel hit you?"

Feeling Nick stiffen, Melissa said hastily, "It's nothing, really, but I would be grateful if we could hire a room here at the inn long enough for me to wash my face and tidy my hair. Also, I'd like a proper breakfast."

Ulcombe smiled, and Nick said, "That shall be done, sweetheart. There is just one more point I must make." He turned back to Yarborne. "Don't think you can draw out your arrangements to leave London until the need to make them eases. If it becomes necessary, I am fully prepared to lay information not only about everything we have discussed to this point but also about your part in Seacourt's death."

Yarborne's eyes widened, but Robert cried, "That's utter rot! He had nothing to do with that, and neither did I!"

At the same time, Melissa turned to Nick and exclaimed, "Papa's death? But what could Lord Yarborne have had to do with that?"

Yarborne was watching Nick, who looked steadily back at him, clearly waiting to hear what he would say. Yarborne said, "I did not kill him, you know."

"I never thought you did."

"Do you know then?"

"I believe I do. If I am correct, I also believe his death

was an accident that arose from a slight miscalculation on your part."

"You are kind to consider it slight. I thought it would be amusing to put two people together to see what mischief they could make. I knew he was a fool. I'm ashamed to say that despite his saying I could control his daughter by force, I never saw that he was also a brute. As to his death being an accident, it was one only if you believe self-defense is accidental and that a man does not write his own destiny."

"You did play a role in the event, did you not? A certain house in Clarges Street is doubtless already closed, and its occupant well on her way to Paris."

"I see that you know more than I'd expected." Yarborne looked at Melissa, then back at Nick, and said, "I applaud your restraint and assure you that I have as much cause as you do to keep the matter quiet. The authorities have accepted the notion of footpads, I believe, so we'll leave it at that."

"Not quite," Nick said. "There are others involved who might meet with difficulty if anyone thinks to accuse them. I won't allow that to happen, and since you can prevent it, I'll want a written statement from you before we leave today."

"Well, I won't say I'm happy to oblige you, but I'll do it, since I trust I'll be safely out of the country before ever you'd have cause to use my words against me."

Yarborne helped Robert up then, and Melissa, seeing a ominous look shoot from father to son, felt a sudden chill. She leaned closer to Nick.

"Cold, sweetheart?"

"I think I'd like to wash my hands and face now, and tidy my hair."

"Yes, of course," he said. "You do that while I see to Yarborne's statement. Oliver, go and find the landlord, and tell him I want to hire a room for a couple of hours and a maid to assist my lady. Then bespeak breakfast for us all."

Ulcombe said, "I'll attend to breakfast while Oliver's

speaking to the landlord. Take your time, Melissa. We'll have a good meal ready for you when you return."

She went with Oliver, and then upstairs with the chambermaid the landlord provided. Twenty minutes later, as tidy as she could make herself under the circumstances, she descended to the coffee room where she found the Barrington men seated at the long table before the fire. Servants were setting platters on the table, and when the smell of bacon wafted to her nose, she realized she was ravenous.

"There you are," Oliver said, getting to his feet when he saw her. "Not only am I starving but now perhaps Nick will tell us what Yarborne wrote in that statement of his. He said we had to wait for you because he didn't want to say it all twice."

As she took her seat, Ulcombe said, "Now, Nick, I hope Yarborne had nothing significant to do with Seacourt's death, because if he did, I couldn't reconcile it with my conscience to let him leave England."

"He didn't kill Seacourt," Nick said. "Unless I missed my guess and he judged to an incredible nicety just how much I missed it, Clara did that."

Melissa said, "Clara? You mean Lady Hawthorne? But why?"

Smiling at her in a way that warmed her through and through, and made her wonder how she could have thought, even for a minute, that he did not care for her, Nick replied gently, "I saw Clara shortly after she had endured a visit from your father. She had got herself entangled with him, you see."

"I knew that," Melissa said. "I saw them together the day of the Vauxhall opening, right before Sir Geoffrey suggested that you were— But go on, sir."

Nick held her gaze for a moment, then said, "Yarborne introduced them. The man couldn't resist trying to ensnare people, to turn them to his own purpose. He put them together because they each had cause to dislike me, never realizing that Seacourt had his own plan. Clara helped him arrange Penthorpe's unexpected journey, and when that went awry, he blamed her for the failure. According to Yarborne's account—which is what Clara told him when she applied to him afterward for help—Seacourt went for Clara, and she fought him off long enough to snatch up a poker and strike him down. He hit his head on something, and when she realized she had killed him, she sent for Yarborne, who had some of his men take the body away. They laid it out in Hyde Park and arranged the scene to look as if footpads had attacked him. It occurs to me that she must have killed Seacourt shortly before I got there. The carpet was wet, and she said she had overturned a vase of flowers. I wonder if his body was still in the house. Ah, but it couldn't have been," he added, looking at Melissa. "Yarborne did not explain how his henchmen managed to get the body from Clarges Street to Hyde Park in broad daylight, but that must be because he didn't know. He was with us by then in Jermyn Street. And Seacourt's body must have been discovered quickly, or Charley would not have known in time to tell us when she did."

Melissa nodded, but Oliver said, "When did you visit Clara, Nick, and when did you and Melissa meet Yarborne in Jermyn Street?"

When Nick glanced at Melissa a second time, she returned his gaze steadily, leaving the decision about how much to reveal up to him. She was not jealous of Lady Hawthorne. She felt sorry for her.

Nick said, "Penthorpe told me he had seen Seacourt go into Clara's house. She was with Penthorpe at Vauxhall when he was abducted, you see. I told you about that during our journey here, but I didn't mention Clara's part. Penthorpe had worried about her safety, albeit not for the right reason, so when he returned to London he drove by her house. He didn't see her, but he did see Seacourt go into the house. After he told me Clara had been involved, I went to find out what part she had played. Because she gave me news that sent me away in a hurry, I did not ask too many questions, but later I realized that she had very recently seen Yarborne."

He shot a speaking look at Melissa, and this time his expression made her shift uneasily, but she understood his reluctance to explain, so she said quietly, "She knew I had an appointment with Yarborne, although I had only just received his message. You put those bits together to deduce his connection to Papa's death, did you not?"

"Yes," he said, "that's it exactly. According to Yarborne's statement, she owed him money and had been doing a number of favors for him." He added blandly, "He did not specify those favors, but recalling that she was the one who first suggested that I'd enjoy the Billingsgate, and knowing now that he owns the club, I'd guess he used her to get other wealthy men to play there. No doubt he ensnared her the same way that he ensnared other dupes," he added, looking from Oliver to Melissa.

She sighed. "Robert Yarborne was right about one thing, at least, that greed is a powerful thing. That was my downfall at the ladies' supper and again yesterday on the road. Both times I wanted the prize so much that I neglected to heed the potential cost. I can't think now how I allowed either of them to entrap me as they did."

"You had barely learned the rules of hazard at that supper," Nick said. "And despite that experience, and at least one other, you hadn't begun to understand the Yarbornes. None of us had." He glanced at Oliver and Ulcombe, but when Melissa grimaced, wondering how much they knew about her dealings with Yarborne, Nick added tenderly, as if he had read her mind, "They know Yarborne played his tricks on you, sweetheart, but I did not tell them the whole story."

"Then I think I will do that myself, if you do not object," she said, feeling relieved by the thought. "I find I do not much care for secrets anymore."

"You can do that on the way home," he said. "At my father's insistence, we came to Newmarket in his traveling coach, so we'll all go home together, too. Before then, however, I want a few moments alone with you upstairs."

"Yes, sir," she said, "I'm sure you do." Turning her attention to her plate, she found her appetite undiminished by anticipation of the forthcoming interview. That he might be a little angry with her was understandable, for she had behaved foolishly and he never tolerated fools gladly, but the warmth she had seen in his eyes told her all she really wanted to know. When she finished, she looked up to find him watching her.

She said, "We can go upstairs now if you like."

He stood up. Ulcombe said, "We'll await you in the yard, Nick. I'll tell them half an hour for the horses, but they can be walked if you need more time."

A few minutes later, upstairs in the little room where she had tidied herself, Melissa faced her husband and said, "I know you must be displeased with me."

"Do you?"

"Yes, for you said I was not to leave the house, but I did, and you said I was not to go out alone, but—"

"But you did. You did not behave very sensibly, that's true, but you certainly proved that you can take care of yourself. I confess, sweetheart, I did just what you accused me of doing. When I couldn't judge what rig was being run, my first instinct was to hide you away, to protect you. What did you mean when you said that yesterday on the road you wanted the prize so much you didn't heed the cost?"

She nibbled her lower lip, but he did not seem to be impatient. She thought she even detected amusement in his eyes, but she saw compassion as well. That she could read so much in his expression made it impossible to say now, to his face, that she had not understood him or known what he felt for her. To insist that she had wanted to hear him express his feelings aloud seemed suddenly small-minded.

At last she said, "I know I insisted once that life is no game, but there are certain similarities in that one never knows what card will turn up until a hand is done. It seemed that every time I took your advice, or tried to do what you seemed to want me to do, I did the wrong thing, just like Robert Yarborne did when he tried to make a gift of me to his father. Yesterday, I let Oliver talk me into what I later thought was one of his pranks. Now, when I try to recall my reasons for leaving, it is difficult, because perceptions are sometimes more powerful than reality. Because you knew more than anyone else about the things Papa had done to me, and because so many people seem to fear your temper, Robert scored a more telling point than he knew when he suggested—just by suggesting it to Oliver, mind you—that people might believe you had killed my father. Oliver scorned the notion, but not until I recalled that no one else knew you might have had cause, did I realize how absurd it was."

"Did you ever think I might have killed him?"

"Not for a minute. But I'm afraid I used the fear Robert ignited (fanned by my own vexation with you) as sufficient cause to go back to Scotland. I pretended to take Oliver's advice, but in fact I know now that I was driven as much by greed as any of Yarborne's other dupes. Even when I thought the whole notion was no more than a prankish attempt of Oliver's to throw us together, I wanted to discover if you still wanted the prize you had won in Newmarket, or would be willing to let it get away."

"Do you know the answer now?"

She looked into his eyes. "Yes, I do."

"I told you once that I hold what is mine, Melissa."

She understood his meaning. "I know you did not come after an errant wife just to keep her, Nicholas."

Reaching out to touch her cheek, he said, "And I think perhaps you were not glad to see your husband merely because he rescued you from a difficult situation."

Pressing her cheek against his warm hand, she smiled. "Robert held me captive overnight, sir, but I got away from him. I daresay I would have managed to get away from them again in time. It was only chance, after all, that no inn servant had come along. When I realized, belatedly, that if I could explain that I was your wife—"

"Yes, perhaps you would like to explain why you did not do that at once."

She shook her head. "It is of no use to discuss each step I took, sir, any more than it is helpful to discuss the cards that ought to have been played in a hand of piquet. I own, however, that I would like to know how you found me. I suppose you must have seen the signs, but you can't have come after me until long after dark, so how did you?"

"You may recall that more than one was attached to the wall of an inn. Inns and inn yards are lighted at night. I've not the least doubt Robert meant to remove those signs long before my appearance on the Great North Road. They expected I would drive hard for the Border, and I might have done just that, had I been alone. When Oliver saw the first sign, I also suspected that he had devised the scheme, but he soon convinced me I was wrong. After that, we watched closely for more signs. I don't suppose we saw them all. Certainly, we saw none between Baldock and Royston."

"I-I suppose you'd like to know how it is that Robert Yarborne knew enough about me—about us, I mean—to be sure such a ruse would work," Melissa said, looking at his waistcoat.

"I know that much," Nick said. "Oliver told me. There were indications even before we left London that you had been maneuvered into leaving. That's why Father and Oliver came with me. Oliver will not make the mistake of discussing our private affairs with his friends again, I promise you."

She looked up then. "I hope you were not too harsh with him, sir. I ought not to have talked to him about such things in the first place."

"Why did you? No, don't tell me," he added, pulling her close. "You are right about debating a hand that's been played. Do you still wonder about my feelings?"

A little shyly, she said, "I think I have known for some

time that you cared for me more than you would say. You are something of a fraud, you know." When he frowned, she chuckled and said, "You pretend not to care about Oliver, you see, but I could tell just by the way you treat him that you do. Your actions do say a good deal, Nicholas, but I own I did wish I could hear you say the words."

"You should have told me more plainly then."

"But they lose much of their force if one has to request them. Besides, Papa was always spouting words. He would tell me how much he loved me just before, or just after, he did dreadful things. Once I realized that your feelings were much more sincerely expressed, I didn't miss the words so much anymore."

He grimaced ruefully. "Sweetheart, I wish I had put up those damned signs, but I didn't even know all I felt, myself, until Oliver told me you might have left London. Even then I didn't realize the depth of my feelings until I realized that you had fallen into some sort of trap. I hope we can do better in the future."

"We will."

Silence fell between them, but when Melissa looked at him, his expression was so understanding that she moved into his arms again and hugged him, saying, "I don't think Papa will be very much missed, Nicholas, and I never thought I'd be grateful to him for anything, but I am."

"I am, too," he said. "I'll admit, sweetheart, when I realized how much money you had cost me in that damned auction, I thought I must have had windmills in my head, but I won a much bigger prize than I knew. I'll be forever indebted to him for that. Being more a man of action than of words, I'll show you how much." He kissed her then, and since the kiss led to other forms of expressing his feelings, it was rather more than half an hour before they rejoined Ulcombe and Oliver in the yard.

Epilogue

The Games End

August, Penthorpe House, Scotland

Watching gentle waves lap against the shore, Melissa paid little heed to the twins' squeals of laughter as they chased each other through the gardens behind her. Cries from a flock of gulls dipping and darting over the bright blue waters of the Firth punctuated the children's laughter, and from time to time she heard masculine chuckles from the terrace, where Susan was supervising arrangements for an alfresco supper with the assistance of Charley and Lady Ophelia, and the more dubious aid of Viscount Penthorpe, Nicholas, Oliver, and Rockland.

Not a cloud stirred in the cerulean sky. Not a leaf rustled in the chestnut tree above her. Smiling at the bickering, greedy birds, she watched sunlight dance on the Firth, savoring the happiness she heard in the children's voices, and the peace she felt within herself. How much her life had changed in a few short months.

A stirring in the air warned her just as a childish voice shrieked, "Melissa, look out!" Before she could defend herself, she was swept off her feet from behind and caught up in her husband's embrace.

"Nick, put me down at once," she commanded, striving

to keep the bubbling laughter from her voice. "Such behavior before the children is most unseemly, sir."

"Is it?" His face was near hers and the look in his eyes revealed his intent the instant before he kissed her. When she responded with a passion that matched his, forgetting the others for long, blissful moments, Nick's eyes began to twinkle, but when he raised his head, he made no move to put her down. Instead, he said, "What are you doing over here all by yourself, love?"

"Just thinking," she said, avoiding his gaze, not wanting to spoil the moment by mentioning past unpleasantness.

He waited patiently, pointedly, saying not a word.

At last, she said, "If you must know, I was thinking about the last time I stood here, for this is where I was when Papa abducted me, and though I know we are agreed that everything came out well in the end—"

"Without Seacourt's assistance, we might never have met."

"Fiddlesticks, Great-Aunt Ophelia had invited me to London several times, offering to sponsor my come-out."

"You'd never have met me at Almack's, and even if we had met normally, sweetheart, do you think anything would have come of it?"

"You would have been smitten by my beauty and my pretty manners, sir. Can you deny it?"

"Easily." He chuckled. "You were a meek mouse then, and I was a callous tiger. I won't say I'd have eaten you alive, for I'm honest enough to admit I'd scarcely have noted your existence had it not been forced upon me to do so."

"No one forced you," she said indignantly. "Now, put me down."

"Have you told the others yet?"

"Told us what?" Charley demanded.

So intent had they been upon their conversation that neither had heard her approach. Giving Nick a speaking look and a tiny shake of her head, Melissa said, "Charley, you know better than to steal up behind someone like that. You startled us."

Charley looked from one to the other, her expression showing that she recognized diversionary tactics when she met them. She said, "It is of no use expecting me to feel guilty when we all saw Nick sneak up and sweep you off your feet."

"Did you have a purpose in interrupting us?"Nick asked. "Because if you don't, I'd like a few more minutes alone with my wife."

"I daresay you would," Charley said, "but Aunt Susan said to fetch you. The servants are bringing out the food." She paused, then added with a grin, "Actually, she asked Oliver to fetch you, but he's busy teaching the twins how to fuzz cards and detect weighted dice, and so—"

"The devil he is," Nick exclaimed, turning to look toward the terrace, where Oliver could be seen talking with the children. "If he thinks he's going to teach those scamps any such thing, he'll soon learn his mistake," he said, putting Melissa down.

"He says he's learned his lesson," Charley said innocently, "so I should think you'd be glad to see him preparing the children to deal with any Captain Sharps they might meet when they grow up."

"Do you?" Nick looked severe, but Melissa chuckled.

"She is just trying to get a rise out of you. Don't leap so swiftly to her bait."

Still frowning, Nick looked around and said, "Where the devil is Rockland? I thought you had taken on the task of entertaining him—or as you so tactlessly put it, of keeping him from taking advantage of the maids at Penthorpe House."

Charley sniffed. "Just because he wormed his way into coming with us by convincing Aunt Ophelia that she would dislike travel less if she had a gentleman escort is no cause for me to pay him heed. As a matter of fact, I mean to borrow some uphills and downhills from Oliver, to teach Rockland a lesson."

Before Nick could join battle with her outspoken cousin, Melissa said, "Should we not join the others? None of us wants to have to explain to Aunt Ophelia why we are dawdling here when food is about to be served."

"Perfectly true," Charley agreed with a laugh, "but we're too late already. Hello, Aunt Ophelia."

The old lady strode briskly toward them on the garden path, swinging her cane to lop off dead flower heads whenever she spied one.

"You've taken an age," she said sharply. "Charlotte, did you not tell them they are beginning to serve?"

When she turned back toward the terrace, Nick, grinning broadly, moved to place a steadying hand under her elbow. She looked up as if she would decline assistance but said only, "I suppose you are feeling mighty proud of yourself."

"Am I?"

She looked at Melissa and back at him. "Well, you ought to be, but if you don't mean to tell anyone else, I daresay I know better than most how to hold my tongue."

Wondering how she had divined their secret, Melissa glanced at Charley, but that young woman's gaze had shifted to the terrace. Following her look, Melissa saw that Rockland had waved away the footman and was holding a chair for Susan. When he had seated her, he took his own seat beside her.

Charley muttered, "Taking a great deal on himself, is he not, but it is always the same with men. They think only of themselves, never of anyone else."

"I cannot agree, Charley," Melissa said, smiling at her husband. "Nicholas has given me little cause to complain of any lack."

"Little indeed," Lady Ophelia murmured, "and with such excellent results."

"Aunt Ophelia, please," Melissa begged.

But this time Charley had not missed the exchange. With dawning awareness she looked at Melissa, then at Nick. "You don't mean— That is," she added, flushing, "are you— Well, what I mean to say is—"

"Get a move on, you lot," Oliver called. "Rockland has already taken his seat and will next devour all the food."

"So we see," Lady Ophelia said testily. "Here, Susan, I've brought them." She glared at Rockland, stepped forward, and prodded him with her cane. "Have you no manners, young man? Despite all their other faults, gentlemen usually stand up when ladies approach them."

Rockland leapt to his feet and bowed, but his eyes were twinkling. Pointedly ignoring Charley, he smiled at Lady Ophelia and said, "My attention was momentarily diverted, and I regret that I did not immediately perceive your arrival."

"Poppycock."

He bowed more deeply.

Charley said abruptly to the company at large, "Nick and Melissa have something of a delicate nature to say to us."

It was not the way Melissa had imagined telling her family, but recognizing that her cousin had received provocation, and seeing delighted expectation radiate from Susan's face, she said, "Charley has stolen our thunder, but I can see that you all have guessed our news. We're going to have a baby."

The meal turned into a celebration, and afterwards, going upstairs with Nick, she tucked her hand into his arm and said, "They are all pleased, I think."

"Not as pleased as we are, but I'd like to have throttled that cousin of yours. Now she's down there, cheating Rockland with those damned dice Oliver gave her, and after the way Rockland's been tormenting her, I couldn't even bring myself to tell him."

Melissa chuckled. "As I told you before, sir, you are a fraud. You are always saying you won't lift a finger to help anyone, but I daresay if the truth were known, you even contribute vast quantities of money to your father's charities.

Now you won't even cry rope on Charley, although she says she means to take Rockland for every penny he brought to Scotland so he will have to walk back to London."

"Well, I *can't* betray her. My own brother is the one who corrupted her morals. What your cousin wants, sweetheart, is a man capable of taming her."

"That's what Rockland thinks he's doing," Melissa said, laughing, "but he won't succeed. The man who could doesn't exist. I can't imagine that Charley will ever find one to suit her, and I own I've never seen one who would. All the men I meet these days seem quite ordinary and insignificant now that you no longer look so large to me."

He grinned at her. "What do you say to measuring me again right now, my love, to see if I can't still overwhelm you with my impressive size?"

Laughing, she linked her arm more tightly with his, and they retired to their bedchamber.

Glossary

banker Whoever holds the bank, the House players, or in some cases, noblemen who could afford to do so.

blacklegs Cheats.

blank (1) In card-point games, a card worth nothing. (2) A hand without court cards, consisting only of numerals.

bonnetters Thimble-rig, to "bonnet" any green one who might happen to win—that is to say, to knock his hat over his eyes, whilst the operator and the others bolted with the stakes.

Captain Sharp A cheating bully, whose office was to bully any *pigeon* who, suspecting roguery, refused to pay what he had lost.

card points The point values of cards in point-trick games (as opposed to nominal face values). In Piquet, for example, the point value of an ace is eleven, not one.

cards and capot A player winning seven or more tricks scores 10 for *cards*. For winning all twelve, he scores an additional 30 (40 in all) for *capot*.

carte blanche A hand without court cards.

carte rouge A hand in which every card counts towards a scoring combination (Piquet).

chance See *main* for full explanation of both Hazard terms.

coppering Placing a copper penny on one's stake in Faro, meaning that one bets on the house card to win. Each play consists of two cards being drawn by the *banker*. One is the English card, for the players, the other the house card.

The banker wins all the money staked on the house card, unless the wager is "coppered."

court cards King, Queen, Jack, etc., as opposed to numeral or pip cards. Also called facecards, and originally coats.

crabs Losing throw in Hazard.

deal To distribute cards to the players at start of play.

declare To show and score for a valid combination of cards in hand (Piquet).

deuce The two of any given suit.

discard (1) To lay aside an unwanted card or cards from hand. (2) To throw a worthless or unwanted card to a trick.

do To cheat.

done up Ruined.

down-hills False dice which run low.

draw To take or be dealt one or more cards from a stock or waste-pit.

dun territory When one's gaming debts are greater than one's assets.

eggers To egg on the dupe to bet (Thimble-rig).

elbow-shaker A gamester.

elder The player obliged or privileged to make the opening bet, bid, or lead. In Piquet, and other two-player games, the Antagonist, or non-dealing player.

en passant A manner of capturing a pawn in chess (in passing).

Faro The most widespread Western gambling game of the 18th and 19th centuries. There was a staking layout of 13 cards, punters bet on individual ranks to win or lose, and the outcome was basically determined by the banker's dealing cards alternately to a winning and losing pile. When only three cards remained, players could bet on the order in which they would appear. According to Andrew Steinmetz (*The Gaming Table,* 1870), some Faro tables were laid out with all 52 cards, but in general the rules required 13. The play described at Lord Yarborne's ladies' supper is from Steinmetz, describing play during the 1820's. The above description of Faro is from *A Dictionary of Card Games* by David Parlett (1992).

flat-catchers Minor members of "the Fancy."

Fulhams Loaded dice.

fuzz To shave cards, to change the pack.

game Bubbles, flats, Pigeons.

Greeks Cheats at play.

green A dupe.

groom-porter That member of a gaming house staff who ran a gaming table. He instructed players in the rules, raked in the losses to the House, and generally was responsible for keeping order.

gull gropers Usurers who lend money to gamesters.

Hazard A game played with two dice. As many men as can stand around the largest round table may play it. According to *The Compleat Gamester* by Charles Cotton: *Hazzard is a proper name for this Game; for it speedily makes a Man or undoes him; in the twinkling of an eye either a Man or a Mouse. There are two things chiefly to be observed, that is, Main and Chance; the Chance is the Caster's, and the Main theirs who are concerned in play with him . . . Certainly Hazzard is the most bewitching Game that is plaid on the Dice; for when a man begins to play he knows not when to leave off; and having once accustome'd himself to play at Hazzard, he hardly ever after minds anything else. . . .*

hedge To secure a bet by betting on the other side as well.

highjinks A gambler who drinks to intoxicate his pigeon.

hunting Drawing in the unwary.

lead To play the first card; or, the first card played.

main In Hazard, the number called by the *caster* before his first *cast*. If it turns up, he wins. If not, the number that does turn up is his *chance*. If he throws *chance* after that point, he wins the stakes on the table. However, except for that first cast, if the caster throws his *main,* he has "thrown out", and (under English rules) must pay every other player an amount equal to that man's stake.

markers Various types, used by gamesters to mark their own rouleaux or other wagers on a tableful of same. When money was raked in by the *groom-porter,* the bettor retrieved his marker(s).

nick In Hazard, a losing cast. Everyone loses his wager, and the house or banker rakes in the money. The caster loses only his stake, and may continue casting.

pawn To hide a card or die.

pigeons Dupes of sharpers at play.

pique If the Elder (non-dealer) reaches 30 upon or after leading to the first trick, and Younger (dealer) has not yet scored anything for combinations or tricks, he adds a bonus of 30 for *pique.* Younger cannot score pique. (Note: In her game with Nicholas, Melissa scores a repique but not a pique because she is dealer.)

Piquet Piquet, or Picket, goes back to the early sixteenth century and has long been regarded as one of the all-time great games for two players. According to *The Compleat Gamester* by Charles Cotton (the standard work on games in England from 1674 till the mid-18th century, and from which Edmund Hoyle gleaned much of the information for his later work on card games): *Before you begin the Game at Picket, you must throw out of the Pack the Deuces, Trays, Fours, and Fives* (by 1800 the sixes were also thrown out) *and play with the rest of the Cards, which are in number Thirty and six* (32 after 1800).

point In Piquet, the total face value of all cards held of any one suit.

repique If either player reaches a score of 30 for combinations alone before the other has scored anything, he adds a bonus of 60 for *repique.*

rook Gambler.

rouleau(x) A roll of sovereigns used for betting, much like a roll of dimes or quarters.

St. Hugh's bones Dice. A bale of bard cinque deuces; a bale of flat cinque deuces; a bale of flat size aces; a bale of bard cater treys; a bale of flat cater treys; a bale of Fulhams; a bale of light graniers; a bale of gordes, with as many highmen and lowmen for passage; a bale of demies; a bale of long dice for even or odd; a bale of bristles; a bale of direct contraries—names of false dice.

stock Cards which are not dealt initially but may be drawn from or dealt out later in the play.

thimble-rig Shell game.

thimble rigger One who runs a shell game.

trick A set of cards equal to the number of players, each having contributed one in succession.

trump (1) A superior suit, any card of which will beat that of any other suit played to the trick. (2) To play such a card.

up-hills False dice which run high.

velvet a. the winnings of a player in a gambling game; b. a profit or gain beyond ordinary expectation (Webster).

Vincent's Law The art of cheating at cards by the banker, who plays booty, Gripe, who bets, and the Vincent, who is cheated. The gain is called termage.

vowel To give an I.O.U. in payment.

younger The player last in turn to bid or play at the start of a game (usually the dealer).

Author's Letter

Dear Reader,

A ladybug met Julius Caesar at a Halloween party, and the seed that had been planted for this story began to grow. Julius Caesar is a psychologist in real life, who specializes in battered women, molested children, and other forms of child abuse. The ladybug was this author. We spent three hours discussing Melissa Seacourt. It was a great party.

Melissa first appeared as a child in *Dangerous Illusions* (Pinnacle, June 1994), and she seemed a natural heroine for this book, but before I could use her, I needed to know if she could enjoy happiness with a would-be domineering male. I also wanted a few ideas about how she could grow and leave the worst of her past behind without modern counseling. To my astonishment and relief, I learned that her cousin Charley was exactly the sort of person most likely to help. The only problem after that was keeping Charley from taking over Melissa's book. I did that by promising her one of her own.

For those of you who like to know about the real bits of history in my books, I came across the account of the chess player and his Almighty opponent in the course of my research, as an example of the sort of con-artistry that was rampant in the late 18th and early 19th centuries, and I couldn't resist using it. When I discovered a carefully detailed description of how to ensnare the minor son of a nobleman, the primary subplot of *Dangerous Games* fell into place.

The conclusion of the book developed from a combination of a recipe for "gulling pigeons," added to a string of signs I encountered last year, while driving to our summer cabin. Beginning with a huge banner strung across the road, it rapidly became clear that two people had quarreled, and the gentleman was determined to make a very public apology.

Also true is the King's Drawing Room. After three postponements, due to his gout, King George IV held a Drawing Room on May 20, 1824, the details of which were printed (down to which window he stood by) in the London *Times*.

I do hope you've enjoyed this book. If you would like to know more about some of the characters (including Charley and Lady Ophelia), I invite you to read *Dangerous Illusions,* and to look for *Dangerous Angels,* Charley's story, from Pinnacle in December 1996.

Hail, Caesar!

Amanda Scott

And for those of you who just can't wait, here's a taste of—

DANGEROUS ANGELS

by

Amanda Scott

—coming this Christmas from Pinnacle Books!

One

Spring 1829, Cornwall

When the large traveling coach increased its speed on the perilous cliff road, the monkey was the first of its dozing passengers to waken. His bristly round head popped out of his small mistress's large fur muff, and his round, inquisitive shoe-button eyes glinted alertly in the light from the gibbous moon hovering over the British Channel and the south coast of Cornwall. The monkey cocked its head, listening intently.

Lady Letitia Ophelia Deverill, a child with nine whole summers behind her, was the next to stir. Her eyes slitted, blinked sleepily, then opened wide. When the monkey began to chatter nervously, she held it closer, murmuring, "Hush, Jeremiah, it's all right." Looking out the nearest coach window, she gasped and added less confidently, "I think it's all right."

Beside her, Miss Charlotte Tarrant shifted, trying to find a more comfortable position, which was no easy task after days of lurching travel with three other persons and a monkey in the close, albeit luxurious, confines of the coach. Inadvertently, she stepped on her father's foot.

Charles Tarrant muttered, shifted his foot, and opened one eye to glare at his daughter.

The carriage rounded a bend and moonlight streamed inside, so that when Charlotte opened her eyes, she was able to see his expression. Smiling ruefully, she said, "Sorry,

Papa. Letty," she added when Charles had shut his eyes again, "whatever is the matter with Jeremiah?"

"I-I don't know, Cousin Charley, but are we not going rather fast? I just looked out the window, and all I can see is the sea, very far down."

Charley leaned forward to look across the child and out the far window. She and Letty occupied the forward seat, facing Charley's parents. Her mother, Davina, wakened just then, frowning.

"Good gracious me, Charles," she exclaimed, "this carriage is swaying like the Royal Mail! Do tell John Coachman to slow down before he has us over the cliff!"

As Charles reached forward to knock on the ceiling of the coach, a shot rang out, followed by a number of others.

"Highwaymen," Davina screamed. "Robbers! Oh, Charles, where is your pistol? Why did we not go through Tavistock? Oh, why did we not hire a guard?"

Charles snapped, "We didn't go by way of Tavistock, my dear, because you insisted that we take the Plymouth Road, that's why. And we did not stay the night in Looe, which would have been the sensible course, because you thought we could reach Tuscombe Park tonight, though why anyone of sense would ever want to drive the Polperro Road, let alone in the dark of night—"

Charley interjected calmly, "We are here, however, but I've got my pistol, Mama, and the big one is in the holster by Papa's door, where it is always kept. John Coachman must have seen them following us, and that is why he increased his pace. However, with only two horses, and on this of all roads, it is a stupid thing to do, and so we must tell him. Shout at him to pull up, Papa. We can deal with highwaymen, but if we should go off the road or lose a wheel—"

As if suggestion had given birth to reality, the coach bounced heavily over a rock, and with a screeching crack, the left hind wheel broke. Had it happened scant moments before, the carriage would have plunged a hundred feet to the jagged, surf-frothed rocks below, but as it chanced, they had reached the unfriendly rough slope of Seacourt Head, the triangular point of land which formed the east boundary of St. Merryn's Bay. The first outcroppings of the jutting headland were behind them. When the wheel broke, the coachman did his best, but the coach was traveling too fast, and when it swerved and lurched off the road, there was nothing he could do to regain control or to save himself. After a few awkward bumps, all forward action ceased and the heavily laden coach began to roll backward on the steep slope of the headland.

The horses strained, but the coach was too heavy and dragged them backward, faster and faster, inexorably toward the edge until it caught on boulders and toppled over sideways, skidding briefly, then beginning to lurch and roll, while the frightened horses screamed in fear.

Dropping the pistol she had snatched from her satchel, Charley held her small cousin tightly. The windows broke and dust flew when first one side, then the other, hit the rocky ground. The nearside door flew open, and when the vehicle hit the ground again, Charley and Letitia were flung out.

Landing hard on her back against a steep slope of loose scree, with Letty on top of her, Charley felt herself sliding rapidly. She heard a sickening scrape of coach against rocks, her father's panicked shouts, and her mother's screams, echoed by those of the horses. The sounds faded abruptly just before she heard a distant, crunching thud, then, except for the sounds of the surf far below, silence. She was still sliding, sliding toward the brink over which the coach had plunged.

Letty was struggling to free herself. Tightening her grip, Charley muttered, "Be still." She scrabbled wildly with her free hand, desperately seeking a handhold, anything to stop their fatal slide toward the precipice.

* * *

From his lookout position, crouching among a cluster of large boulders just above the tide line, as the surf rolled out again, providing a few moments of near silence, Sir Antony Foxearth heard a coach above on the narrow cliff road, moving far too swiftly for safety, then gunshots. Raising his eyes heavenward, he blessed the cliff overhang above him—the same steep overhang he had cursed an hour earlier when he feared that he had misjudged the tide and might be trapped by the unpredictable waves. Several times he had reminded himself that the caves just up the beach were dry enough to store smuggled goods, but as the water inched nearer, and the plump moon had finally slipped behind clouds that his comrades had expected to conceal it much earlier, the darkness and the noise of the surf stirred a primordial fear that had taken much of his overtaxed resolution to defeat. Now, with the moon's reappearance, he had new worries. Smugglers did not generally approve of moonlight.

At the same time that he blessed the overhang that would protect him if the fast-moving coach plunged off the road, he spared a thought for the passengers and the horses. He had not spent so much time alone that he did not still think of others, though he doubted that he would ever again feel the same magnitude of caring and compassion that he had once felt for his family and friends, in long-past days before those emotions withered and died. When they had cast him off for disgracing them with his unsportsmanlike activities during the unpleasantness with Bonaparte thirteen years before, he had found the break wrenching. He had grieved for them then as if they all had died. Remembering the expression on his friend Harry Livingston's face when Harry had accused him of missing his own father's funeral brought only a sigh of depression from him now. He had felt nothing at learning of the old man's death. Any bereavement he might have felt had been expended long before when his father had given him the cut direct in front of everyone at Brooks's Club in London. The wrenching pain of that moment stirred again but was instantly forgotten when he heard the panicked screams of horses and humans. The sound of the surf had briefly muffled noises from above, but he heard the screech of coachwork on rocks from somewhere near the headland at the west end of the little bay. Then came the horrible screams, a muffled crash on the beach, and silence.

Charley's skirt and cloak were caught up around her, pinning her legs together, making it nearly impossible to dig the heels of her half-boots into the unstable mass beneath her. When she banged the back of her hand against a boulder, she managed to catch hold of it, breaking fingernails and crying out at the pain when one ripped below the quick. Feeling the wriggling body atop hers lurch awkwardly forward, almost making her lose her tenuous hold, she nearly snapped at the child to be still before she realized they had stopped sliding.

"I haven't got a very good hold," Letitia said matter-of-factly, "but I think it would be wise to wait till the moon comes out again before I try to gain better purchase."

Aware that her own grip on the rough rock was not reliable, Charley realized that until that moment she had not missed the moonlight. It was much darker than it had been before. She wondered if that was why she had not actually seen the coach topple over the edge, or if she had simply been too concerned about herself and Letty to notice. Knowing that the two of them were far from being safe, she thrust aside all thought of the horror that had overtaken them. Whatever had happened below, she could do nothing about it now. She was not even certain she would be able to do much about her own predicament, but at least she and Letty were still alive. If they slipped over the edge, their chances of remaining in that condition were small. The worst of it was that she did not know exactly how near they were to the precipice.

Letty stirred uncomfortably. "Cousin Charley—"

"Hush," Charley said, for another sound had reached her sharp ears from above them. She nearly called out before she realized that the most likely persons to be at the cliff's edge were the highwaymen. Giving thanks for the clouds that hid the moon, she wondered how long it would stay hidden. Already, she could see a ribbon of silver edging one of the clouds. The cloak she wore was of her favorite dark sapphire blue, to match her eyes, and she knew that the rocks of the cliffs and the slope were dark in more places than they were light, so she could hope the men would not spy them where they lay.

Close to her ear, Letty murmured, "Won't they help us, do you think?"

Giving thanks that the child had not given way to hysterics, Charley decided there was no point in mincing words. "No, darling, they won't. We could speak against them to the authorities, you see, because they caused the accident. They dare not let us see their faces. We must keep very still and hope they do not see us."

"My cloak is gray," Letty whispered, "but they might see my hair when the moon peeks out again."

"See if you can curl up a bit," Charley whispered back, realizing that the child's bright carrot-colored mop of curls might well shine like a fiery beacon. "Move very slowly, and don't let go of the rock if you can help it. I think if I don't move, we won't slide any more, but it's best to be very careful until we can be certain. Pull your cloak over your head and curl up so it covers all of you. And keep very still."

"I don't think they can hear us," Letty muttered. "I can barely hear their voices, or their horses."

"No, but sound travels up better than down, I think, and the quieter we are the less likely we are to draw their notice."

Letty was silent, and Charley noted that she moved very slowly and cautiously as she curled into a ball with her cloak covering her. A piece of wool flopped over Charley's face just as silver moonlight touched the rocks around her.

She heard the men's voices again. Her hearing was acute, but she could not make out their words, nor did she think she would know the voices if she heard them again. The light faded again, but she and Letty kept perfectly still.

She was astonished by her small cousin's calm presence of mind. Charley did not know Letty well, for the child's parents had spent much of the past ten years on the Continent. Letty was nine, but she was an expert horsewoman and more accustomed than most children her age to conversing with adults. Lord and Lady Abreston, unlike most of their friends, had not relegated their three children to the care of nurses and governesses, but spent a great deal of time with them and seemed to enjoy their company. Gideon, Lord Abreston, heir to the marquisate of Jervaulx, having once served with distinction as a brigade major in Wellington's Army, presently held a diplomatic post with the British Embassy in Paris, a position that both amused and astonished those who had long been acquainted with Daintry, his outspoken wife. Soon it would be time for their two sons—both younger than Letty—to return to England for school. Letty herself was being allowed a two-month visit to Tuscombe Park to visit her mama's family. This, Charley told herself grimly, was not the introduction to Cornwall that her Aunt Daintry had intended Letty to have.

Antony hesitated only long enough after hearing the crash to peer through the darkness toward the sea. Still no signal, but he dared not leave lantern or tinderbox behind. Snatching them both up, he raced along the shingle to the broken carriage. He saw at once that both horses were dead, and he nearly sighed with relief. He could not bear to see animals suffer, but he could not have risked a gunshot down here and the mere thought of using his knife to put them out of their misery made him feel ill.

A moan from the carriage snapped his head around. He

had not thought anyone could have lived through such an accident. The moon peeked out again, and he went very still, knowing he might be seen from above. Slowly he tilted his head up, keeping one gloved hand over his face so the moonlight could not catch it. Whoever had fired the shots he had heard earlier might well be peering down at him.

He realized quickly that even if they were up there, they would not see him unless they climbed out onto the headland, and the portion that overlooked his present position was exceedingly treacherous. On the far side, facing St. Merryn's Bay, the slope was less precipitous and a road led out to the point, where a lovely big house perched, overlooking St. Merryn's Bay and a broad sweeping view of the Channel.

Even as these thoughts flew through his mind he had stooped over the wreckage, attempting to see past broken bits of coach to what lay within. He dared not risk a light, and the moon had slipped behind another cloud. The moan came again, more faintly. He moved a piece of the wreckage and found a man's crushed and broken body. The moans were not coming from him.

Moving with more care than ever, Antony shifted another piece of the carriage, and pale silvery light revealed a woman. She was badly injured, and Antony saw at once that there was nothing he could do to help her. She opened her eyes.

"Charley?" The word was clear but faint, and when she tried to speak again, she could not.

Antony took her hand, wanting only to give her comfort. "I'm here," he said gently. "I won't leave you."

"Thank you." Her eyes closed. A moment later, the hand in his went limp. She was gone.

A hail of pebbles from above startled him and reminded him of the men who had undoubtedly been chasing the coach. He did not think it was they who had started the pebbles falling, however. It was far more likely that the careering coach had dislodged them, and perhaps had loosened even bigger rocks. If he were wise, he would move before one fell on him. He would do the Duke of Wellington no good if he were found lying smashed flat on a Cornish beach.

Briefly he wondered if the men would try to ride down to the beach. Having thought the coach worth robbing in the first place, they might still believe it worth searching. There was a path of sorts down the cliff side, one that a good horse could follow, but he had not attempted to bring Annabelle down it in the dark, and she was as sure-footed as an army mule. He did not think they would come.

He had been keeping one eye on the sea, and at last he saw what he had been waiting for. One brief flash of light from a covered lantern, followed a moment later by two more. Swiftly, he opened his tinderbox and lit a sulfur match. Seconds later his lantern was lit. He moved away from the wreckage, and as he did, he saw another flash of light at the eastern end of the beach. So Michael had not trusted him to meet the Frenchmen alone. Not surprising. He had been much more surprised to be ordered to go without a second. A test, no doubt. He wondered if the other watcher had seen the coach go over the cliff. He did not remember seeing carriage lanterns. No doubt they had been broken, and their lights extinguished, soon after the coach had left the road. It had probably rolled several times. He would have to think what to do next about that.

"Cousin Charley, I think they've gone now."

"Keep still a few minutes longer, Letty." But Charley, too, had heard the sounds of departing horses above. She could feel the chill of the rock beneath her, and she could feel the child trembling.

"I-I lost my muff," Letty said in a small voice.

Charley knew she was concerned about much more than a fur muff, and she thought a moment before she said, "We cannot think about what we have lost just now, Letty. We must think about getting ourselves out of this predicament. That is the only thing, right now, that we can do anything about."

"It . . . it is very far down to the beach, is it not?"

"Very far," Charley agreed, "but if we keep our wits about us, we won't fall." She hoped she sounded more confident than she felt. To the best of her knowledge they were twenty or thirty feet below the road, on the slope of the headland where it met the side of the cliff, and perilously near the edge of that slope. It was, after all, little more than the point at which two cliff faces came together at slightly more than a right angle. In broad daylight a man in buckskins and wearing gloves might be able to climb back to the road rather easily. At night, with an unknown enemy still in the vicinity, two females in long skirts and heavy cloaks would not have an easy time of it, even though one of them wore stout half-boots.

"Were you injured, darling?"

"I don't think so," Letty said. "I hit my head on the carriage door, but it was only a bump, and then I fell on you. My hand is a little scraped, I think, where I first grabbed the rock. What about you?"

"I do not want to think about that either," Charley said. "I don't think I broke any bones, but I am beginning to feel a few aches and pains. My cloak protected me from the worst, although I did bang the back of my head when we landed, hard enough to make me see more stars than there are showing above us tonight. I think now that maybe your head hit my chin at the same time."

"The moon is— Listen!"

A rattle of loose stones and pebbles caused both of them to stay quite still, but a moment later a low, almost chirping sound made Letty stiffen, then call out in a low, excited voice, "Jeremiah!"

Another rattle of stones was followed by more low chattering, and then four small paws landed briefly on Charley's shoulder before the little monkey burrowed under Letty's cloak.

"Oh, Jeremiah, I was so worried about you! I thought you must have been killed. Oh, Cousin Charley, do you think Uncle Charles and Aunt Davina might have been thrown clear, too?"

Tempted though she was to say that anything was possible, Charley was a firm believer in honesty. She had loathed being lied to as a child, particularly by grown-ups who later insisted they had done so for her own good. Her Aunt Daintry had always been honest with her. She owed that same honesty to Daintry's daughter. "No," she said with a sick feeling in the pit of her stomach and a shiver of horror as she remembered her mother's screams, "I do not think they were thrown clear. They were still in the coach when it went over the edge."

Letty was silent. Then she said, "Those men on the road are gone. I think we had better see what we can do about finding a safer place for ourselves. I do not think we should try to climb up to the road until we can see what we are doing, do you?"

"No, and you make a very sensible suggestion. I confess, I am rather afraid to shift my position. The rocks under me are very loose and I am afraid the slightest movement might start us sliding again."

"Well, I think I can get behind this boulder I've been holding onto," Letty said. "If I can, then I can brace my feet against it, and if you hold my hand, I believe you can inch your way up behind it, too."

Charley's first, terrified impulse was to tell the child not to move a muscle, but she was getting very cold, and she knew that eventually one of them would have to try. Better to do so now, she decided, while they both still had some control over their limbs, and better that Letty try. The child would have no chance of holding her if she slipped, but she might hold the child.

Letty said, "I can get between you and the boulder, I think, but my cloak and skirt are dreadfully in my way, and these slippers I'm wearing do nothing to protect my feet or to give me traction."

Charley felt her wriggle some more and did not speak, focusing all her attention on keeping her own body flat and perfectly still against the loose scree. She heard Jeremiah protest when Letty removed him from beneath her cloak. When Letty shifted her weight, for a moment Charley felt herself begin to slide again, but the sensation quickly passed.

"I've got my feet against your side," Letty said. "This boulder seems stable. I am going to stand up now."

Charley held her breath. A moment later, Letty spread her cloak over her. Some odd noises and movements followed, and even in the dim starlight, Charley could see that the child was doing something to her own clothing. "What are you doing?"

"Tucking up my skirt," Letty said. "If I should slip, I don't want it getting tangled round my legs again. It's all right," she added, with amusement in her voice. "I've got on my new dimity pantalets, with the Swiss lace, that Mama bought me just before we left Paris, so if anyone should chance to see me—"

"You'll shock them witless," Charley murmured. "I bought a pair, myself, but I am not wearing them because my mama thinks—" She broke off, realizing the tense of the verb was probably wrong, then added calmly, "She thinks that only men should wear pantaloons of any kind, but that is only because of Lady Charlotte Lindsey's losing one leg of hers as she walked down Piccadilly, and causing such a stir. Mine are fashioned in such a way that one leg cannot fall off me the way hers did."

"Mine are, too." Letty was silent for a long moment, then said on a note of satisfaction, "There. Now, I'm holding the boulder with both hands, and it is as steady as a rock ought to be. Just wait one more moment now."

Charley felt loose pebbles sliding past her with each step Letty took, and kept tight hold of the base of the boulder with her left hand. Her arm was stretched to its full reach, however, and she knew that if she attempted to trust her weight to that slight handhold, or to pull herself toward the boulder, she would lose her tenuous grip. Difficult though it was for a woman of her active nature, she knew she had to keep still until the child was as safe as she could be.

Without warning, Letty's cloak was whisked away. "Now, Cousin Charley," the child said, "I am sitting down on my cloak, and my feet are pushing hard against the boulder. It hasn't twitched. If I hold your hand with both of mine—"

"No," Charley said firmly. "You must keep your right hand on the boulder or some other solid object. If both your hands are on mine and I begin to slip, my weight could yank you right out of there. Put your left hand down at the base of the boulder. When you find my hand, grasp my wrist as tightly as you can. Then I'll hold your wrist. Your mother taught—"

"Oh, I know," Letty exclaimed. "It's the way she swings me up to ride pillion behind her."

"Right," Charley agreed.

The little girl's hand seemed very small, her wrist far too slender and fragile for the purpose, but her grip was tight and the slender arm steady when Charley grasped it. Charley's legs were still tangled in her skirts, so she spent long moments moving slowly and carefully, using her free hand to twitch them free. When she could dig her heels into the scree, she managed to inch her way up, but when she tried moments later to sit, the unstable surface beneath her shifted. Only Letty's grip stopped her from sliding.

"Cousin Charley, are you sure sound travels up more easily than down?"

"I think so," Charley said, willing her heart to stop pounding and forcing her breathing to slow. "Why do you ask, darling?"

"Because there are men and lights on the beach," Letty said. "I don't think they can see us, but a lot of loose rock went over the edge just then."

"Do you think they can be the highwaymen?"

"I don't know, but most of them came in a boat, I think. I can just barely see a shape out on the water that might be a ship. And the little boat is leaving again, but at least two men are still on the beach!"

"Hold tight, Letty. I'm going to try again."

Antony thought more than once about Wellington's warning against involving himself in criminal activities as he helped carry cargo from the longboat to the cave where it would be stored until the ponies collected it for transport. If revenuers surprised them, there would be nowhere but the caves to hide. Michael had assured him that the folks in south Cornwall were friendly to fair-traders, but he was risking a lot on Michael's word, and he had little reason to trust the man—no more, in fact, than Michael had to trust him. They had known each other less than a fortnight, after all, and Michael had taken him on faith—that, and the mention of a mutual acquaintance in France who would (if he knew what was good for him) vouch for Antony's "good" character. But Antony knew the locals would continue to test him for some time yet.

The only person in Cornwall who knew him for a government man was the agent for Lloyd's of London in St. Austell. Antony had paid Mr. Francis Oakley a visit, liked the cut of his jib, and had told him he meant to do a little investigating of the coastal gangs for His Majesty's Government. He had confided no more than that to Mr. Oakley. The Fox Cub had learned long since to trust no one but himself with all the facts.

As he hauled kegs to the cave with the others, he was conscious of the wrecked carriage at the west end of the beach. The moon had appeared again, but it had moved west of the headland, and the wreck lay in shadow. Unless someone decided to stroll to that end of the beach for some reason that Antony could not presently imagine, it would not draw anyone else's interest tonight. Daylight was another matter. He did not know who the victims might be. He had seen no crest on the door, and doubted that he would have recognized it if he had seen one. He had found no coachman either, he realized. Perhaps the man had jumped clear and would be going for help. In any case, he would be wiser not to return by daylight, lest his villainous compatriots believe he was after the stored booty. But neither could he reconcile it with his conscience to leave that poor woman and her husband to rot on the beach if their coachman had not lived through the incident. Somehow, he must learn if anyone survived, and if not, get word of the coach's whereabouts to someone in authority.

Tucked between two boulders with a third below them on the slope, Charley and Letty were as safe as they could make themselves. Huddled together inside Charley's thick cloak with Letty's smaller one over them and Jeremiah snuggled between them, they soon grew tired of watching the activity below them on the beach, and fell asleep.

When Charley awoke, it was because Letty had moved away from her and was anxiously calling for Jeremiah.

"Keep your voice down," Charley whispered. "Someone might hear you."

"The smugglers are gone," Letty said, "but so is Jeremiah. I've got to find him! What if he fell over the edge?"

"If he didn't go over with the carriage, you may be sure he did not fall later," Charley said, hoping she was right. "He is very agile, you know, so he is probably only exploring. He will be back soon. Perhaps he will find some food."

Letty giggled. "Are you hungry, too? I did not like to say

anything, but I am starving. There were apples in Aunt Davina's basket, too." The silence that followed was awkward, but for once in her life Charley could think of nothing to say. At last, in a small voice, Letty said, "I'm awfully sorry, Cousin Charley. I-I know that most likely they are dead. At least, don't you think they are?"

"Yes," Charley said firmly. The alternative—that her parents might be lying in dreadful agony at the base of the cliff, while she sat doing nothing to help them—was too horrible to contemplate.

"Well, I am sure they must be, and perhaps it is only that they are not my own parents, but should I not feel like crying, even so? Because, I know I keep saying things that I ought not to say—like about the apples—and . . . and . . ."

Charley reached for Letty's hand and gave it a squeeze, saying, "I am very glad you are not weeping and wailing, darling, because that would only make matters much worse than they are."

"Yes, but ought I not to *feel* like doing so? You are all grown up, and so I don't expect you to fall into flat despair, even though they are your parents, but I don't want to cry. I don't feel anything at all—except cold and a little tired."

"I think we have both had a lot to think about just to stay alive," Charley said quietly. "Moreover, I have heard that it is not unusual to feel numb at first. It was a very great shock, after all, and everything happened very fast, so maybe our sensibilities have not quite caught up with the reality of it all."

"I don't seem to have much sensibility at the best of times," Letty said thoughtfully. "Young Gideon has much more than I do. He cries if a bug gets squashed. I just think what a good thing it is to have one less bug to crawl on me."

Charley chuckled and gave her a hug. "Young Gideon is only five."

"Yes, I know, but I didn't have much sensibility even then.

Papa frequently says I've got more sense than sensibility. Mama said he had that from a book."

"A fine book," Charley said, "I have a copy at home. Do you like to read?"

They talked in this manner for some time, until Charley began to notice that the eastern sky was growing light. It would soon be dawn. She wondered if they would be able to reach the road, and wondered, too, if they would have to walk to Tuscombe Park, and if she could do so without first making her way down to the beach to be sure that what she knew in her heart was really so.

"Cousin Charley, listen! I think it's Jeremiah!"

"Mon Dieu, is someone down there?" The voice from above them was masculine and deep, and it sounded much closer than twenty or thirty feet away.

Charley and Letty kept still, and when Jeremiah leapt to Letty's shoulder and began to chatter excitedly, she grabbed him, shoved him under her cloak, and clapped a hand over his little mouth.

If you liked this book, be sure to look for others in the *Denise Little Presents* line:

Available wherever paperbacks are sold, or order direct from the Publisher. Send cover price plus 50¢ per copy for mailing and handling to Penguin USA, P.O. Box 999, c/o Dept. 17109, Bergenfield, NJ 07621. Residents of New York and Tennessee must include sales tax. DO NOT SEND CASH.

IF ROMANCE BE THE FRUIT OF LIFE—
READ ON—
BREATH-QUICKENING HISTORICALS FROM PINNACLE

WILDCAT (722, $4.99)
by Rochelle Wayne

No man alive could break Diana Preston's fiery spirit . . . until seductive Vince Gannon galloped onto Diana's sprawling family ranch. Vince, a man with dark secrets, would sweep her into his world of danger and desire. And Diana couldn't deny the powerful yearnings that branded her as his own, for all time!

THE HIGHWAY MAN (765, $4.50)
by Nadine Crenshaw

When a trumped-up murder charge forced beautiful Jane Fitzpatrick to flee her home, she was found and sheltered by the highwayman—a man as dark and dangerous as the secrets that haunted him. As their hiding place became a place of shared dreams—and soaring desires—Jane knew she'd found the love she'd been yearning for!

SILKEN SPURS (756, $4.99)
by Jane Archer

Beautiful Harmony Harper, leader of a notorious outlaw gang, rode the desert plains of New Mexico in search of justice and vengeance. Now she has captured powerful and privileged Thor Clarke-Jargon, who is everything Harmony has ever hated—and all she will ever want. And after Harmony has taken the handsome adventurer hostage, she herself has become a captive—of her own desires!

WYOMING ECSTASY (740, $4.50)
by Gina Robins

Feisty criminal investigator, July MacKenzie, solicits the partnership of the legendary half-breed gunslinger-detective Nacona Blue. After being turned down, July—never one to accept the meaning of the word no— finds a way to convince Nacona to be her partner . . . first in business— then in passion. Across the wilds of Wyoming, and always one step ahead of trouble, July surrenders to passion's searing demands!